After thirty-five years as a nurse, **Patricia Davids** hung up her stethoscope to become a full-time writer. She enjoys spending her free time visiting her grandchildren, doing some long-overdue yard work and traveling to research her story locations. She resides in Wichita, Kansas. Pat always enjoys hearing from her readers. You can visit her online at patriciadavids.com.

Debby Giusti is an award-winning Christian author who met and married her military husband at Fort Knox, Kentucky. Together they traveled the world, raised three wonderful children and have now settled in Atlanta, Georgia, where Debby spins tales of mystery and suspense that touch the heart and soul. Visit Debby online at debbygiusti.com; blog with her at seekerville.blogspot.com and craftieladiesofromance.blogspot.com; and email her at Debby@DebbyGiusti.com.

USA TODAY Bestselling Author

PATRICIA DAVIDS

The Shepherd's Bride

&

DEBBY GIUSTI

Plain Danger

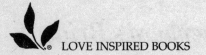 LOVE INSPIRED BOOKS

Recycling programs for this product may not exist in your area.

ISBN-13: 978-0-373-83901-8

The Shepherd's Bride and Plain Danger

Copyright © 2017 by Harlequin Books S.A.

The publisher acknowledges the copyright holders of the individual works as follows:

The Shepherd's Bride
Copyright © 2014 by Patricia MacDonald

Plain Danger
Copyright © 2016 by Deborah W. Giusti

www.Harlequin.com

Printed in U.S.A.

CONTENTS

THE SHEPHERD'S BRIDE

Patricia Davids

This book is dedicated with endearing love
to my lambs, Kathy, Josh and Shantel.

Chapter One

"You can't be serious." Lizzie Barkman gaped at her older sister, Clara, in shock.

Seated on the edge of the bed in the room the four Barkman sisters shared, Clara kept her eyes downcast. "It's not such a bad thing."

Lizzie fell to her knees beside Clara and took hold of her icy hands. "It's not a bad thing. It's a horrible thing. You can't marry Rufus Kuhns. He's put two wives in the ground already. Besides, he's thirty years older than you are."

"Onkel wishes this."

"Then our uncle is crazy!"

Clara glanced fearfully at the door. "Hush. Do not earn a beating for my sake, sister."

Lizzie wasn't eager to feel the sting of their uncle's wooden rod across her back, but it was outrageous to imagine lovely, meek Clara paired with such an odious man. "Tell Onkel Morris you won't do it."

"He won't go against Rufus's wishes. He's too scared of losing our jobs and this house."

It was true. Their uncle wouldn't oppose Rufus. He

didn't have the courage. Rufus Kuhns was a wealthy member of their small Plain community in northern Indiana. He owned the dairy farm where they all worked for the paltry wages he paid. He claimed that letting them live in the run-down house on his property more than made up for their low salaries. The house was little more than a hovel, although the girls tried their best to make it a home.

"Onkel says it is his duty to see us all wed. I'm twenty-five with no prospects. I'm afraid he is right about that."

The single women in their isolated Amish community outnumbered the single men three to one. Lizzie was twenty-three with no prospects in sight, either. Who would her uncle decide she should marry?

"Being single isn't such a bad thing, Clara. Look at my friend Mary Miller, the schoolteacher. She is happy enough."

Clara managed a smile. "It's all right, Lizzie. At least this way I have the hope of children of my own. If God wills it."

It hurt to see Clara so ready to accept her fate. Lizzie wouldn't give up so easily. "Rufus had no children with his previous wives. You don't have to do this. We can move away and support ourselves by making cheese to sell to the tourists. We'll grow old together and take care of each other."

Clara cupped Lizzie's cheek. "You are such a dreamer. What will happen to our little sisters if we do that?"

Greta and Betsy were outside finishing the evening milking. At seventeen, Betsy was the youngest. Greta was nearly twenty. They all worked hard on the dairy farm. With twenty-five cows to be milked by hand twice a day, there was more than enough work to go around.

Without Clara and Lizzie to carry their share of the load, the burden on their sisters would double, for their uncle wouldn't pick up the slack.

Morris Barkman hadn't been blessed with children. He and his ailing wife took in his four nieces when their parents died in a buggy accident ten years before. He made no secret of the fact that his nieces were his burden to bear. He made sure everyone knew how generous he was and how difficult his life had been since his wife's passing.

Lizzie couldn't count the number of times she had been forced to hold her tongue when he shamed her in front of others for her laziness and ingratitude. Her uncle claimed to be a devout member of the Amish faith, but in her eyes, he was no better than the Pharisees in the Bible stories the bishop preached about during the church services.

She rose and paced the small room in frustration. There had to be a way out of this. "We can all move away and get a house together. Greta and Betsy, too."

"If we left without our uncle's permission, we would be shunned by everyone in our church. I could not bear that." Clara's voice fell to a whisper. "Besides, if I won't wed Rufus…Betsy is his second choice."

Lizzie gasped. "She's barely seventeen."

"You see now why I have to go through with it. Promise me you won't tell her she's the reason I'm doing this."

"I promise."

"I know you've been thinking about leaving us, Lizzie. I'm not as strong as you are. I can't do it, but you should go. Go now while you have the chance. I can bear anything if I know you are safe."

Lizzie didn't deny it. She had been thinking about

leaving for years. She had even squirreled away a small amount of money for the day. Only the thought of never seeing her sisters again kept her from taking such a drastic step. She loved them dearly.

The bedroom door opened and the two younger Barkman girls came in. Greta was limping. Clara immediately went to her. "What happened?"

"She got kicked by that bad-tempered cow we all hate," Betsy said.

"She's not bad-tempered. She doesn't hear well. I startled her. It was my own fault. It's going to leave a bruise, but nothing is broken." Greta sat on the edge of the bed she shared with Betsy.

Clara insisted on inspecting her leg. It was already swollen and purple just above the knee. "Oh, that must hurt. I'll get some witch hazel for it."

As Clara left, Lizzie turned to her sisters. "Onkel is making Clara marry Rufus Kuhns."

"Are you joking? He's ancient." Greta looked as shocked as Lizzie was.

"It's better than being an old *maedel*," Betsy said. "We're never going to find husbands if we aren't allowed to attend singings and barn parties in other Amish communities."

Would she feel the same if she knew how easily she could trade places with Clara? Lizzie kept silent. She had given Clara her word. Betsy began to get ready for the night.

Greta did the same. "Rufus is a mean fellow."

Lizzie turned her back to give her sisters some privacy. "He's cruel to his horses and his cattle. I can't bear to think of Clara living with him."

"His last wife came to church with a bruised face more

than once. She claimed she was accident-prone, but it makes a person wonder." Greta pulled on her nightgown.

"Shame on you, Greta. It's a sin to think evil thoughts about the man." Betsy climbed into bed, took off her black *kapp* and started to unwind her long brown hair.

Greta and Lizzie shared a speaking glance but kept silent. Neither of them wanted their oldest sister to find out if their suspicions were true. They remembered only too well the bruises their mother bore in silence when their father's temper flared.

Clara returned with a bottle of witch hazel and a cloth. "This will help with the pain."

Greta took the bottle from her. They had all used the remedy on bruises inflicted by their uncle over the years. He wouldn't stand up to Rufus, but he didn't have any qualms about taking his anger and frustration out on someone weaker. "You can't do it, Clara. You should go away."

"And never see you again? How could I do that? Besides, where would I go? We have no family besides each other."

Lizzie met Greta's eyes. Greta gave a slight nod. After all, they were desperate. Lizzie said, "We have a grandfather."

"We do?" It was Betsy's turn to look shocked as she sat up in bed.

Clara shook her head. "*Nee.* He is dead to us."

"He is dead to Uncle Morris, not to me." Lizzie's mind began to whirl. Would their *daadi* help? They hadn't heard from him in years. Not since the death of their parents.

Greta rubbed the witch hazel on her knee. "We were told never to mention him."

"Mention who?" Betsy almost shouted.

They all hushed her. None of the sisters wished to stir their uncle's wrath. "Our mother's father lives in Hope Springs, Ohio."

Clara began getting ready for bed, too. "You think he does. He could be dead for all we know."

"We really have a grandfather? Why haven't I met him?" Betsy looked as if she might burst into tears.

Lizzie removed the straight pins that held her faded green dress closed down the front. "We moved away from Hope Springs when you were just a baby."

Clara slipped under the covers. "Papa and Grandfather Shetler had a terrible falling out when I was ten. Mama, Papa, Uncle Morris and his wife all moved away and eventually settled here."

"Grandfather raised sheep." Lizzie smiled at the memory of white lambs leaping for the sheer joy of it in green spring pastures. She hated it when her father made them move to this dreary place. She hung her dress beside her sisters' on the pegs that lined the wall and slipped into her nightgown.

"Do we have a grandmother, too?" Betsy asked.

Lizzie shook her head. "She died when our mother was a baby. I'm ready to put out the lamp. You know how Onkel hates it when we waste kerosene.

"Grandfather had a big white dog named Joker," Greta added wistfully. "I'm sure he's gone by now. Dogs don't live that long."

"But men do. I will write to him first thing in the morning and beg him to take you in, Clara." Lizzie sat down on her side of the bed and blew out the kerosene lamp, plunging the small bedroom into darkness.

Clara sighed. "This is crazy talk. Our uncle will forbid such a letter, Lizzie. You know that. Besides, I'm not going anywhere without my sisters."

Lizzie waited until Clara was settled under the covers with her. Quietly, she said, "You will go to Rufus Kuhns's home without us."

"I...know. I miss Mama so much at times like this."

Lizzie heard the painful catch in her sister's voice. She reached across to pull Clara close. "I do, too. I refuse to believe she made your beautiful star quilt for this sham of a marriage. She made your quilt to be her gift to you on a happy wedding day."

Their mother had lovingly stitched wedding quilts for each of her daughters. They lay packed away in the cedar chest in the corner. The quilts were different colors and personalized for each one of them. They were cherished by the girls as reminders of their mother's love.

Lizzie hardened her resolve. "We'll think of something. It's only the middle of March. We have until the wedding time in autumn. You'll see. We'll think of something before then."

"*Nee.* My wedding will take place the first week of May so I may help with spring planting."

Greta slipped into bed behind Lizzie. "That's not right. We can't prepare for a wedding in such a short time."

"Rufus doesn't want a big wedding. It will be only the bishop, Uncle Morris, you girls and Rufus."

Such a tiny, uncelebrated affair wasn't the wedding dream of any young woman. Lizzie felt the bed sag again and knew Betsy had joined them on the other side of Clara.

"I don't want you to leave us." Betsy's voice trembled as she spoke.

"I won't be far away. Why, you'll all be able to come for a visit whenever you want."

A visit. That was it! A plan began to form in Lizzie's mind. She was almost certain she had enough money saved to travel to Ohio on the bus. Their grandfather might ignore a letter, but if she went to see him in person, she could make him understand how dire the situation was.

It was an outrageous plan, but what choice did she have? None.

Clara couldn't marry Rufus. He would crush her gentle spirit and leave her an empty shell. Or worse.

Lizzie bit her bottom lip. She couldn't let that happen. Nor could she tell her sisters what she intended to do. She didn't want them to lie or cover for her. As much as it hurt, she would have to let them think she had run away.

Her younger sisters soon returned to their own bed. Before long, their even breathing told Lizzie they were asleep. Clara turned over and went to sleep, too.

Lizzie lay wide-awake.

If she went through with her plan, the only person she dared tell was Mary Miller. There was no love lost between the schoolteacher and their uncle. Besides, it wasn't as if Lizzie was leaving the Amish. She was simply traveling to another Amish community. If she wrote to her friend from Ohio, she was certain that Mary would relay messages to the girls. If their grandfather proved willing to take them in, Mary would help them leave.

Lizzie pressed her hand to her mouth. Would it work? Could she do it?

If she went, it would have to be tonight while the others were asleep. Before she lost her nerve. She closed her eyes and folded her hands.

Please, Lord, let this plan be Your will. Give me the strength to see it through.

She waited until it was well after midnight before she slipped from beneath the covers. The full moon outside cast a band of pale light across the floor. It gave her enough light to see by. She carefully withdrew an envelope with her money from beneath the mattress and pulled an old suitcase from under the bed. It took only five minutes to gather her few belongings. Then she moved to the cedar chest.

Kneeling in front of it, she lifted the lid. Clara's rose-and-mauve star quilt lay on top. Lizzie set it aside and pulled out the quilt in shades of blue and green that was to be her wedding quilt. Should she take it with her?

If she did, it would convince everyone she wasn't returning. If she left it, her sisters would know she was coming back.

Suddenly, Lizzie knew she couldn't venture out into the unknown without something tangible of her family to bring her comfort. She replaced Clara's quilt and softly closed the lid of the cedar chest.

Holding her shoes, her suitcase and her quilt, Lizzie tiptoed to the door of their room. She opened it with a trembling hand and glanced back at her sisters sleeping quietly in the darkness. Could she really go through with this?

Carl King scraped most of the mud off his boots and walked up to the front door of his boss's home. Joe Shetler had gone to purchase straw from a neighbor, but he would be back soon. After an exhausting morning spent struggling to pen and doctor one ornery and stubborn ewe, Carl had rounded up half the remaining sheep and moved them closer to the barns with the help of his dog, Duncan.

Tired, with his tongue lolling, the black-and-white English shepherd walked beside Carl toward the house. Carl reached down to pat his head. "You did good work this morning, fella. We'll start shearing them soon if the weather holds."

The sheep needed to spend at least one night inside the barn to make sure their wool was dry before being sheared. Damp wool would rot. There wasn't enough room in the barn for all two hundred head at once. The operation would take three to four days if all went well.

It was important to shear the ewes before they gave birth. If the weather turned bad during the lambing season, many of the shorn ewes would seek shelter in the sheds and barn rather than have their lambs out in the open where the wet and cold could kill the newborns. Having a good lamb crop was important, but Carl knew things rarely went off without a hitch.

Duncan ambled toward his water dish. At the moment, all Carl wanted was a hot cup of coffee. Joe always left a pot on the back of the stove so Carl could help himself.

He opened the front door and stopped dead in his tracks. An Amish woman stood at the kitchen sink. She had her back to him as she rummaged for something. She hadn't heard him come in.

He resisted the intense impulse to rush back outside. He didn't like being shut inside with anyone. He fought his growing discomfort. This was Joe's home. This woman didn't belong here.

"What are you doing?" he demanded. Joe didn't like anyone besides Carl in his house.

She shrieked and jumped a foot as she whirled around

to face him. She pressed a hand to her heaving chest, leaving a patch of white soapsuds on her faded green dress. "You scared the life out of me."

He clenched his fists and stared at his feet. "I didn't mean to frighten you. Who are you and what are you doing here?"

"Who are you? You're not Joseph Shetler. I was told this was Joseph's house."

He glanced up and saw the defiant jut of her jaw. He folded his arms over his chest and pressed his lips into a tight line. He didn't say a word as he glared at her.

She was a slender little thing. The top of her head wouldn't reach his chin unless she stood on tiptoe. She was dressed Plain in a drab faded green calf-length dress with a matching cape and apron. She wore dark stockings and dark shoes. Her hair, on the other hand, was anything but drab. It was ginger-red and wisps of it curled near her temples and along her forehead. The rest was hidden beneath the black *kapp* she wore. Her eyes were an unusual hazel color with flecks of gold in their depths.

He didn't recognize her, but she could be a local. He made a point of avoiding people, so it wasn't surprising that he didn't know her.

She quickly realized he wasn't going to speak until she had answered his questions. She managed a nervous smile. "I'm sorry. My name is Elizabeth Barkman. People call me Lizzie. I'm Joe's granddaughter from Indiana. I was just straightening up a little while I waited for him to get home."

As far as Carl knew, Joe didn't have any family. "Joe doesn't have a granddaughter, and he doesn't like people in his house." He shoved his hands into his pockets as the need to escape the house left them shaking.

"Actually, he has four granddaughters. I can see why he doesn't like to have people in. This place is a mess. He certainly could use a housekeeper. I know an excellent one who is looking for a position."

Carl glanced around Joe's kitchen. It was cluttered and dirty, unlike the clean and sparsely furnished shepherd's hut out in the pasture where he lived, but if Joe wanted to live like this, that was his business and not the business of this nosy, pushy woman. "This is how Joe likes it. You should leave."

"Where is my grandfather? Will he be back soon?" Her eyes darted around the room. He could see fear creeping in behind them. It had dawned on her that they were alone together on a remote farm.

Suddenly, he saw another room, dark and full of women huddled together. He could smell the fear in the air. They were all staring at him.

He blinked hard and the image vanished. His heart started pounding. The room began closing in on him. He needed air. He needed out. He'd seen enough fear in women's eyes to haunt him for a lifetime. He didn't need to add to that tally. He took a quick step back. "Joe will be along shortly." Turning, he started to open the door.

She said, "I didn't catch your name. Are you a friend of my grandfather's?"

He paused and gripped the doorknob tightly so she wouldn't see his hand shaking. "I'm Carl King. I work here." He walked out before she could ask anything else.

Once he was outside under the open sky, his sense of panic receded. He drew a deep, cleansing breath. His tremors grew less with each gulp of air he took. His pounding heart rate slowed.

It had been weeks since one of his spells. He'd started

to believe they were gone for good, that perhaps God had forgiven him, but Joe's granddaughter had proved him wrong.

His dog trotted to his side and nosed his hand. He managed a little smile. "I'm okay, Duncan."

The dog whined. He seemed to know when his master was troubled. Carl focused on the silky feel of the dog's thick fur between his fingers. It helped ground him in the here and now and push back the shadows of the past.

That past lay like a beast inside him. The terror lurked, ready to spring out and drag him into the nightmares he suffered through nearly every night. He shouldn't be alive. He should have accepted death with peace in his heart, secure in the knowledge of God's love and eternal salvation. He hadn't.

He had his life, for what it was worth, but no peace.

Joe came into sight driving his wagon and team of draft horses. The wagon bed held two dozen bales of straw. He pulled the big dappled gray horses to a stop beside Carl. "Did you get that ewe penned and doctored?"

"I did."

"*Goot.* We'll get this hay stored in the big shed so we can have it handy to spread in the lambing pens when we need it. We can unload it as soon as I've had a bite to eat and a cup of coffee. Did you leave me any?"

"I haven't touched the pot. You have a visitor inside."

A small elderly man with a long gray beard and a dour expression, Joe climbed down from the wagon slowly. To Carl's eyes, he had grown frailer this past year. A frown creased his brow beneath the brim of the flat-topped straw hat he wore. He didn't like visitors. "Who is it?"

"She claims she's your granddaughter Lizzie Barkman."

All the color drained from Joe's face. He staggered backward until he bumped into the wheel of his wagon. "One of my daughter's girls? What does she want?"

Carl took a quick step toward Joe and grasped his elbow to steady him. "She didn't say. Are you okay?"

Joe shook off Carl's hand. "I'm fine. Put the horses away."

"Sure." Carl was used to Joe's brusque manners.

Joe nodded his thanks and began walking toward the house with unsteady steps. Carl waited until he had gone inside before leading the team toward the corral at the side of the barn. He'd worked with Joe for nearly four years. The old man had never mentioned he had a daughter and granddaughters.

Carl glanced back at the house. Joe wasn't the only one who kept secrets. Carl had his own.

Chapter Two

Lizzie had rehearsed a dozen different things to say when she first saw her grandfather, but his hired man's abrupt appearance had rattled her already frayed nerves. When her grandfather actually walked through the door, everything she had planned to say left her head. She stood silently as he looked her up and down.

He had changed a great deal from what she remembered. She used to think he was tall, but he was only average height and stooped with age. His beard was longer and streaked with gray now. It used to be black.

Nervously, she gestured toward the sink. "I hope you don't mind that I washed a few dishes. You have hot water right from the faucet. It isn't allowed in our home. Our landlord says it's worldly, but it makes doing the dishes a pleasure."

"You look just like your grandmother." His voice was exactly as she remembered.

She smiled. "Do I?"

"It's no good thing. She had red hair like yours. She was an unhappy, nagging woman. Why have you come? Have you brought sad news?"

"Nee," Lizzie said quickly. "My sisters are all well. We live in Indiana. Onkel Morris and all of us work on a dairy farm there."

Joe moved to the kitchen table and took a seat. "Did your uncle send you to me? He agreed to raise the lot of you. He can't change his mind now."

She sat across from him. *"Nee,* Onkel does not know I have come to see you."

"How did you get here?"

"I took the bus. I asked about you at the bus station in Hope Springs. An Amish woman waiting to board the bus told me how to find your farm. I walked from town."

He propped his elbows on the table and pressed his hands together. She noticed the dirt under his fingernails and the calluses on his rough hands. "How is it that you have come without your uncle's knowledge? Do you still reside with him or have you married?"

"None of us are married. Onkel Morris would have forbidden this meeting had he known of my plan."

"I see." He closed his eyes and rested his chin on his knuckles.

She didn't know if he was praying or simply waiting for more of an explanation. She rushed ahead, anxious that he hear exactly why she had made the trip. "I had to come. You are the only family we have. We desperately need your help. Onkel Morris is forcing Clara to marry a terrible man. I fear for her if she goes through with it. I'm hoping—praying really—that you can find it in your heart to take her in. She is a good cook and she will keep your house spotless. Your house could use a woman's touch. Clara is an excellent housekeeper and as sweet-tempered as anyone. You must let her come. I'm begging you."

He was silent for so long that she wondered if he had fallen asleep the way old people sometimes did. Finally, he spoke. "My daughter chose to ignore my wishes in order to marry your father. She made it clear that he was more important than my feelings. I can only honor what I believe to be her wishes. I will not aid you in your disobedience to the man who has taken your father's place. You have come a long way for no reason. Carl will take you back to the bus station."

Lizzie couldn't believe her concerns were being dismissed out of hand. "Daadi, I beg you to reconsider. I did not come here lightly. I truly believe Clara is being sentenced to a life of misery, or worse."

Joe rose to his feet. "Do not let your girlish emotions blind you to the wisdom of your elders. It is vain and prideful to question your uncle's choice for your sister."

"It is our uncle who is blind if he thinks Clara will be happy with his choice. She won't be. He is a cruel man."

"If your uncle believes the match is a good thing, you must trust his judgment. There will be a bus going that way this afternoon. If you hurry, you can get a seat. Go home and beg his forgiveness for your foolishness. All will be well in the end, for it is as Gott wills."

"Please, Daadi, you have to help Clara."

He turned away and walked out the door, leaving Lizzie speechless as she stared after him.

Dejected, she slipped into her coat and glanced around the cluttered kitchen. If only he would realize how much better his life would be with Clara to care for him.

Was he right? Was her failure God's will?

With a heavy heart, she carried her suitcase and the box with her quilt in it out to the front porch. Her grandfather was nowhere in sight, but his hired man was leading a small white pony hitched to a cart in her direction.

He was a big, burly man with wide shoulders and narrow hips. He wore a black cowboy hat, jeans and a flannel shirt under a stained and worn sheepskin jacket. His hair was light brown and long enough to touch his collar, but it was clean. His size and stealth had frightened the wits out of her in the house earlier. Out in the open, he didn't appear as menacing, but he didn't smile and didn't meet her gaze.

He and her grandfather must get along famously with few words spoken and never a smile between them.

It was all well and good to imagine staying until her grandfather changed his mind, but the reality was much different. He had ordered her to go home. How could she make him understand if he wouldn't hear what she had to say? He hadn't even offered the simple hospitality of his home for the night. He wanted her gone as quickly as possible. She would have to go home in defeat unless she could find some way to support herself and bring her sisters to Hope Springs. She didn't know where to start. All her hopes had been pinned on her grandfather's compassion. Sadly, he didn't have any.

Carl stopped in front of the house and waited for her. She bit her lower lip. Was she really giving up so easily? "Where is my grandfather?"

"He's gone out to the pasture to move the rest of his sheep."

"When will he be back?"

"Hard to say."

"I'd like to speak to him again."

"Joe told me to take you to the bus station. It's plain to me that he was done talking."

She stamped her foot in frustration. "You don't understand. I can't go home."

He didn't say anything. He simply waited beside the pony. A brick wall would have shown more compassion. Defeated by his stoic silence, she descended the steps. He took her bag from her hand and placed it behind the seat of the cart. He reached for the box that contained her quilt and she reluctantly handed it over.

He waited until she had climbed aboard, then he took his place beside her on the wooden seat. With a flip of the reins, he set the pony in motion. She looked back once. The house, which had looked like a sanctuary when she first saw it, looked like the run-down farmstead it truly was. Tears stung her eyes. She tried not to let them fall, but she couldn't hold back a sniffle. She wiped her nose on the back of her sleeve.

Carl cringed at the sound of Lizzie's muffled sniffling. He would have been okay if she hadn't started crying.

He didn't want to involve himself in her troubles. Whatever it was, it was none of his business. He glanced her way and saw a tear slip down her cheek. She quickly wiped it away. She looked forlorn huddled on the seat next to him, like a lost lamb that couldn't find the flock.

He looked straight ahead. "I'm sorry things didn't turn out the way you wanted with your grandfather."

"He's a very uncaring man."

"Joe is okay."

"I'm glad you think so."

"He doesn't cotton to most people."

"I'm not most people. I'm his flesh and blood. He doesn't care that his own granddaughter is being forced into marriage with a hateful man."

Carl looked at her in surprise. "You're being forced to marry someone not of your choosing?"

"Not me. My sister Clara. Our uncle, my mother's brother, took us in after our parents died. Onkel Morris is making Clara marry a man more than twice her age."

"Amish marriages are not arranged. Your sister cannot be compelled to marry against her will."

"The man who wishes to marry Clara is our landlord and employer. He could turn us all out of his house to starve. My uncle is afraid of him." She crossed her arms over her chest.

"But you are not." He glanced at her with respect. It had taken a lot of courage for her to travel so far.

"I'm afraid of him, too. Sometimes, I think he enjoys making life miserable for others." Her voice faded away. She sniffled again.

The pony trotted quickly along the road as Carl pondered Lizzie's story. He had no way to help her and no words of wisdom to offer. Sometimes, life wasn't fair.

After a few minutes, she composed herself enough to ask, "Do you know of anyone who might want to hire a maid or a housekeeper?"

"No." He didn't go into town unless he had to. He didn't mingle with people.

"I would take any kind of work."

"There's an inn in town. They might know of work for you."

She managed a watery smile for him. "*Danki.* Something will turn up."

She was pretty when she smiled. Although her eyes were red-rimmed now, they were a beautiful hazel color. They shimmered with unshed tears in the afternoon light. Her face, with its oval shape, pale skin and sculpted high cheekbones, gave her a classical beauty, but a spray of freckles across her nose gave her a fresh, wholesome look that appealed to him.

It felt strange to have a woman seated beside him. It had been a long time since he had enjoyed the companionship of anyone other than Joe. Did she know he had been shunned? Joe should have told her. Carl wasn't sure how to bring up the subject.

He sat stiffly on the seat, making sure he didn't touch her. If she were unaware of his shunning, he would see that she didn't inadvertently break the tenets of her faith. The sharp, staccato *clip-clop* of the pony's hooves on the blacktop, the creaking of the cart and Lizzie's occasional sniffles were the only sounds in the awkward silence until he crested the hill. A one-room Amish schoolhouse sat back from the road, and the cheerful sounds of children playing during recess reached him. A game of softball was under way.

One little girl in a blue dress and white *kapp* waved to him from her place in the outfield. He waved back when he recognized her. Joy Mast immediately dropped her oversize ball glove and ran toward him. He pulled the pony to a stop. Two boys from the other team ran after her.

"Hi, Carl. How is Duncan? Is he with you today?" She reached the cart and hung on to the side to catch her breath.

He relaxed as he grinned at her. He could be himself around Amish children. They hadn't been baptized and wouldn't be required to shun him. Joy had Down syndrome. Her father, Caleb Mast, had recently returned to the area and rejoined his Amish family. "Hello, Joy. Duncan is fine, but he is working today moving Joe's sheep, so he couldn't come for a visit. Has your father found work?"

"Yes, I mean, *ja,* at the sawmill. Mrs. Weaver is glad, too, because that silly boy Faron Martin couldn't keep his mind off his girlfriend long enough to do his work."

Carl heard a smothered chuckle from Lizzie. He had to smile, too. "I'm not sure your grandmother and Mrs. Weaver want you repeating their conversations."

"Why not?"

The two boys reached her before Carl could explain. The oldest boy, Jacob Imhoff, spoke first. "Joy, you aren't supposed to run off without telling someone. You know that."

She hung her head. "I forgot."

Joy had a bad habit of wandering off and had frightened her family on several occasions by disappearing without letting anyone know where she was going.

The younger boy, her cousin David, took her hand. "That's okay. We aren't mad."

She peeked at him. "You're not?"

"Nee."

She gave him a sheepish smile. "I only wanted to talk to Carl."

A car buzzed past them on the highway. Jacob patted her shoulder. "We don't want you to get hit by one of the *Englisch* cars driving by so fast."

"This was my fault," Carl said quickly. "I should have turned into the lane to speak to Joy and not stopped out here on the road."

Joy stared at him solemnly. "It's okay. I forgive you."

If only he could gain forgiveness so easily for his past sins. He quickly changed the subject. "How is your puppy, Joy?"

"Pickles is a butterball with legs and a tail. She chews up everything. Mammi is getting mighty tired of it."

Joy could always make him smile. "Tell your grandmother to give your pup a soupbone to gnaw on. That will keep her sharp little teeth occupied for a few days."

Joy looked past him at Lizzie. "Is this your wife? She's pretty."

He sat bolt upright. *"Nee, sie ist nicht meine frau.* She's not my wife."

Lizzie watched a blush burn a fiery red path up Carl's neck and engulf his face. It was amusing to see such a big man discomforted by a child's innocent question, but she was more interested in his answer. He had denied that she was his wife in flawless Pennsylvania Dutch, the German dialect language spoken by the Amish.

Carl King might dress and act Englisch, but he had surely been raised Amish to speak the language so well.

He gathered the reins. "You should get back to your game, kids. I have to take this lady to the bus station."

He set the pony moving again, and a frown replaced the smile he had given so easily to the little girl. Lizzie liked him better when he was smiling.

"Your Pennsylvania Dutch is very good."

"I get by."

"Were you raised Amish?"

A muscle twitched in his clenched jaw. "I was."

"Several of the young men in our community have left before they were baptized, too."

"I left afterward."

Lizzie's eyes widened with shock. That meant he was in the Bann. Why had her grandfather allowed her to travel with him? Her uncle wouldn't even speak with an excommunicated person. A second later, she realized that she would very likely be placed in the Bann, too. Her uncle would not let her rebellious action go unpunished. She prayed her sisters were not suffering because of her.

She glanced at Carl and noted the tense set of his jaw. The rules of her faith were clear. She could not accept a ride from a shunned person. She was forbidden to do business with him, accept any favor from him or eat at the same table. Her grandfather had placed her in a very awkward situation. "Please stop the cart."

Carl's shoulders slumped. "As you wish."

He pulled the pony to a halt. "It is a long walk. You will miss the bus."

"Then I must drive. It is permitted for me to give you a lift, but I can't accept one from you."

"I know the rules." He laid down the reins and stepped over the bench seat to sit on the floor of the cart behind her.

She took the reins and slapped them against the pony's rump to get him moving. He broke into a brisk trot.

"How is it that you work for my grandfather? Has he left the church, too?"

"No."

"Does he know your circumstance?"

"Of course."

She grew more confused by the minute. "Surely the members of his congregation must object to his continued association with you."

"He hasn't mentioned it if they do."

She glanced toward him over her shoulder. "But they know, don't they?"

"You'd have to ask Joe about that."

As she was on her way to the bus depot, that wasn't likely to happen. "I would, but I doubt I'll see him again." She heard the bitterness in her voice and knew Carl heard it, too.

Her grandfather had made it crystal clear he wasn't interested in getting to know his granddaughters. His rejection hurt deeply, but she shouldn't have been surprised by it. To depend on any man's kindness was asking for heartache.

As the pony trotted along, Lizzie struggled to find forgiveness in her heart. Her grandfather was a man who needed prayers, not her harsh thoughts. She prayed for Carl, too, that he would repent his sins, whatever they were, and find his way back to God. His life must be lonely indeed.

As lonely as Clara's would be married to a man she didn't love and without her sisters around her. Lizzie had failed her miserably.

After they had traveled nearly a mile, Lizzie decided she didn't care to spend the rest of the trip in silence. It left her too much time to think about her failure. Conversation with a shunned person wasn't strictly forbidden. "Is Joy a relative?"

"A neighbor."

"She seems like a very sweet child."

"Yes."

"Who is Duncan?"

"My dog."

His curt answers made her think he'd left his good humor back at the schoolyard. She gave up the idea of maintaining a conversation. She drew a deep breath and tried to come up with a new course of action that would save her sisters.

All she could think of was to find a job in town, but she didn't have enough money to rent a room. She had enough to pay for her bus fare home and that was it. She didn't even have enough left over to buy something to eat. Her stomach grumbled in protest. She hadn't eaten in more than a day. Nothing since her last supper at her uncle's house.

If she returned to his home, she would have to beg forgiveness and endure his chastisement in whatever form he chose. It would most likely be a whipping with his favorite willow cane, but he sometimes chose a leather strap. Stale bread and water for a week was another punishment he enjoyed handing out. She would be blessed if that were his choice. She shivered and pulled her coat tight across her chest.

"Are you cold?" Carl asked.

"A little." More than a little, she realized. There was a bite to the wind now that they were heading into it. A stubborn March was holding spring at bay.

Carl slipped off his coat and laid it on the seat. "Put this on."

She shook her head. "I can't take your coat."

"You are cold. I'm not."

She glanced back at him sitting braced against the side of the cart. "*Nee,* it wouldn't be right."

He studied her for a few seconds, then looked away. A dull flush of red stained his cheeks. "It is permitted if you do not take it from my hand."

"That's not what I meant. I don't wish to cause you discomfort."

"Watching you shiver causes me discomfort."

It was hard to argue with that logic. She picked up

the thick coat and slipped it on. It retained his body heat and felt blissfully warm as she pulled it close. *"Danki."*

"You're welcome."

They rode in silence for the rest of the way into town. As they drove past the local inn, she turned to him. "I wish to stop here for a few minutes. Since my grandfather won't help us, I must try to find a job."

"He told me to take you to the bus station."

"I'll only be a few minutes."

He grudgingly nodded. "A few minutes and then we must go. I have work to do."

"Danki." She gave him a bright smile before she unwrapped herself from his coat and jumped down from the cart.

When she entered the inn, she found herself inside a lobby with ceilings that rose two stories above her. On one side of the room, glass shelves displayed an assortment of jams and jellies for sale. On the opposite wall, an impressive stone fireplace soared two stories high and was at least eight feet wide. Made in the old-world fashion using rounded river stones set in mortar, it boasted a massive timber for a mantel. A quilt hanger had been added near the top. A beautiful star quilt hung on display. Two more quilts folded over racks flanked the fireplace.

At the far end of the room was a waist-high counter. A matronly Amish woman stood behind it. Tall and big-boned with gray hair beneath her white *kapp,* she wore a soft blue dress that matched her eyes. "Good afternoon and *willkommen* to the Wadler Inn. I'm Naomi Wadler. How may I help you?"

Her friendly smile immediately put Lizzie at ease. "I'm looking for work. Anything will do. I'm not picky."

"I'm sorry. We don't have any openings right now. Are you new to the area? You look familiar. Have we met?"

Lizzie tried to hide her disappointment at not finding employment. "I don't think so. Might you know of someone looking for a chore girl or household helper?"

"I don't, dear. If I hear of anything, I'll be glad to let you know. Where are you staying?"

Lizzie glanced out the window. Carl was scowling in her direction. He motioned for her to come on. She turned back to Naomi. "That's okay. I thank you for your time. The quilts around the fireplace are lovely. Are they your work?"

"*Nee,* I display them for some of our local quilters. Many Englisch guests come to this area looking to buy quilts. These were done by a local woman named Rebecca Troyer. I'm always looking for quilts to buy if you have some to sell."

All she had was her mother's quilt, and it was too precious to part with. "My sister has a good hand with a needle. I'm afraid I don't, but I can cook, clean, tend a garden, milk cows. I can even help with little children."

Naomi gave her a sympathetic smile. "You should check over at the newspaper office, *Miller Press.* It's a few blocks from here. They may know of someone looking for work."

Lizzie started for the door. As she reached it, the woman called out, "I didn't get your name, child."

"I'm Lizzie Barkman. I have to go. Thank you again for your time." She left the inn and climbed into the cart again. "They don't have anything. I wish to stop at the newspaper office. There might be something in the help-wanted section of the paper."

"Joe can't move all the sheep without help. I should be there."

"It will only take a minute or two to read the want ads. I'll hurry, I promise. Which way is it?"

He gave her directions and she found the *Miller Press* office without difficulty. Inside, she quickly read through the ads, but didn't find anything she thought she could do. Most of them were requests for skilled labor. It looked as if going home was to be her fate, after all.

With lagging steps, she returned to the cart. She followed Carl's succinct directions to the center of town. When the bus station came into view, she felt the sting of tears again. She'd arrived that morning, tired but full of hope, certain that she could save her sister.

It had been a foolhardy plan at best. She stared at the building. "My sister was right. I'm nothing but a dreamer."

A short, bald man came out the door and locked it behind him. Carl took Lizzie's suitcase from the back of the cart and approached him. "This lady needs a ticket."

"Sorry, we're closed." The man didn't even look up. He started to walk off, but Carl blocked his way.

"She needs a ticket to Indiana."

The stationmaster took a step back. "You're too late. The westbound bus left five minutes ago. The next one is on Tuesday."

"Four days? How can that be?"

The little man raised his hands. "Look around. We're not exactly a transportation hub. Hope Springs is just down the road from Next-to-Nowhere. The bus going west departs at 3:00 p.m. on Tuesdays and Fridays." He stepped around Carl and walked away.

She wasn't going back today. She still had a chance to

find a job. Lizzie looked skyward and breathed a quick prayer. "*Danki,* my Lord."

She wanted to shout for joy, but the grim look on Carl's face kept her silent. He scowled at her. "Joe isn't going to like this."

Chapter Three

"What is she doing back here? I told you to make sure she got on the bus!" Joe looked ready to spit nails.

Carl jumped down from the back of the cart and took Lizzie's suitcase and her box from behind the seat. He knew Joe would be upset. He wasn't looking forward to this conversation.

"She missed the bus. The next one going her way is on Tuesday. I couldn't very well leave her standing on the street corner, could I?"

"I don't see why not," Joe grumbled.

Lizzie got down for the cart and came up the steps to stand by her grandfather on the porch. "I'm sorry to inconvenience you, Daadi, but I didn't know what else to do. I don't have enough money to pay for a room at the inn until Tuesday and get a ticket home. I won't be any trouble."

"Too late for that," Carl muttered. She had already cost him half a day's work.

"What am I supposed to do with you now?" Joe demanded.

"I can sleep in the barn if you don't have room for me in the house."

She actually looked demure with her hands clasped before her and her eyes downcast. Carl wasn't fooled. She was tickled pink that she had missed the bus. He half wondered if she had insisted on making those job-hunting stops for just that reason. He had no proof of that, but he wasn't sure he would put it past her.

Joe sighed heavily. "I guess you can stay in your mother's old bedroom upstairs, but don't expect there to be clean sheets on the bed."

Lizzie smiled sweetly. "*Danki*. I'm not afraid of a little dust. If you really want me to leave, you could hire a driver to take me home."

Scowling, Joe snapped, "I'm not paying a hired driver to take you back. It would cost a fortune. You will leave on Tuesday. Since you're here, you might as well cook supper. You can cook, can't you?"

"Of course."

He gestured toward the door. "Come on, Carl. Those shearing pens won't set themselves up."

She shot Carl a sharp look and then leaned toward Joe. "Daadi, may I speak to you in private?"

Here it comes. She's going to pressure Joe to get rid of me.

Carl didn't want to leave. He enjoyed working with the sheep and with Joe. In this place, he had found a small measure of peace that didn't seem to exist anywhere else in the world. Would Lizzie make trouble for the old man if she allowed Carl to stay on?

Joe waved aside her request. "We'll speak after supper. My work can't wait any longer. Carl, did you pick up the mail, at least?"

He shook his head. "I forgot to mention it when we passed your mailbox."

Joe glared at Lizzie. "That's what comes of having a distraction around. I'll go myself."

"I'll go get your mail." Lizzie started to climb back onto the cart, but Joe stopped her.

"The pony has done enough work today. It won't hurt you to walk to the end of the lane, will it?"

She flushed and stepped away from the cart. "*Nee,* of course not. Shall I unhitch him and put him away?"

"Put him in the corral to the right of the barn and make sure you rub him down good."

"I will."

As she led the pony away, sympathy for her stirred in Carl. Joe wasn't usually so unkind. "I can take care of the horse, Joe."

"If she's going to stay, she's going to earn her keep while she's here. I don't know why she had to come in the first place." Joe stalked away with a deep frown on his face.

Carl followed him. The two men crossed to the largest shed and went inside. Numerous metal panels were stacked against the far wall. They were used to make pens of various sizes to hold the sheep both prior to shearing and afterward.

They had the first three pens assembled before Joe spoke again. "You think I'm being too hard on her, don't you?"

"It's your business and none of mine."

"What did she have to say on your trip into town and back?"

"Not much. She's concerned that her sister is being

made to marry against her will by their uncle Morris. It's not the way things are done around here."

"*Nee,* but it doesn't surprise me much. I never cared for Morris. I couldn't believe it when my daughter wanted to marry into that family. I tried to talk her out of it. I've never met a more shiftless lot. The men never worked harder than they had to, but they made sure the women did. In my eyes, they didn't treat their women with the respect they deserved."

"What do you mean?"

"They spoke harshly to them. They kept them away from other women. I saw fear in the eyes of Morris's wife more than once when he got upset with her."

"Do you believe there was physical abuse?"

"I thought so, but none of them would admit it. Such things weren't talked about back then. I went so far as to share my misgivings with the bishop. The family didn't take kindly to my interference."

"I imagine not."

"My daughter assured me her husband was a kind man, but I saw the signs. I saw the changes in her over the years. My son-in-law and I had some heated words about it. Then one day, the whole family up and moved away. I never saw them again. My daughter never even wrote to let me know where they had gone. Years later, I got one letter. It was from Morris telling me my Abigail and her husband were dead. He said a truck struck their buggy. Her husband died instantly, but Abigail lingered for another day."

Joe's voice tapered off as he struggled with his emotions. Carl had never seen him so upset. After giving the old man a few minutes to compose himself, Carl said,

"I've never heard of the Amish having arranged marriages."

"They don't, but if you dig deep enough in any barrel, you'll find a few bad apples, even among the Amish. Morris was a bad apple. I don't know why my girl couldn't see that, but I was told she lived long enough after the accident to name Morris as guardian of her children. I'm not surprised he thinks he can pick their husbands."

"So, you aren't going to help Lizzie?"

Joe shook his head slowly. "I loved my daughter, Carl. I never got over her leaving the way she did, but she was a good mother. I have to ask myself what would she want me to do. Honestly, I think my daughter would want me to stay out of it. Life is not easy for any of us. I don't want Lizzie to think she can come running to me whenever it seems too hard for her."

"Do you really think that's what she's doing?" Carl asked gently.

"I don't know. Maybe."

Carl didn't agree, but then it wasn't his place to agree or disagree with Joe. It was his place to take care of the sheep.

"What else did she say?" Joe asked. He tried to sound indifferent, but Carl wasn't fooled.

"She wants to find a job around here."

Joe nodded but didn't comment. Carl drew a deep breath. "I had to tell her I'm in the Bann."

"*Ach,* that's none of her business." Joe kicked a stubborn panel into place and secured it with a length of wire.

"She asked. I couldn't lie."

Joe shared a rare, stilted smile. "It would astonish me if you did."

"Will she go to church services with you on Sunday?"

"*Ja,* I imagine so."

"Will my being here cause trouble for you?" He didn't want to leave, but he would. Joe had been good to him.

"Having her here is causing me trouble."

"You know what I mean." Joe could easily find himself shunned by his fellow church members for allowing Carl to work on his farm. The rules were clear about what was permitted and what wasn't with a shunned person. Joe had been bending the rules for more than two years to give Carl a place to live. A few people in Joe's church might suspect Carl was ex-Amish, but no one knew it for a fact. Only Lizzie. If she spread that information, it would change everything.

The old man sighed and laid a hand on Carl's shoulder. "*Sohn,* I know I'm not a good example. I don't like most people, but that's my fault and not theirs. Folks around here are generous and accepting of others. I've known Bishop Zook since he was a toddler. He's a kind and just man. I don't know your story, Carl, but I've come to know you. You seek solitude out among the flocks and in your small hut, but it does not bring you peace. 'Tis plain you carry a heavy burden. If you repent, if you ask forgiveness, it will be granted."

Carl looked away from the sympathy he didn't deserve. "Sometimes, forgiveness must be earned."

Joe's grip on Carl's shoulder tightened. "Our Lord Jesus earned it for us all by his death on the cross. However, it's your life. Live as you must. I've never pried and I never will."

"Thanks, but you didn't answer my question. Will my staying here cause trouble for you?"

Joe dusted his hands together. "I can handle any trouble my granddaughter tries to make."

Carl wasn't as confident.

The evening shadows were growing long by the time they finished setting up the runways and pens. Both men were tired, hot and sweaty, in spite of the cold weather. Carl found he was eager to see how Lizzie was faring. Was she a good cook? Joe wasn't. Carl managed, but he didn't enjoy the task.

The two men entered the kitchen and stopped in their tracks. They both looked around in surprise. The clutter had been cleared from the table. The wild heaps of dishes and pans in the sink had been tamed, washed and put away. The blue-and-white-checkered plastic tablecloth was glistening wet, as if she had just finished wiping it down. Even the floor had been swept and mopped. The scuffed old black-and-white linoleum looked better than Carl had ever seen it. There was a lingering scent of pine cleaner in the air, but it was the smell of simmering stew that made his mouth water.

Lizzie stood at the stove with her back to them. "It's almost done. There's soap and a fresh towel at the sink for you."

She turned toward them and used her forearm to sweep back a few locks of bright red hair that had escaped from beneath her black *kapp*. Her cheeks were flushed from the heat of the oven. Carl was struck once again by how pretty she was and how natural she looked in Joe's kitchen.

If the aroma was anything to go by, this might be the best meal he'd had in months. His stomach growled in anticipation, but he didn't move. The arrangement he and Joe shared might be different now that Lizzie was with them. He locked eyes with Joe and waited for a sign from him.

* * *

Lizzie wasn't sure how to proceed. She'd never fixed a meal for a shunned person. If Carl sat at the table, she would have to eat standing at the counter or in the other room. Eating at the same table with someone in the Bann was forbidden. Had her grandfather been breaking the Ordnung by eating with Carl? If so, it was her solemn duty to inform his bishop of such an infraction. She quailed at the thought. Such a move on her part would ruin any chance of bringing her sisters to live with him.

She watched as her grandfather went to the sink beneath the window and washed the grime off his hands. He used the towel she'd placed there and left it lying on the counter so that Carl could use it, too.

Her *daadi* stepped to the table, moved aside one of the benches and flipped back the tablecloth. Puzzled, Lizzie wondered what he was doing. Then she saw it wasn't one large kitchen table. It was two smaller ones that had been pushed together. He pulled the tables a few inches apart, smoothed the cloth back into place and returned the bench to its original place.

She relaxed with relief. Her grandfather hadn't broken the Ordnung. It appeared that he and Carl maintained the separation dictated by the Amish faith even when no one was around.

She caught Carl's quick glance before he looked away. He said, "Is this arrangement suitable, or should I eat outside?"

He was trying to look as if it didn't matter, but she could tell that it did.

"If my grandfather feels this is acceptable, then it is." It was his home, and he had to follow the rules of his congregation. It wouldn't have been acceptable in her uncle's home. Her uncle wouldn't have allowed Carl inside the house. Her uncle expounded often about the dangers of associating with unclean people.

Joe took his place at the head of the table. Lizzie dished stew into a bowl and placed it in front of him. She dished up a second bowl and gave Carl a sympathetic look before she left it on the counter. She took a plate of golden-brown biscuits from the oven and set it on the table, too.

Carl washed up and carried his bowl to his table opposite her grandfather.

Lizzie got her own bowl and took a seat at her grandfather's left-hand side. When she was settled, he bowed his head and silently gave thanks to God for the meal. From the corner of her eye, she saw Carl bow his head, too.

What had he done that made him an outsider among them, and why was her grandfather risking being shunned himself by having him around?

The meal progressed in silence. Lizzie didn't mind; it was normal at her uncle's home, too. She and her sisters saved their conversations until they were getting ready for bed at night.

The unexpected weight of loneliness forced her spirits lower. She missed her sisters more than she thought possible. Tonight, she would be alone for the first time in her life. She didn't count her night on the bus, for she hadn't been alone for a minute on that horrible ride. She thought she was hungry, but her appetite ebbed away. She picked at her food and pushed it around in her bowl. A quick glance at her grandfather and Carl showed neither of them noticed. They ate with gusto. Maybe good food would convince them they needed a woman around the house full-time.

A woman, yes, but four women?

There was more than enough work to keep four women busy for months. The place was a mess. All the rooms needed a thorough cleaning. There was years of accumulated dust and cobwebs in every corner of the four bedrooms upstairs, although only one room contained a bed. The others held an accumulation of odds and ends, broken furniture and several plastic tubs filled with baby bottles. She assumed they were for the lambs.

The downstairs wasn't as bad, but it wasn't tidy, either.

She was afraid to speculate on the amount of mending that was needed. There was a pile of clothes in a huge laundry hamper beside the wringer washer on a small back porch. The few bits of clothing she had examined were both dirty and in need of repair. It was too bad that one of her days here was a Sunday. She wouldn't be able to engage in anything but the most necessary work on the Sabbath.

She'd simply have to rise early tomorrow and again on Monday and Tuesday mornings to get as much of the washing, mending and cleaning done as she could before her bus left. Her grandfather might not want her here, but she would do all that she could for him before she left, even if she disliked mending with a passion.

It was a shame that Clara hadn't come with her. Clara loved needlework. Her tiny stitches were much neater than Lizzie could manage. Each of the girls had a special talent. Lizzie liked to cook. Betsy was good with animals. Clara, like their mother, enjoyed sewing, quilting and knitting. Greta avoided housework whenever she could. She enjoyed being outside tending the orchard and the gardens.

Just thinking about them made a deep sadness settle

in Lizzie's soul. She had failed miserably to help them thus far, but the good Lord had given her more time. She wouldn't waste it feeling sorry for herself.

She smiled at her grandfather. "I hope you like the stew. I do enjoy cooking. I couldn't help noticing your garden hasn't been prepared for spring planting yet. It's nearly time to get peas and potatoes planted. My sister Greta would be itching to spade up the dirt. The Lord blessed her with a green thumb for sure."

Her grandfather ran his last bite of biscuit around the rim of his bowl to sop up any traces of gravy. "The planting will get done after the lambing."

"Of course. You probably know there's barely any preserved food left in the cellar. I used the last of the canned beef and carrots for tonight's meal. There will be only canned chicken for the next meals unless you can provide me with something fresh or allow me to go into town and purchase more food. What a shame it is to see an Amish cellar bare. At home, my sisters and I have hundreds of jars of meat, corn and vegetables. Do you like beets, Daadi?"

"Not particularly."

"I like snap peas better myself." She fell silent.

"There are plenty of eggs in the henhouse. We men know how to make do."

There had to be a way to convince him of her usefulness. Perhaps after he saw the results of her hard work over the next several days he would agree to let her stay.

Joe pushed his empty bowl away and brushed biscuit crumbs from his beard and vest. "You're a *goot* cook, I'll give you that."

"A mighty good cook. Thank you for the meal," Carl added.

"You're welcome." She wasn't used to being thanked for doing something that was her normal responsibility.

Her grandfather swallowed the last swig of his coffee and set the cup in his bowl. "I reckon it's time to start moving the flocks closer to the barns."

Carl nodded. "I can put the rams and the first of the ewes in the barn tomorrow in separate pens."

"No point penning them inside just yet. Monday will be soon enough. Shearing can start on Tuesday."

Lizzie brightened. Perhaps the sheep held the key to proving her usefulness. "Can I help with that? I'd love to learn more about sheep and about shearing them."

Joe huffed in disgust. "If you don't know sheep, you'll be no use to me."

She looked at Carl. He didn't say anything. She was foolish to hope for help in that direction. Suddenly, she remembered the mail she had collected earlier. There had been a letter for him. She went into the living room and returned with her grandfather's copy of the local newspaper and an envelope for Carl.

Her grandfather's eyes brighten. "*Ach,* my newspaper. *Danki.* I like reading it after supper."

She turned to Carl and held the letter toward him. "This came for you."

When he didn't take it, she laid it on the corner of the table and resumed her seat.

Rising to his feet, Carl picked up the letter, glanced at it and then carried his empty bowl to the sink. Turning to the stove, he lifted the lid on the firebox and dropped the letter in unopened. He left the house without another word.

After the screen door banged shut behind him, Lizzie gathered the rest of the dishes and carried them to the sink. She stared out the window at his retreating back as he walked toward the barn and the pasture gate beyond.

His dog came bounding across the yard and danced around him, seeking attention. He paused long enough to bend and pat the animal. Straightening, he glanced back once at the house before he walked on.

What had he done to cut himself off from his family, his friends and from his Amish faith? Why burn an unopened letter? Why live such a lonely life with only a dog and an old man for company? Carl King was an intriguing man. The longer she was around him, the more she wanted to uncover the answers about him.

"Out with your questions before you choke on them," her grandfather said, still seated at the table.

"I don't know what you mean." She began filling the sink with water.

"*Ja,* you do. You want to know about Carl."

She couldn't very well deny it when she was bursting with curiosity about the man. She shut off the water and faced her grandfather. "I don't understand how you can do business with him. It is forbidden."

"I do no business with him." He opened his paper and began to read.

She took a step toward him in disbelief and propped both hands on her hips. "How can you say that? He works for you. He's your hired man."

"I did not hire Carl. He works here because he wishes to do so. He lives in an empty hut on my property. He pays no rent, so I am neither landlord nor employer."

"You mean he works for nothing?"

Folding his paper in exasperation, he said, "Each year, when the lambs are sold, I leave one third of my profits here on the kitchen table, and I go to bed. In the morning, the money is always gone."

"So you do pay him?"

"I have never asked if he's the one who takes the money."

She crossed her arms over her chest. "Don't you think that is splitting hairs?"

"No doubt some people will say it is."

"Aren't you worried that you may be shunned for his continued presence here?"

He leaned back in his chair. "What would you have me do?"

"You must tell him that unless he repents, he must leave. What has he done to make all your church avoid him?"

"I have no idea."

"But all members of the church must agree to the shunning. How can you not know the reason? It is not a thing that is done lightly or in secret."

"In all my years, I have seen it done only a handful of times. It was very sad and distressful for those involved. Carl is not from around here. He has not been shunned by my congregation. I would not have known he was anything but an Englisch fellow in need of a meal and a bed if he hadn't told me. It seems to me that he holds our beliefs in high regard."

"Then for him to remain separated from the church is doubly wrong, and all the more reason to send him away."

Her grandfather let his chair down and leaned forward with his hands clasped on the table. "Child, why do we shun someone?"

"Because they have broken their vows to God and to the church by refusing to follow the Ordnung."

"You have missed the meaning of my question. What is the purpose of shunning an individual?"

"To make them see the error of their ways."

"That is true, but you have not mentioned the most important part. It is not to punish them. Shunning is done out of love for that person so that they may see what it is to be cut off from God and God's family by their sin. It is a difficult thing to do, to care for someone and yet turn away from them."

"But if they don't repent, we must turn away so that we do not share in that sin."

"If I give aid to a sinner, does that make me one?"

"Of course not. We are commanded to care for those in need, be they family or stranger."

"As the Good Samaritan did in the parable told by our Lord."

She could see where his questions were leading. "*Ja,* if you have given aid to Carl, that is as it should be."

A smile twitched at the corner of his mouth. "I'm glad you approve. The first time I met Carl, I discovered him sleeping in my barn. It had rained like mad in the night. His clothes were ragged and damp. They hung on his thin frame like a scarecrow's outfit. Everything he owned in the world he was wearing or had rolled up in a pack he was using as a pillow, except for a skinny puppy that lay beside him.

"Carl immediately got up, apologized for trespassing and said he was leaving. I offered him a meal. He declined, but said he would be grateful if I could spare something for the dog."

Lizzie's heart twisted with pity for Carl. To be homeless and alone was no easy thing. "I assume you fed the dog?"

"I told Carl I had a little bacon I could fry up for the pup. I coaxed them both into the house and fried enough for all of us. I put a plate on the floor and that little Duncan gobbled it up before I got my hand out of the way. Bacon is still his favorite food. When I put two plates on the table was when Carl told me he could not eat with me."

"At least he was honest about it."

"If you had seen the look in that young man's eyes, you would know, as I do, that he cares deeply about our faith. He was starving, but he was willing to forgo food in order to keep me from unknowingly breaking the laws of our church."

"Yet, he never told you why he had been placed in the Bann?"

"*Nee,* he has not, and I do not ask. I told him I had an empty hut he could use for as long as he wanted. His dog took naturally to working the sheep and so did Carl. He has a tender heart for animals."

"What you did was a great kindness, Daadi, but Carl no longer requires physical aid."

"True. The man is neither hungry nor homeless, but his great wound is not yet healed. That's why I have not turned him away."

She scowled. "I saw no evidence of an injury."

Her grandfather shook his head sadly. "Then you have not looked into his eyes as I have done. Carl has a grave wound inside. Something in his past lies heavy on his mind and on his heart. My instincts tell me he will find his way back to God and to our faith when he has had time to heal. Then there will be great rejoicing in heaven and on earth."

Maybe she came by her daydreaming naturally, after all. "*If* it happens."

Her grandfather sighed, rose from his chair and headed toward his bedroom. Before he closed the door, he turned back to her. "It will happen. It's a shame you won't be here to see it when it does."

Chapter Four

He wouldn't go up to the house today.

Carl stood in the doorway of his one-room hut and stared at the smoke rising from Joe's chimney a quarter of a mile away. The chimney was all he could see of the house, for the barn sat between it and his abode.

It hadn't taken Carl long to decide that avoiding Lizzie would be his best course of action. It was clear how uncomfortable his presence made her last night. He didn't want her to endure more of the same.

Her presence made him uncomfortable, too.

She made him think about all he had lost the right to know. A home, a wife, the simple pleasure of sitting at a table with someone.

No, he wouldn't go up to the house, but he knew she was there.

Was she making breakfast? If it was half as good as supper had been, it would be delicious. He couldn't remember the last time he'd had such light and fluffy biscuits.

Even for another biscuit, he wouldn't go up the hill.

He could make do with a slice of stale bread and

cheese from his own tiny kitchen. He didn't need biscuits. He didn't even need coffee.

And he sure didn't need to see her again.

Lizzie Barkman's pretty face was etched in his mind like a carving in stone. All he had to do was close his eyes, and he could see her as clearly as if she were standing in front of him.

He hadn't slept well, but when he dozed, it was her face he saw in his dreams and not the usual faces from his nightmares.

In his dream last night, Lizzie had been smiling at him, beckoning him from a doorway to come inside a warm, snug house. He wanted to go in, but his feet had been frozen to the ground as snow swirled around him. Sometimes, the snow grew so thick it hid her face, but as soon as it cleared a little, she was still there waiting for him—a wonderful, warm vision in a cold, lonely world.

Carl shook his head to dispel the memory. No, he wouldn't go up to the house today. She wouldn't beckon him inside, and he shouldn't go in if she did. He was a forbidden one, an outcast by his own making.

He needed to stop feeling sorry for himself. He had work to do. He glanced toward the sturdy doghouse just outside his doorway. "Come on, Duncan. We have sheep to move today."

Duncan didn't appear. Carl leaned down to look inside and saw the doghouse was empty. Puzzled, he glanced around the pasture. His dog was nowhere in sight. Carl cupped his hands around his mouth and hollered the dog's name. Duncan still didn't come.

This wasn't like him. The only time the dog occasionally roamed away from the farm was when school was in session. He liked to play fetch with the kids and visit with the teacher's pretty female shepherd. It was too early for the children or the teacher to be at school yet, so where was Duncan?

Maybe Joe had taken him and gone out after some of the sheep already. If that was the case, Carl had better see that the fences in the hilltop enclosure around the lambing sheds were in good repair.

He headed up to the barn and found Joe pitching hay down to the horses in the corral. If he hadn't gone after the sheep, where was the dog? "Joe, have you seen Duncan this morning?"

Joe paused and leaned on his pitchfork handle. "*Nee,* I have not. He's not with you?"

Carl shook his head. "He was gone when I got up."

"He'll be back. Lizzie should have breakfast ready in a few minutes. Tell her I'll be in when I'm done here." Joe resumed his work.

"I'm not hungry. I'm going to fix the fence in the little field at the top of the hill, and then I'll move the ewes in the south forty up to it. They'll be easier to move into the barn from there when it's time to shear them."

"All right."

Carl knew if he took two steps to the left, he'd have a good view of the house from around the corner of the barn. "It'll make it easier to keep an eye on them for any early lambs, too."

"It will." Joe kept pitching down forkfuls of hay.

"I don't expect any premature births from that group. They've all had lambs before without any trouble."

"I know."

Carl folded his arms tight across his chest and tried to ignore the overpowering urge to look and see if he could catch a glimpse of Lizzie. "We might have to cull a few of them. We've got five or six that are getting up there in years."

Joe stopped his work and leaned on his pitchfork again. "I'm not senile yet. I know my own sheep. I thought you were looking for your dog."

"I was. I am."

"Have you checked up at the house?"

"No." Carl unfolded his arms and slipped his hands into his front pockets.

"That granddaughter of mine was singing this morning. Could be the dog thought it was yowling, and he's gone to investigate."

"Is she a poor singer?" Somehow, Carl expected her to have a melodious voice to match her sweet smile.

"How do I know? I've been tone-deaf since I was born. It all sounds like yowling to me." Setting his pitchfork aside, Joe vanished into the recesses of the hayloft.

Now that he was unobserved, Carl took those two steps and glanced toward the house. He didn't see Lizzie, but Duncan sat just outside the screen door, intently watching something inside.

"Duncan. Here, boy!"

The dog glanced his way and went back to staring into the house. He barked once. Annoyed, Carl began walking toward him. "Duncan, get your sorry tail over here. We've got work to do."

The dog rose to his feet, but didn't leave his place.

Carl approached the house just as the screen door opened a crack. The dog wagged his tail vigorously. Carl saw Lizzie bend down and slip Duncan something to eat.

After deciding he wouldn't see her at all today, that tiny glimpse of her wasn't enough. He wanted to look upon her face again. Would she welcome his company or simply tolerate it?

It didn't matter. He had no business thinking it might.

What had Joe told her about him last night? Carl kept walking in spite of his better judgment telling him to go gather the flock without his dog.

By the time he reached the door, Lizzie had gone back inside, but the smell of frying bacon lingered in the air.

Carl stared down at his dog. "I see she's discovered your weakness."

Duncan licked his chops.

Carl grinned. "*Ja,* I've got a strong liking for bacon myself."

"Come in and have a seat before these eggs get cold. I hope you like them scrambled." Her cheerful voice drove away the last of his hesitation. She was going to be here for only a few days. Why shouldn't he enjoy her company and her cooking until she left?

He moved Duncan aside with his knee and pulled open the screen door. The dog followed him in and took his usual place beneath the bench Carl sat on. Duncan knew better than to beg for food, but he would happily snatch up any bits his master slipped to him. It was a morning ritual that had gone on for years.

The house smelled of bacon and fresh-baked bread. Lizzie must have been up for hours. She stood at the stove stirring something. There were two plates piled high with food already on the counter. Carl sat down and waited. "Joe will be in shortly."

She took her pan from the stove and poured creamy gravy into a serving boat on the counter beside her. "*Goot.* I ate earlier. I have a load of clothes in the washer I need to hang out. Having a propane-powered washer is so nice. At home, we do all the laundry by hand." Turning around, her eyes widened with shock. "No! Out, out, out!"

Carl leaped up from his seat. "I'm sorry. I thought it was all right if I ate here."

"You, yes. The dog, no."

It took him a second to process what she meant. "But Duncan normally eats with me at breakfast."

She plunked the gravy boat on the table. "Then he will be thrilled when I'm gone. But until I leave this house, I won't tolerate a dog in my kitchen at mealtime. Look what his muddy feet have done to my clean floor. Take him outside." She crossed her arms over her chest and glared at them both.

So much for basking in the glow of her smile this morning. Carl looked down and saw she was right. Muddy paw prints stood out in sharp contrast to the clean black-and-white squares. The dog must have gone down to the creek before coming to the house.

Duncan sank as flat against the floor as he could get. He knew he was in trouble, but Carl was sure he didn't understand why.

"Come on, fella. Outside with you."

Duncan didn't move.

Carl took hold of his collar and had to pull him out from under the table. His muddy feet left a long smear until Duncan realized he wasn't welcome. Then he bolted for the door and shot outside as Joe came, in nearly tripping the old gent.

"What's the matter with him?"

"His feet are muddy," Carl said. He left the kitchen and went out to the back porch. He returned with a mop and bucket. He started to wipe up the mess.

Already seated at the table, Joe said, "Leave the woman's work to the woman."

"It was my dog that made the mess." Carl met Lizzie's eyes. They were wide with surprise. Suddenly, she smiled at him. It was worth a week of mopping floors to behold. He leaned on the mop handle and smiled back.

Lizzie realized Carl's bold gaze was fixed on her. And why shouldn't it be? She wasn't behaving in the least like a modest maiden. She averted her eyes and schooled her features into what she hoped was a prim attitude. It was hard when his presence made her heart race. He was a handsome fellow, but she shouldn't be staring at him.

"Am I getting breakfast, or should I go out and get the rest of my work done?" Joe snapped.

"I'm sorry, Daadi. I have it right here." She hurried to bring both plates to the table. Keeping her eyes downcast, she said, "I'll take the mop out to the porch. I'm going that way. It was kind of you to help."

"It's no trouble. I'll take it out."

"As you wish." She scurried ahead of him out the back door and stopped when she had the tub of the wringer washer between them.

He emptied the pail out the back door and placed it with the mop in the corner. When he didn't go back inside the house, she realized he wanted to say more.

"Is there something else?" *Please let it be quick and then please let him go away.* He made her nervous, but in a strange edgy way that she didn't understand.

"I know you hope your grandfather will let you and your sisters live here. I can see you're trying to please him. I don't think Joe will change his mind, but there are a few things you should know about him."

"Such as?"

"He mentioned you were singing this morning."

So her grandfather had noticed. She brightened. "I was. Did he like it?"

"Joe is tone-deaf. Singing is just noise to him."

"Oh." That was a letdown. She hoped a happy attitude and a cheerful hymn would soften his heart.

"And there is something else," Carl said.

She crossed her arms. "What?"

"Don't jump to do his bidding. He doesn't like people who are spineless."

Indignation flared in her. "Are you saying I'm spineless?"

"No, not at all. It took courage to come here. Just stand your ground and don't pander to him."

She relaxed when she realized he was honestly trying to help. "I appreciate your advice. I imagine you think I'm being underhanded by seeking to worm my way into his affections."

"No, I don't. Just don't get your hopes up."

"I'm afraid hope is all I have at this point. If nothing changes by Tuesday afternoon, I will go home a failure. My sisters are all I have. My sisters and my faith in God. I can't believe our Lord wants Clara in an unhappy marriage any more than I do."

"I respect what you're trying to do, but Joe has lived alone for a long time. He's old and he's set in his ways."

"He has you around every day."

"I'm sort of like Duncan. I'm useful and tolerated because of that."

She shook her head. "You don't know my grandfather nearly as well as you think. He cares deeply about you.

He cherishes the hope that you will one day find your way back to God and salvation."

There was no mistaking the sadness that filled Carl's eyes. "Then I reckon you aren't the only one who shouldn't get their hopes up. God isn't interested in my salvation."

He went back into the house and left Lizzie to puzzle over his words. What had happened to make him lose faith in God's goodness and mercy?

What a strange man Carl King was. He was polite and kind, he liked dogs and children, he was more helpful than most men she knew, and yet he seemed to believe God had abandoned him. Why?

If he had grown up in the Amish faith then surely he must know that God loved all His children. No sin was greater than God's ability to forgive.

With a tired sigh, she unloaded the washer and carried the wet clothes to the line outside. One by one, she hung the shirts, pants, sheets and pillowcases to dry in the fresh morning air until she had filled both clotheslines. She pulled a brown sock out of the basket and then had to search until she found its mate. They had both been neatly darned at the heels. She suspected it was Carl's work. She pinned them together on the clothesline. The next pair she put together had holes in both toes. More mending work for her.

She finished hanging up the load, and as she started for the back steps, movement caught her eye out in the pasture. Carl was striding toward the sheep dotting the far hillside. Duncan stayed close to his side until some unheard command sent him bolting toward the sheep in a wide, sweeping move.

As she watched, her grandfather joined them. The

dog gathered the scattered flock into a bunch and began moving them toward the pens just beyond the barn. Carl and the dog worked together until the group was safely penned. After Joe swung the gate shut behind the last ewe, Carl knelt. Duncan raced to him and the two enjoyed a brief moment of play before Carl rose to his feet. He and her grandfather headed farther afield with the dog trotting behind them.

As intriguing as Carl was, she couldn't add him to her list of people to be rescued. First and foremost, she was here to find a home and jobs for herself and her sisters. If there was any chance that her grandfather would change his mind, she had only these few days to prove how valuable she could be and how comfortable a woman in the house could make his life.

She went back to the washing machine and by late afternoon, the pile of clothing had dwindled to a few pieces that she considered rags. The pants that were dry had been folded and laid on her grandfather's bed. His shirts that were clean and mended hung from the pegs along his bedroom wall. The kitchen and bathroom towels had been sorted and put away. The socks that needed mending could wait until after supper. The jeans and shirt she knew were Carl's were piled on a chair in the living room where he was sure to see them.

Eggs from the henhouse and the last of the flour in the bin made a large batch of noodles that she simmered together with some of the canned chicken from the cellar. She discovered two jars of cherries and made an oatmeal-topped cobbler that she hoped would please both the men.

When everything was ready, she walked out onto the porch and rang the dinner bell hanging from one of the posts. A beautiful sunset was coloring the western sky with bands of gold and rose. Such powerful beauty before the darkness of night was another reminder of God's presence at the close of day.

Tomorrow would be a new day and a new chance to find a way to save her sisters.

Bright and early the next morning, Lizzie hurried to get in the buggy, where her grandfather was waiting impatiently. She said, "I hope I have not made us late."

The moment she was seated, Joe slapped the reins against the horse's rump. "Do not expect the horse to make up the time you've lost."

"I don't. Is the service far away?"

"*Nee*, it's less than two miles. It's at the home of Ike and Maggie Mast. I will tell you now that I don't stay for all the visiting and such afterward. We'll go home as soon as the service is over."

"But what about the meal?"

"I eat at home."

Lizzie hid her disappointment. Her family always stayed to eat and visit until late in the afternoon. Sunday service was a huge social event. She had hoped to meet as many local families as possible and see if anyone had work for her. Perhaps she could convince her grandfather to let her stay while he went home. "I would like to meet some of your neighbors and friends. I can walk home after the service."

"No point in getting friendly with people you'll never see again." He kept the horse at a steady trot until they came even with the small shepherd's hut that was set back a little way from the road. He stopped the buggy by the pasture gate and waited.

Lizzie realized he was waiting for Carl. When Carl

didn't appear after a few minutes, her grandfather's shoulders slumped ever so slightly. He clicked his tongue and set the horse moving again.

Lizzie glanced back as they drove away. "You were hoping that he would join us."

"He will when he is ready. All things are in God's own time."

"Some people never come back to the Amish life."

"Carl will." He slapped the reins again and the horse broke into a fast trot.

Would Carl ever seek forgiveness, or would he remain an outcast? It seemed so sad. He respected their ways, but something kept him from accepting them. If only she knew more about his past, she might be able to help him, but it wasn't likely she would get to know him that well.

The journey to the preaching service took less than half an hour. When they arrived at the farm home set into the side of a tree-covered hill, Lizzie saw the yard was already filled with buggies. Her grandfather's congregation was a large one. Several young men came to take charge of the buggy and the horse.

Her grandfather got down without waiting for her. Lizzie clasped her hands with trepidation. It was the first time she had attended a prayer meeting at a church besides her own. She wouldn't know anyone here. It was an uncomfortable feeling, but one she was determined to overcome.

Today was for praising God and giving thanks to Him for His blessings.

The singing of the first hymn started by the time they reached the front doors. Inside the house, the living room held four rows of backless wooden benches with a wide center aisle dividing them. The women and girls sat on one side, while the men and boys sat on the other. Her grandfather walked straight ahead to where the married men and elders sat. She made her way to an empty spot on the women's side of the aisle near the back.

She gathered many curious glances. The only face she recognized was the woman from the inn, Naomi Wadler. Smiling and nodding to the woman, Lizzie took a seat and picked up a copy of the Ausbund.

The hymnal was the same one used in the services she attended at home. The weight of the book felt familiar in her hand and gave her a sense of comfort. She might be far from home, but she was never far from God.

When the first hymn ended, she joined in silent prayer with those around her.

Please, Lord, protect and keep my sisters. If it be Your will, let Grandfather change his mind and allow us to live with him. And please, Heavenly Father, help Carl King to find his way back to You. Amen.

When the Sunday prayer service was within walking distance, Carl followed Joe to the neighboring farms. He never went near the buildings, but often, like today, he found a place beneath a tree and settled himself to listen. The sound of solemn voices raised in song came to him on the light spring breeze. The hymns, hundreds of years old, were sung by the Amish everywhere. The words and the meaning remained unchanged by the passage of time. They were as familiar to him as the clothes on his back or the worn boots on his feet.

Sometimes, like now, he softly sang along. The birds added their songs to the praising as the sun warmed the land. Spring was coming. A time of new births, a time of new beginnings. A time for the new lambs to join the flock.

For years, Carl had been waiting for a sign from God that he had been forgiven, that he could return to the fold of worshippers and be clean and whole again, but no sign had been forthcoming.

God had not yet forgiven him for killing a man.

Chapter Five

Lizzie sat patiently through the three-hour-long church service at the home of her grandfather's neighbors, Ike and Maggie Mast. She enjoyed the preaching, singing and prayers. The entire morning lifted her spirits.

When the last notes of the final hymn died away, Lizzie was immediately welcomed by a young woman seated near her, a redhead with a set of freckles that rivaled Lizzie's.

"Hello, and welcome to our church. I'm Sally Yoder. Did I see you arrive with Woolly Joe, or did my eyes deceive me? I didn't know he had any family."

"If you mean Joseph Shetler, then yes, I came with him. I'm his granddaughter from Indiana. I'm Lizzie Barkman."

"Are you Abigail's daughter?" someone asked from behind her. Turning, Lizzie saw it was Naomi Wadler, the woman from the inn.

"*Ja,* my mother's name was Abigail. Did you know her?"

"Very well. No wonder I thought you looked familiar. You resemble her a great deal. How wonderful to see you all grown up. I'm sure you don't remember me, but when you were very young, your mother and I spent many happy hours together. We were dear friends. You have more sisters, don't you?"

"Yes, there are four of us."

"I'm so happy that Joseph has mended the breach with your family. He was deeply saddened when your mother moved away. He never really got over it. I was so sorry to learn of her death. You must come visit me at the inn so that we can catch up. I'd love to hear what Abigail's daughters are doing."

Lizzie didn't care to share information about her strained relationship with her grandfather. Instead, she changed the subject. "I'm still looking for work. Have you heard of anything?"

"I have, and it may be just the thing for you. Come meet Katie and Elam Sutter. Elam's mother mentioned the couple has been thinking of hiring a girl to live in and help with the children and the business."

Excited by the prospect, Lizzie asked, "What kind of business?"

"Elam runs a basket-weaving shop. He and his wife are opening a store to sell their wares here in Hope Springs in addition to taking them to Millersburg to be sold there. We have so many tourists stopping by these days that it makes sense to have a shop locally."

Sally said, "I've worked for Elam for ages, and I've known Katie for several years. They are wonderful people."

Naomi led Lizzie to a group of young mothers seated on a quilt on the lawn. They were keeping an eye on their toddlers playing nearby while several infants slept on the blanket beside them. "Katie, have you found a chore girl yet?" Naomi asked.

Katie picked up a little boy and rose to her feet. She deftly extracted a pebble from his mouth. He yowled in protest. "Jeremiah Sutter, rocks are not for eating. *Nee,* Naomi, I have not found anyone willing to take on my horde."

"They are not a horde. They are adorable. Katie, this is Lizzie Barkman, and she may be just the woman you and Elam are looking for if you don't scare her away."

Lizzie met Katie's gaze and liked what she saw. The young mother had black hair and intelligent dark eyes. Her coloring was a stark contrast to her son's blue-eyed blondness.

"I don't know anything about basket weaving, but I'm willing to learn. I have two younger sisters, so I know something about taking care of children."

Katie put her little boy down and tipped her head slightly as she regarded Lizzie. "You aren't from around here, are you?"

"I was originally. My family moved to Indiana when I was small. My grandfather is Joseph Shetler."

"I didn't realize that Woolly Joe had any family," Katie said.

Sally propped her hands on her hips and rocked back on her heels. "That's exactly what I said."

Naomi smiled sadly at Lizzie. "After your mother and father moved away, your grandfather became a recluse. I hope that will change now."

"I don't believe it will." Lizzie glanced toward the line of buggies. Sure enough, her grandfather was hitching up his horse. He was ready to go. He wouldn't be happy if she kept him waiting.

"I pray that his eyes will be opened and he will see how many of his old friends still care deeply about him and miss him." There was something oddly poignant in Naomi's tone. Lizzie looked at her closely, but Naomi's gaze was fixed on Joe.

After a moment, Naomi sighed and looked back to Katie. "I'll leave you women to get acquainted while I go help set up for the meal. It was wonderful talking to you, Lizzie. I'm serious. You must come by the inn so we can catch up. I want to hear all about Abigail's daughters."

As Naomi walked away, Sally leaned close to Katie. "Did I just hear what I thought I heard?"

Katie wore a puzzled expression, too. "If you just heard Naomi Wadler sighing over Woolly Joe Shetler, then yes."

Lizzie pointed at Katie's son. "Jeremiah just ate another rock."

Katie rolled her eyes. She grabbed her son and swiped a finger through his mouth to pull out a pebble. "Come by our farm on Tuesday of this week and meet my husband. If he agrees, we'll work out the details. How soon could you start?"

"As soon as you would like."

Lizzie could barely contain her excitement. Once she had a job, she would be able to send money home, enough to get all of her sisters to Hope Springs. She had no idea where they would all live, but she put her faith in God. He would provide. She bid the women goodbye and rushed across the yard to where her grandfather was waiting.

A man approached their buggy as they were preparing to leave. "Might I have a word with you, Joe?"

"If it's a short word." Reluctantly, her grandfather nodded toward her. "This is my granddaughter Lizzie Barkman. This fellow is Adrian Lapp."

Adrian smiled at her. "Pleased to meet you. Joe, has Carl King had any experience shearing alpacas?"

Her grandfather scratched his cheek. "I've never heard him mention it."

"But he does all your sheep, right?"

"He does."

"My wife didn't like the man I hired last year. She said he was too rough with them. She's very attached to her animals. I'm looking for someone local who is willing to take on the task."

Joe stroked his beard slowly. "I've heard that they spit on folks."

"Only if they are frightened or very upset. Normally, they are as gentle as lambs."

"I heard the one you call Myrtle spit on the bishop's wife."

Adrian smothered a grin as he glanced over his shoulder. "It was a very unfortunate incident."

To Lizzie's surprise, Joe chuckled. "I would have given a lot to see that."

"Faith would rather the whole thing be forgotten, but a number of people feel as you do. Myrtle spit on me, too, the first time we met. The smell fades in a few days."

"I'll make sure Carl knows that."

"If he's willing to take on the work, just have him drop by tomorrow and let me know. We're in a hurry to get them done, but I know you'll be shearing soon, too. It could wait until after lambing season if need be, but Faith is anxious to get started on a batch of new yarns before our baby arrives. Her orders are already coming in. She's going to need help if she is going to keep up with them."

Lizzie leaned forward. "Are you looking to hire someone?"

Adrian shrugged. "We've been talking about it."

"I have a sister who is looking for work. The pay doesn't have to be much if she can get room and board."

"Does she have experience with carding wool and spinning?"

"She does." It had been years ago, but Lizzie remembered Clara and her mother working together on the big wheel. Before their mother died and Uncle Morris sold it.

"I'll let my wife know. She isn't here today. She wasn't feeling well this morning. Why don't you come over with Carl if he decides he wants the job? That way, you and Faith can discuss it."

"I'll do that." Lizzie didn't want to get her hopes up, but it was a promising lead. She glanced at her grandfather. "Before I go home on the bus."

"Which is Tuesday," he stated.

"But not until in the afternoon," she added. "Please tell your wife I'll stop by even if Carl decides not to take the work."

"All right, I will."

As Adrian walked away, her grandfather turned the buggy and headed down the lane. "I thought I told you to accept your uncle's wishes in the matter of your sister's marriage."

Lizzie remembered Carl's advice and spoke with firm resolve. "I appreciate your wise counsel, but my sister deserves a choice. Nothing good can come from marriage vows made without love."

Joe glanced at her but didn't say anything more. Lizzie relaxed when she realized he didn't intend to argue the point.

It had been a productive morning. So far, the Lord had provided two promising opportunities. Lizzie wasn't going to ignore them. She might be able to offer Clara a job and a place to live, but unless she could find something for all her sisters, Clara wouldn't take it. She wouldn't leave Betsy behind to marry Rufus Kuhns in her stead.

That evening after supper, Joe mentioned Adrian's offer to shear his alpacas to Carl.

Carl remained silent. Lizzie noticed that he didn't rush into making decisions. He always thought before he spoke. "The extra pay would come in handy. I've never clipped an alpaca, but it can't be too much different than a sheep. I'll give it a try. Can we spare the time tomorrow? We have the sorting pens to build yet."

"We can spare half a day. If we don't get them put together on Monday, Tuesday will be soon enough. Take the job if you want it."

Lizzie broached the subject that couldn't be avoided much longer. "Adrian Lapp cannot do business with you, Carl."

"True, but the man needs help. I'll find a way that is acceptable."

Joe said, "Lizzie will go with you. She can handle the money. Adrian's wife is looking for help with her yarn business."

Carl sat up straighter. "So you may not be leaving?"

"Not if I can find a job and a place to stay."

She thought for a moment that Carl looked happy at the prospect, but he quickly looked away.

Would it please him if she stayed in the area? It shouldn't matter, but for some reason, it did. "The spinning job with Faith Lapp is for my sister Clara. I go Tuesday morning to see if Elam Sutter will hire me to work in his basket-weaving business. It is my hope to bring all my sisters to live here."

Joe pushed his chair back from the table. "The next thing you know, I'm going to be surrounded by a gaggle of women. Well, I won't have it. I like my peace and quiet. You and your sisters can move anywhere you want, so long as you leave me be."

He stomped out of the kitchen and slammed his bedroom door behind him, leaving Carl and Lizzie alone.

"He doesn't mean that." Carl looked embarrassed by the outburst.

She began to gather the dishes. "I think he does. I've done everything I can think of to show him having a woman in his house is a good thing. I've cooked. I've cleaned until my fingers are raw. I've been quiet. I have stayed out of his way to the best of my ability, and still he treats me like a millstone around his neck."

"I appreciate your work, especially your good cooking. I'm sure Joe does, too. I don't think housekeeping skills will impress him enough to let you and your sisters stay here. Joe loves his solitude."

"And you do, too?"

He couldn't meet her gaze. "Yes, I do, too."

She felt so sad for them. They were two lonely men living apart from the world. It seemed that they both planned to remain that way.

Carl woke in the middle of the night bathed in sweat and shaking. He sat up gasping for air. Slowly, his nightmare faded. He wasn't in a grass hut in Africa. He was in a stone shepherd's hut in Ohio.

He had left the door open, and Duncan came in. The

dog laid his muzzle on Carl's hand and whined. As soon as Carl's thundering heart slowed, he said, "It's okay, boy."

He had not been forgiven. Every time the events of the past played out in his nightmares, he knew God was reminding him of his sin.

He rose from the bed and got a glass of water. Walking to the door, he looked out at the star-strewn sky and wondered how much more he had to endure.

The events of that terrifying day were as clear to him as the water glass in his hand. He had gone to Africa to be with his sister, Sophia, on her wedding day.

Born with a burning desire to share God's salvation with the world, Sophia chose not to join the Amish faith of her parents, but to become a Mennonite and go out into the world to spread God's word.

His family, like all the Amish, did not believe in seeking converts, but they supported missions of mercy. Sophia's first mission trip took her to Africa. She fell in love with the land and the people, and eventually, with another young missionary. They chose to marry in the village they called home. Sophia wrote and begged that at least one member of her family come to attend her wedding. Carl, being the oldest and unmarried, chose to go.

Although the land and the people were strange, Carl quickly saw why his sister loved the place. He soon became a favorite with some of the village children, particularly a young girl named Christina.

She called him Kondoo Mtu, a name that meant "sheep man" or "shepherd" in her native tongue. His sister told him it was because *ja,* his word for *yes,* sounded like the noise the sheep and goats made. He sometimes wondered if that was why he had decided to stay on Joe's farm and become a true shepherd instead of a carpenter like his father.

The day before Sophia's wedding, Carl had gone out to help Christina find her lost goat when he heard the first gunfire. There had been talk of a civil war, but no one believed it would happen. The frightened child raced back to the camp. Sophia's home was on the edge of the village. Carl caught up with Christina and took her there. When he opened the door, he saw a dozen women from the village huddled together with his sister. The fear in their eyes was terrible to see.

Christina's mother stood up. "Run, Carl. Take my daughter and run away."

Christina began screaming, "Where's Daddy?" She bolted toward the fighting. Carl raced after her. He saw a dozen villagers lying dead in the street. Christina found the body of her father among them. She sobbed over him and begged him to get up.

As if in slow-motion, Carl saw it all again. A soldier came around the corner and spotted her. He raised his gun. Christina's father's rifle was lying in the dirt at Carl's feet. Carl had grown up hunting. He knew how to use a gun. With barely a thought, he snatched it up and fired.

A second later, he watched the surprise on the soldier's face fade away. The light went out of his eyes as he fell dead.

Carl couldn't get that picture out of his head.

He had killed a man.

Nonviolence was a pillar of the Amish faith. For centuries, they suffered persecution without reprisal as the Bible commanded.

But I say unto you, That ye resist not evil: but who-
soever shall smite thee on thy right cheek, turn to
him the other also.

It was a creed Carl believed in with all his heart, but
his faith hadn't been strong enough. He did not face
the death of that child, nor his own certain death, as he
should have. God was the giver and taker of life, the judge
of men, not Carl King.

He threw down the gun, grabbed Christina and hid as
more soldiers scoured the area for him. He managed to
make his way back to his sister's home, but he was too
late. The women had been found by the soldiers looking for him.

He lived while everyone else died. He should have
been brave enough to face his own death as his sister
had done, with her Bible in her hands and peace in her
soul. Instead, he'd broken a most sacred law: "Thou shalt
not kill."

Each morning, he prayed for forgiveness. On those
nights when his nightmare didn't come, he began to hope
that God had taken pity on him.

But always, like tonight, the nightmare came back.
He was forced to watch a man die by his hand over and
over again and to know that his actions had cost his sister her life, too.

No, he had not been forgiven.

Later the next morning, Carl loaded his equipment in
the back of the wagon and waited for Lizzie. He didn't
have to wait long. She came rushing out of the house,
still drying her hands on her apron.

She was out of breath by the time she reached him. "I

hope I haven't kept you waiting. I had to get the break-fast dishes done and then I had to get something started for Grandfather's lunch. I pray that God wants Clara to work for Faith Lapp. I really do."

Her cheeks were rosy and her eyes sparkled with excitement. How could someone who had been up before dawn and hard at work for hours look so fresh and adorable?

He dismissed the thought as unworthy the moment it occurred. He had no right to look upon an Amish maid with such delight. He laid the reins on the bench seat and scooted over.

Lizzie climbed aboard and picked them up. "You will have to tell me the way."

"Go past the school and turn right at the next road. Then it's about a mile."

"I'm excited to see an alpaca up close. Do they really spit at you? How far can they spit?" She was like a kid on her way to the county fair.

"I have no idea."

"My sister Greta would love to visit a farm with such exotic creatures. She loves animals. She has a special way with them, even the stubborn and mean ones."

"You should write and tell her all about it."

"That is exactly what I will do."

She grew silent and some of the happiness faded from her face.

"What's wrong?" he asked.

"I miss them. I've never been away from them before."

"You will see them again soon enough." He wanted to offer more comfort, a shoulder to cry on if she needed one, but he held himself rigid beside her.

"If I fail to get a job, then I must return home on the

bus tomorrow afternoon. As much as I miss them, I don't want to go back and face them having accomplished nothing, for I know my leaving has caused great heartache."

"But it was a brave thing, nonetheless."

Lizzie thought Carl looked tired and sad this morning. She wondered why, but didn't wish to pry. She sensed that he needed comforting. After riding a while in silence, she glanced at him. "Are you okay?"

"I'm fine. I didn't sleep well, that's all."

He just needed cheering up. "I find a cup of herbal tea in the evenings helps me sleep like a babe. I haven't seen any in Grandfather's cupboards, but I'm sure you can buy some in town. I will write down the name for you, if you'd like."

"Thanks."

"If my constant chatter gets on your nerves, just shush me. I can take a hint."

He closed his eyes and rubbed his brow. "A little peace would be nice this morning."

"Absolutely. I understand completely. I often find I'm not at my best until almost noon. Isn't it a nice morning? March is such a funny month. A person would think winter is over when we have such a pretty day, but then, bang, the cold weather comes back."

"Lizzie."

"What, Carl?"

"Shush."

"Oh. Shush as in stop talking?"

"Is there another kind of shush?"

She opened her mouth, but he held up one hand. "No, don't explain. Shush as in stop talking."

She managed to be quiet for the rest of the trip, but

it was hard. How could she cheer him up if she couldn't speak to him?

When they reached the Lapp farm, she met Adrian and Faith's son, Kyle. A nine-year-old boy with bright red hair, freckles and an outgoing personality, he was happy to share his knowledge of shearing alpacas with everyone. Lizzie could have spent all day just gazing at the beautiful, graceful creatures. An adorable baby alpaca, which she learned from Kyle was called a cria, bounced around on stiff legs and darted under the adults standing in a small herd.

Inside the barn where the men were getting ready to work, Kyle indicated a number of bags stacked on nearby hay bales. "These bags are for the fleece. Alpacas have three kinds of fleece. There's prime—that's the best fiber. It's from their back and ribs. The fleece that we get off their thighs, neck and the legs is called seconds. The rest is called thirds and it isn't used by spinners. It's trash, but we keep some for batting inside the cria blankets if the babies are born during cold weather. Our little ones, the ones less than one year old, have prime all over because they've never been shorn."

"Is he bending your ear?" Faith asked as she entered the barn. She walked with a slight limp and wore a metal brace on her lower leg. Adrian came in with her, leading a white alpaca with a brown-and-white baby trotting at her heels.

"Not at all," Lizzie said with a smile for the boy. "I'm enjoying learning all about your beautiful animals."

The baby came to investigate the hem of Lizzie's dress. She had never seen a more adorable creature. She looked at Faith. "Is it all right if I pet him?"

"Of course. We like to keep the ones we have as tame

as possible so that they get used to handling. It makes working with them so much easier. The important thing to remember is that they need to respect humans. We don't make pets of them. An alpaca that is spoiled with a lot of petting and treats can become aggressive when they are grown, especially the males. Once they have lost respect for a human, they can't be trusted."

"It's the same with sheep," Carl said. "It's often the bottle-fed lambs that become the most aggressive ones."

Kyle knelt and gathered the baby in his arms. "This is Jasper."

Lizzie stroked his velvety head. The mother watched them intently and made soft humming sounds to her baby. "I'm afraid I could not raise them. I would constantly want to hug them. They are so soft and they have the most beautiful eyes."

Carl walked around the mother. "If she was a sheep, I'd pick her up and set her on her rump to shear her. With those long legs, that looks a little tricky."

Adrian laughed. "I tried that the first time I attempted to shear Myrtle. She jumped straight up in the air a good four feet off the ground and sent me tumbling backward. Then she spit on me. Don't worry. We have a sock we use for a muzzle now. You'll be safe."

"I have it right here," Faith said and came up to put it on.

Carl tipped his cowboy hat back with one finger. "So how do we do this?"

Adrian led Myrtle forward until she was standing on a large rubber mat. "It's a three-person job. Someone needs to hold her head. That will be me. We put ropes around her legs and just stretch her out until she is flat on the ground. It looks a little awkward, but it doesn't hurt them. I will warn you, some of them really hate this, and they will scream. Others simply lie still until it's all over and never make a sound. Once we have this girl down on the ground, I'll tell you how we need the fleece to be cut. Kyle will gather the blanket as it comes off and put it in the bags. Are you ready to start?"

"As ready as I can get," Carl said with a lack of certainty.

Lizzie watched as Faith wrapped loops around each of Myrtle's legs, then she and Kyle pulled on the ropes until Myrtle was lying on her belly. Several of the other alpacas wandered over to watch what was happening. Having them and her baby nearby kept Myrtle quiet.

Carl followed Adrian's instructions and quickly learned the best way to shear the animal. In a matter of a few minutes, Myrtle was released and scrambled to her feet.

Lizzie giggled. "She looks positively ridiculous."

Myrtle's big woolly body was now skinny and scrawny except for the thick fleece that had been left around her head and a pom-pom at the end of her tail.

Kyle grabbed the rest of the fleece from the floor around Myrtle's feet. "They always looked shocked. Like, what just happened to me?"

Lizzie met Carl's gaze, and they both chuckled. He said, "She looks like that is exactly what she's thinking."

"Are you from Texas?" Kyle asked.

Lizzie perked up. Perhaps she would learn something about Carl's past today.

Carl frowned. "What makes you think that?"

Kyle pointed to his head. "Your cowboy hat. I'm from Texas. Lots of people wear hats like yours out there."

Kyle was from Texas? Lizzie glanced at his parents.

Faith smiled and said, "*Ja,* our boy is a Texan. Confusing, isn't it? Tell them how you came to live in Ohio, Kyle."

The little boy grew solemn and crossed his arms over his chest. "It went like this. My dad, my first dad, was my aunt Faith's brother. He moved away from his Amish family and married my first mom. I was born in Texas. Are you with me? Then they died in a car accident. After that, I was really scared and sad. I lived in this home with other kids without parents.

"I didn't like it much, but I did like my foster mom. Her name was Becky. Anyway, a social-worker lady brought me here to Ohio to live with my aunt Faith. Then we met Adrian. He had the farm next to our house. Only, it's our farm now, and someone else lives in my aunt's house. A nice fellow named Gideon Troyer and his wife, Rebecca. He used to be a pilot.

"Anyway, Adrian became my new dad because he fell in love with my aunt and married her and they adopted me, so now they are my new *mamm* and *daed.* And that's how I got to be Amish.

"I do miss having a TV, but I like having alpacas a lot. I have one named Shadow. He's black as coal, and I get to keep all the money from his fleece when we sell it." Kyle's solemn expression dissolved into a wide grin.

Lizzie struggled to take in all of the information he had dished out so quickly. Faith laughed. "Did you get that?"

"I think so. Kyle is from Texas."

Adrian handed the lead rope to the boy. "Take Myrtle back to the pen and bring one of the others."

Kyle rushed to do as he had been asked. He was a charming child, but Lizzie was disappointed that she hadn't learned anything about where Carl was from.

Would she ever?

Chapter Six

Carl soon relaxed and grew more confident with each animal he sheared. As Adrian had said, some of the animals screamed in protest, but most lay quietly and allowed him to do his job without worrying about injuring them. He was spit at once but managed to jump aside, and only his boot took a direct hit. After that, Faith put muzzles on every animal.

Lizzie, of course, dissolved into laughter as he scraped his boot clean on a nearby hay bale. Each time she caught him looking at her after that, she pinched her nose and made a face.

He tried to keep his attention strictly on the task at hand, but having Lizzie working beside him made that difficult.

Her good humor never lagged as she pitched in to help without being asked. She was soon tying up alpacas as if she'd been doing it for years. When one was a particularly bad squirmer, Lizzie lay down on the ground beside him to help hold the animal still.

When she wasn't needed to help control the animals, she was helping to sort and bag the fleece. The whole time, she was smiling and cheerful, chuckling at the antics of the alpacas and making the morning one of the most pleasant he'd had in a long time.

When noon rolled around, Faith brought a picnic hamper down from the house. Lizzie followed with a large quilt over her arm and a pitcher of lemonade in her hand.

"Lizzie suggested we eat out here. I think a picnic is a wonderful idea. It's the first one of the year," Faith said as Adrian took the hamper from her.

Lizzie glanced at Carl and then looked away. "It's such a beautiful spring day that I thought it would be a shame to spend it eating at the table inside."

"Adrian, would you spread the quilt in a sunny place for us?" Faith indicated the spot she wanted and her husband quickly did as she asked.

Within a few minutes, they were all settled on the quilt except for Carl. He carried a bale of hay out and put it where he could sit and lean against the trunk of an apple tree.

Faith withdrew a plate full of ham sandwiches made with thick slices of homemade bread from the hamper. They all helped themselves as Lizzie poured glasses of fresh lemonade. She handed them out to everyone except Carl. When she approached, he was busy wiping his hands with a wet towel. "Just set it on the ground. I'll get it in a minute."

She caught his glance and nodded. It was acceptable.

"When do you plan to start shearing Joe's sheep?" Adrian asked.

"Tomorrow."

"How many sheep does Joe have?" Kyle asked as he examined the large clippers Carl had laid aside.

"He has four rams and about two hundred ewes."

Kyle's eyes widened. "And I thought shearing ten alpacas was a lot of work. How long will it take you?"

"If the weather holds and nothing goes wrong, we'll be done in three or four days."

Kyle was holding Carl's shears trying to squeeze the big scissor-like blades together. "Doesn't your hand get tired?"

Carl almost choked on his lemonade. "It does. By the end of the week, my hand is very tired. I'll show you how to use those. A good shearer can earn a tidy sum of cash in the spring."

Kyle handed them back. "No, thanks. I'm gonna farm with my dad and grow peaches. How did you learn? Did your dad shear sheep?"

"*Nee,* my father is a carpenter." A sharp stab of regret hit Carl. He hadn't seen his father since he left home when he was twenty-four years old. He would be twenty-nine this fall. Five years was a long time. When would he be able to go home? When would God grant him the forgiveness he craved?

"Where does he work?" Lizzie asked softly.

"Pennsylvania." He didn't share more details. "Lizzie mentioned you are looking for a spinner to work with you, Faith."

Faith smiled. "Lizzie has a sister who might be interested in the job."

"My oldest sister, Clara. She used to spin with our mother, but that was many years ago."

"Did she like it?" Adrian asked.

"She loved doing it, but our uncle sold the spinning wheel after our mother died."

Adrian pushed his straw hat back a little and regarded her intently. "Is she staying with Joe, too?"

"*Nee.* Clara is at home in Indiana, but I know she would come if she knew she had a job."

Adrian gave Faith a speaking glance and then said, "I would rather meet your sister first and see her skill level before we offer her a job. Faith's work has gained a good reputation among the shops that purchase her yarns. We don't want to start selling an inferior product."

Lizzie nodded. "I understand. It's just that it's very important that Clara have a job soon."

"And why is that?" Adrian asked.

Lizzie looked to Carl. He was pleased that she valued his opinion. He nodded. "Tell them."

She drew a deep breath. "My uncle is making Clara marry a cruel man. Rufus Khuns is our landlord. We live and work on his dairy farm. Clara doesn't want to marry him, but Onkel Morris is afraid Rufus will turn us out if she doesn't. He told Clara that he'll make our youngest sister wed Rufus if Clara won't. Betsy is barely seventeen."

"That's terrible. Oh, Adrian, we have to help them," Faith cried.

Adrian took his wife's hand in his and patted it. "Calm yourself. Remember, the midwife said getting upset isn't good for your blood pressure."

"I know. And sitting for a long time at the wheel makes my feet swell, so I shouldn't do that, either. I will be glad when this babe makes an appearance."

Adrian turned to Lizzie. "Tell your sister she has a job here for as long as she needs one."

"But what about your other sisters?" Faith asked. "They can't stay and be abused in your uncle's home."

"I have a job interview tomorrow at Elam Sutter's home. Once Clara and I both have jobs, we'll be able to take care of our little sisters. I don't care what it takes. I won't leave them behind."

Faith reached over and squeezed Lizzie's hand. "Of course you can't. I will pray for the success of your mission every day."

Lizzie felt as if she had finally found people who understood what she faced. It was a deeply comforting feeling.

She and Faith carried the quilt and lunch items back to the house as the men returned to shear the final four alpacas. After the dishes were washed, Faith said, "Come see my spinning room. You will want to tell your sister about where she'll be working."

She led the way to a bright room that had been built off the kitchen on the east side of the house. In it were three spinning wheels of various sizes and dozens of skeins of yarn. The windows overlooked a small orchard where the shorn alpacas were gathering beneath the trees.

Lizzie admired the largest spinning wheel. "This is the kind that my mother had. What a lovely place you have to work."

"Adrian built it for me when I first moved here. He knew how much I liked to watch my animals."

"He seems like a caring husband."

Faith cupped her hands over her pregnant belly. "He is a wonderful man. I never thought I would find someone like him. My first husband was a very demanding and hard man. Life was not…easy with him. It wasn't all his fault. He had a very tragic childhood. Then we had two little daughters who were stillborn early in our marriage, and he was never the same after that."

"I'm so sorry for your loss."

"*Danki.* I know they are with God in Heaven and I will see them again someday. You must tell your sister not to give up hope and not to marry without love. God brings special people into our lives exactly when we need them. If it is His will, your sister will find a man like my Adrian, and she will know the joy of being a true wife."

"I will tell her. Thank you for giving her a job. I can't believe how fortunate I've been since coming to Hope Springs."

"I felt the same way when I first arrived. So many people came to give me a hand getting my house and my farm in order. My husband and I had moved around a lot, so I'd never known the sense of community that exists here. You and your sisters will see. You'll be welcome by all."

"I hope so."

"You have not mentioned how Joe feels about your sisters coming here. Is he glad? I have only known him as the recluse who shuns the company of all others except for Carl."

"Grandfather doesn't want us here."

"How sad for you."

"Honestly, I think it is sad for him."

"You're right. We can't change how people feel. We can only do what we know to be right, and bringing your sisters here sounds right to me."

"Bless you for understanding."

"I do. Now, we must get back to the shearing or I'll find black thirds mixed in with my white firsts." She chuckled. "I have good men, but they still need supervision."

It didn't take long to finish shearing the rest of the animals. Faith led the last one back to their enclosure while Adrian pulled a wallet from his pocket.

He counted out the amount and held it toward Carl. "My wife is very satisfied with your work. I hope I can count on you for next year."

"If I'm still in the area. Give the money to Lizzie while I go wash up. They might be prized for their fleece, but it makes me itch." Carl walked to a nearby stock tank and began to rinse his arms.

Adrian seemed a bit surprised, but offered the payment to Lizzie. She accepted it and put it in her pocket.

Later, back at her grandfather's farm, she left the bills on the table and went down to the cellar for a jar of vegetables. When she came up, the money was gone. Carl had been as good as his word. Everything had been done carefully so as not to have Adrian or Faith unknowingly break their church's Ordnung.

Once again, Lizzie was puzzled by Carl's behavior. Adrian and Faith had no idea that Carl was a shunned person. He could have gone about his business as an Englischer and no one would've been the wiser. Why did he take such great care to protect the people when he was no longer a member of their faith? If he cared so much, why didn't he ask forgiveness for his sin, whatever it was, and be welcomed into the church again?

It didn't make sense. Nothing about Carl made sense. And yet she spent a great deal of time thinking about him and wishing she could find a way to help.

When her grandfather came in for supper that evening, he hung his hat on the peg by the door as usual. "Carl won't be joining us."

"Why not?" She set a platter of noodles on the table.

"Said he wasn't hungry. How did the alpaca shearing go?"

"Fine. Is Carl unwell?"

"Not that I could see."

"Is it unusual for him to miss a meal?"

"He's a grown man. If he doesn't want to eat, he doesn't want to eat. Could be he's tired of your cooking."

She snatched the dish off the table. "There's nothing wrong with my cooking. If you don't want it, I'll feed yours to the dog."

"I never said I didn't want it," he admitted grudgingly.

She glared at him. "I'm a good cook."

"I said that before, didn't I?"

"Then you shouldn't suggest otherwise. It's hurtful."

It took him a few seconds, but finally, he said, "I didn't mean to hurt your feelings. Now can I eat?"

It was as close to an apology as she was likely to get. She set the platter on the table again and turned away to hide a smile. Her grandfather needed someone to stand up to his cantankerous ways. Carl was right about that.

She went to the window and looked out, but she couldn't see his hut beyond the barn. "Carl was quiet on the ride home from the Lapp farm. I didn't give it much thought. I assumed he was tired, but perhaps he was ill."

"I hope not. We need to get started on our beasts first thing in the morning. The lambs are due to start arriving in two to three weeks."

"I hope I can be here to see it." She turned around and went back to the table. "I remember watching the new lambs when I was little. They jumped, ran and played with each other, and it looked like they were having so much fun. Mother said they were leaping with joy."

"Did she?"

"She said the lambing season was the hardest work of the year, but it was all worth it."

A sad, faraway look came into his eyes. "*Ja,* my girl was right about that."

He bowed his head to pray and didn't speak again during the meal. He went to his room directly afterward, leaving Lizzie alone. Perhaps she had been wrong to mention her mother in front of him. It seemed to bring him pain.

She went to bed that night and lay under the quilt her mother had made. Outside her open window, a chilly breeze blew by and carried the sounds of the night with it. An owl hooted nearby. In the distance, a sheep bleated and another answered. A dog barked somewhere.

This was her last night in the house where her mother had grown up. Tomorrow, if she got the job with Elam Sutter, she would stay with his family and work to bring her sisters to Hope Springs. If she wasn't hired, she would be forced to go home, back to Indiana. At least she'd found a job for Clara, but she wasn't sure her sister would take it if it meant leaving the rest of them.

She slipped out of bed and got to her knees. "Please, Lord, I'm begging You. Give me the strength and wisdom to find a place for all of us."

Knowing that she could do nothing more and that it was all in God's hands, she climbed into bed and quickly fell asleep.

Lizzie finished her chores the next morning and hurried outside. She was surprised to see Carl waiting with the pony already hitched to the cart. "*Danki,* Carl, but you should not do this for me."

"It's not a favor, Lizzie. It's part of the work I do here. Do you know how to get where you're going?"

"I have a general idea."

"I drew a map. It's on the seat if you need it."

"That was very thoughtful of you."

"Good luck. I hope you get the job."

"I shall know soon enough." She stood beside the cart knowing that she should hurry, but she was reluctant to actually get under way.

What if it didn't work out? What if she was back here in two hours to pack and board the bus this afternoon? The thought was depressing.

Carl stepped close to her. "The journey of a thousand miles begins with a single step."

"I thought I took that first step when I walked out of my uncle's house last week."

"Then you are well on your way to where you want to be. This next step cannot be as difficult as that one."

She smiled softly. "You are right about that. You are right about a lot of things, Carl King."

"And I will be right if I tell you to hurry up and go or you won't get back in time to make us lunch."

She laughed. "I declare, you men think with your stomachs."

"I'm going to miss your cooking, Lizzie Barkman."

"I'm going to miss cooking for you."

"You will have Sundays off if Sutter gives you the job. Feel free to come out here and cook to your heart's content."

"That is only if I get the job."

"I don't know Elam Sutter, but he is a fool if he doesn't hire someone as hardworking as you are. Now, get going. Joe and I need to get our sheep sheared."

Lizzie climbed into the cart and picked up the reins. "At least you know they won't spit on you. See you soon."

She slapped the reins against the pony and left Carl standing in the yard watching her. When she reached the end of the lane, she looked back. She lifted a hand and waved. Carl saw her gesture and waved back.

Lizzie drove toward town with a light heart that had nothing to do with a job prospect. Her happy mood was because Carl cared about her comfort and because he said he would miss her if she left.

Lizzie arrived at the Sutter farm and was immediately welcomed by a little girl about four years old, followed by a puppy that reminded Lizzie of Duncan.

"Guder mariye," the little girl called out. She turned and shouted toward the house, "Mamm, we have company."

Lizzie stepped down from the cart. "Thank you. You must be Rachel."

"Ja, I am. Who are you?"

"My name is Lizzie Barkman, and I'm here to see your father about a job."

"Papa is in his workshop. Shall I get him?"

"That would be nice, *danki.*"

The little girl turned to her puppy and patted her leg. "Come on, Peanut Butter. Let's go find Papa."

Together they ran toward the barn. Lizzie heard the door of the house open and saw Katie come out with Jeremiah balanced on her hip. "Lizzie, I'm so glad you are here. Come in the house. My husband should be in shortly."

"Rachel just went to tell him that I'm here."

"Oh, *goot.* She is quite the little helper. She makes me

wish for another girl. She is much less trouble than my boys have been."

"What has Jeremiah tried to swallow today?"

"My sewing bobbin. I can't take my eyes off him for a minute. Thankfully, the baby isn't much trouble yet, but I'm sure he'll be just like his brother when he is old enough to get into mischief."

Lizzie held out her arms for Jeremiah and was delighted when he grinned and reached for her in return. She propped him on her hip and followed Katie into the house. They were settled at the kitchen table when Elam came in. He hung his hat on a peg by the door.

Jeremiah, who until that moment had been quiet seated on Lizzie's lap, started whining to get down. Elam plucked him away from Lizzie.

"Charming the girls already, are you?" Elam took a seat at the table and allowed the little boy to sit on his lap.

"Indeed, he has been," Lizzie replied.

"My wife tells me you are interested in working for us. Have you any experience at basket weaving?"

"None, but I would be interested to learn. I can help with the children, of that I'm certain."

"Well, then, come down to the shop and let me show you what you will need to know. You may decide the work isn't for you. It can be tedious."

He handed his son to his wife, and Lizzie followed him outside and into his shop. It was part of the barn, but had been walled off to separate it from the rest of the structure. The moment Lizzie stepped inside the room, the aromatic scent of cedar and wood shavings enveloped her. The walls had been painted a bright white. Tools hung from the pegs neatly arranged on one wall. A long table sat in the middle of the workshop, and a small stove in one corner held a simmering vat of something reddish-brown. Around the table sat three women, each with partially completed baskets in front of them.

Elam said, "This is Mary, Ruby and Sally. They all work for me part-time."

Sally put down the basket she was working on. "Lizzie, how nice to see you again."

Lizzie met the other women, who, as it turned out, were Elam's sister and sister-in-law. After seeing how they turned the thin strips of poplar wood into beautiful baskets, Lizzie realized this was something she would like to learn. She thanked the women for their demonstrations, asked a few questions and then followed Elam back to the house.

Katie was setting out mugs of coffee. Everyone took a seat at the kitchen table. "Well, what did you think?" Katie asked.

"I think I have a lot to learn, but it looks like something I would enjoy."

"How soon would you be able to start?" Elam asked.

"Today," Lizzie said quickly.

Elam and Katie exchanged amused glances.

"I'm afraid I don't have a room ready for you yet," Katie said.

"Why don't you start tomorrow? If you think you'll like the work, let's give it a two-week trial," Elam suggested.

Lizzie grinned as excitement bubbled up inside her. She took a sip of coffee. "Tomorrow will be fine."

Carl secured the last panel into place with a length of wire and glanced out the barn door to see Lizzie returning. Even from across the yard, he could see the grin on her face. She caught sight of him and jumped down from the cart. "I got the job," she yelled.

He couldn't believe how relieved he was. She wouldn't be going back to Indiana. She had a job and a place to stay in the neighborhood. He would see her again. Even if only from a distance.

Joe came up to stand beside him. "What did she say?"

"She said she got the job."

Joe gave a disgusted humph and walked away, but Carl wasn't fooled. Joe might not admit it, but he didn't want her to leave, either.

A few minutes later, Lizzie came out of the house and raced down the lane with something in her hand. Intrigued, Carl watched until she slipped whatever she was carrying into the mailbox and raised the flag to let the mail carrier know there was mail to pick up. Was it a letter to her sisters? Probably.

Carl hoped everything would work out for them, but he knew what people desired was not always what God had planned for them. His poor little sister's short life was proof of that.

Turning back to his work, Carl began getting ready to shear. He had three days of hard work ahead of him. He wouldn't get much done if he couldn't stop thinking about Lizzie. He didn't need the constant distraction of having her near, but…oh, how he desired it.

After spending much of yesterday in her company, he had retreated to his hut, thinking that the distance would help him stop thinking about her. It hadn't worked.

The mixture of foolish longing and painful reality swirling through his brain left him feeling hopelessly muddled.

Lizzie had a way of turning him inside out with just

a smile. How was he going to get through another day, let alone the years ahead, if she stayed in Hope Springs?

Lizzie could barely control her excitement as she walked back from the mailbox. Everything was falling into place. The letter she mailed to Mary contained a second letter to her sisters explaining everything: Lizzie's job, Clara's job and her fervent hope that they would all be together soon.

In with the letter, Lizzie had put all of her money. It was enough for a one-way ticket for Clara. She prayed that Clara would come. Together, they would soon earn enough to pay for Betsy and Greta to join them and keep the younger women from being forced into marriage instead. It wasn't a foolproof plan, but it was all Lizzie had to offer.

What they needed now was a place to stay. The Lord had provided jobs. Lizzie was sure He would provide them with a home, too. She just had to have faith.

Bubbling with happiness and optimism, she went to the barn to watch the men at work. A small group of sheep had been gathered in a pen inside the barn. The air was filled with sounds of their bleating as they milled around. A narrow passageway had been built from the large pens outside to a smaller one where Carl was preparing to start the work.

A large piece of plywood had been put on the ground outside the gate of the smallest pen. Carl was down on one knee on the board tying on wool moccasins. When he finished, he reached for the clippers and affixed them to his right hand.

Moving closer, Lizzie said, "Why the special shoes?"

"They keep my feet dry and keep me from slipping on the oils from the fleece."

"Are you going to shear the rams first?" She eyed the four big fellows separated in a pen by themselves.

"That's right." Carl didn't look at her but kept his eyes downcast.

"Why?"

"They're bigger and harder to work with. It's best to get them out of the way so the rest of the work goes more easily. We only have four rams. It doesn't normally take long."

"And you said two hundred ewes." It sounded like a tremendous amount of work for one man and her elderly grandfather.

"That's right."

"I vaguely remember watching the shearing when I was little. A man used electric clippers. He brought his own generator with him. I thought it was very worldly at the time. Doesn't it take longer to clip the fleece by hand?"

Unlike the clippers she remembered, Carl had what looked like a giant pair of scissors strapped to his hand. The blades hooked together at the handle ends instead of in the center.

"It takes me about six minutes per sheep instead of four minutes if I were to use electric clippers. Joe likes them shorn the old way."

"In keeping with our faith. That's understandable."

"He likes it because the fleece isn't cut so close to the skin. Hand-sheared sheep are left with a short coat instead of looking naked. It gives them better protection against foul weather. It's also less stressful for our pregnant mothers without the buzzing sound of the clippers and the smell of gasoline fumes from a generator."

"Are the two of you gonna keep yacking or can we get some work done?" Joe shouted from just outside the pen where the sheep were milling.

Carl waved. "I'm ready."

"What do you need me to do?" she asked.

"There needs to be a clear flow of sheep entering and leaving the shearing area. This barn is divided into two parts. Where the sheep come in and where they go out. The catch pen, the small one here, is connected to the outside corrals by movable panels."

"I see that." The narrow alleyway was just wide enough for one single ram to walk down to the actual shearing pen.

"After I'm done shearing the sheep, I'll turn him into this second alley. I need you to close the gate behind him so he can't run back into this area."

"Got it."

"Once I'm done with all of them, you'll need to close that big gate by the barn door and open the smaller gate beside it so the ewes go out to a separate corral."

"So you just want me to chase them outside for you?"

"Basically. Don't get in with the rams. They can be mean."

"I will remember that."

"Joe may need help giving the animals their worm medicine while I have them still. He'll take care of the fleece that's cut off, too. You can make notes in our logbook for us. Each sheep has an ear tag with a number on it. Joe will tell you what to write."

"Sounds easy enough."

"It is if the sheep cooperate. The only thing they do without protest is grow wool. Ready to start?"

"Sure."

Lizzie quickly learned that sheep were not the cute, cuddly animals of her memory. They were much stronger than they looked, horribly stubborn, smelly and incredibly loud. The bleating grew to a deafening din inside the barn.

Duncan nipped at the heels of the rams as the reluctant animals filed into the catch pen.

Carl opened a small gate and pulled out the first struggling ram. Grasping the heavy wool, he tipped the sheep backward until it was sitting. The second the sheep's feet were all off the ground, it stopped struggling. The animal looked as if it were being held still by the force of Carl's will.

With the ram braced between his legs, Carl quickly set to work clipping first the belly fleece and then around the entire animal until the wool came off in one large piece.

Joe pulled the fleece aside, folded it and placed it on a nearby table. He made a few quick notes in a ledger, gave the animal a dose of medicine and then went to move the next ram into the catch pen with Duncan's help.

Lizzie watched how it was all being done as Carl sheared his second ram. She noticed the first ram had come back inside to be with the others. While Joe was busy rolling up the fleece, she went to shoo the fellow outside.

The ram balked and wouldn't leave. She opened the gate to go in and move him along. In the next second, she realized her mistake. The ram, seeing a new way out, bolted past her, knocking the gate wide open.

Lizzie cried out a warning, but it was too late. The

ram didn't slow down. He plowed into Joe and sent him flying before charging through the open barn door beyond. She stared in horror at her grandfather's crumpled figure as Carl raced to his side.

Chapter Seven

Lizzie drove the buggy as fast as she dared. Carl sat in the back cradling Joe, but with every bounce and jolt, her grandfather moaned in pain. The sound made her cringe with remorse. It was all her fault. In her foolish need to prove she could be useful, she'd simply proven she was careless.

After what seemed like an eternity, the outskirts of Hope Springs came into view. Thankfully, there was very little traffic on the streets. She was able to follow Carl's directions and they arrived within a few minutes at the front doors of the Hope Springs Medical Clinic.

Carl lifted Joe out of the buggy and carried him inside. The tiny, elderly receptionist behind the desk jumped to her feet. "Oh, my. What has happened?"

"Joe's been hurt bad," Carl said.

"Bring him this way. I'll get the doctor."

Carl and Lizzie followed her down a short hallway and into an examination room. Carl gently laid Joe on the bed. "It's okay, Joe. You're going to be fine."

A young man in a white lab coat hurried into the room. "I'm Dr. Zook. What seems to be the matter?"

"Where is Dr. White?" Carl asked.

"He's not in today. I'm his partner. Is that a problem?" Carl shook his head.

"Are you related to Bishop Zook?" Lizzie asked.

"Very distantly, if at all. Zook is simply a common name in these parts."

Outside the door, the receptionist asked, "Should I call for an ambulance, Doctor?"

"Give me a few minutes to see how serious this is, Wilma. Have Amber finish with Mrs. Lapp and then ask her to join me. Can someone tell me what happened?"

"It's my fault." Lizzie clasped her hands together. "I left one of the gates open and a ram got out. He ran into Grandfather and knocked him down. Grandfather hit his head on one of the steel fence posts. It was bleeding terribly."

The doctor began to unwind Lizzie's apron from around Joe's head. "Head wounds are notorious for bleeding a lot. Has he been unconscious long?"

Carl took a step back from the bed to give the doctor more room. "He's been in and out for the past half hour or so. He complains that his right leg hurts. I think it's broken."

The doctor looked kindly at Lizzie. "You might want to step out and let us get him undressed. I'll let you know the extent of his injuries as soon as I've finished examining him."

Lizzie nodded and left the room. She found her way back to the waiting area. Taking a seat on one of the upholstered chairs that lined the wall, she put her head in her hands and prayed.

A short time later, she heard a door open and she looked

up. It wasn't the doctor. It was a blonde Englisch woman in a pale blue smock. She walked beside Faith Lapp.

"Everything looks good with your pregnancy, Faith. I'll see you back in two weeks. Sooner if you have any problems. You know I'm available day or night. I'd love to stay and chat a little longer, but I'm needed for another patient."

"*Danki,* Amber. I will see you in two weeks," Faith said. She turned to leave and caught sight of Lizzie. Her eyes widened with surprise. "Lizzie, what are you doing here?"

"Grandfather has been hurt."

"I'm so sorry to hear that. Is it serious?" She sat down beside Lizzie and took her hand.

Her comforting gesture was all that was needed to push Lizzie's shattered emotions over the edge. She burst into tears.

Faith wrapped an arm around Lizzie's shoulder. "There, there, don't cry. He is in God's hands, and God is good."

Lizzie nodded but couldn't speak. She was too choked with tears and worry.

Faith stayed with her until the doctor finally came out to talk to her. She could tell by the look on his face that it wasn't good news. She rose to her feet. "How is he?"

"He's resting comfortably at the moment. I've given him something for pain. The head wound was not serious. It required a few stitches, but he did sustain a minor concussion. The problem is that Joe has a broken hip. We can't treat that here. He needs to go to the hospital. He'll need surgery to pin the broken pieces together."

"Surgery? Is that dangerous at his age?" Faith asked.

"All surgery comes with risks, but I'm afraid there's

very little choice. The fracture won't heal unless it can be immobilized."

"Do what you think is best, Doctor. Can I see him now?"

"Of course. I'll make arrangements for an ambulance to transport him to the hospital in Millersburg."

Faith laid a hand on Lizzie's arm. "I'll let Bishop Zook know what has happened. Don't worry. Everything will be taken care of."

Lizzie nodded and walked down the hall, but hesitated before going into the room. What could she say except that she was sorry? She wiped the tears from her cheeks and opened the door.

Joe lay on the same bed with his eyes closed. A sheet was pulled up to his chin. A white bandage stood out starkly on his forehead. He looked pale and helpless.

Carl sat in a chair beside him. He glanced up as Lizzie peered in. "It's okay. He's awake."

"Of course I'm awake," Joe growled. "Who could sleep with all this commotion?"

"Oh, Daadi, I'm so sorry. I was only trying to help. Please forgive me."

"Things happen. That old ram has had it in for me since I bought him. Carl, it will be up to you to get the shearing done. It'll be hard to do it all yourself."

"I can handle it, Joe. You just rest and get better."

"You won't be able to manage the lambing alone."

Lizzie stepped closer to the bed. "I'll help. I know I made a mess of things today, but I want to make it up to you."

"What about your new job?" Carl asked.

"I'm sure when the Sutters hear what's happened, they will understand if I can't start work for a few more days."

"It will be a few weeks."

"Oh."

Joe shifted uncomfortably on the bed. "The girl won't be any use to you, Carl."

"She'll be better than no one."

It wasn't much of a recommendation, but Lizzie was thankful that he spoke up for her. "Faith Lapp is out in the waiting room. She said she'll let Bishop Zook know what has happened."

Joe pushed up on one elbow, his eyes blazing. "I don't want that busybody Esther Zook in my house, do you hear me?"

Lizzie was stunned by his outburst. Carl rose and eased Joe back on the bed. "I thought you liked the bishop. You told me he was a good man."

"He's a good man married to a shrew of a woman. She'll turn her nose up at everything I own and tell folks what a pity it is that I've let the place go to ruin. I don't want her to set foot inside my door."

Lizzie moved to stand beside him on the other side of the bed. "I won't let her in. I promise."

The outside door opened and the nurse entered. "The ambulance is here. I'm going to have you both step into the waiting room while they get Mr. Shetler ready for transport. Which one of you is going to ride with him?"

"I will," Lizzie said quickly.

"*Nee,* you go home. I want Carl to come."

Lizzie had to concede. Of course he wanted his friend, not the careless granddaughter he barely knew who put him here in the first place.

The nurse gestured to Lizzie to come with her. When they were outside in the hallway, she said, "We haven't met. I'm Amber White. I'll make arrangements for a driver to take you to the hospital."

Embarrassed, Lizzie shook her head. "I have no money to pay a driver."

"Don't worry about that. We have a fund set up for just such an emergency. All the local Amish churches donate to it. The driver will make sure you get to the hospital and that you get home when you are ready. Just let the receptionist have your name and address."

"I don't know how to thank you."

"Of course you do. Someday, you will see a person in need, and you will help them. That is all the thanks I require." Amber went back to the room and Lizzie went to speak to the woman behind the desk.

Carl rode in the back of the ambulance strapped into a small seat out of the way of the crew, but situated where he could see Joe. His friend's color was so pale that Carl began to worry something else was wrong. At the hospital, Carl stood aside and tried to keep out of the way as they admitted Joe and readied him for surgery.

When a lull in the activity finally occurred, the two men were alone for a few minutes.

Joe looked over at him. "With that long face, you make a man think you're on your way to a funeral."

"It will be a long time before anyone plants you in the ground, Woolly Joe."

"I hope so, but a man never knows what the good Lord has in store for him. Could be that I'm on my way to see Him now and just don't know it."

"Lizzie feels bad enough. If you decide to die, she's gonna feel awful."

"She should go stay with the Sutters instead of staying on the farm."

"If you are worried about her safety or anything else, don't be."

"No, it isn't that. I know you'll watch over her. I have no worries on that score. It's just that a sheep farm isn't any place for a woman."

"You don't give Lizzie enough credit. She can handle the work and then some."

"I bought the place a year before I married Lizzie's grandmother. My wife, Evelyn, hated it. She hated the sheep. She hated the smell of them. She hated the long hours and the hard work during the lambing season. I thought she would grow to love it as I did, but that never happened. After a few years, I realized it wasn't the farm. She was never happy with me."

"I'm sorry to hear that."

"The Lord didn't bless us with a child until we were close to thirty. I thought having a baby on the place would make a difference to Evelyn, but it didn't. She died when Abigail was only two. I didn't want the girl to grow up hating the place the way her mother did. I sent her to live with my wife's sister until she was fourteen. I visited her every week, but I'm not sure it was enough. Maybe if I had kept her with me from the start, she would've felt differently about leaving the way she did. Maybe she thought I didn't care about her, but I did. I loved my little girl."

Carl laid a hand on his friend's shoulder. "Joe, if you give Lizzie half a chance, she will grow to love you as I do."

Joe shook his head. "It's better to be alone. You take care of my sheep while I'm laid up, you hear me?"

"I hear you. The sheep will be fine."

"I know they will be with you looking out for them. You and I, we get along okay. We don't need anyone else."

Carl had spent the past five years believing that was true, but now he wasn't so sure. He was learning that a life spent alone could be painfully lonely.

A nurse in surgical garb entered the room. "Mr. Shetler, your granddaughter is here. Would you like to see her before we take you to surgery?"

"*Nee,* let's get this over with."

The nurse looked surprised, but said, "I'll show her where the waiting room is."

A few minutes later, more people came in. Joe was wheeled from the room. Carl followed them to a large set of double doors.

One of the nurses gestured toward a side hall. "The waiting room is the first door on the left. The surgeon will come talk to you as soon as he is finished."

Carl laid a hand on Joe's arm and leaned close. "God is with you, my friend."

"I know. I just hope He is with the Englisch *doktor,* too."

Carl managed a smile. When they took Joe through the double doors, he walked down to the waiting room.

Lizzie was seated alone by the window. Her hands were clasped together and her eyes were closed. He knew that she was praying. As if she sensed his presence, she looked up and rose to her feet. "How is he?"

"They just took him into surgery."

She sank back onto her chair. "He didn't want to see me."

"Don't dwell on it. When he gets out of here, you can ply him with more of your wonderful cherry cobbler."

"I don't think my cooking can undo the damage I've done today. Do you?"

He didn't have an answer for that.

They waited together in silence until the surgeon finally came in to tell them Joe's surgery had gone well. Later, when Joe was moved to a room, he refused any visitors. Carl, knowing Joe wouldn't change his mind about seeing her, convinced Lizzie to go home.

By the time the driver delivered them to the farm, it had grown dark. Carl stood on the bottom porch step as Lizzie opened the front door. She looked back at him. "I wish there was more that I could do for him. I feel so bad about this."

The urge to take her in his arms and comfort her was overpowering. He clenched his hands into fists at his sides to keep from reaching for her. "We are to take care of his sheep. That is all Joe wants from us. Get some rest, Lizzie. Tomorrow will be a long, busy day."

In the days to come, she would be working by his side. The joy the thought brought him was bittersweet. They would have a few days together, maybe a few weeks if she stayed through the lambing, but she wouldn't stay with him forever.

Carl wasn't surprised to see Lizzie just after dawn the next morning. He hadn't slept well and he doubted she had, either. She came down to the barn dressed in a faded green dress with her hair covered by a matching green kerchief instead of her usual black *kapp*. She carried a basket over one arm. When she drew near, he could see the puffiness in her eyes. She must have cried herself to sleep.

He longed to offer a comforting hug, but knew she wouldn't welcome such a gesture.

She held out the basket. "I have some cold biscuits and sausage with cheese and a thermos of coffee. It's not much."

"It's fine. I'm not that hungry."

"Neither am I."

"Save them for later."

She set the basket aside and pulled on a pair of her grandfather's work gloves. "I promise to do only what you tell me and exactly what you tell me. Where do I start?"

"You can start by not being so hard on yourself."

"I have put my grandfather in the hospital and made twice as much work for you. I'm not being hard on myself."

"Okay. First, we need the floor clean around where I'm working. You'll need to keep it raked and swept to prevent hay and other bits of debris from getting into the wool."

She grabbed a broom and began cleaning the old wooden floor of the barn with a vengeance.

Carl smiled at her eagerness. She was determined to be as much help as another man. He knew she felt badly about the accident, but she was going to wear herself out if she kept trying so hard. "Pace yourself, Lizzie. We have a lot more to do."

When they had the floors cleared, Carl brought in the rams that hadn't been shorn the day before. He wouldn't let Lizzie help until they were done and outside in their own separate enclosure.

He kicked the fleece aside and said, "Now we can move the first bunch of ewes into the catch pen. I'll need you to catch a sheep and bring her to me. When I pull her out and hold her, you need to squirt a dose of medicine into her mouth and then make note of it in our record book."

"I'll do whatever you need me to do."

She made a grab for the first animal and tried to pull it to where he stood. It was amusing to watch a one-hundred-and-twenty-pound girl trying to pull a two-hundred-pound animal with four splayed feet and a lot of determination across the pen. Finally, she gave up and the ewe scampered away from her.

Carl started to laugh until he caught sight of Lizzie's face. There were tears in her eyes. "I can't do any of this," she wailed.

"Sure you can. You just have to learn how to control sheep." He caught a ewe in the corner and said, "Come here. You place your hand firmly under her jaw and around her nose like this." He demonstrated. "Then you lift their nose up. This move will keep an ewe still if you press her against a wall or fence so she can't spin away."

Lizzie wiped her cheeks with the back of her hands. "So how do I get her to you?"

"You keep her nose up, put a hand on her hind end, and you walk her backward like this." He demonstrated moving the reluctant ewe to the shearing gate. "They won't all come easily, but most of them can be convinced this way."

He proceeded to give the sheep her medicine and then said, "Now I want you to hold this one here while I step out."

Lizzie looked dubious, but she did as he asked. The sheep, sensing a weaker hand, began to struggle, but Lizzie leaned into her, pushing her against the wall and holding her still.

"Good girl."

He stepped out of the shearing gate, grabbed the sheep from her, took it down to the ground and began to snip away. "While I'm cutting the fleece off, I want you to look up the ear-tag number in our flock record book and mark that she has been wormed. You'll see a place for a checkmark for the medication, a place to write a note if the animal needs a closer checkup because she's sick or acting strange."

"Okay." She flipped through the pages of the book and quickly made a note.

By the time she finished making the entry, he had the fleece off and allowed the ewe to regain her feet. Bleating loudly, she scampered down the runway and out into the corral beyond.

"Ready to bring me the next one?"

"Aren't you going to roll up the fleece?"

"I'll wait till we have a few piled here, and then we will clean and bag them."

From the group milling in the small pen, she grabbed the next one and moved it within Carl's reach. He pulled it from the pen and proceeded to shear it. In this way, they went through the morning. Sometimes, Lizzie managed to have one ready for him. Often, he had to step in and help her. By midmorning, he made the catch pen smaller so the sheep had less room to evade her.

At noon, Lizzie dusted off the front of her apron. She was breathing hard, but looked pleased at her accomplishments. "That was the last one."

"Twenty down, one hundred and ninety left to go."

Her eyes widened. "One hundred and ninety more?"

"Give or take. There will be a half dozen or so that we will cull, so they won't be sheared."

"What will we do with them?"

"I'll take them to the sale barn later this spring. Some will be purchased for slaughter, but a lot of them become fluffy lawn mowers. It's not a bad way for a sheep to live out its days. Come, I'll show you how we take care of the fleece."

He laid the first one from the pile on the table. "We pick off the really dirty wool and any grass or hay that might be stuck in it. Then we fold them up like this." He demonstrated and carried it to a gigantic plastic bag that was held upright by a large wooden frame with boards a few feet apart like a ladder on the sides of it.

"I've been wondering about this thing. It looks like a windmill without a top."

"The slats are so that I can climb up and get inside the plastic bag to tromp down the wool."

"That sounds like something I can do for you. It's got to be easier than wrestling sheep."

"It is easy, but, honestly, you don't weigh enough to pack down the fleece."

She looked for a second as if she wanted to argue with him but quickly thought better of it. "I'll fold the fleece, and you stuff the bag."

"It's a deal."

"Is it time for me to bring in more sheep?"

"It's time for a rest and some lunch. After that, I'll sharpen my shears, sweep off the platform and we'll start all over again."

She grimaced as she rubbed her hands together. "I had no idea their wool could be so greasy."

"It's lanolin. It gives you soft skin." He held out his hand. She ran her fingers across his palm. In a heartbeat, his mouth went dry. He inhaled sharply as his heart beat faster.

She must've sensed something, because her gaze locked with his. He wanted more than the brief touch of her fingers. He wanted to hold her hand. To reach out and pull her close. He wanted to learn everything there was to know about this amazing woman.

She quickly turned away. "I'd better get something ready for lunch. I hope cold sandwiches will be okay."

"That will be fine."

"Goot."

He watched her hurry away and wished he had a reason to call her back.

Lunch and the rest of the afternoon passed in an awkward silence. Carl tried to keep his mind on his work, but he was constantly aware of where she was and what she was doing. Her boundless energy began to lag in the late afternoon. He called a halt to the work even though he hadn't finished nearly as many animals as he had hoped to.

He went to clean up while Lizzie returned to the house. An hour later, he came in to find his supper waiting for him. Lizzie was seated in her usual place, but she was fast asleep, slumped over the table with her head pillowed on her arms.

Carefully, so that he wouldn't wake her, he picked up his plate, meaning to take it outside. Instead, he found himself frozen in place watching her sleep.

He studied the wisps of wild red curls that wouldn't be contained beneath her scarf, the high cheekbones of her face, the way her eyebrows arched so beautifully. He had never seen a more lovely woman.

Once, he would have had the right to court her. To

drive her home after a Sunday singing or to slip away with her after dark to attend a barn party or simply take a long walk in the woods. Once, but not now.

Such a thing was impossible. He had failed God with his weak faith. He should have died alongside his sister. He should have accepted the fate God willed for him and for one small girl and joined them in Heaven. Instead, his cowardice made him break his covenant with God.

Any future he might imagine with Lizzie was nothing but a wisp of smoke pouring from the barrel of a fired gun. A puff of white mist lost in the wind that could never be called back.

Lizzie squirmed into a more comfortable position and sighed deeply. He had no future with her, but he had this moment to remember all his days.

His food was cold by the time he let himself out the door. Duncan was lying on the porch waiting for him. The dog sat up. "Stay. Guard," Carl told him.

The big dog moved in front of the door and lay down. Knowing Duncan would alert him to any problems, Carl walked down the hill to his cold and dark hut.

Chapter Eight

For Lizzie, the following day started out much like the day before, except she ached from head to toe. There wasn't a muscle in her body that didn't hurt.

She wasn't used to such physical labor. She kept house for her uncle and sisters and did all the cooking, canning and most of the laundry. Twice a day she helped with the milking, but she didn't have to wrestle the Holsteins into their stanchions.

Sheep were stubborn, smelly and loud. She had no idea why her grandfather thought so much of them. But he did, and she would help Carl care for them until Joe was able to do so himself. For however long it took.

By midmorning, she was working some of the kinks out of her shoulder when she spotted a wagon turning into the drive. She looked at Carl. "Are you expecting someone?"

He finished clipping the ewe he had between his knees and then straightened to look out the barn door. "No, I'm not expecting anyone. Joe doesn't get visitors."

A buggy turned in behind the wagon. "I hope it's not

the bishop's wife." Lizzie had no idea how to prevent the woman from entering Joe's house if she wanted to.

Together, she and Carl walked out of the barn. On the front seat of the wagon, she recognized Adrian Lapp and his son, Kyle. Several young Amish men she didn't know jumped down from the wagon bed behind them.

The buggy pulled in with Katie Sutter and Sally Yoder on the front seat. They got out and began pulling large picnic hampers from the back.

Lizzie glanced at Carl. He just shrugged. "It looks like we've got some help."

Adrian and his young men approached them. Adrian said, "I've heard that your animals don't spit when you shear them. I thought I would come see this wonder for myself."

He gestured to a gray-haired man in blue jeans and a plaid shirt behind him. "This is Sheldon Kent. He's not Amish, but he says he knows how to get the wool off a sheep."

The man held up a pair of hand shears identical to the ones Carl used. "It's been a few years, but I reckon I still know my way around a fat woolly," he said in a thick Scottish brogue.

Carl broke into a wide smile. "Fat woollies I have aplenty. This way and thanks for the help."

Lizzie turned to Katie and Sally. "How did you know?"

"Faith Lapp told Bishop Zook about Joe's accident. He knew Sheldon Kent from over by Berlin and went to see if he could help shear. It's a blessing that Sheldon was free and could come. The bishop stopped by to tell us yesterday about his plan. We found a few more volunteers to help and here we are. Where would you like this food?"

"In the house, I guess. Is the bishop's wife coming?"

"Not today. Why?" Katie asked slowly.

"For some reason, Grandfather doesn't want her in the house."

Katie and Sally looked at each other and burst out laughing.

"What's so funny?" Lizzie asked.

Katie struggled to control her giggles. "Esther told my mother-in-law that she wouldn't set foot on Woolly Joe's property."

"The bishop's wife said that? I wonder what it's all about." Lizzie knew her grandfather wouldn't explain even if she asked him.

"We may never know. Grab that box off the backseat, Lizzie. We'd best get ready to feed our men." Katie marched ahead into the house.

Sally waited until Lizzie extracted the box and then walked beside her to the house. "Tell me, have you found out anything about your grandfather's hired man?"

Lizzie looked at her sharply. "What do you mean?"

"He is something of a mystery around these parts. No one knows where he came from. He rarely speaks to anyone except the children. Some people think he's ex-Amish. Some people say he's a weird Englisch fellow that's soft in the head."

Lizzie bristled. "Carl is not soft in the head, but he was raised Amish."

"I'm sorry. I didn't mean to insult your friend."

"We're not friends. He lives and works here, that's all. He works hard, and he's a good shepherd. He cares about the sheep. My grandfather respects Carl's privacy and I do, too."

"You are right to do so. I was being nosy. Forgive me."

Lizzie realized she had spoken too harshly. "There's nothing to forgive. I'm tired and short-tempered today and worried about my grandfather."

Sally smiled. "Of course. I think a hot cup of tea is called for. Come in and rest."

With so much help, the shearing was finished by the end of the day. Carl thanked the men who had come. Joe would be happy to learn the job had been finished in record time. When the wagon finally rolled out of the yard in the late afternoon, Carl looked at Duncan sitting beside him. "This will give us a few more days to get ready for the lambing."

He knew how to do that, but he didn't know how to take care of a convalescing patient with a broken hip. Or a young woman who was so determined to make a place for her family.

Would Lizzie stay and help take care of her cantankerous grandfather, or would she move to the Sutters' farm as she had planned? It was something they should talk over. Perhaps now Joe could be convinced that he needed his granddaughters to come stay with him. Lizzie would be thrilled if they could all stay together.

Carl went to his hut and changed out of his grimy work clothes. Wrapping them and a few other items in his sheets, he carried them all to the back porch. It was his intention to do his own laundry, but Lizzie heard him filling the machine with water and came outside.

"I can do those for you, Carl."

"I can manage."

She took the box of laundry soap out of his hand. "You have been working all day, while I wasn't allowed to do anything harder than brew a pot of coffee."

"You've been working nonstop since you arrived. I think you deserve a few hours of rest."

"And now I've had them. Supper will be ready in a little while. I'm going to walk over to the telephone booth and call the hospital to check on my grandfather."

While the Amish did not allow telephones in their homes, Carl knew that Joe's congregation allowed a shared telephone that was located centrally to several farms. "I'll walk over with you when you go."

Was he being too bold? Hadn't he convinced himself last night that he didn't deserve her interest? Even so, he held his breath and waited for her answer.

She smiled and nodded. "I would be glad of the company. *Danki*."

He grinned, giddy with relief. "I'm anxious to hear how he is doing, too."

The phone booth was a half mile from the end of the lane. To Carl's knowledge, Joe had never used it. Carl had used it only once. A year ago, he had called the Englisch bakery where his sister Jenna worked to let her know that he was okay. He knew she would relay his message to their parents. Jenna begged him to come home, but he couldn't face his family yet. Not until he believed he had earned God's forgiveness. In a moment of weakness, he gave Jenna his address.

She had been writing to him every week since that day. He had read the first two without answering them, but he couldn't bear to read them after that. It was too great a reminder of his shame and his loss.

He thought a lot about that phone call as he walked beside Lizzie. He missed his family just as Lizzie missed hers. Although he knew he might never see his home again, he wanted Lizzie to have the people she loved around her.

It had been a long time since he'd given a thought to what someone else needed. He said, "The doctor told Joe that he was going to need extra help when he came home."

"I've been thinking about that. I reckon I should tell Katie Sutter that I won't be able to work for her and that she should look for someone else."

"Actually, I was thinking that your sisters might be able to come help care for him."

She shook her head. "They don't have the money to get here. I sent all that I have, but it is only enough for one of them. I don't know if Clara will come without Greta and Betsy."

"Have you written to them about their grandfather?"

"I haven't. I don't know how to explain what a mess I've made of things here."

"Perhaps knowing that you need help taking care of him will convince Clara to come."

"I hadn't thought of that. You may be right."

"It happens sometimes."

She gave him a puzzled look. "What happens sometimes?"

"Sometimes it happens that I'm right. I was making a joke, Lizzie."

She pressed her hand to her mouth and giggled. It was the cutest sound he'd ever heard. They arrived at the phone booth all too soon for him.

He waited outside the door until she came out. "How is he?"

"The nurse said he is doing very well except for a

small fever. She said he is cranky, and he's been complaining about the food."

"That doesn't surprise me. If he wasn't complaining about something, I'd be really worried."

"She said to expect him to stay there for a week or so depending on how well he does with his physical therapy."

"I almost wish they would keep him longer."

"Why?"

"Once the lambing season starts, I'm not going to have time to look after him. Knowing Joe, he's going to want to be out helping."

She sighed. "We must be thankful that he is recovering. If he allows me to stay, I will take care of him while you take care of the lambs."

"I hate to see you give up a paying job that means so much to you."

"It's my family that means a lot to me. Grandfather is part of my family even if he doesn't want to be. I'll stay until he's fit, and then I will find a job. Clara's wedding isn't until the first week of May. I have time yet to earn the money my sisters will need to join me."

"Knowing that you'll stay until Joe is mended takes a load off my mind."

She blushed and smiled sweetly. "I'm glad."

"What else did the nurse say?"

She updated Carl on what was said as they walked home. He tried to slow the pace to make the trip last longer, but Lizzie wasn't one to drag her feet. Was her haste because of the work she had yet to finish, or was it his presence that she was eager to escape?

He couldn't blame her if that was true. He didn't belong in the company of an Amish maid. Most Amish people would frown on even this harmless activity because of his exclusion from their faith. Those who didn't know that he had been placed in the Bann could criticize Lizzie for spending time alone with an outsider. Either way, he was putting Lizzie's reputation at risk. Today, the community had rallied around her. He wanted it to stay that way. The less time he spent with her, the better it would be for her.

He stopped walking. "I've got a ram out in the upper pasture that I need to check on. I noticed an abscess on his back when I sheared him."

She shot him a perplexed look. "But it's almost suppertime. Can't it wait until tomorrow?"

"I'm not hungry. Go ahead and eat without me. Don't look for me tomorrow, either. I've got a lot of lambing pens to get set up."

"You have to eat, Carl."

"I've got food at my place. It's not as good as your cooking, but I'll make do."

"I'm not going to let you go a whole day without a hot meal and that's that."

"Okay, you can feed me supper tomorrow." He started backing away.

"Are you sure?" She sounded reluctant to see him go.

That was all the more reason for him to leave, but he couldn't believe how difficult it was to walk away. "I'm sure. Have a good night, Lizzie."

"*Guten nacht,* Carl."

He stopped a few feet away from her and turned back. "My place is only a quarter of a mile away if you need something."

She smiled softly. "I know."

"Right." He gestured toward the pasture. "I should get going."

"Be careful around those rams. I have no idea how to run a sheep farm."

If anyone could do it, she could. "I don't think it would take you long to learn."

Although Lizzie's thoughts and prayers frequently turned to her grandfather and to her sisters while she worked the next day, she was amazed at how often they strayed to Carl. A dozen times during the morning, she stopped what she was doing to look out the window in the hopes of catching a glimpse of him. Each time, she was disappointed.

Was he avoiding her, or did he really have so much work to do that he couldn't even stop in for a cup of coffee? She kept a pot warm on the stove just in case. In the early afternoon, she poured herself a cup, took one sip, grimaced and poured the rest down the drain. It was strong enough to float a horseshoe. She was glad that Carl hadn't had a chance to sample it.

She finally caught a glimpse of him and Duncan walking across the pasture toward his hut around six o'clock. She realized if she made another trip to the phone booth that their paths would pass close to each other in front of his home. That way, she could pretend she hadn't set out to meet him deliberately.

Quickly, she changed her stained apron for a clean one. She patted any stray hairs into place and went out the door, but she was doomed to disappointment. She didn't meet Carl or Duncan on her walk. Had Carl seen her coming his way and changed directions?

She continued along the path feeling let down and

more disappointed than she should have been. When had she come to depend so heavily upon Carl's presence to cheer her?

Today, like yesterday, the sun shone brightly in the sky. The same flowers bloomed in the grass along the roadside and the trees pushed the same green leaves open. A lark sang a happy song from the fence off to one side. The sights, sounds and the smells of spring were still all around her, but they seemed muted without Carl's companionship.

The realization troubled her.

As soon as her grandfather was able to live on his own again, she would have to leave. She had grown far too fond of Carl in the short time that she'd known him. She couldn't delude herself into thinking otherwise. Wasn't she out here hoping that he would join her? Such feelings were a recipe for disaster, for both of them.

When she reached the phone booth, her call to the hospital only added to her worries. The nurse she spoke to seemed reluctant to share much information. She did relay the fact that Joe still had a fever and that he was undergoing more tests.

On the way back to the farmhouse, Lizzie picked up the mail. It was too soon to expect an answer from Mary, but Lizzie was disappointed anyway when there wasn't anything for her.

Her grandfather's newspaper was there. She wondered if the hospital would supply him with a copy. Tomorrow, when she called again, she would ask. She thumbed through the rest of the mail. There were a few pieces addressed to her grandfather and a letter for Carl that caught her attention.

She studied it briefly. Was it from the same person

that had written to him last week? She hadn't paid attention to the previous letter, so she had no way of knowing. The return address on the one she held was Reedville, Pennsylvania. Was that where he was from? The sender's name was Jenna King.

A sister or his mother? A wife? The block printed letters of the address had a childlike quality. His child perhaps? He could be married with a half dozen *kinder* for all she knew. It was an unsettling thought. The envelope in her hand sparked far more questions than answers about the man. She was curious to see what Carl would do with this letter.

She didn't see him until she rang the bell for supper that evening. He came in and washed up without looking at her. Was he still upset with her for causing Joe's accident? She couldn't think of anything else she had done to make him avoid her.

Maybe he sensed her interest and wanted to stem it. She blushed at the thought.

"Have you heard anything about Joe?" he asked.

"I called the hospital again. They told me he was running a fever. I got the feeling the nurse wasn't telling me everything."

He leaned a hip against the counter as he dried his hands. "You think Joe is worse than they are letting on?"

"I don't know what to think."

"What did the nurse say?"

"That he is still running a fever and they are doing more tests."

"Maybe I should go see him."

"Would you? That would be wunderbar."

"If it will ease your mind, I'll see if I can get a ride with Samuel Carter tomorrow. He's a local English fellow who uses his van to drive Amish folks when they need to travel farther than a buggy can go."

She bit her lower lip, then said, "You must not do it as a favor to me."

"Right. No favors. Okay. It will ease *my* mind to see how he's doing firsthand."

"Goot." The small distinction seemed silly, but it relieved her conscience.

The sound of a car pulling up outside and Duncan's mad barking made them both glance outside. "Who is that?" she asked.

"I have no idea."

Lizzie opened the door and saw Dr. Zook get out of a dark blue car. He wasn't dressed in his white coat this evening. He was wearing a light gray sweater and a pair of faded blue jeans.

He nodded to her. "Good evening, Miss Barkman. I thought you might like an update on Joe's condition."

Lizzie stepped back from the door. "Of course. We were just talking about him. Please come in. Can I get you a cup of coffee? We were about to have supper. You are welcome to join us. Several of the local women have left desserts with us. I understand that Nettie Imhoff's peach pie is quite good."

"It is. I've had it on several occasions, but I don't need anything tonight, thank you. I can only stay for a few minutes. I wanted to let you know that your grandfather isn't getting along as well as I had hoped. Unfortunately, there have been some complications."

Lizzie pressed a hand to her heart as fear made it thud painfully. "What type of complications?"

"His blood work shows that he has an infection. We believe it's in the surgical site."

"Is it serious?" Carl asked from the kitchen.

The doctor turned to include Carl in the conversation. "It can be, but at this point it's not life-threatening. It is, however, something we need to keep a close eye on. What this means is that Joe will have to remain in the hospital for at least another week of IV antibiotics. I'm sorry. I know this is not what you want to hear."

No, Lizzie had been hoping to hear that Joe would be home soon and up and around in no time.

Carl held out his hand to the doctor. "We appreciate you stopping by in person to give us the news."

"It was on my way home from making rounds at the hospital. We'll let you know if there's any change in his condition. I also wanted to visit with you about his care when he does get to come home. He's not going to be able to live alone for at least six weeks."

"Six weeks?" Her heart sank at the news. It was only six weeks until Clara's wedding. She wouldn't be able to get a job and make enough to pay Greta and Betsy's way here.

"Will that be a problem?" Dr. Zook asked.

Lizzie raised her chin. "*Nee,* I'll be here for as long as he needs me."

"And I'll be close by," Carl added.

"I know the Amish take care of one another, but I've also heard that Joe is something of a recluse. The nurses at the hospital tell me he's turned away all his visitors, including the bishop."

"He can be cantankerous," Carl admitted.

"That's what worries me. I don't want him trying to do things by himself too soon."

"I'll see that he behaves. He'll listen to me." Carl's tone reassured Lizzie and the young doctor.

"Good. Joe's caseworker will come to visit with you about his needs before he comes home. If you have any questions, feel free to stop by my office or give me a call." With that, the young doctor nodded goodbye and went out the door.

Lizzie pressed a hand to her forehead. "Daadi has to be all right. I've only just gotten to know him again. I can't bear the thought of losing him."

Carl looked worried, too, but he said, "Joe is a tough old goat. He's going to be fine. We have to believe that."

He was trying to reassure her and she was grateful for his effort. "You're right. I'm borrowing trouble to worry about something I can't change. All things are in God's hands."

"I'm sorry that I can't do more to ease your worries." His tone was soft and filled with regret.

"I appreciate that." Lizzie looked away from the sympathy in his eyes. It was becoming much too easy to accept his kindness when she knew she shouldn't.

She indicated the packet of mail on the table. "Would you go through this and see what needs to be taken to Joe? There's a letter for you, too."

"Thanks." He picked up the bundle and leafed through it. He separated one letter, carried it to the stove and dropped it into the fire. She knew without asking that it was the one addressed to him.

It was none of her business what Carl did with his correspondences, but she was still shocked. Her curiosity about him rose tenfold. Who was the woman who wrote to him, and why did he burn her letters?

Chapter Nine

After a hectic week, Lizzie expected a day of rest on Sunday, since there was no church to attend. Amish congregations gathered for worship every other week. The "off" Sunday, when there was no preaching service, was reserved for quiet reflection, visiting and family time.

At home, it would have been the day for reading quietly or perhaps going to visit a friend or neighbor. Because she and her sisters didn't have the extended family so common among Amish communities, they seldom visited anyone but a few close neighbors. Her uncle wasn't a popular man. It was rare that anyone came to visit them.

The morning passed much as she expected, but a little before noon, Elam and Katie Sutter drove in. Sally Yoder sat in the back holding Jeremiah while Rachel leaned out the window with wide round eyes.

Glad for the distraction that would prevent her constant worry about her sisters, Lizzie went out to greet them. Three people emerged from the back of the buggy. As she was being introduced to Levi and Sarah Beachy and Naomi's daughter, Emma Troyer, several more buggies turned into the lane. Lizzie looked around for Carl, but he remained out of sight. The second buggy held the Lapp family, and the last vehicle belonged to a couple she hadn't met. Faith introduced them to her as Joann and Roman Weaver.

Joann, a plain woman with amazing green eyes, said, "I think I remember you. Didn't you go fishing with your grandfather when you were little?"

"Now that you mention it, I do remember going to a lake with him, but I remember throwing rocks into the water, not fishing. Are you the little girl who could skip stones so well?"

Joann laughed. "I don't know that I did it well, but I did it often, until I learned that it scared the fish away. I'm so happy to see you again. I feel like I have discovered a long-lost friend."

Her husband wore a sling on his left arm. "I believe you have. Just remember, I'm still your number-one fishing buddy."

"Like I could forget that." The smile the couple shared made Lizzie wish that someone would smile at her that way.

It was a silly thought. She never expected to be courted. She never wanted to be courted. So why would she long for such closeness with any man?

"Newlyweds," Sally whispered in Lizzie's ear as she walked past. "They only have eyes for each other."

The children ran past her and greeted Duncan. Then they immediately went down to the barn to look at the sheep. The next time Lizzie glanced their way, she saw Carl was with them. He was holding Rachel and letting her pet one of the ewes. She squealed each time she touched the animal's soft wool, making Carl laugh at her antics. Joann and Roman went down to visit with Carl. Were they friends of his? Did they know his history?

Sally bounced down the steps of the porch and stopped beside Lizzie. "Good, those two have gone to make sheep's eyes at the sheep instead of at each other. For two people who couldn't stand one another just a year ago, they certainly get along well now."

Lizzie watched Carl explaining something to Joann and wondered if there was someone in his past that he loved, or was loved by in return. Were the letters he burned from his mother or a sister? Or were they from a wife that he'd left behind? How many letters had he ignored? More important, why?

Katie soon claimed her attention, and Lizzie went inside to discover a lunch had been laid on her table with enough food to feed an army.

She passed an amazing day with her new friends. They laughed and told stories about each other and about her grandfather. They made Lizzie feel as if she had always been a part of their circle of friends.

Their closeness reminded her of her sisters. Katie was a lot like Clara. They were both quiet, deep thinkers. Greta, with her love of animals, would find a kindred spirit in Faith. Sally was only a little older than Betsy, but Lizzie could imagine them as friends and confidantes, boldly speaking their minds and giving the local boys a heartache or two.

If only she could get her sisters to Hope Springs, life would be so much better for all of them.

The afternoon passed quickly, and when the last of her visitors had gone, Lizzie walked out onto the porch and took a seat on one of the two green metal chairs along the side of the house. From the scuff marks in the railing's white paint, she suspected that both Carl and her grandfather spent evenings here with their feet propped up.

She had been sitting only a few minutes when she saw Carl leave the barn. He glanced in her direction. She raised a hand and waved. He hesitated, as if torn between coming to the house or going to his hut. Duncan had no difficulty making a decision. He loped across the yard and up the steps to sit between the chairs. Lizzie reached down to pet him. He licked her hand in doggy gratitude.

When she looked up, Carl was coming her way. He silently climbed the steps and took a seat. She almost giggled when he tipped his chair back and propped his feet on the rail in front of him. "You've had a busy day."

"I have been overwhelmed with visitors, that's true. You will be amazed at the amount of food that is on the table. They insisted on leaving everything. I may not have to cook for a month."

"That would be a shame. You're a mighty good cook."

She blushed at the compliment. "It seems that Grandfather has many friends. I had no idea. Do they visit often?"

"Not since I have been staying here, and that's almost four years now. Naomi Wadler comes a few times a year, but she never stays long. She keeps Joe's larder stocked with jars of garden produce, jam and fruit from her orchard and puts up the stuff he grows, too."

"Really? I wonder why. Are they related?" It was common practice for Amish families to care for their elders.

"Not that I know. I always thought she was sweet on him. I'm glad she does it or we would end up eating nothing but muttonchops and crackers."

"Sweet on my grandfather? Are you serious? He's old!"

Carl chuckled. "He may be old, but he can keep out

of her way fast enough. She may be chasing, but he isn't ready to be caught."

"Naomi wasn't here today, but I met her daughter, Emma. I like her very much."

"I've never met her, but if she is anything like her mother, she is a formidable woman."

"I noticed you talking to Joann and Roman Weaver. Are they friends?"

"Don't you mean do they know I have been shunned?"

"*Nee,* I meant no such thing." Maybe she had been wondering that, but she wouldn't admit it now.

"Joann and Roman like to go fishing at Joe's lake. I speak to them now and again. A few times, they have left their catch with us. Joann is something of a bookworm. She was telling me today that llamas make good guard animals for sheep, plus, you can sell their fleece."

"Do they spit?"

He chuckled. "Worse than an alpaca."

"Let's stick with Duncan. He never spits." The dog wagged his tail at the mention of his name. She reached down and stroked his head.

"Is this what the off Sundays are like where you come from?" Carl asked.

"*Nee.* We seldom have visitors. Uncle Morris doesn't like it when our friends come over. He complains that we can't afford to feed everyone. What about you? What were Sunday afternoons like when you were growing up?"

"A lot like this. My mother has twelve brothers and sisters, and my father has five, so we were always inundated with cousins, aunts and uncles or we were traveling to visit them."

"You must miss that."

"Sometimes, but I like my privacy." He shot her a pointed look.

She ignored it. "Do you keep in contact with your family?"

"No."

"How sad. I thought perhaps the letters that came for you are from someone in your family. I saw the name on the return address was Jenna King. I know it's not my business..."

"You're right. It's not," he said abruptly.

She took offense at his attitude. "If you intend to be rude, I'm going inside."

He quickly stretched his hand toward her. "No, wait. Don't go yet. I'm sorry. It's just that I don't like to talk about my past."

"Talking helps, Carl."

"It can't change what has happened."

"No, but it can show us that we aren't alone in our troubles."

"In case you haven't noticed, Lizzie, I like being alone."

"In case *you* haven't noticed, Carl King, *you* don't." She rose and stomped into the house.

Duncan whined, sensing the tension that Carl tried hard to control. Lizzie enjoyed needling him. He reached out and ran his hand over the dog's silky head. "We used to like being alone, didn't we?"

Until Lizzie showed up and constantly made him aware of how barren his life was. Working, eating, sleeping and watching over the sheep had been satisfying enough for him until a week and a half ago. How could such a little slip of a woman turn things topsy-turvy in a matter of days?

Maybe he was drawn to her because she reminded him so much of Sophia. Like his youngest sister, Lizzie's enthusiasm sometimes outweighed her common sense. Still, he liked that about her. She saw what she wanted, and she worked to achieve it. But no matter how hard she worked at prying into his past, she was going to find herself up against a dead end. His crime was his own. He wouldn't share the story of how he fell so far from grace. He couldn't bear to see the look on Lizzie's face if she found out he had murdered someone.

The door opened and Lizzie came outside again. Her normally sweet expression was cold. She thrust a foil-wrapped plate into his hands. "Enjoy your supper…alone. I won't be cooking tonight."

She turned on her heel and marched back into the house. She didn't quite slam the door, but she shut it with conviction.

Duncan lifted his nose toward the plate. Carl held it out of his reach. "Oh, no, you don't." He raised his voice and shouted, "This is mine, Duncan, and I'm going to enjoy it alone!"

Somewhere in the house, a door slammed. Feeling slightly gratified at having had the last word, he walked down the hill toward his hut. At the door, he paused. As much as he hated to admit it, Lizzie was right.

There was a wooden chair outside his front door. He grabbed it and carried it toward the small creek that meandered through the pasture. He stopped beside an old stump that he could use for a table. From this vantage point, he could see the house up on the hill. Somehow, just knowing she was up there was a comfort.

He settled down to snack on cold fried chicken, carrot sticks and biscuits that were flaky and good, but they didn't measure up to Lizzie's. Not by a long shot.

The next day began with a flurry of work. Knowing that her grandfather would be unable to put in his garden or do such chores for several weeks, Lizzie attacked his garden plot with a vengeance. The weather had turned cold again. The taste of spring had been just that, a taste. March wasn't going to go out like a lamb.

It was nearly noon when she noticed Carl standing outside the fence watching her. Finally, she couldn't bear his stoic silence any longer. She thrust her spade into the ground. "What are you staring at?"

"I have some composted manure and straw I need to get rid of. Shall I haul it over here? I don't want to do you any favors."

"Shall I go in the house so you can do it alone?"

He struggled to keep a grin off his face and lost. "I reckon I deserved that. I'm sorry I was cross with you yesterday."

"And I am sorry for being a nosy busybody. Your life is your own, Carl. It was wrong of me to pry. Can we be friends again? I really dislike eating alone."

"So do I, but can we be friends?"

She smiled. "I don't see why not. You are invaluable to my grandfather, and I wasn't joking when I said I didn't know how to run a sheep farm."

"You have been a good learner. Next year, you'll be able to wrestle the sheep to me with barely a thought. I may even teach you how to use the shears." He opened the garden gate and carried in a spade. He took a spot beside her and began to turn over the dirt.

"Next year. I hadn't thought that far ahead. I've been so focused on getting my sisters here. Will I even be here a year from now? So much depends on my family."

"Have you heard anything from them?"

Lizzie shook her head. "I only sent them my letter a week ago. I should hear something soon. I have another letter that I need to mail today. I had to explain how my foolishness has landed our grandfather in the hospital. I want them to be prepared for what they will find when they arrive."

"Did you tell them about me?"

"Only that you live on the property and you take care of the sheep."

He stopped digging to look at her. "Nothing else?"

"Nothing else."

He nodded and began to spade up the soil again. Working together, they finished half of the garden before Lizzie called a halt to the work. "I want to get my letter to the mailbox before the mail carrier goes by. We can finish the rest tomorrow."

Carl stepped on his spade, driving it deep into the earth. "I thought I would call the hospital and see how Joe is today."

"Let me get my letter and I'll walk with you part of the way. That is, if you don't mind?"

He chuckled. "I don't mind. Is there any coffee left from this morning?"

"I have tried keeping some on the back of the stove, but it just gets bitter. It won't take me long to make a fresh pot. You must tell me what vegetables Grandfather will want planted this spring."

"He's fond of kale and radishes, I know that. He likes

cucumbers and the squash casserole Naomi brings over in the summer."

"I'll check with her for the recipe and see what variety of squash she uses." Lizzie walked through the garden gate ahead of Carl, happy to be on good terms once more.

The day became a pattern for the rest of the week. Over a cup of coffee in the midmorning, they discussed what work needed to be done and made plans to get as much done as they could before the lambs began to drop. Carl finished building the sheep pens while Lizzie continued to work on the garden until rainy weather put a stop to her outdoor activity. In the late afternoon or early evening, they would walk together to the phone booth. Normally, Lizzie was the one who spoke to the nurses and relayed the information to Carl. Joe refused to take phone calls in his room. It was permitted by their church in such circumstances, but the hospital staff respected his wishes.

As the days passed, Lizzie began to worry that she hadn't heard from Mary or from any of her sisters. It was likely that Uncle Morris had forbidden them to contact her, but she hoped and prayed they would find a way. It was during those worry-filled times that Lizzie came to rely on Carl's words of reassurance.

It was strange that a man who had been shunned by others could be such a comfort to her. More than ever, she wanted to help him find his way back to the community that meant so much to each of them.

One evening, after hearing from the nurses at the hospital that Joe was doing better, Lizzie and Carl stopped at the mailbox on the way back to the house as had become their habit. Lizzie opened the front panel and pulled out the mail. Excitement sent her pulse racing when she saw an envelope with her name on it. She clutched it to her chest. "Finally! It's a letter from my friend Mary. Please, Lord, I hope she tells me that Clara is coming."

She handed Carl the rest of the mail and quickly tore open her letter. As she read, her excitement turned to shock.

She felt Carl's hand on her shoulder as her knees threatened to buckle. "Lizzie, what's wrong?"

She managed to focus on his face. "Mary writes that Uncle Morris was furious at my running away. He and Rufus have decided to push the wedding up. The banns were read at last Sunday's church service. The wedding will take place two weeks from today." Lizzie pressed a hand to her cheek.

"I'm so sorry. I don't know what to say."

Tears welled up in her eyes and trickled down her cheeks unheeded. He pulled his hand away. She missed his comforting touch immediately.

"What does Mary say about the money you sent? Clara may decide to come now that she knows how little time is left."

"She can't. Mary hasn't been able to see them or get my letters to them. Uncle Morris has forbidden her to visit. They don't know where I am or that I haven't abandoned them. Two weeks! I can't even return for the wedding. I sent all the money I had to help Clara leave. It was all for nothing. For nothing!"

She fled down the lane and rushed into the house, leaving Carl standing alone behind her.

Lizzie went through the motions of fixing a meal, cleaning the house and readying the garden for planting. The work kept her busy, but it couldn't take her mind off the fate of her sisters. She felt marooned in the ramshackle house with no hope of seeing them again. Even Carl's softly spoken words of reassurance and quiet strength couldn't lift her spirits.

She often felt his eyes on her. She tried to put on a brave front, but inside she was miserable. When she went to bed at night, she prayed fervently for the Lord's intervention and for the courage to accept her failure as His will.

Late one afternoon, she came in from feeding the chickens and saw an envelope on the kitchen table. She picked it up. Inside was several hundred dollars. For an instant, she thought her prayers had been answered, then she realized who had left the money.

It was the answer to her prayers, but it was one she couldn't accept.

Her hands trembled as she placed the envelope back on the table and turned away.

Carl was standing outside the screen door watching her. She realized in that moment how much she had come to care for him.

"You have not taken it from my hand," he said quietly.

"But I know it's from you."

"Your grandfather would say this way is acceptable."

"It is a wonderful gesture, but I can't take your money, Carl."

He pulled open the door and came in. "Tell me how to make it acceptable to you and I'll do it. It's all I have. Please, take it."

"I could not accept such a favor."

"Would you accept it from me if I had not been shunned?"

"But by your own admission you have been. I must

hold true to the vows I spoke before God." Her grandfather once said shunning was a difficult and painful thing. Until this moment, she hadn't realized how right he was.

Carl's shoulders slumped in defeat. "You won't accept it even if it means never seeing your sisters again?"

"Even if it means that."

"You live your faith, Lizzie Barkman. God will surely smile on you."

"Just as He smiles on all His children," she said quietly.

Carl stared at the floor. "I could not hold true to my faith as you do. He has turned His face away from me."

She moved to stand in front of him. "That isn't true, Carl. God never turns away from us. It is we who turn away from Him. We give in to doubt and fear, but He knows our hearts. He knows we need His love. Forgiveness and acceptance are ours for the asking."

He shook his head. "I have asked for forgiveness many times, but I have not received it. I don't know that I ever shall."

"If anyone knows you, they must surely see your goodness. Your desire to help me means more than I can say. I know now what my grandfather sees in you. You have such a generous heart."

He raised his eyes and stared at her for a long moment. "And you are a strong, brave woman."

"Not at the moment." She picked up the envelope and held it out to him. He took it from her and left the house. She sat down at the table and wept.

Chapter Ten

Lizzie stood by the mailbox waiting for the letter carrier to reach her. She spotted the white van stopped at a farm down the road and knew he would come her way next.

She couldn't let go of the hope that Mary would write and tell her something had changed. It had to change. Clara couldn't marry Rufus. It was unthinkable.

When the van pulled up beside her, she waited impatiently as the man in the gray uniform behind the wheel sorted through the stack in his hand. "Looks like only one today."

He held it toward her. "I haven't seen Joe for a couple of weeks. I hope he's okay."

She glanced at the letter and saw it was addressed to Carl. She put it in her pocket. "My grandfather is in the hospital with a broken hip."

"Man, that's tough. I'm sorry to hear that. My son and I were planning to stop in and buy a club lamb from him later this spring. Should we rethink that?"

"I'm afraid I don't know what a club lamb is, but Carl King is here. I'm sure he can help you."

"Great. A club lamb is one that's raised by a kid in

4-H or FFA, Future Farmers of America. Carl was the one who helped my son choose a lamb last year. It took second place at the county fair. My boy is hoping for first place this year."

"I'm sure Carl will be happy to help you again."

"He's really good with kids. My son learned more about how to take care of his lamb from Carl than he did from his 4-H leader. Well, give Joe my best." He nodded and drove away.

Lizzie started toward the phone booth next. Was it only two days ago that she strolled along this path with Carl at her side? It seemed as if a century had passed since then. So much had happened. So much had changed. Her mad scramble to get her sisters to Hope Springs had come to a painful stop.

As had her growing friendship with Carl.

Her refusal of his gift put his shunning front and center between them. As it should have been all along, she acknowledged.

Leaving the security and close-knit circle of her family had put her adrift in a sea of change. Nothing was as she imagined it would be. Nothing worked out as she had hoped. Carl's quiet, reserved strength had offered her shelter from the storm of events taking place around her. It was no wonder she grew to cherish his friendship so quickly.

He was a good man. She didn't doubt that, but he no longer believed as she did and that was unacceptable. He knew it, because he had stopped coming by the house. She had seen him out and about on the farm, but he didn't come in for coffee in the morning or for lunch, or for supper, for that matter.

In short, he left her alone.

And she missed him terribly.

She reached the phone booth and saw Duncan lying outside it. Her traitorous heart gave a happy leap before she could put her hard-won resolve into place. A few moments later, Carl emerged. He stopped short at the sight of her.

"*Gutenowed,* Carl." She was pleased that her voice sounded composed with just the right touch of reserve.

"Good evening." He looked haggard and worn, as if he hadn't been sleeping well.

"Were you checking on Joe?" she asked.

He hitched his thumb over his shoulder toward the phone. "Yes. He's doing much better today. He's been up walking with a walker. There's no sign of fever. Looks like the antibiotics have done the trick."

"That's wonderful news."

He shifted uncomfortably. "It is. He should be home in a week. Look, I've got to go. Are you doing okay?"

"I'm fine, and you?"

"I'm managing. Have a nice night." He tipped his hat and walked past her.

She watched him until he disappeared around a bend in the path that led to his hut. He never looked back. She wanted to call out to him, but she couldn't think of a reason to do so. She didn't want him to know how much she missed having him around.

Should she have taken the money he offered? It would have been enough, more than enough. She could have taken it, confessed later to the bishop and accepted his forgiveness. There were ways around the rules, but they weren't just rules to her. They were the glue that bound her Christian community together against the forces that would break it down, both from the outside and from within.

Because of the Ordnung, every Amish man and woman knew what was expected of them. They knew their purpose in life. The rules of their society weren't made to be broken or ignored. They were made to guide and to guard against the disruptions of the world that could come between the faithful and God. Accepting the Amish faith came at a great price. It was never done lightly.

She might regret not using Carl's gift, but she knew she had done the right thing.

If only she had her own money or something she could sell, but she owned nothing of value. She had little more than the clothes on her back. Her heart ached as she thought about the life Clara would be forced to live with an abusive husband.

It would be their mother's life all over again.

Lizzie remembered all too well the desperate attempts to keep peace in the house, waiting in agony for the simple spark that would set their father's temper ablaze. He was always sorry afterward, but his repentant behavior never lasted, yet their mother forgave him time and again.

Lizzie shuddered at the memories. Clara deserved better.

Lizzie was lost in her thoughts and didn't realize a buggy had stopped on the roadway until someone called her name. Sally Yoder waved and beckoned Lizzie to her side. Lizzie didn't recognize the woman seated beside her. She wore dark glasses and looked to be several years older than Sally.

"I'm so glad we ran into you. We were just on our way

to a quilting bee at my cousin's house. Have you met Rebecca yet?" Sally asked.

Lizzie shook her head. "I don't believe so."

The woman in the dark glasses leaned around Sally. "Hi, I'm Rebecca Troyer. It's a pleasure to meet you, Lizzie. Everyone has been talking about the sudden appearance of Woolly Joe's relative. Almost no one knew he had a family. How is he doing?"

"He's better. He may be home in a week."

Sally smiled in relief. "That's wonderful news. The reason I wanted to see you was to ask if you would like to ride with my family to the church service on Sunday."

"That's very thoughtful of you, Sally. That would be great as long as it's not out of your way."

"Not at all. We will go right past your lane. How are you doing living by yourself out here?"

"It's very quiet, but there's no one to interrupt my work during the day. Grandfather's house is getting the scrubbing it deserves. I found some half-empty paint cans on the back porch, so I plan to spruce up the kitchen."

"That sounds like a monumental task. Are you free this afternoon? Would you like to come to the quilting bee with us? We are making a quilt for my aunt's fiftieth birthday."

"We would love to have you join us," Rebecca added.

"I'm afraid I have limited skill with a needle. Rebecca, did I see one of your quilts for sale at the inn in Hope Springs?"

"Yes, my Lone Star quilt. Naomi sold it yesterday. I'm always amazed when someone buys one."

"You shouldn't be," Sally said. "You have a wonderful talent. People recognize the value of your work. We should get going. Lizzie, we'll pick you up at eight o'clock on Sunday morning."

"I look forward to it." Lizzie waved as they drove away, but her mind was already reeling. She did own something of value. Something of enormous value to her, but was it valuable enough to buy one-way bus tickets for three young women from Indiana to Hope Springs?

She had her mother's beautiful wedding-ring quilt.

The very idea of parting with the only thing she had to remember her mother by was painful to contemplate. What if she sold it and her sisters still didn't come? Then she would have less than nothing.

She walked the rest of the way home and wrestled with her choices. She could break down and use Carl's money, sell her mother's quilt or accept that she could do nothing. None of them were good choices, but there was only one she could live with.

When she entered the house, she was surprised to see Carl in the kitchen with a box of oatmeal in his hand. He gave her a sheepish look and set it on the counter, like a little boy caught with his hand in the cookie jar. "I'm out of oatmeal. I knew Joe had an extra box. Do you mind if I use it?"

"Is that what you've been living on?"

He stuffed his hands in his front pockets. "I like oatmeal."

"So do I, but not for three meals a day. I'm having chicken and dumplings for supper. There's plenty. You're welcome to have some."

He hesitated, glanced at the oatmeal box, then said, "Thanks. Don't mind if I do."

She turned aside to hide the surge of happiness that engulfed her.

It was just supper. She had to make sure she didn't let her emotions get out of hand again. "I may have discovered a way to earn the money I need to send for my sisters."

"Have you found another job? I can manage without you until Joe comes home."

"*Nee,* I saw Sally Yoder and Rebecca Troyer a little bit ago. They were on their way to a quilting bee. It reminded me that Naomi sells quilts for local women at the inn. She sold one of Rebecca's recently. I have a wedding-ring quilt. I thought I would take it to her and see if she could sell it for me."

She busied herself putting plates on the table and avoided looking at him. She didn't want him to see how hard her decision had been.

He was a difficult man to fool. "A wedding-ring quilt is often a part of a young woman's hope chest."

"I don't plan to marry, so I have no need of the quilt." She tried to sound offhand but failed miserably.

"I thought marriage was the goal of every young Amish woman."

She turned to face him and wrapped her arms tightly across her middle. "It's not the goal of this Amish girl. Every family needs a maiden aunt to help care for the elderly and to help look after the children. That's the life I want."

"I can't see you living a life without love in it. What has given you a distaste for marriage?"

"I didn't say I have a distaste for it. I just said it's not the life I want." She stuffed her hands in the pockets of her apron and encountered the letter she'd forgotten to give him.

She held it out. "This came for you. I'm sorry I didn't remember sooner."

He took it from her, stared at it for a long moment,

then put it in his shirt pocket. At least he didn't toss it in the fire this time. Was that a good sign?

She finished putting supper on the table and they ate in silence. She was afraid he would resume his questions regarding her feelings about marriage, but he didn't. It was fully dark by the time supper was over. Low clouds had moved in, bringing with them a chilly wind.

Carl put on his cowboy hat and coat and took a lantern from a hook by the door. He raised the glass and used a match to light the wick. "I have one ewe out in the hill-top pen that I need to check on. I may have to move her into the barn if she isn't better by morning."

"All right. Is there anything I can do?"

"No, I'm just letting you know so you don't worry if you see a light out in the field. Good night, Lizzie."

"*Guten nacht,* Carl," she said and watched him go out. She carried the dirty plates to the sink and glanced out the window. Carl had stopped at the corral gate. He set his lantern on the fence post and took something out of his pocket. Was he going to read his letter? She held her breath.

He brought the envelope to the top of the lantern chimney. After a few seconds, it caught fire. He held it between his fingers, turning it slightly to keep from being burned until there was only a tiny bit left. He dropped the piece to the ground and watched until the fire consumed all of it. Then he picked up the lantern and walked out into the field.

Lizzie turned away from the window. Her heart ached for Carl and for the woman who wrote him every week. How she must love him to keep writing in the face of his continued silence.

Who was she?

* * *

It wasn't his intention to take supper with Lizzie when he went to the house earlier. He really did need the oatmeal. Even a large box didn't last long when a man ate it three times a day. Cereal was his only reason for being in her kitchen.

At least, that was what he told himself as he crossed the dark pasture with a lantern in his hand. He might have been able to convince himself of that fact if he had actually taken the oatmeal with him when he walked out.

It was still sitting on the counter where he'd left it. He was hungry, but not for food. He craved Lizzie's company. He longed for a glimpse of her smile, to see her look upon him with kindness and maybe something more.

Duncan came out of the dark to walk beside him. He glanced at the dog. "I'm a fool, you know."

Duncan's only response was to lope away.

"So much for venting my troubles to a friend." Carl walked on. The dog couldn't help him with his dilemma. It was something he would need to come to grips with on his own. Although he had only known Lizzie Barkman for two weeks, he was falling for her in a big way.

He'd tried staying away from her, but his efforts had been futile. He was drawn to her in a way that had nothing to do with a home-cooked meal and everything to do with the way she made him feel when she smiled. He was drawn to the warmth of her soul.

He hadn't questioned the wisdom of staying in Hope Springs since the day Joe offered him a place to live. Until she showed up, the farm had been a sanctuary for him. A place where he could retreat from the world and the harm he'd caused. Only, now his self-imposed solitude had abruptly lost its appeal.

Lizzie's rejection of his offer to help hurt deeply even though he had half expected what her reaction would be. It was his inability to help that hurt the most. It kept him awake at night and made him realize how truly separated he had become from those of his faith.

As it turned out, she didn't need his help. She'd found a way without breaking her promise of faith.

He stopped walking and looked back at the house. The light from the kitchen window went out. He watched as the faint light of her lamp passed through the living room and vanished briefly before it reappeared in the window of her second-story bedroom. Would she sleep beneath her wedding-ring quilt tonight? He recognized the distress she tried to hide when she talked about selling it. The decision hadn't been an easy one for her.

He watched her window until the light went out. It was one thing to be alone when it was his choice. It was another thing when he ached with the need to comfort Lizzie but could only watch her struggles from afar.

A new thought occurred to Carl as he stood beneath the brilliant stars strewn across the night sky. Was Lizzie's arrival the way the Lord had chosen to call him back to the faith he'd grown up in?

The next morning, Lizzie finished her chores and left a note for Carl telling him she had gone into town. After that, she climbed the stairs to her small bedroom and stared at the quilt on her bed. It was all she had to remind her of her mother. It was the only thing of value she owned in the world.

She pulled it off the bed and wrapped it around her shoulders. It wasn't the same as being hugged by her mother, but it was as close as she could come until they met again in Heaven.

Tears filled her eyes. She would never feel her mother's arms again, but she could have her sisters' embraces to comfort her. She would have to sell her heirloom to make that happen. In her heart, she knew her mother would understand.

Laying the quilt on the bed again, she folded it carefully. Then she placed it in the box and tied it shut with a length of string. With it tucked firmly under her arm, she walked down the stairs and out the door with a purposeful stride.

It took her over an hour to reach Hope Springs. At the door of the Wadler Inn, she hesitated. She took a moment to gather her courage, then she opened the door and walked in.

Naomi Wadler wasn't behind the desk. An elderly Englisch gentleman greeted Lizzie. "Good morning. How may I help you?"

Lizzie laid her box on the counter. "I have a quilt that I would like Naomi to sell for me."

Naomi appeared in the doorway of a small office behind the counter. "Did I hear my name? Lizzie, how nice to see you again. How is Joe getting along? We have all been praying for him."

"The doctor told us that he developed an infection, but he has improved with the antibiotics they are giving him. He could come home in a week, but he'll still need care and physical therapy."

"I'm glad to hear that. What can I do for you, child?"

"I have a quilt I would like you to sell for me."

"Is this it?" She motioned toward the box.

"*Ja,* it's not a new quilt." Lizzie broke the string and

opened the box. She pulled out the quilt and tears stung her eyes again at the sight of the intricately pieced fabrics in muted blues, pinks and soft greens.

"This is lovely. Was it all done by one person? My buyers prefer quilts done by a single hand rather than the ones done at a quilting bee."

"My mother made it by herself. It's very dear to me, but I have no idea what it is worth to someone else."

Naomi's eyes softened. "Are you sure you want to sell it?"

"I don't want to, but I must." Lizzie choked back tears. "It's the only way I can afford to pay for my sisters to move here. It is desperately important that they come. I know my mother would understand and approve. That makes selling it a little easier."

Naomi came around the counter and slipped an arm across Lizzie shoulders. "Surely your grandfather would loan you the money."

"I can't ask him now. He has hospital and doctor bills to pay. His accident was my fault. Besides, you know what a recluse he is. He doesn't want us here."

"Doesn't want you here? You must be mistaken."

"I wish I were. I left my home and traveled here with the hope that my grandfather would take us in. Things have become very…difficult at home. He refuses to help."

"I thought Joe would do anything for Abigail's children."

"I know he is old and set in his ways. A house full of women would be disruptive for him. I try to understand and forgive him. Can you sell the quilt for me?"

Naomi smiled sadly. "Absolutely. I know someone who might treasure this as you would."

Lizzie stroked the quilt one last time. "*Danki.* I hope

it will be useful to them. Do you know how soon I could expect it to sell?"

"A quilt of this quality will be snatched up in no time. Don't worry about that. I'll send my son-in-law out to the farm with the money for you as soon as I can. Take heart, Lizzie. Something good will come of this, you'll see. Our Lord is watching over you and your sisters."

Lizzie nodded. If only she could be sure this was the path He wanted them to travel.

Naomi began folding the quilt, but her sharp eyes were fixed on Lizzie's face. "Tell me, how are you getting along with Carl King? He's an interesting young man, isn't he?"

Chapter Eleven

Lizzie hoped she wasn't blushing as she looked away from Naomi Wadler's pointed gaze. "I think Carl is doing well enough. Frankly, I don't know what my grandfather would do without him. He's been a tremendous help with all the farmwork. I know that grandfather trusts him to take care of the place and everything on it," she added with a rush, all the while wondering if she had given away too much of her own feelings about Carl.

"I was more interested in how you are getting along with Carl."

"Me? I have barely seen him the past few days. He has a lot to do to get ready for the arrival of our lambs." It wasn't a lie. Carl had been making himself scarce. She didn't need to explain why.

"I've always liked that young man. It is a pity he no longer follows our Amish ways. I know that Joe is terribly fond of him."

Naomi was one of the few people that had visited the farm with any frequency. Lizzie couldn't pass up the opportunity to see if she knew something about Carl's past. "Grandfather told me a little about how they met. Did he ever tell you?"

It was Naomi's turn to look uncomfortable with the conversation. "Joe and I don't really talk a lot when I visit. Even when Abigail lived at home, Joe wasn't one to make idle chitchat."

"You mentioned you were a friend of my mother's. I would love to hear about her when she was young."

Naomi spoke to the gentleman behind the desk. "Charles, Miss Barkman and I will be in the café if you need me." She handed him the box with Lizzie's quilt. "Put this in my office, please."

Naomi came around the counter and hooked her arm through Lizzie's. "Let me treat you to some of the best shoofly pie you've ever had. My daughter makes it. I can tell you so many funny things about your mother."

Lizzie smiled at her. "What was she like when you knew her?"

"She came to live with us when she was only two and I was fifteen. I became her little mother. Did she ever tell you that I was the one who chipped her front tooth with a baseball bat when we were playing ball? Of course, it was an accident, but I felt so terrible about it every time I saw her smile."

"She never told us that." Lizzie allowed Naomi to lead her through a set of French doors to the Shoofly Pie Café that adjoined the inn.

Carl peeked in through the front window of the Wadler Inn. He didn't see Lizzie inside. He'd waited more than an hour after she left home to come into town, as well. He was sure she would have come straight here. He didn't want her to know what he had planned, but he was determined to help her reunite with her sisters.

When he stepped inside the lobby, the elderly Englisch gentleman behind the counter smiled brightly. "Welcome to the Wadler Inn. How may I help you?"

"I understand that you have quilts for sale."

"Yes, we certainly do. You will find our area quilters are some of the very finest. Their creations are true works of art, although the Amish do not view them as such. The ones around the fireplace are the only ones we have at the moment, but more come in all the time."

"I'm actually interested in a wedding-ring quilt that was brought in this morning."

The man looked perplexed for a moment and then said, "Let me get Mrs. Wadler to help you. That quilt is not on display."

Carl relaxed. It hadn't been put on display, so it must be still available. The man went into the café next door and returned a few moments later with Naomi. Her eyes widened in surprise. "Why, Carl, what are you doing here? Joe is doing okay, isn't he?"

"As far as I know, Joe is being his cantankerous self with the hospital staff who get paid to put up with him. I'm here to buy a quilt."

Naomi's eyebrows inched higher. She glanced over her shoulder into the café and then back to him. "Did you have something special in mind?"

"It's a wedding-ring quilt."

She steered him toward the fireplace. She took a seat and he sat across from her on a plush sofa. "Do you know who made it?" she asked.

"I'm not sure who's stitched it, but Lizzie Barkman,

Joe's granddaughter, would have been the one who brought it in."

"I see. It's a shame you didn't buy it from her before she left the farm this morning. It would have saved you both a lot of time."

He was going to have to admit why he was here. "I don't want Lizzie to know that I'm the one buying it."

"Why not?"

There was no way he was going to reveal his entire reason, but he said, "I know it means a lot to her, and I don't want her to feel beholden to me."

"I can understand that, but I'm sorry to tell you the quilt is no longer available."

"Do you mean you sold it already?"

She kept her gaze on the door to the café. He wondered if he had interrupted her lunch. "I haven't actually sold it, but I am holding the quilt for someone. If they choose not to purchase it, I will be sure and let you know."

He rubbed his palms on his thighs. "Lizzie has an urgent need for the money the quilt will bring. Please, let me know as soon as possible."

"By Monday. I will let you know by Monday. And now I must get back to my guest." She rose to her feet and he did the same.

"Thanks for your help." He had done all he could. One way or the other, Lizzie would get the money she needed.

Naomi tipped her head slightly to one side as she stared at him. "Joe has placed a lot of faith in you, Carl. Please don't let him down."

"Don't worry. His sheep are safe with me."

"I wasn't actually thinking about the sheep."

He was too stunned to reply. She gave him a wink and

walked to the desk. "Charles, would you please arrange a driver for me on Sunday evening?"

"Yes, ma'am."

She waved to Carl. "I'll be in touch."

Sally and her family picked up Lizzie on Sunday morning and they joined the long line of buggies traveling single file along the country road. The line moved only as fast as the slowest horse. No one would dream of passing a fellow church member on the way to services. Such a move would be seen as rude and prideful. Even the young men with their high-stepping horses and topless courting buggies held to a sedate pace.

Lizzie found her gaze drawn to Carl's front door when they drove by the pasture gate. The door was closed. There was no sign of him. No smoke came from the chimney even though the morning was crisp.

Surely he must miss being part of a community that made God the center of their lives. Lizzie knew that she couldn't live cut off from her faith. She prayed that she never had to find out how it felt.

Like the previous prayer service, Lizzie was captivated by the simple but eloquent sermon delivered by Bishop Zook. He had a rare gift for preaching the word of God.

About an hour into the service, she noticed Katie Sutter was having trouble managing Jeremiah and the new baby. Both of them were fussing. Katie got to her feet and came to the back of the room where a set of stairs led to the upper level. When Jeremiah saw Lizzie, he reached for her and began hollering at the top of his lungs. Lizzie immediately got up from her seat and took charge of him.

"Bless you," Katie whispered. "I think he needs changing, and the baby wants to eat."

Lizzie wrinkled her nose. "He does." She followed Katie upstairs to one of the bedrooms. After she changed Jeremiah's diaper, she took him to the window to entertain him while Katie nursed his baby brother.

She pointed to a cardinal in the branches of the tree. "See the bird? Can you say *bird?*"

He babbled happily, but none of his words sounded the least like *bird*. He pointed a chubby finger at something and jabbered louder. Lizzie looked to where he was pointing and saw a dog. She realized it was Duncan. He was lying under the last buggy parked at the end of the row.

Lizzie leaned closer to the window. Was that Carl standing at the rear of the buggy?

It was. She straightened. What was he doing here? When the next hymn began in the room beneath her, she realized that Carl was singing, too. She couldn't hear him, but she could see the rise and fall of his chest and the movement of his lips.

She pressed a hand to her heart as pity welled up in her. How often had he stood apart from the worshippers and worshipped from afar? How sad that he wouldn't allow himself to return to what he clearly loved. More than ever, she wanted to find out what had driven him away.

Naomi softly opened the door to Joe's hospital room. The blinds were drawn. The room was dark. He was sitting up in bed, but he had fallen asleep with the newspaper spread over his chest. He wore a hospital gown. It was the first time she had ever seen him in something other than his blue work shirt or his black Sunday coat. He looked...helpless and alone.

The sight only strengthened her resolve. She walked

to the side of the bed and took a seat in the single chair beside him. He slowly opened his eyes and focused on her. For a second, she thought she saw a glimmer of happiness before he frowned. He yanked the bedspread up to his chin. The newspaper went flying. "What are you doing here?"

"I came to see you."

"I'm not in the mood for company."

"That's hardly surprising. You haven't been in the mood for company for the past twenty years."

She laid the package she carried on his lap. "I brought you something."

He looked at it as if it might contain a snake. She almost laughed. It would be funny if it weren't so sad. "Go ahead, open it."

"You have no call to bring me presents."

"I declare, you can make a mountain out of a molehill faster than anyone I've ever met. Just open the package."

"I always knew you were a bossy woman."

"And I have always known that you are a stubborn man."

He lifted the lid of the box and gazed at the fabric with a perplexed expression on his face. "I don't have need of a quilt, but thank you. The stitching is quite fine."

"Abigail made it."

That shocked him. "Abigail? You don't mean my Abigail?"

"Yes, Lizzie brought it to the inn. She wants me to sell it. It's the only thing she has to remember her mother by. Abigail made a quilt for each of her daughters before she passed away. Lizzie was in tears when she handed it over."

Joe ran a hand lovingly over the fabric. "My Abigail

always had a fine hand with a needle. You taught her well."

They both fell silent as thoughts of a shared past over-whelmed them. Naomi drew a deep breath. "She also had a stubborn streak. I suspect she got it from you."

"Why would Lizzie sell this?"

"Because she is desperate to bring her sisters here. Joe, we are old friends. What is Lizzie so afraid of?"

"Morris is making Clara marry a man that Lizzie feels is unsuitable. Harsh, even. That's why she came to Hope Springs. She was hoping I would take them in."

"And why have you turned your back on them? The truth, Joseph," she demanded when she saw the bellig-erent glint in his eyes.

His expression slowly softened. "Lizzie is so much like her."

"But she is not Abigail. I know your daughter broke your heart when she married that man. She broke my heart, too. I saw what he was long before she would admit it. But hearts mend, Joe. Love mends a broken heart."

"I haven't any love left in me."

"You can't fool me, you old goat. Your heart is full of love for that young man you've taken in and for Abigail's daughter. You're just afraid to admit it. You're afraid of being hurt again."

"What if I took them in and they turned against me the way she did? I couldn't bear it."

"So you think it's better not to care at all? That's self-ish. Has trying not to care for Lizzie made you happy, Joseph? The truth, now!"

"*Nee,* it has not."

"Then I see that you have two choices. Risk loving that wonderful child and her sisters and enjoy the best of what God has given you, or turn your back on His gift and keep on being a miserable shell of a man. What's it going to be, Joseph Shetler?"

"You shouldn't speak harshly to me, woman. I'm a sick man."

She leaned forward and laid a hand on his cheek. "Not so sick that you can't see how much I care for you, I hope."

He looked away. "I don't know what you're talking about."

"I had such a crush on you when I was young."

"A *maedel*'s foolishness. I'm almost twenty years older than you."

"Fifteen years. And while that was a lot when I was eighteen, it's not so much now that I'm sixty."

"You've gone soft in the head or something to be talking like this. You married a good man. The right man."

"Yes, I did, and I loved him dearly, but he's been gone for eight years now. Did you really think I brought all those canned vegetables and preserves to you out of Christian duty for the past five years?"

"Well...*ja,* I did."

"You silly man. I was trying to get your attention. I see now that the only way to accomplish that is by plain speaking. I'm right fond of you, Joseph Shetler. I would know now if you feel the same way."

"You can't expect a man to answer a question like that when he's under the influence of Englisch pain medicine."

"When I heard you had been taken to the hospital, I realized what a fool I have been to stay silent for so long hoping that you would speak first."

"You could have your pick of upstanding fellows.

There's no reason for you to chase after a rickety old sheepherder. I can't even walk. What kind of husband would I be? Besides, a sheep farm is no place for a woman."

"Nonsense. So Evelyn hated sheep. So what? I like sheep. And I happen to like rickety old shepherds. Are you going to make me ask the question?"

He scooted up uncomfortably in bed and smoothed the spread over his chest. "What question would that be?"

She shook her head and began to gather up her things. "I reckon I'm a foolish old woman who thought that maybe, just maybe, I could have a second chance to love a man and be loved in return. I see I was wrong. Good night to you, Joseph. May the Lord bless and keep you." She rose and headed for the door.

"Wait," he called out.

She kept her gaze fixed on the doorknob. "I have been waiting, Joseph. I'm not going to wait anymore."

"All right, all right, have it your way."

Joy surged through her. She turned slowly to face him. "What does that mean exactly?"

"I'm not going to come courting in some fancy buggy."

"I don't need a fancy buggy."

"Well…it'll be lambing season soon. Any plans you've got will have to wait until summer."

She smiled broadly, walked back to his side and took his hand. "A quiet little summer wedding sounds wunderbar."

Worry filled his eyes. "Are you certain about this, Naomi?"

She bent down and kissed him. Then she whispered in his ear, "I've never been more certain of anything."

"I think I'm too old to be this happy." He wiped a tear from the corner of his eye.

"The good Lord didn't put an age limit on happiness, darling. Will you buy Abigail's quilt? If not, I will put it up for sale in my shop."

He looked down at the soft fabric. "I wish I knew what my daughter would want me to do."

Lizzie was raking up the previous year's litter from the vegetable garden when she saw a buggy coming up the lane on Monday. She didn't recognize the man driving, but she walked out to meet him. He drew up beside her and tipped his hat. *"Guder mariye."*

"Good morning and welcome."

"Are you Lizzie Barkman?"

"I am."

"I'm Adam Troyer. Naomi Wadler is my mother-in-law. She wanted me to deliver this to you." He leaned forward and held out an envelope.

"What is it?"

"I believe it is payment for your quilt."

"My quilt has been sold already? I only left it there on Saturday."

"I'm afraid I don't know the details, but it must've sold."

Lizzie opened the envelope. She looked up at Adam in shock. "This can't be right. There's far too much money here."

"Many of the quilts we sell fetch fine prices. The Englisch don't seem to care what they have to pay. I've seen some of the larger quilts at auction go for thousands of dollars."

Overwhelmed with gratitude and excitement, Lizzie

realized she had more than enough to buy bus tickets for all her sisters.

"*Danki.* Please tell Naomi that I am eternally grateful for her help. Now I have to get this in the mail." As Adam turned the buggy around, Lizzie sprinted toward the house.

There is still time. There is still time. The refrain echoed in her mind.

"Carl! Carl, where are you?" She knew he had gone to town earlier, but she had seen him return. She wanted to share her joy and she wanted to share it with him. She raced up the steps, yanked open the screen door and ran full tilt into him.

Carl wrapped his arms around Lizzie to keep her from falling as they both struggled to catch their balance. Fear clutched at his heart. "What is it? What's wrong?"

She looked up, grinning from ear to ear. She patted his chest with both hands. "Nothing's wrong. Everything's right and God is good."

She didn't seem to notice that he was holding her. He noticed. She was close enough for him to see the flecks of gold in her bright hazel eyes. She was close enough to kiss. More than his next breath, he wanted to taste the soft sweetness of her lips.

Duncan nosed open the screen door and joined in with exuberance. He jumped up and planted his front feet on Lizzie's side, barking wildly. Carl slowly lowered his arms and reluctantly released her.

She turned her beautiful smile on the dog. "Yes, everything is fine, and you, Duncan, are a *goot, goot hund.*"

She took hold of his front feet and turned in a circle as the dog hopped to keep up with her. Laughing, she grabbed his face and ruffled his fur. Duncan dropped back to all fours, but continued to wag his tail as he fixed his eyes on her.

Carl folded his arms over his chest and tried not to be jealous of a dog. "Have you had good news about Joe?"

"I haven't heard anything about Grandfather today, but my quilt has been sold. I have money, Carl. Enough money to bring my sisters here and some left over."

"That's great news. Are you sure your sisters will come? They haven't written to you."

"I pray that they will. I pray with all my heart that they will find the courage to leave my uncle's house. I used to think that everyone's lives were like ours. That words of compassion were spoken at church but not practiced at home. Since coming here, I realize there are kind and generous people who live their faith as our Lord commanded and do more than pay it lip service. I'm so glad that I came."

"I'm glad that you came, too."

She blushed at his words, but nothing dimmed her happiness. "I have to get this in the mail to Mary. What will you do if three more women show up on your doorstep?"

"I'll hide."

She laughed as she rushed up the stairs. She didn't believe him. If only she knew the truth. The last thing on earth he wanted was a house full of women to look after.

Just the thought of it made his blood run cold.

Chapter Twelve

Lizzie carried the coffeepot to the sink and began filling it with water. It had been two days since she put her quilt money in the mail to Mary. It should arrive today or tomorrow. How soon would she hear something?

Joe would be home before long. Would that mean less time working beside Carl? She enjoyed his company. She glanced out the window and noticed a speck of white in the green grass on the hillside beyond the barn. She leaned closer.

"A lamb. That's a lamb. Oh, my goodness, they're coming." She left the pot in the sink, ran out the door and raced down the hill to Carl's hut.

The door was open. He was seated on the edge of his bunk pulling on his boot.

"Carl, I saw one. I saw a lamb!"

A slow grin spread across his face. Why wasn't he as excited as she was? "We have been expecting them, Lizzie."

"You don't understand. It's out there all alone. The mother isn't with it. What if she has abandoned it?"

"Then you will get to bottle-feed one, but let's hope the mother is nearby."

Lizzie waited impatiently for him to pull on his other boot. "I don't see how you can be so matter-of-fact when a baby has been left all alone out in the wilds."

Her patience gave out. She turned and ran back up the hill toward the pasture. She was out of breath and panting when she reached the baby sleeping quietly in the grass. She held her aching side as she sank to her knees beside it.

It was so small and so precious. She wanted to scoop it up and cuddle it in her arms, but she was afraid to touch it.

She heard a noise nearby and realized the mother was less than ten feet away on the other side of a bush. Her second lamb was busy nursing and twirling its tail.

"You didn't leave your baby. What a good mother you are."

Lizzie was still gazing at the beautiful sleeping creature when Carl joined her. He had a large navy blue bag slung over his shoulder. Duncan trotted at his heels.

Carl leaned down and picked up the lamb. It came awake with a start and struggled in his hands. Its frantic cries brought the ewe running back. She immediately began bleating loudly in protest. At a word from Carl, Duncan went out to distract her.

"What are you doing?" Lizzie demanded.

"When a lamb is born, some processing is required."

"What does that mean?"

"First, I checked to see if the lamb is healthy, and this one looks like she is. Then I put iodine on the navel to prevent infection. I give her a numbered ear tag because we will need to know which babies belong with which mothers. The numbers are easy enough to see when the lamb is standing still, but when they are running about, it's a lot harder, so I mark them with these waxy crayon sticks. I put the ewe's number on like so."

He demonstrated by marking the number forty-two on the lamb's left side with a yellow marking stick.

"If it's a single birth, the lamb will get marked with one stripe across its back from side to side. If it's a twin, two stripes and so on. Always mark them on the left side."

The mother continued to bellow her displeasure and lowered her head in a threatening gesture. Lizzie took a step away from Carl. "Are we done? She's very upset."

"Almost. I just have to put this rubber band over the tail. It's a bloodless way to dock the tail. The part below the rubber band will simply die and fall off in a couple of weeks. A shorter tail allows for cleaner sheep."

"I could've gone my entire life without knowing that fact."

He chuckled as he put the lamb on the ground. She quickly scurried to her mother's side. The mother stopped protesting and nuzzled her baby before moving away with it only to go through the entire process all over again when Carl caught and marked her other lamb.

He gave Duncan the command to gather, and the dog began herding the sheep and lambs toward the barn.

From that moment on, Lizzie had very little time to think about her sisters coming, about Joe getting out of the hospital and about how much she enjoyed working beside Carl. She was too busy with the newborn lambs.

Things went well until the weather took a turn for the worse. April began with an unusually cold and rainy week. It was a potentially disastrous combination for the newborns.

Some of the newly shorn mothers sought the shelter of the sheds and the barn, but some chose less suitable birthing places, such as dense thickets and groves of trees in the pasture.

Carl worked tirelessly to move the reluctant mothers and their newborns into the sheds. He built additional pens inside the barn and even moved the horses out so that he could turn their stalls into sheep maternity wards. Lizzie divided her time between bottle-feeding a pair of orphans every three hours and making sure Carl had food, hot coffee and warm, dry clothes.

When he wasn't assisting an ewe with a difficult birth or checking on the condition of the lambs, he combed the pastures for the few expectant mothers who had wandered away from the flock.

After three days of nonstop birthing, Lizzie could see how tired Carl was. "Please, let me help more. Tell me what to do."

"You're doing enough."

"I can do more."

"Lizzie, that's the trouble with you. You always think you can do more."

"Try me. If I can't manage, what have you lost?"

"Very well. In the smallest shed are the ewes that lambed three days ago. I need you to take hay to them and make sure they have plenty of water."

"I can do that. What else?"

"Add fresh straw to the pens if they look dirty. That will keep you busy for the next hour."

It didn't take her an hour to complete the tasks. She was back at his side as soon as she was able. He had delivered a set of twins from one ewe and was helping a second one deliver a lamb that was breech. "I've given them hay and water and new straw. Now what?"

"Check on number fifty-four. She had twins, but she wasn't letting one of them nurse a while ago. Let me know if they're both doing okay."

Lizzie walked down the aisle looking into the small pens where the mother sheep stood with their new babies until she saw the one whose ear tag was fifty-four. One of her babies was up and nursing. The other lay in a small huddle in the corner. Lizzie stepped into the pen and tried to rouse the little one, but it seemed too weak to stand. She rushed back to Carl.

"One of them is lying down and won't get up."

"Can you check his temperature for me?"

"If you tell me how." She felt so stupid. How could she be of help to him if she had to constantly run to him for information and instructions?

He grabbed a thermometer from his box of equipment and explained what she needed to do. "A lamb's temperature should be about 102°. If he's colder than that, take him to the warming boxes I have set up by the stove in the house." He extended the thermometer to her. She hesitated, then took it from him. This wasn't about Carl's shunning. This was about saving as many lambs as possible.

The lamb was much colder than he should have been. She bundled him up in a blanket and carried him up to the house. Carl had set four boxes around the stove in the kitchen. She put the lamb in one and made sure there was plenty of wood to last the night before going out to the barn again. She paused and groaned when she stepped outside. The bitter-cold rain was mixed with snow. How much worse could it get?

Carl's second ewe had successfully delivered her lambs. Both were trying to get to their feet while their mother nuzzled them. He gave Lizzie a tired smile. "These will be fine. I'm going back out to the hilltop pen. I saw two more ewes laboring up there an hour ago."

"Carl, it's snowing."

"Let's hope it doesn't last. Go back to the house. I'll be in shortly."

She did as he asked, but he wasn't back soon. She moved a lamp to the window to let him know she was still up in case he needed her, then she sat down in her grandfather's chair to wait. Carl would need some of the warm soup she had simmering on the stove when he came in.

Sometime later, she was jolted awake when the kitchen door flew open. Carl came in along with a flurry of wet snow. His black cowboy hat and coat were dusted with white. She hurried toward him. "You must be chilled to the bone."

He had something buttoned up inside his coat. Crossing to the stove, he knelt there. "I need your help. Bring me blankets, old ones if you have them, or towels."

He opened his jacket enough for her to see he had two tiny wet lambs bundled against his body for warmth.

Lizzie sprang into action. She raced up the stairs and pulled towels and blankets from the linen closet. Returning to Carl's side, she waited as he extracted one lamb and handed it to her. "Dry her good. She might make it. I'm not so sure about her brother."

"Did their mother reject them?" Lizzie knew it sometimes happened. She wrapped her baby in a towel and handed a second towel to Carl.

"Yes, she had triplets, but she would only nurse one."

Lizzie put the little one down for a minute and put

several of the towels in the oven to warm. She went back and dried her charge as best she could. When the towels in the oven were warm, she wrapped the lambs in them.

"They'll need colostrum," Carl said. His baby remained lethargic.

Lizzie had learned it was the first milk the ewes produced and was essential to the newborn's health. A supply was kept frozen in a small propane-powered freezer in the barn. "I'll get some and warm it up."

She handed him her lamb and jumped to her feet. Carl caught her hand as she walked by and looked up at her. "Thank you. For everything you've done. I don't know what I would have done without you."

"I'm glad I was here to help."

"So am I."

He slowly released her hand and she missed the comfort of his touch more than she imagined was possible. "You're an amazing man, Carl. I don't know how you do it. I admire your dedication, your skill, your selflessness. This has been a time I will never forget."

After that, the following days became something of a blur for Lizzie. Two more orphans joined the collection in the kitchen. Each morning at five o'clock, Lizzie rose, made a mug of strong tea and checked on the orphaned lambs. Most times, Carl was already there feeding them their breakfast before getting his own. It was amusing to see him seated on the floor with a baby bottle in each hand and lambs climbing on his lap in the hopes of being next.

After the babies were fed, she and Carl walked together to the pasture looking for lambs that had arrived during the past few hours or for ewes that were in obvious distress. When they found lambs, they would carry them back to the barn with their anxious mothers following alongside.

During the peak lambing season, the new arrivals came fast and furious. The ewes delivered late at night, in the early hours and throughout the day. At times, it seemed to Lizzie that there were baby sheep in every nook and cranny on the farm.

Through the rough parts, it seemed to her as if Carl never slept. She knew, because she slept very little herself. But no matter how tired or busy she was, she always made time to run down to the end of the lane and collect the mail. Every afternoon she hoped for a message from her friend or her sisters, but none came. Slowly, her hope began to fade.

The bad weather finally broke on Sunday morning and the sun came out. Lizzie had never been so glad to lift her face to the warming rays and simply soak them up. It was the off Sunday, so there was no need to travel to church.

Carl opened the gates of one shed and let the ewes with lambs several days old out into a larger enclosure. The ewes, thrilled to be back outside, got busy eating the new green grass where the sun had melted patches free of snow. The lambs, not used to being ignored, discovered each other.

They gathered in a bunch and began butting each other. Suddenly, they broke and ran, jumping and leaping for the sheer joy of it over the ground until they noticed that they had strayed too far from their mothers. In what looked like a race, they all came galloping back. Only an occasional mother even raised her head from the green grass to check on them.

Lizzie leaned on the fence beside Carl and watched

it all with a feeling of deep contentment. "'This is the day which the Lord hath made; we will rejoice and be glad in it.'"

"Psalm 118:24," he said quietly.

Her heart turned over as she looked at him. "Isn't it wonderful how God brings us joy in the simplest ways? It's a sign of His endless love."

She didn't turn away from the warm look that filled his eyes. "You almost make me believe that, Lizzie."

Drawn to the change she sensed in him, she stepped closer and laid her hand over his heart. "Then I'm happy to be His instrument. The Lamb of God gave up His life on the cross so that we might know salvation. It is up to each of us to cherish or to deny that gift."

He looked away. "It's more complicated than that."

She let her hand fall to her side. "When you come right down to it, it's not."

Bracing his forearms on the fence, he stared at the ground. "There are other people involved."

"God didn't create us to live alone. There are always people who touch our lives, for better or for worse. None of them can change God's love for you or for me. It is eternal."

"So they say, but it doesn't feel like it to me. I'd better finish checking the pens in the barn. We have a dozen mothers-in-waiting left."

He walked away, leaving her aching for his pain. He was so lost. If only there was some way to help him.

When the last pregnant ewe gave birth, Lizzie gave a huge sigh of relief. After more than a week of nonstop work, the worst was finally behind them.

On Friday, just like clockwork, another letter arrived

for Carl, but this time there was a letter from Mary, as well. Lizzie had been on the verge of giving up hope. Clara's wedding was less than a week away.

She quickly opened her letter and read the bitter news. Mary had been unable to see her sisters, but she would keep trying to get Lizzie's money to them.

Lizzie nearly screamed with frustration. She wanted to hear from her family so badly, while Carl ignored letters from his. It wasn't fair.

Back in the kitchen, Lizzie started supper, but she was drawn to Carl's letter. She picked it up and spent a long time looking at the envelope. Was Carl ignoring an olive branch extended by his family? Lizzie had no way of knowing unless she opened the letter and read it.

It was so tempting. Carl would never know if she burned it for him. She laid the letter on the kitchen table with the rest of the mail and went to the stove. Turning back quickly, she snatched the envelope up and held it in the steam rising from the eggs she was boiling to make egg-salad sandwiches. The steam burned her fingers before the glue on the envelope gave way.

Ashamed of herself, she put the letter back where it belonged and continued fixing supper. A dozen times, she glanced at the table as she worked. Finally, she covered the distraction with a kitchen towel.

It was not her letter. It was not her life. To read or to destroy the correspondence was up to Carl. She removed the towel and put the letter under the newspaper.

It was nearly dark by the time he came in. She was seated at the table with a cup of coffee in her hands. "Do we have any sick ones?"

He hung his cowboy hat on a wooden peg beside the

door. "Not yet. At least, none that I've found, but I think we're missing one."

"An ewe or a lamb?"

"A lamb. Number eighty-three had twins, but she's only got one lamb with her now."

"Maybe one of the others stole it." An ewe without a lamb of her own would sometimes try to steal another's baby.

"Maybe. Is there any coffee left?"

"In the pot. It's fresh."

He poured a cup, blew on it to cool it and took a sip. "Before you leave, will you please teach Joe how to make good coffee? I can't go back to drinking the shoe polish that he makes."

She chuckled. "I will do my best."

He looked around the house. "This is nice."

She looked around to see what he was referring to but didn't see anything unusual. "What's nice?"

"Coming into a clean house with supper simmering on the stove. You have no idea what a difference it makes after a long, hard day of work outside."

"I'm happy that I can ease your way, for you work very hard. Supper will be ready in about twenty minutes." She pointed to the pile of mail on the corner of the table. "The paper came today, if you want to read it while you wait."

"After supper."

Lizzie bit her bottom lip to keep from mentioning his letter. Maybe this time he would open it. She got up and began to set the table.

When they finished the meal, Carl took the mail into the other room while Lizzie cleaned up. She was putting away the last plate when he walked past her, opened the firebox of the stove and dropped the letter in.

"Supper was good. Thank you. I'll see you in the morning." He walked to the pegs by the door and put on his coat and hat.

Her heart sank. Someone was desperately reaching out to him, and he was just as desperately keeping that someone at bay. She couldn't remain silent any longer. "If you mark them Return to Sender, perhaps she will stop writing."

He paused with his hand on the doorknob, but didn't look at her. "I tried that once, but it didn't work."

Lizzie heard the pain in his voice and wanted to throw her arms around him and hold him close. It was impossible for her to do so, but knowing that didn't lessen her desire to comfort him. "I think only someone who loves you very much would remain so persistent."

He walked out and closed the door behind him without a word.

Carl continued toward his hut in the dark. He knew the path by heart. He didn't need to see where he was going. Duncan walked beside him. He looked down at the dog, who had been his best friend for a long time. "Lizzie is like a dog with a bone about those letters. In fact, she's worse than you are. She's not going to bury it and leave it alone."

She was every bit as persistent as Jenna was. He wished now that he'd never told his sister where he was staying.

He sat down on the chair outside his door and stared out over the pastures. The white sheep dotting the hillsides stood out in stark contrast to the dark ground. They looked like little stars that had fallen from the sky. Duncan lay down beside Carl and licked his paw.

Only a month ago, Carl would have enjoyed the peaceful calm of a night like this, but tonight he didn't appreciate the pastoral serenity. Tonight, he was restless and edgy.

Lizzie was eager to find out more about him. He saw it every time she looked at him. He heard it in her voice each time she mentioned his letters. She cared for him. He saw that in her eyes, too, even as he struggled to keep his feelings for her hidden.

If he gave in and told her the truth, what would he see in her eyes then? How would she look at him when she learned he had killed a man? Would he see horror? Revulsion? Pity?

He leaned his head back against the wall. Maybe it was time for him to move on. It would be best to go before he fell deeper in love with the amazing little woman with smiling eyes. A woman he could never hold.

Duncan suddenly sprang to his feet and growled deep in his throat. The hair on his neck stood up as every muscle in his body tensed.

Carl stared out into the darkness, trying to see what had riled his dog. It took a bit, but finally he saw a darker shadow streaking along the hillside on the opposite side of the creek. He stood up to get a better look. Was it a coyote or a dog?

He realized as the animal crested the hill that it carried one of his lambs in its mouth. A second later, it was lost from sight. Duncan took off after it at a run.

Chapter Thirteen

The day Joe came home from the hospital was the day of Clara's wedding.

Carl watched Lizzie try to keep a brave face as they waited for the van that would bring Joe home, but he could see the strain she was under. The days since she had mailed her quilt money had gone by without a single word from her sisters. He had no idea what had gone wrong with her plan, but she wore the look of a woman who was barely hanging on to hope.

He wondered how long it would be before he saw her smile again.

Outside, the sun was shining. A soft breeze turned the windmill beside the barn and stirred the new grass in the pastures in small, undulating waves. Carl had moved the entire flock close to the house, but he was still losing a lamb every other night.

Lizzie became as nervous as a June bug in a henhouse when the van finally rolled in. And well she should be. She was the reason Joe ended up in the hospital in the first place. Carl knew Joe had forgiven her, but he was worried that Joe might not let her forget it anytime soon.

When the driver got out and opened the door, she rushed down the steps with an offer of help. To Carl's surprise, Joe calmly accepted Lizzie's offer and allowed her to help him out of the car. He walked haltingly with a walker, but managed well enough.

With Carl on one side and Lizzie on the other, they were able to help Joe up the steps and into the house. Once inside, he looked around and sighed deeply. "You have no idea how good it feels to come home."

"I have your room ready, Daadi. Would you like to lie down now?"

"No, I'm sick of being in bed. I would like to sit in my chair for a while."

"Of course." She hovered beside him as he crossed into the living room and sank with a deep sigh of relief into his overstuffed chair. She quickly arranged a footstool and pillows so he could elevate his legs. She had been paying close attention to the home-care instructions the hospital had mailed to her.

Carl was delighted to see his friend looking so well, if a bit weak and worn-out. "You have two hundred and seventy-eight new lambs."

"How many ewes did we lose?"

"Only two."

"And how many lambs have we lost? Every day I watched the rain running down the windows of the hospital I was thinking about my poor babies out in such weather."

"We didn't lose any to the weather."

"Are you serious?"

"Lizzie has been busy bottle-feeding six of them."

"That's a lot of work," Joe said, looking at her with admiration.

"I don't mind. They're adorable, but any praise must go to Carl." She turned her earnest eyes in his direction and he saw admiration in them, but also something more. He saw an echo of the way he felt about her.

"Carl worked day and night to make sure the sheep had the best possible care. He went out in a snowstorm to look for lambs. He brought back two that lived because of his dedication."

Carl decided the bad news could wait until after Joe had rested.

Joe looked around the room. "Where's Duncan? I didn't see him when we came in. He normally raises a ruckus when there's a car around."

"I have him on guard duty with the flock."

Lizzie knelt beside Joe. "We can talk about this later. Daadi, you need to rest."

"Coyotes?" Joe's sharp eyes drilled into Carl and ignored Lizzie.

"A big one."

"How many has he gotten?"

"Four."

Joe pushed himself up straighter in the chair. "You know what has to be done?"

"I won't touch a gun, Joe. You know that."

"A gun?" Lizzie's eyes widened with shock. "You aren't thinking about shooting it, are you?"

Joe gave her an exasperated look. "A coyote that starts killing sheep won't stop. It has to be put down."

"Isn't there another way?"

"What other way?" Joe asked.

"I don't know, but it doesn't deserve to be shot without trying something else. We could trap it."

Carl remained silent. Each word of Lizzie's protest cut

like a knife. She couldn't bear the thought of him killing a wild predator. How appalled would she be if she knew the truth about his deed? He grew sick at the thought.

Joe patted her hand. "Women! Soft hearts and soft heads. My rifle is in my room, Carl. You know I wouldn't ask you to do this if I could do it myself. The sheep can't defend themselves."

Carl nodded. Lizzie's eyes begged him not to do it. He looked away. He didn't want to kill anything, but better that she hate him for thinking about shooting a coyote than to know the truth. Maybe this way she would see that he wasn't worth trying to save.

Maybe he could stop loving her if she stopped looking at him as if he was her hero.

Lizzie couldn't decipher the expression on Carl's face. It was as if he had suddenly turned to stone. There was a lack of life in his eyes that troubled her.

"I'm surprised your sisters aren't here," Joe said, pulling Lizzie's attention away from Carl.

"I have not heard from them," she said. Her disappointment and worry were too heavy to hide.

"Oh. I thought they had the means to join you. Naomi Wadler stopped in to see me and she mentioned that you were selling a quilt to pay for their bus fare. Did you change your mind?"

"I sent them money. However, it may have been too late or my uncle may have intercepted it. Clara's wedding was moved up after I left. The ceremony was to take place today."

He sank back in his chair. Lines of fatigue and pain appeared on his face. "So she is married to him, the man you don't like and don't trust. I'm sorry for her. And for you."

"It must be God's will for her. Perhaps her kindness will change his heart and make him a husband she can respect and admire."

Joe laid a hand on Lizzie's head. "I have been a fool and so I must pay the price, but I'm sorry you must pay it, too. What will you do now?"

"I love it here. The people of this community are so warm and loving. I even like the sheep now much more than I did when we had to shear them."

"But you aren't going to stay," Carl said softly.

"I can't leave them there. I have to go back." She tried to gauge his reaction to her decision, but she couldn't. Tears blurred her vision.

"You can't go until I'm fit," Joe grumbled.

She rose to her feet. "Of course not. I promised I would stay as long as you need me. I should go feed the orphans. Carl will stay with you to make sure you don't overdo it."

"I don't need a babysitter."

Lizzie escaped out the door before she heard Carl's reply. He was used to handling Joe. She knew he would manage without her. She gathered the baby bottles and milk replacer and went down to the barn where the orphans lived now. After only a week, they had outgrown their warming boxes. They slept now in an empty stall at the back of the barn.

She sat down on the hay among them, and as they pushed and shoved for her attention, she held their soft bodies close one at a time and gave in to her tears.

She was responsible for her own heartbreak. She knew better than to fall for Carl, but that hadn't stopped her from embracing every dear quality he possessed. It was so easy to love him.

In the long years ahead, she would look back on their days together and remember what it was like to share the joys and pains of everyday life with him. She would never forget the way he made her feel.

If only she knew he would find his way back to his faith, she wouldn't mind leaving so much.

After she finished feeding the orphans, she returned to the house and went up to her room. She pulled a sheet of paper from the small desk by the window and sat down to write a letter. She raised her pen to her mouth and nibbled on the end of it as she considered what to say. Finally, she started writing.

Dear Jenna,
You don't know me, but I am a friend of Carl King's. He lives and works on my grandfather's sheep farm here in Ohio. I have only recently moved here, but I soon became aware that you write to Carl every week. I hesitate to tell you this, but Carl burns your letters without reading them. He does not know that I am writing to you.

When I first met Carl, he told me he is in the Bann, but he will not say why he has been shunned. His situation weighs heavily on my heart for I have come to care for him a great deal.

Lizzie lifted her pen from the paper. She didn't just care for Carl. She loved him. She always would.

A tear splashed onto the page as she began writing again.

Carl keeps all rules of our faith, except that he will not attend our services. I have seen him standing outside of our place of worship, close enough to hear the preaching and singing and yet not be a part of it. His separation from God is painful to see, for I know that it is painful to him, too.

It is my hope that with some understanding of Carl's past, I can help him to return to the faith he clearly loves. He refuses to tell me anything. I'm hoping that you will. I value Carl's friendship and his trust. I risk losing that which is most dear to me by writing to you, but what Carl stands to gain is so much more important.

Please forgive me if you find this intrusion into your affairs offensive. I mean no harm. I don't do this lightly, but only with the very best of intentions. If you do not answer this letter, I will not bother you again.

Your sister in Christ,
Elizabeth Barkman

When she finished the brief missive, she folded it and slipped it into an envelope before she could change her mind. Carl was stuck in limbo. He couldn't move forward with his life until he had received forgiveness from someone in his past. If that person was the author of his letters, then perhaps letting her know how much Carl desperately needed her forgiveness would spark their reconciliation.

She didn't delude herself into thinking Carl would approve of her actions. He would be furious with her.

She composed a second letter. This one was to her sisters telling them that she would be returning in a few weeks. As much as she longed to see them, she dreaded returning to life in her uncle's home. How would she bear it after knowing a better way existed?

She took her letters down to the mailbox in the early afternoon when she knew the mailman was due to go by. If there was a letter from Mary or from her sisters and they were coming, Lizzie wouldn't send the ones she had written, for it meant she would be staying in Hope Springs.

The postman handed over the mail. "I see you have a new crop of lambs out there. How did it go?"

"Busy. Joe is home from the hospital now. You are welcome to bring your son and pick a lamb whenever you like."

"We're going to be gone on a family vacation for a week, but we'll do it sometime after we get back. Do you want to mail those letters?" He pointed to the ones in her hand.

She finished looking through a handful of junk mail. There was nothing from her family. She nodded. "I guess I do."

Her conscience pricked her all through the day and kept her awake until long into the night. She had no right to interfere in Carl's personal affairs. It was prideful on her part to think what she said would matter.

Where was Clara tonight? Was she at the home of her new husband? How was he treating her?

Lizzie pulled her pillow over her face to shut out her fears. It didn't work.

Carl attributed Lizzie's long face to her grief at not being able to help her family. She didn't say a word as they finished the morning chores and turned out the youngest lambs with their mothers. She barely spoke to the orphans as they clamored for her attention.

On the way back to the house, he said, "You're awfully quiet today."

"Am I?

"Do you have something on your mind?"

"A lot of things."

"Such as?"

"Number ninety-four doesn't seem to have enough milk for her triplets. We may need to supplement one of them with milk replacer."

"Just what we need, another mouth to feed in the orphan pen."

"I'll take care of moving him this afternoon," Lizzie said as she walked up the steps ahead of him. She opened the front door and stopped so abruptly that he almost ran into her. She shrieked, dropped the bucket she was carrying and charged into the room. Carl rushed in behind her to see what was wrong.

Suddenly, the room echoed with shrieks as three women rushed to embrace Lizzie. They were all laughing, crying and hugging each other. Joe stood leaning on his walker on the far side of the room.

Carl skirted the women and moved to stand beside him. "I take it these are the rest of your granddaughters?"

"They are. Have you ever heard such a noisy bunch? They're worse than a barn full of sheep."

Although Joe tried to hide it with his gruff words, Carl heard the happiness in his voice. Carl was happy, too, that Lizzie's dream had come true. Now she wouldn't be leaving.

Lizzie had tears of joy rolling down her face but she didn't care. "How did you get here? I thought the wedding was yesterday. I didn't know when I would ever see you again."

Greta said, "The wedding *was* yesterday, but the bride failed to show up for it."

Clara grasped Lizzie's hands. "I don't know how I can ever thank you. We would have come sooner, but we didn't know Mary had the money you sent until the morning of the wedding. Uncle Morris wouldn't let us have visitors until then."

Betsy wrapped her arm around Clara's waist. "Mary showed up at the house demanding that she be allowed to attend Clara on her wedding day. There were already people at the house, so I think uncle didn't want to look bad in front of them by saying no."

Greta took up the tale. "The moment Mary was in the room with us, she gave us your letters and then handed each of us a bus ticket and said that her buggy was waiting for us outside."

"We climbed out the window and drove into town as fast as we could. We barely made it to the bus station on time," Betsy added with a dramatic flourish.

Lizzie pressed a hand to her heart. "Oh, I wish I had been there to see it."

Clara shook her head. "If you had been there, none of us would be here now. You showed us the way. Your courage gave us courage."

"I prayed that you had guessed what I was trying to do and that you didn't think I had simply run away."

The three sisters exchanged glances. Greta laid a hand on Lizzie's shoulder. "We knew."

Joe came forward with his walker. "Now that all the screaming is over, I hope a man can have his lunch in peace."

Lizzie drew a deep breath. "*Ja,* Daadi. We will have your lunch ready in no time."

She caught sight of Carl as he was slipping out the back door. She left her sisters and caught up with him on the back porch. "Where are you going? You must stay and meet my family."

"Another time." His voice held a sad quality that made her want to fold her arms around him.

"But I want them to meet you. Stay for lunch with us."

"Half the table won't be big enough for all of you, Lizzie." It was a pointed reminder that he could not eat with them.

"They don't have to know. I won't say anything. They will think you are an Englisch hired hand."

"But I will know, and you will know, Lizzie. I'm glad your plan worked. I'm really happy for you."

"Will you be in for supper?"

"I don't think so."

It was then that Lizzie realized the arrival of her sisters spelled the end of her time alone with Carl. "You have to eat."

"We've had this conversation before. You like to feed people."

"It's what I'm good at."

"Fix me a sandwich, then. I'm going to camp out in the pasture and try to keep that coyote from killing any more lambs.

"Will you shoot it?"

"Not if I don't have to."

"*Goot.* That makes me feel better."

"It's a wild animal, Lizzie."

"Every life is valuable, Carl. We are all God's creatures."

She saw him flinch at her words. Maybe she was being too hard on him. The lambs were God's creatures, too. She didn't want any of them to die. "You'll do the right thing. I know that."

He nodded and walked away, but she had the feeling that she had somehow let him down.

Lizzie spent the rest of the day surrounded by her sisters. They were eager to hear about everything that she had done since leaving home. Her stories about shearing alpacas and sheep had them all laughing. Her grandfather sat on the edge of their group and added a few stories of his own. When she recounted Naomi's stories about their mother, she caught a glint of tears in Joe's eyes.

She made up sandwiches for Carl, but he never came to the house to pick them up, so she left them in the refrigerator for him and left a note telling him where they were on the kitchen table.

The next morning, he came in while her sisters and Joe were all seated around the kitchen table. Carl's face was grave. He held a bloody bundle in his arms. Lizzie jumped to her feet. "Are you hurt?"

"No, but this poor little girl is." He unwrapped part of the cloth to show them a lamb with a gaping wound on its hind leg.

Lizzie immediately came over to examine the animal. "It's a deep laceration. She's going to need stitches. We should get her to a vet right away. She may go into shock from blood loss. We need to keep her warm." She lifted the lamb out of Carl's arms and moved to stand close to the stove with it.

Greta filled a hot-water bottle and gave it to Lizzie, who tucked it in with the lamb. She looked at Carl. "Was it the coyote?"

"Yes. It came within fifty feet of me. It has no fear of humans. I think it's a coydog. A coyote and dog cross. That's why it's so big. It's not killing for food. It's killing the sheep for fun. Duncan drove it off but not before it had a chance to kill one and maim this poor little one. I'll go hitch up the wagon."

Joe said, "Take the buggy. My trotter is faster than the pony. Greta, you and Lizzie take the lamb to the vet. Carl, you and I need to figure out what we're going to do about this."

"We should notify the sheriff. The animal is big enough to start attacking cattle, too, if it hasn't already."

"All right. Go call him. Then take my gun out and practice with it. I'm not going to lose my whole lamb crop. I can't afford to lose even one more."

Carl knew Joe was right, but the last thing he wanted in his hands was another gun.

Chapter Fourteen

Sheriff Bradley came to the farm, and Carl filed a report with him. The sheriff suggested Carl put a notice in several of the local newspapers with a description of the coydog in the unlikely event that it was a pet and not a wild animal. After an entire week passed without another attack, Carl joined Lizzie and Joe in the living room.

Carl leaned forward and propped his forearms on his thighs. "Maybe the sheriff was right and the coydog isn't wild. Maybe the owner read about his pet in the paper and decided it was time to keep Fido in his kennel at night."

Joe nodded. "Another explanation is that someone else took care of the problem for us."

"I'd rather think that he's home and safe with his family," Lizzie said.

Carl looked around. "Speaking of family, where are the girls?"

"Clara has gone to meet Adrian and Faith and see if she wants the job they have to offer. Sally Yoder took Betsy to meet the Sutter family."

He frowned at her. "Wasn't that the job you were going to take?"

"I would have been happy to work for them, but I think Betsy will be happier."

"You just want to stay here and boss me around," Joe grumbled.

"You're right. That's exactly why I want to stay. It's time for you to do some more walking. You can't sit around all day like a king on his throne."

Joe muttered under his breath, but he stood up with his walker. "I'll be outside with Greta. I've never seen anyone so happy to be hoeing in the dirt. My garden will be twice its size when she's done. Lizzie, I meant to tell you what a good job you've done with that crippled lamb. She's almost as good as new."

"Danki." Lizzie was smiling as she watched Joe make his way out the door.

"Is this what you imagined it would be like when they came?" Carl asked.

By mutual consent, they had avoided spending time alone in each other's company. She kept her eyes lowered modestly. She rarely looked him in the eyes anymore. "This is so much more wonderful than I dreamed. It fills my heart with joy to see them meeting new people and going to new places."

"It does my heart good to see you happy, Lizzie."

She turned her face aside. "You should not say such things."

"I know it's not proper, but I wanted you to hear it anyway. You didn't used to be so proper."

"Things were different then. Now I have my sisters to think of."

He'd done a lot of soul-searching while he was patrolling Joe's pastures over the past few nights. Soul-searching and longing for a life within the community that had welcomed Lizzie and her sisters with such joy and kindness.

He had arrived at an answer. He hoped. He would go home and beg forgiveness for Sophia's death and the killing of the soldier from his parents, his siblings and his church. If they granted him what he sought, then the past would stay in the past. When a sinner was forgiven, the sin need never be mentioned again. Lizzie would never have to know what he had done.

"I'm going away for a while, Lizzie."

She looked up and locked eyes with him. "For how long?"

"I'm not sure."

"But you'll be back."

"It is my dearest hope to return to you as soon as possible." He couldn't say too much, but he longed to tell her of his love.

"Are you going home, Carl?"

"*Ja.*"

She smiled. "*Goot.* I miss you already. When are you leaving?"

"The day after tomorrow."

She reached out and laid her hand on his. "Then I wish you Godspeed."

He left the house feeling hope for the first time in five long years. Lizzie had brought hope into his life. She was the sign he had been waiting for.

"Is that a car I hear?" Joe asked from his chair. The crippled lamb, now known as Patience, was asleep on his lap. Greta was out checking the pasture with Carl and Duncan. She expected them back at any time.

Lizzie looked out the living-room window. "It is a car. Maybe it's one of your therapists."

"I don't have physical therapy scheduled for today."

She pointed a finger at him. "That doesn't mean you get to skip your exercises."

"Nag, nag. Don't worry, I'll do them. I don't intend to be glued to a walker for the rest my life. Don't just stand there. Go see who it is."

Lizzie brushed off the front of her apron, straightened her *kapp* and went to the door. An Amish woman and an ebony-skinned girl of about thirteen dressed in Englisch clothes emerged from the backseat.

The girl darted away from the car and came running up the steps. "Is Kondoo Mtu here? Where is he? I want to thank him for the good life he has given me."

Her thick accent kept Lizzie from understanding who she was looking for. "You must have the wrong house. There's no one by that name here."

The Amish woman came and stood behind the girl with her hands on her shoulders. "*Kondoo Mtu* means 'Sheep Man.' When Carl would say, *'Ja. Ja,'* to her, it sounded like 'Baa. Baa.' Hence, Sheep Man. Hello, I'm Jenna King. And this bundle of energy is my adopted daughter, Christina. Her English is improving, but she still has trouble with many of our words. Are you Elizabeth Barkman?"

"I am." Lizzie wasn't sure what else to say. She had expected a letter in response to the one she wrote, not a face-to-face visit.

"Who is it?" Joe shouted from the living room.

"I'm Carl's sister," the woman said with a knowing smile.

Lizzie went weak in the knees with relief. Not a wife.

A sister. "Oh, I'm very glad to meet you. Come in and meet my grandfather."

"Where is Carl?"

"He's out checking the lambs. He should be in soon. He still doesn't know I wrote to you."

"I'm very glad you did. When you wrote that Carl had burned my letters, I was hurt. I knew I had to come see him in person. Besides, I wanted to meet the woman who cares so much about him. "

Lizzie's face grew hot. "I do care about him. He's a good man."

"Then perhaps together we can help him find his way back to his family and his faith. You said Carl hasn't told you why he was shunned. Is that still true?"

"He won't speak of it."

"It's a tragic story, but one I think he must share with you himself. If he isn't ready to do that, then my coming here may have been a mistake."

Was it a mistake? Lizzie prayed she hadn't done the wrong thing by writing to Jenna. "I don't think it was a mistake for you to come here. Carl told me yesterday that he planned to go home."

Relief brightened Jenna's eyes. "That's good to hear."

"Please come inside while you wait for him."

"Danki." Jenna held out her hand and Christina dashed to her side. Together, they entered the house.

Lizzie scanned the hillside, looking for Carl. There wasn't any sign of him. A sick feeling settled in her stomach. What was he going to say when he found out what she'd done?

In the living room, Jenna and Christina took a seat on the sofa. Lizzie introduced them to her grandfather. Christina couldn't sit still. She was up and down a dozen times to pet the lamb in Joe's lap and look out the window. Jenna gave Joe an apologetic smile. "I'm sorry. She's just so excited to see Carl again. She hasn't seen him since they came back from Africa."

"Carl was in Africa?" Joe was clearly shocked.

Lizzie leaned forward knowing she was finally going to learn about Carl's past.

Jenna nodded. "We had a younger sister named Sophia. She was drawn to missionary work. She chose not to be baptized and left home to work with a Mennonite group in Africa. She fell in love with a young man working there and they decided to marry. Sophia wanted someone from the family to attend her wedding. You can't blame her. My mother's health wasn't good. I didn't want to go, so Carl went."

Christina beamed. "He came to my village. He made us all laugh. He made Sophie happy. We liked him."

Jenna's eyes grew sad. "The wedding never took place. The village was raided by rebel soldiers and everyone was killed, including Christina's parents. Carl and Christina were the only survivors."

Christina left the window to stand in front of Lizzie. "The bad men came and shoot, shoot, shoot. Kondoo Mtu, he saved me."

Jenna leaned forward. "Christina, no! We don't speak of this."

But the excited child continued, "He get gun and kill the bad man who killed my father. He shoot him dead. We hide. Then more soldiers find Sophia and my mother. They kill them, too."

Lizzie went rigid with shock. A loud buzzing filled her ears. No Amish man would raise a gun to another human. She couldn't believe what she was hearing.

Jenna jumped to her feet and put her arms around Christina. Regret was etched deeply in her face. "I'm so sorry, Lizzie. This isn't how I wanted you to find out."

Lizzie couldn't draw a breath. It was as if the air was gone from the room. "Carl killed a man? He shot him?"

"Yes, I did," Carl said from the doorway.

Lizzie turned to stare at him, but she couldn't speak. Never had she imagined such horrible things could happen to someone she knew.

Christina dashed across the room. She threw her arms around him. "Kondoo Mtu, do you remember me?"

"Yes, I remember you." He kissed her cheek and she beamed at him.

"Thank you for bringing me to Jenna. She is good lady."

"I know. Why don't you go down to the barn and tell the lady there that you would like to feed the lambs? Tell her that I sent you. Her name is Greta."

When the child did as he asked, he looked straight at Lizzie. "Now you know."

What should she say? She hadn't been prepared for anything like this.

After a long minute, he looked down and gave a deep sigh. Then he turned and started to walk away.

Behind her, Lizzie heard Jenna call his name. He stopped. He spoke without turning around. "You shouldn't have come here, Jenna. Why did you?"

"She's here because I wrote to her," Lizzie admitted. Why wouldn't he look at them?

"You shouldn't have done that, Lizzie." He shook his head sadly. "I knew this was too good to last."

He walked away without another word, leaving Lizzie in shock and wondering what to do next.

Jenna put her arm around Lizzie's shoulders. "I'm so very sorry."

Lizzie managed to speak without breaking down in tears. "Don't be. It's Carl's choice to remain apart." Apart from her and the love she would so willingly give him.

"Come, sit down and I'll tell you the rest of the story."

Lizzie followed her back to the sofa.

When they were seated, Jenna said, "Carl returned to our family a broken man. He was haunted by his actions and Sophia's death. At night, he would wake up screaming. We did all we could to console him, but it didn't help. He refused to ask for forgiveness. He didn't believe he deserved it. He stopped going to church services and eventually our bishop had no choice but to place him in the Bann until he repented. Instead, Carl left without telling anyone where he was going."

Joe sighed heavily and straightened his leg with a grimace of pain. "He didn't have a destination in mind. He told me he'd been walking the back roads and getting odd jobs to get by. It wasn't until he found a starving puppy that he decided to stay in one place. The Lord blessed me when He led Carl here."

Jenna smiled at him. "Our family is grateful for your generosity. Carl didn't contact us until two years ago. He called the business where I work. I thought it signaled a change for the better, something we had all been praying for. I wrote him every week thinking that reading my letters would help him see that we still loved him and wanted him to come home."

"He would have gone home if I hadn't interfered." Lizzie bit her lower lip, rose from the sofa and went outside.

After hearing Jenna relate the entire sad story, she finally understood a little of what Carl had gone through. She gathered her shattered emotions and went to find him and beg his forgiveness.

Following the path that led to his place, she tried to imagine what she would say to him. Nothing formed in her mind. It was as if a dark curtain had been pulled across her emotions. She paused in the open door of the shepherd's hut. He had his back to her. He was stuffing his clothes in a black duffel bag.

"Carl, I must speak to you."

He stopped what he was doing and straightened, but he didn't turn around. "Don't bother. I already know what you have to say."

She took a step inside the door. "I don't think you do."

"You know what I did. You don't have to say anything. I'm leaving. All I ask is that you take good care of Duncan for me."

"All I ask is that you turn around and look at me."

His shoulders slumped. "Don't make this harder, Lizzie."

If he wouldn't turn around, she would just have to apologize to his back. "It is not my intention to make anything harder, but my good intentions have not turned out as I hoped. I'm sorry for interfering, Carl. I shouldn't have written to Jenna without your knowledge. I betrayed your trust, and I'm truly sorry. I wanted you to confide in me."

"When is the right time to tell the woman you love that you're a murderer?" He closed his eyes and bowed his head.

In two quick strides, she crossed the room and cupped his face with her hands. There were tears on his cheeks. "I cannot begin to comprehend the horror and the terror you faced. Under such ghastly circumstances, a man does not know how he will react until he is in the situation."

"Our faith tells us what a man must do, no matter what circumstances he faces. 'Thou shalt not kill.'"

He pulled free of her touch and resumed packing. "I made a choice. I decided another man's life was less valuable than mine, or Christina's. I became his judge and jury, and I snuffed out his life in the blink of an eye. In his fellow soldier's fury to avenge him, I brought a terrible fate upon my sister and the women with her. They all died because of me. I'm the one who should have died, not Sophia and her friends. I see them in my dreams. I can't get their faces out of my head. I never wanted you to know what I did."

"Don't torture yourself. I know your sister has forgiven you."

"Go back to the house, Lizzie. I don't want to see you again. I can't bear the way you look at me now. Tell Jenna to go home. I don't want to see her, either."

"But you told me yesterday that you intended to go home."

"I was wrong to think I could. I see now there is no reason to go back. Nothing has changed for me."

Lizzie struggled to find the right thing to say, but she was at a loss. She didn't know how to help him deal with his crushing burden of guilt. "I was shocked by what I heard. I'll admit that."

"Can you say your feelings for me haven't changed?"

"Give me some time to come to grips with this."

"That's what I thought."

"Please, do not judge me harshly. I'm not sure how I feel, but I do care about you. I forgive you for what you did. There's no question about that in my heart. Have you forgiven yourself?"

"I don't know how to do that."

She couldn't get through to him. "Where will you go?"

He stopped packing and raised his face to the ceiling. "Away." Then he began stuffing his clothes into his pack again.

"Carl, don't shut me out."

"Go away, Lizzie. Please."

Lizzie felt as if the ground had vanished from beneath her. She couldn't reach through the prison walls he had erected around his heart. With no other choice, she left and went back to the house. When she reached the porch steps, she broke down and sobbed as if her heart were breaking.

Because it was.

Carl stood in the hut after Lizzie left without moving. It hurt to breathe. He had no place to go. He was adrift without a compass of any kind. What now? Where could he find a hole deep enough to hide in so that he never had to face himself again? Where would he find peace?

Nowhere. So why was he running away? What was he running to?

He raked a hand through his hair. It wasn't right to leave while Joe was crippled. He owed the man too much.

If he left, he would never see Lizzie again. She didn't hate him, but had he lost her love?

He fell to his knees with his hands at his sides and gave vent to his pain. "God, why are You doing this to me? Because I dared to love her? You made her the way she is. How could I not love her?"

He had no idea how long he knelt slumped on the

stone floor. His legs grew numb. His eyes burned from the tears that streamed down his face. All he could say was "God, help me. I'm sorry. I'm sorry. Forgive me."

Gradually, his despair faded and a gentle calm replaced it. He felt something rough on his face. He realized that Duncan was licking his tears.

He wrapped his arms around the dog and held on. "Am I forgiven? Have you been the sign from Him all along but I refused to see it? Was Joe the sign I had God's forgiveness? Is it Lizzie? How many signs do I need to tell me that life is good if I choose to live it as He wills?"

As He wills, not as Carl King would have it.

For the first time, he understood that he couldn't hide from what he had done. He had to accept his failure, not wallow in it, and go forward. He would face other tests in his life. Some great and some small, but all were by the will of God. He prayed for the strength to meet them with humility and peace in his heart.

Struggling to his feet, he walked to the door, surprised to see it was almost dark. Duncan growled low in his throat. The sounds of frantic sheep cries reached Carl. Looking east, he saw part of the flock scattering in a terrified panic just across the creek. The large coydog raced among them.

Joe's gun sat just inside the door. Carl picked it up. The feel of the cool wooden stock made him sick to his stomach. He tightened his grip. He owed it to Joe to protect the sheep. It was just a wild animal, not a man. He'd done much worse. He could do this. He just hadn't expected God to test him so soon.

He tightened his grip on the gun. He wouldn't let Joe down.

He made Duncan stay inside and closed the door, then

he sprinted toward the sheep in trouble. The frenzied bleating of a lamb guided him to his target. The coydog had a lamb down at the edge of the creek. He saw Carl and stood over a struggling lamb with his head lowered and his teeth bared.

Carl raised the gun and sighted along the barrel. His finger curled over the trigger but he couldn't pull it. He drew a shaky breath and lowered the gun.

He couldn't do it. Not even to save the lambs. He couldn't take a life, even that of a predator.

He stepped closer and yelled. The coydog flinched, but stood his ground.

"I won't kill you, but maybe you'll think twice about going after sheep again."

Carl sighted carefully. He let out a sharp whistle. The coydog lifted its head and perked its ears. Carl fired. The bullet hit the rocks in front of the animal, peppering him with bits of stone. He yelped and took off, shaking his head as he ran.

Carl crossed the creek and hurried to the downed lamb. It struggled weakly as he picked it up. Its injuries appeared superficial. It was suffering from exhaustion and shock as much as anything. "Joe's going to have to invest in a few more guard animals to keep the rest of the flock safe in case that big fellow didn't get the message. I've heard llamas make excellent guardians."

He picked up the lamb and cuddled it close. "Don't worry, little one. I reckon Lizzie will have you fixed up in no time. I only pray that I can mend the harm I've caused her."

He started toward the house with long, sure strides. He had wounded Lizzie as surely as the coydog had wounded the lamb in his arms. If it took him the rest of his life, he would show Lizzie how sorry he was. If she gave him a second chance, he'd never shut her out of his life again.

Surrounded by her sisters and her grandfather, Lizzie sat at the kitchen table and tried to gather up the pieces of her broken heart. Jenna and Christina had gone to the inn in Hopes Springs for the night. They would travel home tomorrow.

Lizzie propped her chin on her hand. "I've made such a mess of things."

Clara laid a hand on Lizzie's shoulder. "You were trying to help."

"My interference didn't heal a family breach. It has driven Carl farther from those who love him." Including her.

"He'll come back," Joe said. "In time, he'll see that you meant well. Everyone makes mistakes."

"I've made more than my share lately." She looked out the window as the lights of a car swept into the yard and stopped.

"Now who is here?" Joe asked.

"I don't know. I don't recognize the car. It's not the one that brought Jenna earlier."

She had her answer a moment later when her uncle Morris and Rufus Kuhns stormed through the door.

Chapter Fifteen

"**O**nkel, what are you doing here?" Lizzie demanded. Her voice trembled with fright.

"I have come to take you and your wayward sisters home. How dare you defy me in this fashion?"

"How did you find us?" Betsy had tears in her eyes.

"Lizzie wrote a letter to you, but you were already gone. When I saw the postmark, I knew you had come here. You will be disciplined for this disrespect of your elder. Get your things and get in the car." He slapped a thick wooden yardstick on the table, making them all jump.

Rufus advanced on Clara. She shrank back in fear. He raised his fist and shook it at her. "You have made me the laughingstock of our community. You will come back and wed me." He grabbed her arm.

"*Nee,* I will not."

He struck her across the face. The women shrieked in outrage. Lizzie grabbed Clara and moved to put her own body between Rufus and his victim. "Leave her be."

Joe rose to his feet. "Get out of my house."

Morris pushed him back into his chair. Joe fell and grimaced with pain.

Rufus glared at Lizzie. "I'll teach you to interfere between a man and his betrothed." He raised his hand to hit her. She cowered before him.

"Enough!"

Everyone turned to see Carl in the doorway. He held a rifle in one hand and a lamb in the other.

Rufus eyed the gun. "This is a family matter, Englisch. It's none of your concern."

Carl set the gun against the wall and ignored the red-faced man. "Are you all right, Joe?"

"Right as rain. What's the matter with my wee woolly?"

Carl spoke softly to Lizzie. "He's been mauled. I need your help. We need to clean his wounds."

She was frightened, but his calm words gave her courage. She moved away from Rufus, pulling Clara with her. "Go get some towels, Clara. Greta, put some water on the stove to heat. Betsy, would you fix some milk for him? It's in the barn. We need to get fluids into him."

"Sure." Betsy started for the front door.

Morris smacked the table with his stick again. Clara and Betsy flinched, but Clara went up the stairs and Betsy went out the front door.

Lizzie heard Duncan barking in the distance and hoped he would stay away. Her uncle wasn't fond of dogs.

She took the lamb from Carl's arms. It cried pitifully. "It's all right. We'll fix you up."

"Stop what you're doing and get your things. We're leaving," Morris shouted.

Lizzie looked into Carl's serene eyes. "I think he may need stitches."

"You know best. Should we take him to the vet?"

Rufus and Morris exchanged puzzled looks. Lizzie knew they weren't used to being ignored.

"Obey me, you ungrateful child." Morris raised his stick and stepped toward Lizzie.

She closed her eyes and tried to shelter the lamb. She knew what was coming. Suddenly, Carl's arms were around her, shielding her. She felt him flinch with each blow her uncle struck, but he never made a sound.

A crash followed by screaming made her open her eyes. Duncan had charged through the mesh of the screen door and launched himself at Morris. Her uncle fell in his attempt to evade the dog. He was lying on the floor, trying to beat the dog off and screaming for Rufus to help him.

Rufus aimed a kick at Duncan. The dog easily evaded it and turned his attention to his new attacker. Darting in and out, he sought a hold on Rufus's leg and found it. Rufus hollered in pain.

Morris saw his chance and made a dash for the front door. Duncan, seeing his prey on the run, charged after him. Morris barely made it out, slamming the wooden door behind him. Rufus made a limping run for the back door. Carl spoke quickly. "Leave it, Duncan. Down."

The dog dropped to the floor and lay panting as he watched his master for his next command. Outside, the car engine sprang to life and the vehicle roared up the lane. Lizzie had to wonder what the Englisch driver must think of the evening's events.

She realized she was still in Carl's arms. She relaxed against his chest and drew several shuddering breaths. He lifted her chin with his hand and gazed at her face. "Are you all right?"

"I should be asking you that."

A tender smile pulled at the corner of his mouth. "At this moment, I've never been better in my life."

"Then maybe I can stay here a little longer?"

He pulled her close and tucked her against him. "You definitely should."

The front door flew open. Betsy stood there gasping for breath. Clara ventured down the stairs with towels in her arms and Greta moved to Joe's side to check on him. He patted her hand. "I'm fine."

Carl smiled at Betsy. "Duncan was shut in my hut. How did he get out?"

She was still panting. "I opened the door for him because it sounded like he wanted out. Onkel Morris doesn't like dogs. I thought they should meet."

Clara dropped to her knees to hug Duncan. "You are a wunderbar guard dog."

He wagged his tail happily. Joe said, "Bacon for that boy tonight for sure."

Everyone began to talk at once except Lizzie. She was content to rest in Carl's arms. She never wanted to move. It seemed her grandfather finally noticed.

He cleared his throat loudly. "We should get that lamb fixed up."

Carl reluctantly released her as her sisters came to take the lamb from her. He said, "We need to talk."

She pressed a hand to his cheek. "The past is over and done. It need never be mentioned again."

He flicked her nose with one finger. "It's not the past I want to talk about, Lizzie Barkman.

"After this baby is fixed up, would you care to drive into town with me? I need to see Jenna and Christina. I have a lot of explaining and apologizing to do. To all of you."

* * *

Naomi Wadler greeted them with some surprise as they came into the lobby of the inn. Carl approached the counter. "My sister Jenna King is staying here. Would you let her know that I'd like a word with her?"

"She and Christina are in the café. I'll show you the way. How is Joe getting along?"

"Fine. You should come by for a visit," Carl said with a slight smile for her.

She blushed. "I'll do just that. Tell him I'll be by with some canned goods on Sunday."

He and Lizzie followed her to the café doors. Lizzie caught his arm. "If you want to speak to your sister alone, I can wait in the lobby."

He covered her hand and gave her a reassuring squeeze. "I want you by my side."

The smile she gave him warmed his heart. The Lord had truly blessed him when He brought her into his life.

They found Jenna and Christina seated in a booth in the corner. Christina saw him first and jumped up to hug him. "Kondoo Mtu, I thought I would never see you again."

Lizzie took a step to the side as he hugged the child in return. Jenna looked uncertain about what her response should be. He kept one arm around Christina, but he held out his free hand. Jenna scooted out of the booth and threw her arms around him.

He choked back the tears that threatened to keep him silent. "I'm sorry, Jenna. I'm so sorry for the hurt I've caused you and everyone. Can you forgive me?"

"All is forgiven. All is forgiven. Come home, Carl. We love you. We miss you so much."

He looked over Jenna's head at Lizzie. "I don't deserve such unselfish love."

"Yes, you do," Lizzie said softly.

He read in her eyes what she wanted to say. She loved him, too. Soon he would be able to tell her how he felt, that he loved her with his whole heart and soul. For now, he had to believe she could see his love for her shining in his eyes.

After everyone's tears were dried, Naomi brought them slices of pie and cups of coffee with a mug of hot chocolate for Christina.

Jenna took a sip of coffee and sniffed once. "What are your plans now, Carl?"

"I thought since you have already hired a driver that I would ride home with you."

"Mamm and Daed with be so happy to see you. It will be a wunderbar surprise."

"I'd like to see the bishop first thing and explain myself."

Jenny reached across the table and took his hand. "You know that he and everyone in the church will rejoice that you have returned."

"I know. The thing is, I'm not going to stay, Jenna. I'm coming back here."

She glanced between him and Lizzie, who was blushing bright red. "Although we will hate to lose you again so soon, I think everyone will be happy for you."

"I won't be happy," Christina said with a pout.

He ruffled her hair. "I'll come visit a lot. You'll come to visit me here, too."

"Can I feed the lambs again?"

They all chuckled. He nodded. "Sheep Man said you may always feed the lambs."

When they were finishing their pie, Naomi approached again with a large box in her arms. "Lizzie, I have something for you."

Lizzie's eyebrows shot up. "For me? What is it?"

Naomi laid the box on the table. "Open it and see."

Lifting the carton lid, Lizzie squealed in delight. "It's my mother's quilt!"

Naomi smiled at her. "The buyer thought you should have it back."

Lizzie's eyes narrowed as she met his gaze. "Carl, did you do this?"

He held up both hands. "I tried, but someone beat me to it."

"Who?" Lizzie looked at Naomi.

"I promised not to tell."

Lizzie pulled the quilt from the box. "But it was so much money. I need to pay someone back. I can't accept such a gift."

Naomi fisted her hands on her hips. "You can and you will."

Lizzie's eyes narrowed again. "Naomi, did you do this? Do I owe you money?"

"*Nee,* it wasn't me. I'm just glad the quilt is back where it belongs. Your mother made it as a wedding gift for you. I know, and the buyer knows, that she would want you to have it. She would be so pleased that you used it to help your sisters find a safe home."

Lizzie held the quilt to her face and closed her eyes. "Please give my thanks to the buyer. I can't believe it came back to me."

Naomi patted Carl's shoulder and winked at him. "Now all that is needed is a wedding."

* * *

On the last Sunday in April, the congregation of Bishop Zook found itself in for a few surprises.

Carl had gone to meet privately with the bishop a few days before. Lizzie didn't know what they talked about, but she knew Carl planned to join their church if the congregation would ultimately accept him. It had to be a unanimous vote of all baptized members, so she knew Carl would be under close scrutiny for the next few months.

He looked very handsome in his dark coat and flat-topped black felt hat. He spent a lot of time running his hands up and down his suspenders. She could tell he wasn't used to them after wearing jeans for more than four years. There were a lot of surprised looks when the bishop introduced him after the service.

Faith Lapp had delivered a healthy seven-pound baby girl the week before. She brought her to church for the first time and everyone, including the Barkman girls, took turns admiring her. Adrian stayed by his wife's side, playing the role of proud papa with ease.

Lizzie, like everyone else, dropped her jaw when the banns between her grandfather and Naomi Wadler were read aloud by the bishop as the last item of the morning. She turned to her sisters. They all shrugged. None of them knew anything about it. Joseph, in his usually abrupt manner, left early after church and avoided a ton of questions. Naomi climbed into his buggy with him and they drove off, leaving people to speculate wildly on their whirlwind romance.

Only Sally Yoder said, "I knew something was up between them all along."

Later that afternoon, when Lizzie and her sisters arrived home in Carl's new buggy, they all piled out and rushed into the house.

Naomi held up a hand to forestall their questions. "He was supposed to tell you."

Joe looked defensive. "The time never seemed right. It's my decision to wed. If it doesn't suit any of you, too bad."

The sisters surrounded him with hugs and best wishes. No one objected to having a new grandmother in the family.

After supper that night, Carl asked Lizzie to come for a buggy ride with him. Her heart raced as she agreed.

They had been careful to keep things low-key during his transition from an Englisch to an Amish sheepherder. His presentation to the church was the next-to-last step on his road back to the faith of his heart. It opened the way for him to court Lizzie without damaging her reputation.

Carl drove them out to the lake. It was an old stone quarry that had filled with water a century before. It was a favorite fishing spot for some of the locals, but they had the place to themselves that evening. They got out of the buggy and found a large flat rock to sit on by the water. Lizzie got up and threw a half dozen stones into the lake to ease her jitters.

Carl rested back on his elbows and watched her. "Can I ask you a question, Lizzie?"

"Of course." She came to sit beside him.

"On the night your uncle showed up, what did you think when I walked in with a gun in my hand?"

"I saw the gun and lamb at the same time. I thought you had been out protecting the flock from the coydog."

He studied her intently. "You didn't think I would use the gun?"

"On my uncle? *Nee,* that never crossed my mind. Can I ask you a question?"

"Sure."

She hesitated a moment. "Did you shoot the coydog?"

"*Nee,* I could not."

She grinned with relief. "He hasn't been back. I'm grateful for that."

"I found out who owns him."

"Did you? Who does he belong to?"

"Our postman."

"He's the mailman's dog?" Lizzie laughed.

"He and his son stopped in to buy a club lamb a few days ago. He had the coydog with him. He said the boy wanted the dog to get used to sheep so he wouldn't bother the one they took home."

"Oh, dear. Did you tell them that he can't be trusted around the lamb?"

"I had to tell them he's been killing our sheep. They offered to pay for all the damages. They felt bad about it, especially the boy. Joe wouldn't take their money."

"He's too happy these days to worry about money."

"Naomi is making a new man of him, that's for sure."

"Speaking of new men, you look very Plain in your new suit."

"I am a new Plain man, and I'm in love with a beautiful Plain woman." Carl leaned close and Lizzie knew he was about to kiss her. She had never wanted anything more.

His lips touched hers with incredible gentleness, a featherlight caress. It wasn't enough. She cupped his cheek with her hand. To her delight, he deepened the kiss. Joy clutched her heart and stole her breath away.

She had been waiting a lifetime for this moment and she didn't even know it.

He pulled her closer. Her arms circled his neck. The sweet softness of his lips moved away from her mouth. He kissed her cheek and then drew away. Lizzie wasn't ready to let him go. She would never be ready to let him go.

"I love you, Lizzie," he murmured softly into her ear. "You have made me whole again. I was broken, and you found a way to mend me. I lived a life of despair, ashamed of what I had done. I thought I was beyond help. And then you came into my life and I saw hope."

"I love you, too, darling, but it is God that has made us both whole."

"And the two shall become as one. I never understood the true meaning of that until this very moment."

He kissed her temple. "Will you marry me, Lizzie Barkman?"

Lizzie had never felt so cherished. The wonder of his love was almost impossible to comprehend. This man, who had seen so much of the world, wanted her to be his wife. Emotion choked her. She couldn't speak.

He drew back slightly to gaze at her face. "Am I rushing you? Please, say something."

"Can't you hear my heart shouting *yes?*"

"No, for mine is beating so hard that I can't hear anything."

"Yes, Carl King. I will marry you."

Suddenly, he lifted her off her feet and swung her around, making her squeal with delight.

"I love you, Lizzie. I love you. I love you. I will never get tired of saying that."

When he stopped spinning, her feet touched the

ground again. She gazed into his eyes. "And I will never grow tired of hearing it. I can't believe this is real. I'm afraid that I'm dreaming."

"Shall I pinch you?"

"Don't you dare."

"Then I will simply have to kiss you again. If I may?"

She put her hands on his chest. "You may. For as often and as long as you would like once we're married."

"Then say it will be soon."

"November will be soon enough."

He growled and pulled her snugly against him. "November seems an eternity from now."

She wavered. "It does, doesn't it?"

"I think we should have a June wedding."

"June will be too soon, but I think October will be about right."

He leaned close. "As you wish, but this is the last kiss you will get until our wedding day."

She gave him a saucy smile. "Then you had better make it a good one."

He proceeded to show her just how wonderful a kiss could be.

* * * * *

PLAIN DANGER

Debby Giusti

This story is dedicated to the wonderful readers
who buy my books and share them with their friends.
Your encouragement and support
mean so much to me. Thank you!

Store up treasure in heaven,
where neither moth nor decay destroys,
nor thieves break in and steal. For where
your treasure is, there also will your heart be.
—*Matthew* 6:20–21

Chapter One

Bailey's plaintive howl snapped Carrie York awake with a start. The Irish setter had whined at the door earlier. After letting him out, she must have fallen back to sleep.

Raking her hand through her hair, Carrie rose from the guest room bed and peered out the window into the night. Streams of moonlight cascaded over the field behind her father's house and draped the freestanding kitchen house, barn and chicken coop in shadows. In the distance, she spotted the dog, seemingly agitated as he sniffed at something hidden in the tall grass.

"Hush," she moaned as his wail continued. The neighbors on each side of her father's property—one Amish, the other a military guy from nearby Fort Rickman— wouldn't appreciate having their slumber disturbed by a rambunctious pup who was too inquisitive for his own good.

Still groggy with sleep, she pulled on her clothes, stumbled into the kitchen and flicked on the overhead light. Her coat hung on a hook in the anteroom. Slipping it on, she opened the back door and stepped into the cold night.

"Bailey, come here, boy."

Black clouds rolled overhead, blocking the light from the moon. Narrowing her eyes, she squinted into the darkness and started off through the thick grass, following the sound of the dog's howls.

She'd have to hire someone to mow the field and care for the few head of cattle her dad raised, along with his chickens. Too much for one person to maintain, especially a woman who knew nothing about farming.

Again the dog's cry cut through the night.

Anxiety tingled her neck. "Come, boy. Now."

The dog sniffed at something that lay at his feet. A dead animal perhaps? Maybe a deer?

"Bailey, come."

The dog glanced at her, then turned back to the downed prey.

A stiff breeze blew across the field. She shivered and wrapped the coat tightly around her neck, feeling vulnerable and exposed, as if someone were watching… and waiting.

Letting out a deep breath to ease her anxiety, she slapped her leg and called to the dog, "Come, boy. We need to go inside."

Reluctantly, Bailey trotted back to where she stood.

"Good dog." She patted his head and scratched under his neck. Feeling his wet fur, she raised her hand and stared at the tacky substance that darkened her fingers.

She gasped. Even with the lack of adequate light, the stain looked like blood.

"Are you hurt?"

The dog barked twice.

Bending down, she wiped her hand on the dew-damp

grass, then stepped closer to inspect the carcass of the fallen animal.

A gust of wind whipped through the clearing and tangled her hair across her eyes so she couldn't see. Using her unsoiled hand, she shoved the wayward strands back from her face, and holding her breath to ward off the cloying odor, she stared down at the pile of fabric that lay at Bailey's feet.

Her heart pounded in her chest. A deafening roar sounded in her ears. She whimpered, wanting to run. Instead she held her gaze.

Not a deer.

But a man.

She stepped closer, seeing combat boots and a digital-patterned uniform covering long legs and a muscular trunk.

Goose bumps pimpled her arms as she glanced higher. For half a heartbeat, her mind refused to accept what her eyes saw.

A scream caught in her throat. She turned away, unable to process the ghastly sight, and ran toward the house, needing the protection of four walls and locked doors.

The setter followed behind her, barking. Between his yelps, she heard a branch snap, then another. Straining, she recognized a different sound. Her chest tightened.

Footfalls.

Heart skittering in her chest, she increased her pace, all too aware that someone, other than Bailey, was running after her.

Coming closer.

She sprinted for the house and slipped on the slick grass as she rounded the corner. Catching herself, she climbed the kitchen steps and pushed open the door. Pulse pounding, gasping for air, she slammed it closed after Bailey scooted in behind her. Her hands shook as she fumbled with the lock. The dead bolt slipped into place.

She ran into the family room. Drawing the curtains with one hand, she grabbed the phone with the other and punched in 911.

Listening, she expected to hear footsteps on the porch and pounding at the door. The only sound was the phone ringing in her ear.

Grateful when the operator answered, she rattled off her father's address. "I found someone…in the back pasture. Military uniform. Looks like he's army."

Her father—a man she hadn't known about until the lawyer's phone call—had died ten days earlier. Now a body had appeared on his property. Touching the curtain that covered the window, she shivered. The horrific sight played through her mind.

"Someone c…cut the soldier's throat." She pulled in a breath. "So much blood. I…I heard footsteps, coming after me. I'm afraid—"

Her hand trembled as she drew the phone closer. "I'm afraid he's going to kill me."

Working late at his home computer, Criminal Investigation Division special agent Tyler Zimmerman heard sirens and peered out the window of his rental house. A stream of police sedans raced along Amish Road, heading in his direction.

For an instant, he was that ten-year-old boy covered in blood and screaming for his father to open his eyes. The memory burned like fire.

He swallowed hard and took in the present-day scene that contrasted sharply with the tranquility of the rural Amish community where he had chosen to live specifically because of its peaceful setting.

Eleven years in the military, with the last six in the army's Criminal Investigation Division, had accustomed him to sirens and flashing lights at the crime scenes he investigated, but when the caravan of police cruisers turned into the driveway next door, Tyler's mouth soured as thoughts from his youth returned. Once again, violence was striking too close to home.

Leaving his computer, he hurried into the kitchen, grabbed his SIG Sauer and law enforcement identification before he shrugged into his CID windbreaker and stepped outside. The cool night air swirled around him. He hustled across the grassy knoll that separated his modest three-bedroom ranch with the historic home next door.

The flashing lights from the lineup of police cars bathed the stately Greek revival in an eerie strobe effect. The house, with its columned porch and pedimental gable, dated from before the Civil War when life wasn't filled with shrill sounds and pulsating light.

Men in blue swarmed the front lawn. Others hustled toward the field behind the main house. A woman stood on the porch, next to one of the classical white columns. Her arms hung limp at her sides. She was tall and slender with chestnut hair that swept over her shoulders and down her back. Her eyes—caught in the glare—were wide with worry as she stared at the chaos unfolding before her.

Gauging from the number of law enforcement officials who had responded, something significant had gone down. For a moment, Tyler switched out of cop mode and considered the plight of the stoic figure on the porch.

Whatever had happened tonight would surely affect her life, and not for the better. Ty was all too aware that everything could change in the blink of an eye. Or the swerve of an oncoming car.

Approaching a tall officer in his midthirties who seemed in charge, Ty held up his identification. "Special Agent Tyler Zimmerman. I'm with the CID at Fort Rickman."

The guy stuck out his hand. "You've saved me a phone call to post. Name's Brian Phillips."

He pointed to a second man who approached. "This is Officer Steve Inman."

Tyler extended his hand and then pointed to his house. "I live next door and saw your lights. I wondered if you needed any assistance."

"Appreciate your willingness to get involved," Inman said with a nod.

"You probably know that the owner of the house, a retired sergeant major named Jeffrey Harris, died ten days ago," Ty volunteered.

"I remember when the call came in about his body being found." Phillips pursed his lips. "Seems he lost his footing on a hill at the rear of his property and fell to his death. Terrible shame. Now this."

Tyler pointed to the forlorn figure on the porch. "Who's the woman?"

"Carrie York. Evidently she's the estranged daughter of the deceased home owner." The taller cop glanced down at a notepad he held. "Ms. York called 911 at twelve-thirty a.m. She had arrived at her father's house approximately six hours earlier after traveling from her home in Washington, DC. She was asleep when her father's dog alerted her to the body. Supposedly the deceased is in uniform."

"Army?"

"Camo of some sort. Could be a hunter for all we know. Some of my men secured the crime scene. I'm headed there now. You're welcome to join me."

"Thanks for the offer."

Phillips turned to Inman. "Get Reynolds and question Ms. York. See what you can find out."

"Will do." Inman motioned to another officer and the twosome hustled toward the porch, climbed the steps and approached the woman. She acknowledged them with a nod and then glanced at Tyler as he fell in step with Phillips and passed in front of the house.

In the glare of the pulsing lights, she looked pale and drawn. A stiff breeze tugged at her hair. She turned her face into the wind while her gaze remained locked on Tyler.

Warmth stirred within him, and a tightness hitched his chest. The woman's hollow stare struck a chord deep within him. Maybe it was the resignation on her face. Or fatigue, mixed with a hint of fear. Death was never pretty. Especially for a newcomer far from home and surrounded by strangers.

He dipped his chin in acknowledgment before he and Phillips rounded the corner of the house and headed toward the field of tall grass that stretched before them.

"How well did you know your neighbor?" Phillips fixed his gaze on the crime scene ahead.

"Not well. I'm new to the area. We exchanged pleasantries a few times. The sergeant major seemed like a nice guy, quiet, stayed to himself."

Tyler had spent the last month and a half focused on his job, leaving his house early each morning and returning after dark. Being new to post and getting acclimated into his assignment didn't leave time for socializing with the neighbors.

The cop glanced left and pointed to the Amish farm house on the adjoining property. "What about the other neighbors?"

"Isaac Lapp's a farmer. He and his wife and their eight-year-old son are visiting relatives in Florida."

"Probably for the best, especially so for the boy's sake. No kid should witness a violent death."

Tyler's chest constricted. Without bidding, the memory returned. His father's lifeless body, the mangled car, the stench of gasoline and spilled blood. He blew out a stiff breath and worked his way back to the present. Why were the memories returning tonight?

Two officers had already cordoned off an area near the rear of the field and stood aside as Ty and Phillips approached. Ducking under the crime scene tape, they headed to where battery-operated lights illuminated the body. The victim lay on his side, his back to them. No mistaking the digital pattern of the Army Combat Uniform or the desert boots spattered with blood.

Grass had been trampled down as if there'd been a struggle. The earth was saturated with blood. The acrid smell of copper and the stench of death filled the night.

Ty circled the body until he could see the guy's face and the gaping wound to his neck. He paused for a long moment, taking in the ghastly sight of man's inhumanity. What kind of person would slice another man's throat?

The victim's hands were scraped. His left index finger was bare, but then not all married guys wore rings. Blood had pooled around his head.

Ty hunched down to get a closer view. *Fellows*, the military name tag read. The 101st Airborne patch on his right sleeve indicated he had served with the Screaming Eagles in combat. The rank of corporal was velcroed on his chest. The patch on his left arm identified that he was currently assigned to the engineer battalion at Fort Rickman.

"Looks like he's one of ours." Tyler stood and glanced at Phillips. "I'll contact the CID on post as well as his unit."

Pulling his business card from his pocket, Tyler handed it to the cop. "Let me know what your crime scene folks find. I'd like a moment with Ms. York as soon as Officers Inman and Reynolds end their questioning."

"No problem. Tell them you talked to me." Phillips pocketed the business card. "I'll keep you abreast of what we find."

Tyler retraced his steps to the house, climbed to the porch and tapped lightly on the door before he turned the knob and stepped inside. A young officer glanced at the identification he held up and motioned him forward.

Inman and Reynolds stood near the fireplace in the living room. Ms. York sat, arms crossed, in a high-back chair.

Inman excused himself and quickly walked to where Tyler waited in the foyer. "Was the victim military?"

Tyler nodded. "From Fort Rickman. I'll notify his unit." He handed the cop his business card. "The CID's resources are at your disposal. Let me know what you need."

"Glad we can work together." Glancing into the living room, Inman kept his voice low as he added, "I presume you want to talk to her."

"Whenever you're done. Has she provided anything of value thus far?"

"Only that she works as a speechwriter for a US senator in DC. Probably a big-city girl, with big-city ideas." Inman smirked. "She asked whether the FBI would be notified."

"And you told her—"

"That we'd handle the initial investigation."

Noting the agitation in the cop's voice, Tyler was grateful for the good relationship between the Freemont Police Department and the Fort Rickman CID, which hadn't always been the case from the stories he'd heard around the office. Things could change again, but currently the two law enforcement agencies worked well together. A plus for Tyler. Getting in at the onset of a case made his job easier and pointed to a faster resolution, especially on a death investigation.

"Maybe there's a reason she requested the feds," he suggested. "If she works for a senator, there might be something she's not telling you."

"Could be. We can check it out. She claims to have heard footsteps as she ran back to the house."

"Did she get a visual?"

"Unfortunately, no. She didn't see anyone. Could be an overanxious imagination, especially after finding the body. Still, you never know. People have been known to fake grief and shock."

"Did you get her boss's name?"

Inman glanced down at his open notebook. "It's here somewhere."

Tyler turned his gaze to the living area, feeling an emotional pull deep within him. Usually he didn't allow his feelings to come into play during an investigation. This case seemed different. Perhaps because her father had been a neighbor. The close proximity might have triggered a familiarity of sorts. Or maybe because she'd lost her father. Tyler could relate. Still, he hadn't expected the swell of empathy he felt for her.

"Here it is." Inman stepped closer and pointed to his notebook. "Ms. York works as a speechwriter for Senator Kingsley."

Any warmth Tyler had sensed disappeared, replaced with a chilling memory of a man from his past.

"Senator Drake Kingsley?" Ty asked.

Inman nodded. "That's right. You know the name?"

Worse than that, Tyler knew the man—a man he would never forget and never forgive. Drake Kingsley had killed his father, yet he'd never been charged for the crime.

Chapter Two

Carrie's head throbbed and her mouth felt dry as cotton. Officer Reynolds appeared oblivious of her discomfort and continued to ask questions that seemed to have no bearing on the terrible crime that had happened tonight.

"Has Senator Kingsley had attacks against his person?" he asked. "Or have there been attacks on anyone with whom you work?"

"Not that I know of, but I don't see how what happens in Washington could have bearing on a soldier's murder in rural Georgia."

"Yes, ma'am, but I just want to cover every base."

"Bases as in baseball, Officer Reynolds, or the investigation?"

He looked peeved, which was exactly how she felt. Peeved and tired and more than a little frightened to think of what had occurred just outside her window while she slept. She'd never expected following the trail to her estranged father would hurl her into a murder investigation.

If she wasn't so confused, she would cry, but that wouldn't solve the problem at hand, namely to answer the officer's questions. Plus, she didn't want to appear weak.

She'd been living alone long enough to know she had to rely on her own wherewithal. A lesson that had been one of the few good things she'd learned from her mother.

Not what she wanted to bring the memory of her deceased mother into the upheaval tonight.

"I'm sorry," Carrie said with a sigh. "My rudeness was uncalled for, to say the least."

"I know this must be hard for you, ma'am, but if you can endure a few more questions."

Which she did until her head felt as if it were ready to explode. She glanced at the leather-bound Bible on the side table, the stack of devotionals and religious texts on a nearby shelf and a plaque that read As for Me and My House, We Will Serve the Lord. All of which made her wonder if she had stumbled into the wrong house. How could she be so closely related to a man she didn't even know?

Exhausted and exasperated, she finally held up both hands as if in submission. "If you don't mind, I need a glass of water."

"Certainly. Why don't we take a break?" Officer Reynolds acted as if pausing had been his idea. "Officer Phillips will probably want to talk to you later."

She sighed. "I've told you everything I know."

"Yes, ma'am. I'll pass that on, but I'm fairly confident he'll have additional questions."

"Of course, he will." She stood, her gaze flicking to the man in the foyer wearing the navy jacket. He and Officer Inman were whispering as if they were talking about her.

Turning back to Reynolds, she asked, "May I bring you something? Water? Coffee?"

"No, thank you, ma'am. I'm fine." He closed his notebook and pointed to the door. "I'll step outside for a bit while you relax."

As if she could with so many police officers swarming over her father's property. Hurrying into the kitchen, she ran water in a tall glass and drank greedily, hoping to slake her thirst as well as the headache. She arched her shoulders to ease the tension climbing up her neck and glanced out the window at the neighboring brick ranch.

George Gates, her father's lawyer, had mentioned the army man who lived next door. She'd seen him come home earlier, when she fixed a cup of tea and nibbled on the chicken salad croissant the lawyer had been kind enough to have waiting in the fridge for her.

Tall and well built with short dark hair and a thick neck, the neighbor had US Army written all over him. Hard to mistake a guy who looked that all-American. She hadn't expected to see him walking across the front lawn earlier in his CID windbreaker. Now he was waiting for her in the foyer.

Did he even have jurisdiction this far from post? As much as she didn't want to answer any more questions, she didn't have a choice. Placing the glass on the counter with a sigh, she then returned to the living room.

Reynolds and Inman had left the house, leaving the younger cop guarding the door and the army guy standing in the entryway. She extended her hand and walked to meet him. "Carolyn York. My friends call me Carrie."

"Tyler Zimmerman. I'm a special agent with the Criminal Investigation Division at Fort Rickman. The CID is involved because the victim was military."

His handshake was firm and confident.

"Fort Rickman is where my father was last stationed,"

she stated in case he wasn't aware of her father's military past.

"Yes, ma'am. I understand you just arrived in Freemont."

She nodded. "A little before five and in time to talk to my father's lawyer briefly. Mr. Gates asked me to return to his office in the morning to discuss my father's estate, but—" She spread her hands and looked out the window. "I'm not sure if everything will settle down by then."

"I understand your concern, Ms. York."

She tried to smile. "Carrie, please. Since we're neighbors."

He quirked an eyebrow.

Had she revealed too much? "The lawyer mentioned that someone from the CID was my father's neighbor," she quickly explained. "I put two and two together. You do live next door?"

"That's correct." He motioned toward the living room. "Shall we sit down? I know you've answered a lot of questions already, but I'd like to hear your take on what happened."

She settled onto the couch while he pulled a straight-back chair close. Mr. Zimmerman seemed to be a man of few words with no interest in social niceties that could take the edge off the tension hovering in the air. She wouldn't make another mistake by trying to be neighborly.

As much as she struggled to remain stoic, a picture of what she'd seen played through her mind again.

The gaping wound, the bloody ground—

She dropped her head in her hands. "I'm sorry, but I...I can't get the image—"

"The man in the field?" the special agent filled in.

Pulling in a ragged breath, she glanced up and nodded. "The memory keeps flashing through my mind."

"Which is understandable." He hesitated a long moment, before asking, "What alerted you to go outside, ma'am?"

"It was Bailey." The dog lay by the chair where she had sat earlier. Hearing his name, he trotted to her side.

"I had let him out a little before midnight," she explained. "When he hadn't returned, I must have fallen back to sleep."

She rubbed the dog's neck, finding comfort in his nearness. "At some point, Bailey started barking. I went outside to get him, thinking he'd found an animal."

Mentally she retraced her steps, seeing again the mound that had turned into a man. "I never expected to find a dead body."

"Did you see anyone else or hear anything?"

"Footsteps behind me when I ran back to the house. I locked the door and called 911."

"After you made the call, did you hear or see anyone outside?"

"No, and I was too afraid to pull back the curtain. The only sounds were the sirens."

"Could you describe what you saw when you discovered the victim?"

"Blood, a military uniform, boots. At first, I thought he might have tripped and fallen. When I saw his face, I…I knew he…he was dead." Her hand touched her throat in the exact place the soldier's had been cut. "The wound was—"

She dropped her hand into her lap and worried her fingers. "I can't describe it."

"But you saw no one the entire time you were outside the house."

"That's correct."

"How did you learn of your father's death, Ms. York?"

"George Gates called five days ago with the news. That's when I learned Sergeant Major Harris was my father."

The agent glanced up from his notes. "Sorry?"

"I thought my father had died soon after I was born."

"Why did you think that?"

"My parents weren't married. My mother evidently fabricated a version of what had happened."

"She told you he had died?"

"That's correct. In a covert black ops mission."

The special agent narrowed his gaze. "And you believed her?"

Carrie bristled. "Don't children usually believe their mothers?"

A swath of color reddened his cheek as if he were embarrassed by his lack of sensitivity. "So you grew up not knowing Sergeant Major Harris was your father?"

"My mother told me my father's last name was Harrison, probably to keep me from learning the truth. I searched through military channels when I was in college, but the army disavowed having a record of a Jeffrey Harrison from Radcliff, Kentucky." She glanced up at the tall ceiling and crown molding, thinking of the lie her mother had perpetuated for too many years. Lowering her gaze, she focused on the photo of a muscular man in uniform. The name tag on his chest read Harris. "Now I find out my father lived in Georgia."

"What did your mother say after Mr. Gates notified you of the sergeant major's death?"

"My mother died three years ago of a heart attack."

"I'm sorry."

Carrie had grieved deeply for her mother, but she wasn't sure how she felt now. After the phone call from Gates, she'd been numb and confused. Since then, the word betrayal had come to mind, although she knew her mother wasn't totally to blame for the disinformation she had passed on to Carrie. Surely the sergeant major bore some of the guilt, as well.

She hugged her arms, suddenly cold and overcome with fatigue. Once again, the line of questioning seemed to have digressed off track.

"Mr. Zimmerman," she said with a sigh. "I have no idea what is going on here. My father supposedly died from an accidental fall ten days ago. Finding another military man dead on his property tonight has me wondering if something suspect could be underfoot."

The agent leaned in closer. "Like what?"

She shrugged. "You tell me. Was my father involved in some nefarious or illegal operation?"

"Do you think he was?"

"I have no idea. According to his lawyer, Jeffrey Harris stipulated in his will that I was not to be notified of his death until after his burial. Mr. Gates presumed that my father didn't want me to feel coerced to attend his funeral. I must admit that I question my father's logic. It seems strange that he would be considerate of a daughter he'd never tried to contact."

Giving voice to what troubled her the most about her father brought even more unease to her already-troubled heart. Why hadn't her father wanted a relationship with his only child?

She glanced at the fireplace with its wide hearth and

sturdy oak mantel and shook her head to ward off the hot tears that burned her eyes. She usually could control her emotions. Tonight was different. More than anything, she didn't want to seem needy in front of the agent with the penetrating eyes and questioning gaze. "I feel like I'm drowning, as you might imagine. No buoy or life preserver in sight."

"Ms. York…uh, Carrie, I'm sure things will sort themselves out over the next few days. How long do you plan to stay in Freemont?"

"I'm not sure. Mr. Gates mentioned that someone is interested in buying the property. He encouraged me to sell, and initially, I had planned to put the house on the market as soon as possible."

"And now?" the CID agent asked.

"Now I'm not sure."

"Then you plan to stay?"

"No." She didn't know what she planned to do. "I have a job in DC, but I can work here for a period of time. I'm sure the police won't want me to leave the area."

"Not until the investigation is over," he confirmed.

"Then that settles the problem. I'm forced to stay, although I'm concerned about safety issues with a man dead in the backyard. Still, I'll remain here, at least until the ceremony downtown."

"I'm unaware of any ceremony."

"Honoring veterans from the local area. Mr. Gates said a plaque with my father's name and years in service will be added to the War Memorial and unveiled at the end of the month. I'll stay until then."

"And if the investigation is still ongoing?"

Her shoulders slumped ever so slightly. "Eventually I'll have to return to my job."

"You work for Drake Kingsley?"

"That's right. I'm his speechwriter."

"Do you believe everything you write in his speeches?"

The personal nature of the question surprised her as much as the sudden hard edge to his voice.

Any residual tears instantly dried. "What does that mean?"

"He's not a friend of the military."

"Senator Kingsley is a good man." With a big heart, she almost added.

"If that's what you believe, then he's got you fooled."

The door opened, and Inman stepped into the foyer. "Officer Phillips needs to see you, sir."

The special agent pushed out of the chair and stood. "Excuse me, ma'am. I have work to do."

He turned on his heel and followed Inman outside, leaving her alone, except for Bailey and the young cop who stood guard at the door.

Recalling the special agent's curt tone and abrasive comment, she felt her heart pounding. The senator had been like a father to her over the past eighteen months that she'd worked for him. Demanding at times, but he was also generous with his praise, and her writing had improved under his tutelage.

Why would Special Agent Zimmerman be so antagonistic toward a noted public servant who played such an important role in her life? The senator had changed a few of her speeches over the months to tone down her exuberant support for the military. She had never purposefully maligned anyone in uniform, nor would she ever do so. The special agent didn't understand that she was a paid employee on Kingsley's staff and had to comply with his requests in regard to his talks.

Evidently Mr. Zimmerman was unaware of the number of people Carrie admired, all dedicated men and women who were serving in the military. She—and indeed, the entire nation—was indebted to their sacrifice.

Admittedly Senator Kingsley had been somewhat vocal in his disregard of those in uniform in private settings, and she had heard him say that the military wasn't to be trusted, but that was the senator's belief and not hers.

Unlike Kingsley, she was wholeheartedly pro-military.

Except she did wonder about the special agent neighbor. Not because he was in the army, but because he lived next to a murder scene and had so quickly appeared on site. Was it purely coincidental?

Carrie needed to be careful until she knew if the CID agent was trustworthy or someone to watch.

Tyler left the house and descended the porch steps to where Officer Phillips stood on the sidewalk, cell phone at his ear. Disconnecting, the cop acknowledged Tyler with a nod.

"The victim's wallet confirmed Fellows's name and provided an address." Phillips pointed into the wooded area behind the Harris home. "A dirt road winds along the rear of the property. The sergeant major kept a trailer in the woods and rented it out. Fellows was his latest tenant. Some of my guys are there now looking for anything that can shed light on his murder."

Tyler glanced back at the house. "I wonder if Ms. York was aware of the trailer. She plans to talk to her father's lawyer in the morning."

"George Gates?" Phillips asked.

"You know him?"

"I know of him," the cop acknowledged. "His office is just off the square. He's well thought of in town. Has a pretty wife, a couple kids. The wife is some kind of designer. Works with Realtors by staging the homes that are on the market. All high-end properties."

"Thanks for the information," Tyler said. "I'll pay him a visit in the morning."

"Doubt he'll provide anything new." Phillips smirked. "You know lawyers and client privilege."

"You're saying Harris had something to hide?"

"I'm saying you never know about neighbors." Phillips made a clucking sound as he stared into the wooded area before turning back to Tyler. "Did you ever see Fellows hovering around Harris's property?"

"Never. But then I've haven't been in Georgia long."

"Where were you stationed before Rickman?"

"Germany for three years. A little town called Vilseck."

"Near the Grafenwohr training area."

Surprised that Phillips knew of Grafenwohr, Tyler smiled. "You're prior military?"

"Roger that." The cop chuckled. "I enlisted after high school."

Tyler liked Phillips. Knowing he had served elevated him in Tyler's opinion even more. "Thanks for your service."

"My contribution was insignificant compared to most. Present company included."

Tyler appreciated the comment. At least Phillips would understand the role the CID could play in the investigation.

"With the army's concern about fraternization between the ranks, something seems strange to me," Phillips said as he pocketed his cell. "Why would a sergeant major rent his trailer to some young soldier?"

"Harris was retired, and even if he had been on active duty, it wouldn't have been a problem if they were from different units. The sergeant major probably advertised on-post. Fellows may have been a country boy. Liked the outdoors and wanted to move out of the barracks."

The cop rubbed his jaw. "Maybe, although I wonder if anything else was afoot."

"I'll talk to his first sergeant and the other soldiers in his platoon," Tyler said. "They might provide a better picture of who Fellows was."

Phillips nodded. "And why someone wanted to kill him."

"What about questioning the neighbors?" Tyler asked.

"I've got a couple officers checking the folks who live nearby. I'm not sure how cooperative the Amish will be. They're good people, but they stick to themselves."

Tyler glanced at where the body was found. "The killer could have skirted Amish Road, by using the dirt road you mentioned. If he paid Fellows a late-night visit, they could have argued and gotten into a fight. Fellows might have run this direction to get away from the assailant. The killer follows and attacks after Fellows stumbled into the clearing."

"Did you hear anything unusual?"

Tyler shook his head. "Not a peep."

"Something must have alerted Ms. York."

"She said her father's dog found the body and started barking."

Phillips pursed his lips. "Might seem like a stretch, but I wonder if she could be involved."

Tyler hadn't expected the comment, but as any law

enforcement officer knew, no one could be ruled out at this point.

The cop slapped Ty's shoulder. "My turn to talk to her."

Tyler pulled out his phone as the officer climbed the steps and opened the door. Carrie stood in the foyer and glanced around Phillips to where Tyler lingered at the bottom of the steps. She tilted her head ever so slightly as if questioning why he was still hanging around outside. The door closed, leaving Tyler with a strange sense of being shut out.

He had allowed his emotions to get the best of him when he questioned her. A mistake he shouldn't have made and wouldn't make again. Still, he hadn't expected an investigation in Georgia to open a painful memory from his past.

Pulling up his phone contacts, he tapped the number for the CID special agent on call. Everett Kohl's voice was heavy with sleep when he answered. "What's going on, Ty?"

"A soldier was murdered along Amish Road."

"Fill me in on the details."

Tyler shared what he knew about the case.

Once he had finished providing information, Everett asked, "Want me to notify the post duty officer? He'll inform General Cameron. The commanding general needs to know what happened."

"Sounds good. Thanks."

"Any witnesses?" Everett inquired.

"Not at this point. The sergeant major's daughter arrived in town late in the day. She knew nothing about her father until his lawyer called informing her of the property she had inherited."

"Welcome to Freemont."

"You've probably heard of Drake Kingsley, the senator from Ohio?" A ball of bile rose in Ty's throat. Not that he would share his past with Everett.

"As I recall, the senator's not enamored with the military."

"You're exactly right." Tyler paused for a moment before continuing. "Kingsley is talking about the need to slash the defense budget even more than last year. He was also instrumental in convincing the president to cut troop strength."

"What's the connection with this case?"

"Carolyn York, the woman who found the body, works as a speechwriter for Senator Kingsley."

Everett groaned. "She could be as vocal as her boss. We don't need any more bad press or do-gooders from Washington interfering with our investigation."

Tyler understood bad press. He also understood Everett's concern. Budget cuts and troop reduction had decimated the army. Combat readiness was a thing of the past.

"How'd you get involved, Ty?"

"I heard the sirens. Came to see what was going down and found out the deceased was military, assigned to the engineer battalion."

"That's interesting."

"In what way?" Tyler asked.

"Let me check the post paper. Seems I read the sergeant major's obit not long ago."

Tyler waited until Everett came back on the line.

"Here it is. 'Sergeant Major Jeffrey Harris, recently retired from the US Army.' This is the part that's of interest. 'His last duty station was Fort Rickman, where

Harris was the command sergeant major of the engineer battalion.'"

"So he and Fellows could have served together, depending upon how long ago the corporal transferred to the battalion."

"Doubtful the sergeant major would rent a trailer to someone in the same unit, unless they had some prior connection." Everett voiced the same concern as Phillips had earlier. "Having a superior as a landlord could be seen as a conflict of interest."

"Something to consider."

Ty looked back at the Harris home. Carrie's arrival the night Fellows died could also be significant.

"This case could explode in our faces," Everett continued. "Especially since the woman has ties to Washington. I'll confirm with Wilson tomorrow to ensure that the boss is in agreement, but the way I see it, you'll need to keep tabs on Ms. York. Two folks have died on that property in less than two weeks. Keep her safe and as happy as can be expected under the circumstances. I'll let you know any information we find out about Fellows."

Everett was right. Tyler needed to keep an eye on his neighbor and see what he could learn about the estranged daughter and the young soldier who had died on her father's property. Maybe the pretty newcomer to Freemont knew more about her father than she was willing to admit.

Chapter Three

The first light of dawn glowed on the horizon as the Freemont police climbed into their squad cars. Phillips stood next to Tyler, watching their departure.

"Our crime scene folks will expand their search over the entire field," Phillips said. "So far they haven't found anything that seems to have bearing. I'm hoping Forensics might provide more information. I'll let you know what we uncover."

"Earlier you mentioned that the sergeant major's body was discovered in the woods," Tyler said. "Do you know who found him?"

"Inman handled the call, but if my memory is correct, an Amish teenager took a shortcut through the property and stumbled across the remains."

"Was there anything suspect about Harris's death?"

Phillips shook his head. "Nothing that seemed questionable at the time."

"Might be worth reviewing the report," Tyler suggested.

"I'll do that. And I'll talk to Inman."

Tyler glanced at the lights glowing in the downstairs

windows of the stately home. "Are any of your people still inside the house?"

"One of our rookies."

"I'll tell him you're wrapping up." Tyler hustled up the porch steps and rapped lightly on the door. The young cop he'd seen earlier answered his knock. Tyler stepped inside and repeated the message from Phillips. The officer hurriedly left the house and climbed into one of the squad cars.

Footsteps sounded from the kitchen.

"Ms. York?" Tyler called from the foyer.

She stepped into the hallway. Her eyes widened ever so slightly. "Agent Zimmerman, I didn't expect to see you again. Do you have more questions?"

"No, ma'am, but I wanted to apologize for my comments."

"Which comments are you referring to?" She squared her shoulders in a defensive gesture he had half expected after his earlier outburst.

"My comments about Senator Kingsley." Not that they weren't true. Still, he hated hearing the cool aloofness in her voice.

She stepped closer. "Evidently I said something wrong, something that upset you. Let me assure you that I'm not the senator."

He pointed a finger back at himself. "I in no way thought you were."

"Nor do I put words in his mouth."

"Actually…" Tyler hesitated. "If you write his speeches, that's exactly what you do."

She frowned.

He wasn't making points.

"Senator Kingsley is quite explicit on what he wants

covered in each speech," she said with an icy stare. "His policies are exactly that—his policies. They reflect his opinions and what he believes to be true and do not reflect the way I think or feel."

"That's good to know."

"I admire all who defend our nation, Agent Zimmerman. They sacrifice greatly. Many give their lives for our security. I am indebted to their service, as the entire nation should be."

"Then we see eye-to-eye on that point, but I still hope you'll accept my apology."

"Of course."

He handed her his business card. "Some of the crime scene personnel will remain on-site for a while. I'm heading to post. My phone will be on if you think of anything else."

"I've told you everything."

"Yes, ma'am, but I'm sure you're anxious and concerned. Keep your doors and windows locked. Be alert to any danger."

Her stiffness crumbled. She drew her hand to her neck. "Y-you're worrying me."

Which he hadn't intended to do. "I just want to ensure that you use caution."

"Thank you for your concern."

When he'd entered the house the first time, his focus was on the murdered soldier and on finding information. Now that the immediate urgency was over, he paused to glance at the expansive living area with two brick fireplaces, tall ceilings and hand-hewn hardwood floors.

"Your home is beautiful."

"My father's home," she corrected. "I still feel like an outsider."

"In time, that should change."

Her face softened for a moment, exposing a vulnerability he hadn't expected. Then she pulled in a quick breath and returned to her former polite, but somewhat perturbed, self.

"I hope the investigation is wrapped up quickly, Agent Zimmerman."

"It will be." Tyler sounded more optimistic than he felt. "My cell's always on. You can call me if you hear anything worrisome. I'm home most nights by seven."

"Bailey's a good watchdog."

"I'm sure he is."

Tyler started for the door.

A phone rang. Carrie reached for her cell and checked the caller identification. "If you'll excuse me, it's the senator's office."

"You notified Washington?"

She quirked her brow. "Did you want me to keep the soldier's death secret?"

"Of course not." He opened the door. "I'll be in touch."

He hurried off the porch and started across the front lawn on his way home. Phillips waved from his sedan as he and Inman pulled onto Amish Road and headed back to town.

Tyler needed coffee and a shower before he drove to post, but he couldn't get past the churning in his gut, knowing Carrie York was on the phone to DC.

This case came with baggage. Not what he needed or wanted. He had to focus on the investigation instead of getting into a war of words with the senator's speechwriter whose arrival in Freemont felt suspect.

Was Carrie York an innocent bystander? Or was she somehow involved in the soldier's death?

* * *

After the congestion and traffic in DC, driving along the gentle, rolling hills and fertile farmland was a refreshing change of pace for Carrie. Some of the anxiety she'd felt through the night had ebbed by the time she arrived downtown.

She parked her car behind the lawyer's office and hurried inside. George Gates had been nice enough yesterday when he gave her the keys to her father's house as well as the information about Bailey and the kennel where the dog had been boarded. Everything had seemed like a dream, especially when she realized the huge white home with Greek columns had belonged to her father.

Thankfully the dog's frisky playfulness and demand for attention had filled the expansive house with activity that added warmth and welcome to what could have been a difficult homecoming. She and Bailey had quickly become fast friends, and she was grateful for his attention. The pup had stayed close by her side, until he'd whined to go out shortly after midnight.

All too soon, the initial charm of the historic home had been marred by the discovery of Corporal Fellows's body. She hoped the lawyer would provide some clue to the soldier's death, which was the first question she asked George Gates once they'd exchanged pleasantries and she'd taken a seat in the chair across from his desk.

The lawyer was midforties, with whitened teeth, bushy eyebrows and a ruddy complexion that made her wonder if he frequented a tanning salon.

"I heard something had happened along Amish Road," he said, his voice somber. "Although I wasn't sure if the information I received was accurate. So you're saying a soldier was killed behind Jeff's house?"

"In the open field but close to the woods. As you can imagine, I'm upset and confused. Is there something you failed to tell me about my father?"

Surprise registered on his puffy face. "Surely you're not implying your father was involved in anything that would lead to a soldier's death."

"You tell me."

"Jeff was a good man, Carrie. He did a lot for Freemont and was well respected. The Harris family has been a part of this town's history since the early 1800s. Your father inherited the house and property from his maiden aunt some years back. He worked hard to restore the home to its former beauty, and since then, he's been a pillar of the town."

"Pillars can crumble."

He laughed off the comment. "I told you someone has expressed an interest in buying the property. It's something to consider. You're probably eager to return to Washington. I can handle the paperwork and expedite the sale."

She held up her hand. "It's too soon, George. I'm not ready to sell."

"You're upset, no doubt, about what happened last night. Take a few days to think it over. I'm sure the offer will please you."

"I came here today to find out more about my father's estate and especially his property. You didn't mention the trailer he rented."

"My mistake. You were tired yesterday. I hesitated taking up more of your time."

He taped a manila envelope on his desk. "A plat of the property is inside. Your father owned a hundred and twenty acres and the house. He rented out a trailer, usually to one of the soldiers from post. Almost half of his land is prime farmland. The rest is wooded."

"And you have an interested buyer for both the land and the house?"

"That's correct."

"Can you assure me the property won't be cut up for development?"

"I'm not sure what the buyer's plan would be, but it's nothing you need to concern yourself with at this point."

She leaned closer. "But it is my concern, George. I don't want to disrupt the beauty of the Amish community."

"Yes, of course. I understand."

Did he? Carrie wasn't sure about George Gates or his too-accommodating responses.

By the time she shook his hand in farewell, she had even more questions about her father, his past and her future.

Leaving the office, she hurried to her car and clicked the remote opener. Before she reached for the door handle, someone called her name. Turning, she spied Tyler Zimmerman climbing from a car parked on the opposite side of the lot.

In the light of day, he looked even taller and more muscular. Maybe it was the navy slacks and tweed sports coat he wore. For a moment she wondered why he wasn't in military uniform before recalling that CID agents wore civilian attire when working on a case. She'd stumbled upon the information while researching a speech for Senator Kingsley. Something about not wanting rank to interfere with their investigation.

"I didn't expect to see you here," she said in greeting.

He smiled as he neared. "I wanted to talk to Mr. Gates."

"You need a lawyer?"

His eyes twinkled, making him appear even more handsome.

"I want to talk to Mr. Gates about your father's rental property," he explained. "And see if he can provide information about your dad's relationship with Corporal Fellows."

When she didn't respond, he added, "I'm just gathering information, Ms. York."

"Carrie, please."

He smiled again.

Her heart skittered in her chest, making her feel like an adolescent schoolgirl. Too young and too foolish. Needing to shield herself from his charm, she clutched the manila envelope close as if it could offer protection.

He cocked his head. "What are you up to today?"

She tried to sound nonchalant. "In search of a grocery store."

"There's one on the way out of town. Turn left at Harvest Road. The supermarket's two blocks down on the left."

"Thanks." She opened her car door and slipped behind the wheel. "Good seeing you, Tyler."

Leaving the lot, she glanced back as the special agent opened the door to Gates Law Firm and stepped inside. Rounding the corner, she passed an Amish teenager who watched her turn right. Seeing the special agent had put her on edge. The pensive stare of the Amish boy added to her unease.

After a quick stop at the grocery store, she drove out of town, heading back to her father's house. Even the pretty countryside couldn't lessen her anxiety. In the distance, dark clouds filled the sky. Her heart felt as heavy as the thick cloud cover.

If only she could go back to the stories her mother had told her about the handsome army man who had swept her mother off her feet. They'd been young and in love and...well, things happened, including babies, or so she had explained when Carrie was old enough to learn the truth.

Only part of it had been a lie.

Her father hadn't died in a covert black ops mission as her mother had led her to believe. He wasn't part of the military's elite Delta Force, and the army hadn't covered up his death and withheld information from the grieving girlfriend who was pregnant with his child.

Now Carrie knew the truth, but counter to what scripture said, it hadn't set her free. Instead she felt tied in knots and suddenly connected to a man and a past she didn't understand, which only confirmed her upset with God. Why would He turn His back on a woman who always longed for a father's love? Evidently she and her problems didn't carry weight.

The special agent only confused her more. He'd been civil enough today, and his smile had seemed sincere, yet she had to be careful and cautious, especially after his antagonistic comments last night.

Carrie glanced again at the sky and turned on the windshield wipers as the first drops of rain began to fall. A road sign warned of a sharp curve ahead. She lifted her foot from the accelerator and placed both hands on the wheel as the car entered the turn.

A bolt of lightning cut through the dark clouds, followed by a clash of thunder that made her flinch. The tires lost traction for a heartbeat on the slick roadway. She turned the wheel to the right and tapped the brake, relieved when the car responded.

Coming around the curve, she glanced ahead and gasped. A semi-trailer was bearing down on her, going much too fast. Heart in her throat, she intensified her hold on the steering wheel, feeling the pull as the truck flew past with less than an inch to spare.

Too close.

Clunk-clunk-clunk.

Startled by the sound, she gripped the wheel even more tightly. The car shimmied, then jolted as the rear left side dropped. She glanced back, seeing a tire roll across the roadway.

A grating sound. Metal dragging against pavement. Her heart raced. The car veered left, crossed the center line and crashed into the ditch that edged the roadway.

Rain pelted the windshield. She struggled to free herself and clawed at the door, unable to push it open.

"Help!" she cried, knowing no one would hear her.

"Carrie!"

She turned, seeing Tyler.

He grabbed the door handle and ripped it open. Reaching around her, he unbuckled her seat belt. "Are you all right?"

She nodded. He pulled her free.

Rain pummeled her face as she looked into eyes filled with concern.

"Where are you hurt?" He touched her arms, the back of her neck and head as if searching for an injury. "Talk to me."

She swallowed down the fear and nodded. "I…I'm okay. How—"

"I was driving home and saw your car enter the turn. A semi passed. Then I saw you in the ditch. Did you get sideswiped?"

She shook her head. "The tire came off."

"What?"

He turned to study her car, then glanced back to where the wheel lay on the edge of the roadway. Retrieving the tire, he pried off the hubcap. "Three of your lug nuts are missing. Have you gone to a mechanic recently?"

"I had my oil changed before I made the trip to Georgia."

"This just happened. Since you last drove the car."

"I...I don't understand."

"In town. While you were talking to Gates. Someone removed three of your lug nuts."

Her ears roared, and she shivered in the chilly rain.

"Someone tampered with your wheel, Carrie," he repeated, his voice deathly calm. "They wanted the tire to fall off."

"But why?"

"Two reasons come to mind. Either to scare you—"

Her heart quickened.

"Or to do you harm."

Chapter Four

The police sedan's flashing lights drove home the seriousness of what had happened. Tyler glanced at his own car where Carrie sat, protected from the stiff breeze that had picked up once the rain eased.

"You must be working the twenty-four-hour shift," Ty said when Officer Steve Inman climbed from his patrol car.

Ignoring the dampness, the officer smiled. "You and Ms. York are keeping me busy."

Much to Tyler's frustration, Carrie left the warmth of his car and hurried to join them at the side of the road.

"Ma'am." Officer Inman nodded a greeting. "You mind telling me what happened?"

She quickly filled him in on losing control of the car and the missing lug nuts.

"Any chance your folks can dust the hubcap for prints?" Tyler asked. "You'll find mine, for sure, and the last mechanic who checked the tire."

"That won't be a problem." Inman pulled a notebook from his pocket. "So you think the lug nuts were purposely removed."

Tyler nodded. "I'm guessing when Ms. York was in town."

"I made two stops," she added. "The Gates Law Firm and the supermarket on Harvest Road."

Inman made note of the information. "I'll see if we have video cameras in either area that might have picked up activity."

"You'll let me know what you uncover," Carrie insisted.

"Yes, ma'am." He turned to Tyler. "You were following Ms. York home?"

"I had talked briefly with George Gates and ended up not too far behind her car, which was fortunate."

"Ma'am, did you see anyone behind you when you drove to town this morning?" the cop asked.

Carrie shook her head. "No one."

Inman turned to Tyler. "What about you, sir?"

"Negative. But I left my house early and went to post first so I could brief Chief Wilson, the head of the CID, on Corporal Fellows's murder. General Cameron has been informed, as well."

"He's the post commanding general?"

"That's right. As you can imagine, the general's upset about the corporal's death and has given us free rein to support you in any way we can."

"I'll pass that on. The chief of police is out of town, so Phillips is in charge. Last I heard, he contacted the Georgia Bureau of Investigation to rush the forensics on the case. Freemont is indebted to the military. We'll do everything we can to bring Corporal Fellows's killer to justice."

All of them turned at the sound of an approaching vehicle. Earl's Tow Service was painted on the side of the tow truck that pulled to a stop. A man hopped to the pavement.

"Craig Owens." The driver provided his name as he approached the threesome. "Special Agent Zimmerman?"

Tyler nodded. "That's right. I talked to Earl."

He pointed to Carrie's car, wedged in the ditch. "The vehicle needs to be towed. Earl said he'd order a new rear tire. Tell him to check the underbelly and ensure that nothing else is wrong."

"Will do." The driver held up a clipboard. "You mind signing the request for service?"

Tyler passed the clipboard to Carrie. "The car belongs to Ms. York."

"Do you need payment now?" she asked.

"No, ma'am, just your signature."

After she'd signed the form, the driver tossed the clipboard into his cab and climbed behind the wheel. He backed to the edge of the ditch and used a winch to hoist the vehicle onto the flatbed.

Once the car was safely locked down, he handed Carrie a business card. "Earl will call you with an estimate if your car needs repair work. As soon as the new tire comes in, he'll notify you. Appreciate your business."

Tyler stopped Owens before he climbed into his truck. "Any idea how long a wheel would stay attached with only two lug nuts?"

The tow man scratched his head. "Not long. The tire would start to shimmy and work the remaining lug nuts off in a short time."

Which was exactly what Tyler thought. "Thanks for getting here so quickly."

"We aim to please."

Inman slipped the notebook into his shirt pocket as the

tow truck headed back to town. "I'll let you folks know if we find any prints." He rolled the tire to his sedan and placed it in the trunk.

Then turning to Carrie, he added, "I might be jumping to the wrong conclusion, ma'am, but it looks like someone's not happy that you're in Freemont."

Tyler had to agree.

"Lock your doors and windows. Call my number or Special Agent Zimmerman if you feel threatened in any way or if anything else happens."

"Good advice," Tyler said to Carrie. "We're both worried about your safety."

"Use caution, ma'am," Owens continued. "As I said before, seems someone wants to do you harm."

Her face twisted with concern. "But why?"

The cop pursed his lips. "No clue, except it might tie in with the soldier's death."

"Or my father's," she added.

Tyler needed to learn more about the sergeant major. He wouldn't give voice to his suspicions, because it would upset Carrie even more, but just as she had mentioned earlier, her father could have been involved in something illegal that could play in to the corporal's death and have bearing on her accident today.

Inman nodded to Carrie and slapped Tyler's arm before he slid behind the wheel of his police sedan.

After ushering Carrie to his car, Tyler held the door for her as she settled onto the passenger seat. "I'm grateful Officer Inman responded to the call," he said as he climbed into the driver's side. "Someone without knowledge of what happened last night might not see the significance of the accident."

Her face was drawn and her eyes reflected both fatigue

and worry. "How would someone know where I was or which car in the lot was mine?"

"Your out-of-state tags would be easy to spot. Information travels fast in small towns. No telling who knew you planned to visit George Gates."

She shook her head. "But I didn't have an appointment."

"You told him yesterday that you would return in the morning."

"What if losing the tire was just a random act?"

Tyler sighed. "Having three lug nuts go missing is more than happenstance, Carrie."

"Then either someone's trying to scare me off, or it involves Corporal Fellows, as Officer Inman mentioned."

When Tyler failed to reply, she turned her gaze to the road. "Whatever the reason, the person responsible doesn't understand my determination to learn more about my father."

"Might be a good idea to program my cell number into your phone, Carrie."

"I already have."

They drove in silence until Tyler turned into the Harris driveway and parked at the side of the antebellum home. He glanced at the barn and the small chicken coop at the rear, seeing movement. His neck tingled a warning.

"Looks like someone's prowling around your property, Carrie. Stay here until I give you the all clear."

Before she could object, he slipped from the car and cautiously approached the barn, keeping his right hand close to the weapon on his hip. He stopped at the corner and watched as a man peered over the top of the coop.

"You're trespassing." Tyler raised his voice. "Put your hands in the air and turn around slowly."

The man complied without hesitation. Only he wasn't much over fifteen, with a shaggy haircut, suspenders and black pants. A hat lay on the ground, along with a bucket half filled with what looked like chicken feed.

"State your name and the reason you're on the Harris property."

"Eli Plank."

His clothing identified him as Amish. "Isaac Lapp asked me to feed the chickens while he and his family are out of town." The kid blinked. "I have done nothing wrong."

Tyler realized his mistake. "You can put your hands down, Eli. I didn't know anyone was helping out."

The boy lowered his arms. "Isaac has been caring for the chickens since Mr. Harris died. He asked me to lend a hand so he and his wife and Joseph could visit the boy's *Grossdaadi*. His grandfather."

"Where do you live?"

He pointed south. "The next farm. You know my *Datt*?"

Tyler shook his head. "I've seen him working in the fields, but we haven't met."

"Tyler?"

Hearing Carrie's voice, Tyler peered around the barn. She was walking toward them.

"Is everything okay?" she asked.

"Everything's fine." He introduced Carrie to the Amish boy and explained the reason Eli was on the property.

"Thank you for taking care of the chickens." Carrie opened her purse. "I'd like to pay you."

The boy shook his head. "I was helping Isaac. That needs no payment, but I must go home now." After returning the unused feed in the barn, Eli waved goodbye and hurried across the road.

"I don't think Eli is anyone to fear." Carrie watched as the boy approached the two-story farmhouse visible in the distance.

"Probably not, in fact, it's doubtful any of the Amish are involved, but you never know. Remember Corporal Fellows was a neighbor."

She tilted her head. "You're a neighbor too."

He nodded. "The difference is that you can trust me. I'm going back to post this afternoon to talk to Corporal Fellows's first sergeant. He worked in the same unit as your father. If you want to join me, I'd be happy to show you around Fort Rickman."

She hesitated for a moment and then nodded. "What time?"

Tyler glanced at his watch. "After lunch. Say one o'clock."

"I'll be ready."

Ty pulled his SUV to a stop in front of the large white home with the tall columns and yesteryear appeal. He stepped onto the driveway, rounded the car and climbed the porch. The front door opened before he had time to knock.

Carrie stood in the doorway, looking far too pretty in a flowing skirt and matching sweater. She had changed out of the rain-damp clothes she'd worn this morning. With a nod of greeting, she grabbed a jacket from the rack in the foyer and stepped onto the porch, closing the door behind her.

He reached for the coat and helped her slip it on. "The sun's out, but it's still chilly and damp."

"Thanks."

He pointed to the door. "It's locked, right?"

She nodded, then dug for keys in her purse. "But I'll engage the dead bolt." Flicking a worried glance at him, she added, "Just in case."

"That's right." Ty didn't want to belabor the point, but he was relieved that she understood the need for caution.

"Do you think Corporal Fellows's uniform may have made him a target?" she asked.

"You're concerned terrorism might have been involved?"

"Probably a long shot, but Senator Kingsley talks about some of the groups in the Middle East targeting young men and some women here in the States. Home-grown terrorism, lone wolf, whatever you want to call it, he believes we're going to see more acts of aggression and violence in the days to come."

Although Tyler hated to agree with the senator, he knew his assessment was right.

"I don't understand," Carrie continued, "how people can be brainwashed into thinking that killing has a greater good."

"They're looking for something to believe in, to give them an identity. A cause bigger than themselves. Without a good foundation of faith and morality, kids can confuse evil for good, especially when the message is coated with affirming rhetoric."

"Sounds as if you know what you're talking about."

He shrugged. "Our military is built on guys who want to do good and fight for a cause bigger than themselves. Thankfully they've found what all kids want—a stable foundation."

"Did you have that growing up?"

He laughed ruefully. "I had a strong-willed father who loved the Lord."

Tyler hadn't planned to talk about his childhood.

"I'm sure he's proud of you."

He hadn't expected her comment either. "Maybe he would have been, but he died when I was a kid."

"I'm sorry."

Opening the passenger door, he helped her into the seat. Before he slipped behind the wheel, he glanced at the nearby Amish farms and the expansive fields. His own life had been shattered years ago, which was probably why he had been drawn to the serenity of Amish Road. Just as had happened in his youth, death now threatened the peace and well-being of those who lived nearby.

No matter the reason for the crime, the murderer needed to be apprehended sooner rather than later. Otherwise the tranquil countryside would be torn apart, especially if the killer struck again.

Chapter Five

Fort Rickman, with its stately oaks and tall pine trees, wasn't what Carrie had expected. She had a preconceived notion of army posts filled with men in uniform marching across parade fields accompanied by flags and a band. Her false ideas had probably been the result of watching too many military movies as a kid that featured army heroes. Silly of her, but since she'd never known her father, she'd hoped the movies would help her understand the life he had lived.

Ty made a quick stop at CID headquarters and insisted she come into his office, which turned out to be a cubicle big enough for a desk and two chairs. He brought her coffee and asked for her to wait while he talked to one of the other agents about the case.

As she sipped the hot brew, she couldn't help noticing the lack of photos and other knickknacks on his desk. Everything was neat and tidy but unadorned with anything that smacked of family or gave her a clue about who Ty Zimmerman really was.

He returned and smiled. "Ready to go to your father's unit?"

She continued to be pleasantly surprised as they drove across post. A stream meandered next to a walking trail that bordered a grassy knoll. The plentiful stands of trees and expansive green spaces reminded her of a national park. She'd been to Fort Meyer and Fort Belvoir in Virginia with the senator. Both posts were beautiful, but they weren't troop posts where soldiers trained for war. Somehow she hadn't expected anything as lush at Fort Rickman.

"It looks so peaceful," she said as they drove along a quiet two-lane road, overhung with a canopy of live oaks. "I expected dusty training areas with little or no vegetation."

He pointed left and then right. "The training areas stretch east and west on either side of the main post garrison. If you'd like, we could drive there."

She held up her hand. "That won't be necessary. I'm not even sure about stopping by my father's unit."

"I thought you wanted to know more about who he was and what was important to him."

"I do. It's just that…" She hesitated. "I don't know what to expect."

"Not to worry. From what I've heard, Sergeant Major Harris was well liked and well respected. I'm sure his men and colleagues will enjoy meeting you."

Tyler made a number of turns that eventually led to the engineer battalion. He pointed to a one-story brick building with a military flag hanging in front. To the side and rear were a number of three-story buildings.

"The taller structures are the barracks where the soldiers live. Battalion headquarters sits in the middle. That's where the commander works, along with his staff and the command sergeant major."

"Which was my father's position."

"That's correct. He was the ranking noncommissioned officer in the battalion."

All around them soldiers scurried from building to building. In the distance, she saw men standing in formation, and beside one of the barracks, military personnel were scrubbing trash cans. A soldier picked up a scrap of paper and tossed it in a nearby receptacle.

"Looks like everyone takes pride in maintaining the area."

"I'm sure your father stressed that to his men."

"They look so young."

"That's because they are, Carrie. Many of them are right out of high school."

"And going to war."

"If their unit is deployed."

Pulling to a stop, he again opened her door and then ushered her toward the headquarters.

Stepping inside, she was surprised when three soldiers, sitting at desks, all rose to greet her. She hadn't expected their manners or their welcoming smiles.

"Afternoon, ma'am," they said practically in unison. The tallest of the three men turned to Tyler. "How may I help you, sir?"

He showed his identification and gave his name and Carrie's. "I'd like to talk to Corporal Fellows's first sergeant."

"Yes, sir. That would be First Sergeant Baker. I'll call him and ask him to come to headquarters."

Tyler glanced at the office to the rear. The nameplate on the door read Command Sergeant Major Adams, evidently the man who had taken her father's position.

"Is the sergeant major in?" Tyler asked.

"Ah, no, sir. He's tied up at main post headquarters along with the commander."

"Ms. York is Sergeant Major Harris's daughter. I'm sure she'd appreciate seeing her father's former office, if you don't mind."

One of the other men came from around his desk. "Your dad was a fine man who did everything he could to help the troops. I'd be happy to show you around."

She followed the soldier into a corner office. A large desk sat in front of two windows. Three flags, including the American flag, stood nearby.

"Your father had the side wall filled with awards and commendations, ma'am. Close to thirty years on active duty. That's a career to be proud of, although I don't have to tell you."

She nodded, unable to think of anything to say that wouldn't expose her mixed emotions. "How did he treat the other men in the unit?" she asked, searching for something to say that wouldn't reveal her lack of knowledge of the military.

"He was by the book, if that's what you mean, ma'am, although the sergeant major liked to laugh. A deep bellowing sound that would fill a room. If you heard him laugh, you knew everything would be okay." Her guide suddenly looked embarrassed. "Forgive me, ma'am. I'm not telling you anything you didn't already know."

His statement took her aback. Confusion swept over her as it had too many times over the last twenty-some hours. If only she had heard her father's laughter.

Tears stung her eyes and a lump filled her throat. Not wanting the sergeant to realize her upset, she choked back her thanks and returned to the main area where Ty stood to the side talking to another man in uniform.

"I'll wait for you outside," she managed to say in passing as she hurried out the door and toward the car. Breathing in the fresh air, she stared at the pristine grounds that had been her father's life for close to thirty years. She knew so little about the military, and everything she thought she knew was proving to be wrong.

A breeze stirred the trees and made her hair swirl in front of her face. She pulled it behind her ears and wiped her hand across her cheeks. She needed to be strong, especially here, surrounded by men and women in uniform who sacrificed so much for the nation.

Carrie thought she had known who she was and where she'd come from. Since George Gates had called her, she had realized how her past had been clouded by her mother's lies. Regrettably the foundation upon which she'd built her life had been false.

Before arriving at Tyler's car, someone shouted her name. She turned, seeing a soldier, late thirties, blond hair visible under his beret. He ran toward her.

"Ma'am, one of the men said you were Sergeant Major Harris's daughter."

"That's correct."

He held out his hand. "Sergeant Oliver, ma'am. Pleased to meet you."

She returned the handshake.

"I was with your father in the Middle East and served with him here at Fort Rickman. His death was hard on all of us who knew him. If there's anything I can do, don't hesitate to ask."

"Thank you, Sergeant."

"You've heard about the ceremony at the end of the month for Freemont veterans?"

"My father's lawyer mentioned that a plaque would be unveiled honoring my father."

"Yes, ma'am. The unit's putting together a slide slow that will be played during the ceremony. The photos highlight the work our soldiers do within the civilian community. I want to add a portion about your father since he's being honored."

"That's very thoughtful."

"It's the least I can do to recognize his contribution. He did a lot of good for a lot of people, but then I don't have to tell you. Although I've got a number of pictures that the Public Affairs Office has taken, I'd like to include a few more. Any chance I could borrow some of the snapshots he had at home?"

"He has an office in the rear of the house. I could search through his papers."

The sergeant handed her his business card. "Call me if you find some that might work. I can pick them up anytime."

"Give me a day or two, Sergeant."

"That's fine, ma'am, and I don't want to pressure you."

"You're not, it's just that I've got a lot to take in when it comes to my father. Being on post today seems to be affecting me emotionally."

"Grief is hard, ma'am."

She appreciated the sergeant's understanding. Turning to regain her composure, Carrie gazed at the various military structures, surprised to see a wooden building with a steeple and cross on the next block. "Is that a church?"

Oliver nodded. "Yes, ma'am. It's Soldiers Chapel. The sergeant major's funeral was held there."

"Not in Freemont?"

"He worshipped on-post, ma'am, and as I understand it, he requested to have his service at the chapel."

When Carrie had met with George Gates this morning, she had expressed her desire to see her father's grave, although she hadn't thought to ask about the funeral and where it had taken place. The realization hung heavy on her shoulders. That should have been one of her first questions. "Do you know where he was buried?"

"Freemont Cemetery. It's on Freemont Road, which connects the post to town. You probably passed it on your way to Fort Rickman."

"I'm sure we did." But her mind had been on other things rather than burying the dead.

"I wasn't able to attend the graveside service," Oliver admitted. "The men said the chaplain did a good job."

Oliver glanced back at the headquarters. "I won't take any more of your time, and I'd better get back to work."

"Thank you, Sergeant. If you see Special Agent Zimmerman inside, would you mind telling him I plan to visit the chapel?"

"Will do, ma'am."

The sun peered through the clouds and warmed Carrie's back as she hurried toward the chapel. A group of soldiers doubled-timed along the nearby road, the rhythmic cadence of their Jody calls sounding in the quiet afternoon. Under other circumstances, she would have smiled at the lighthearted jingle about military life that set the pace as the soldiers ran in formation, but at this moment and after everything that had happened, the slap of their boots on the pavement reminded her of the long line of men and women who had gone to war.

Today their sacrifice seemed especially hard to bear. While she had been getting her degree and living the good life, so many had shipped off to the Middle East. Some hadn't returned home. Others had been maimed, wounded or psychologically or emotionally scarred.

Greater love hath no man...

The words from scripture played through her mind in time with the passing unit.

Arriving at the chapel, she climbed the steps, pulled open the glass door and stepped into the small narthex. Religious magazines and pamphlets hung on racks to the left. A door on the right led to an office. Seeing no one inside, she continued on into the sacristy, where she was welcomed by reflected sunlight that angled through the stained glass windows.

The scent of candle wax hung heavy in the air. She inhaled deeply and recalled the few times in her youth that she'd attended Sunday services. A relationship with the Lord hadn't been one of her mother's priorities. Regrettably Carrie had followed in her mother's less-than-faithful footsteps.

She slipped into a pew midway down the aisle and closed her eyes. Pictures flashed through her mind of the bigger-than-life hero she had envisioned in her youth. That make-believe dad had been repeatedly berated by her mother who had little to say that was positive about the military. Landing a job with the senator had further eroded any idealized concept that remained of her father.

Opening her eyes, she gazed at the cross hanging on the wall behind the altar, knowing she had hardened her heart not only to her parents, but also to the Lord.

Instead of embracing Christ's message of love and forgiveness, she had turned her focus inward, to her own self-serving needs. Just like many of the people with whom she worked with in Washington, the emphasis was on their own lives and not the true well-being of the nation.

Could she have been so wrong?

A door opened. She turned to see two men in uniform enter the chapel. The older of the two—a man in his forties—nodded before stepping inside the office. The younger man, early twenties, followed.

Feeling suddenly ill at ease, she left the pew and headed for the door, which opened again. Ty entered the chapel, his gaze filled with question as if he wondered why she was seeking solace in this place of worship.

Glancing into the office, he raised his hand in greeting. "Afternoon, Chaplain."

The older man met him in the narthex. The two shook hands. "Good to see you, Tyler. I have a feeling your visit involves Corporal Fellows. Terrible shame. We've lost too many soldiers in the Middle East. Tragic some succumb to violence in our own country."

"Yes, sir." Tyler introduced Carrie to the chaplain.

She accepted his handshake. "Nice to meet you, sir. I'm Carolyn York. I believe you officiated at my father's funeral. Sergeant Major Harris."

The chaplain's square face softened. "Less than two weeks ago. My sympathies. Your father was a good man with a strong faith. Knowing him was an honor."

She tried to smile, but the twisted feelings of inadequacy tangled around her heart. "I didn't know my father, and only learned of his death a few days ago. I'm trying to piece together a picture of who he was."

The chaplain nodded as if he understood. "Be assured that he loved the Lord."

"Which seems strange for a man of war."

"A man of peace," the chaplain corrected. "The military protects and defends against forces of evil that threaten our way of life. Our soldiers provide a deterrent against aggression. God would not have us stand idly by when evil looms so close and threatens those who cannot protect themselves."

"I never thought of it that way."

The chaplain turned to the younger man and introduced his assistant, Jason Jones. "Can you find one of the programs from Sergeant Major Harris's funeral for Ms. York?"

"Yes, sir." The soldier rummaged in a file cabinet and then handed her a folded program. A cross with lilies adorned the front.

She turned it over and stared at the photo of the man in uniform pictured on the back cover, the father she had never known.

"Thank you for your kind words, Chaplain. I'd like to visit his grave site at some point."

"Of course." He turned to Tyler, who had remained silent. "You know the Freemont Cemetery. It's not far from post if you go out the main gate."

Tyler nodded. "On the left off Freemont Road."

"That's correct. Enter the cemetery and make a right at the dead end. The grave sits on a small knoll around the first bend. You'll see the newly covered grave about twenty feet from the road on your right. The sergeant major had chosen the grave site just a few days prior to his death."

"Was there some urgency in selecting a burial spot?" Carrie asked. "My father wasn't that old. Had he been ill?"

"He told me that he thought about selling his property and moving to Florida, but reconsidered. Evidently his ancestors had settled around here in the 1800s. Once he made the decision to stay in Freemont, he made arrangements for his burial, although I don't think he realized how timely his decision would be."

"Did he ever talk about other family members?" she asked.

"He mentioned a daughter he had never seen." The chaplain's gaze was filled with compassion. "I presume that's you, Carrie. But he had no other family."

"Thank you, Chaplain." She nodded to the soldier who had found the funeral program before she turned to Tyler. "If we have time, I'd like to stop at the cemetery."

"Of course." He shook hands with the chaplain. "Good seeing you, sir."

Stepping outside, she glanced at the building where her father had worked. A soldier, yet a man of God and a man of peace, which went counter to what she had believed about him for the past few years. Pulling her coat around her neck, she and Tyler hurried back to the car. He opened the door, and she slipped into the passenger seat, still struggling with both confusion and grief. She had come to Fort Rickman hoping to get answers as to who her father was, but what she had learned only bewildered her more. A good man, a role model to his soldiers, a man who loved the Lord?

He'd chosen his grave site just days prior to his death and had been killed in a fall nearly two weeks before another soldier from his unit was tragically and heinously murdered on her father's property. Surely the two deaths had to be intertwined. But how?

Tyler sensed Carrie's tension as they left Fort Rickman and headed north along Freemont Road. She'd been hit with a lot of information about her father, all good, but probably hard to sort through, as well.

"I'm glad you met the chaplain, Carrie. He's a good man. Seems he thought highly of your father."

"Thank you for taking me to post. I...I don't think I could have found his unit on my own."

"The cemetery isn't far, but I know you're probably worn out. Do you want to stop now or would you rather return another day?"

"Now, if you have time."

"It's not a problem."

"What did you find out from the first sergeant?" she asked.

"Only that Corporal Fellows did his job, although he kept to himself. The first sergeant will talk to the guys in his platoon and see if anyone knows anything about his private life."

"Did the rental situation concern you?"

"Only if your father was Fellows's boss. The CID learned Fellows hadn't been here long and arrived well after your father's time on active duty ended."

"I wonder if they were friends or ever did things together. I keep thinking it's more than a coincidence that they both died in the same area so closely together."

Tyler had to agree, but he knew investigations could change direction in the blink of an eye when the right piece of information was revealed. The CID was looking into Fellows's past. The Freemont police were investigating the murder from the civilian angle, and Tyler was keeping tabs on the newly found daughter whose arrival in Freemont corresponded with Fellows's death.

A coincidence?

Maybe yes.

Or maybe no.

Chapter Six

Tyler turned into the cemetery and followed the chaplain's directions. Seeing the newly covered grave, he pulled to the side of the road. Carrie opened the passenger door and sighed as she stepped from the car.

Together, they walked to where dried flower arrangements still covered a mound of soil. A small stone indicated the number of the grave but not the name of the deceased buried there.

She stared at the ground for a long moment, her voice a whisper when she finally spoke. "I need to ask George Gates about a monument."

"The military will provide a marker. We can contact the funeral home and inquire about what's been arranged."

"If a marker hasn't been ordered, it's something I could do." She glanced at Tyler. "Something to show deference to my father."

"That would be very appropriate, Carrie, and would honor his memory."

"A memory I don't have." She clasped her hands. "I don't even know how to pray for him."

Tyler lowered his eyes, sensing Carrie's anguish and wishing he could comfort her. From deep inside, words sprang. "God bless Carrie's father. Draw him close to You in the everlasting life where You dwell, O Lord. Amen."

"Thank you, Tyler." She offered a weak smile. "Your words were far more meaningful than anything I could manage. Ever since Gates called and told me about my father, I've felt empty and unable to pray. Not that prayer was part of my life before, but the void has gotten bigger these last few days."

"God knows how you feel, Carrie."

"Does He?" She shook her head. "I don't think He's happy with the type of person I've become. I'm sure my father would wonder about my faith and lack of trust in the Lord. I never thought finding information about the man I wanted to know my whole life would make me so conflicted."

The low whine of a car engine turned Tyler's attention to the crest of the hill where a dark sedan pulled to a stop. The driver of the car extended something through his open window and raised it to his eyes.

Tyler's heart stopped as realization hit like a two-by-four. He grabbed Carrie's shoulders and threw her to the ground behind the mound of turned earth and dried flower arrangements. She gasped. In less than a heartbeat, the bullet whizzed past them.

"Stay down," Tyler warned.

Tires squealed in the distance.

Raising his head, he searched the hill, then flicked his gaze around the surrounding area, looking for any sign of the shooter. "The car's gone."

"Who was it?" Carrie moaned as she worked to free herself from under Tyler's hold.

"Sorry." He scooted aside, all the while keeping his eyes on the hillside.

Satisfied the shooter and car had both left the area, Tyler stood and helped Carrie to her feet. "Let's get back to my vehicle. Hurry."

Keeping his hand on the small of her back, he ushered her forward. Once they both were in the car, he headed out of the cemetery and onto Freemont Road, where he reached for his cell and called Officer Inman.

"I'm driving Carrie back to her father's house," Tyler quickly told the law enforcement officer. "The shot came from a dark sedan parked on the crest of the hill. See if one of your men can find tire prints or anything the shooter might have left behind. You know how to contact me. My cell's on."

Disconnecting, he glanced at Carrie. Tears filled her eyes, and although her shoulders were braced against the seat, her hands trembled and her sweet face was pulled tight with fear.

"You're okay. The person fled." Tyler rubbed his hand over hers, hoping to offer reassurance.

She dabbed at her eyes. "Did…did you see the shooter's face?"

"Negative. Just the car and rifle."

"Who knew I was at the cemetery?"

"It could have been anyone, Carrie."

"What about the chaplain?" she asked.

"I don't think Chaplain Simmons is involved, but questioning his assistant might be prudent."

Tyler called Everett at CID headquarters and filled him in on what had happened. "Send someone to Soldiers Chapel ASAP. Chaplain Simmons doesn't worry me, but he can provide information about his assistant.

See if Jason Jones remained at the chapel. If not, he could have followed us to the cemetery."

"I'm on it," Everett said before he disconnected.

"I mentioned wanting to see my father's grave to George Gates," Carrie admitted, once Tyler placed his phone on the console.

"Did you tell him you planned to stop by the cemetery today?"

She shook her head. "I merely said that I wanted to at some point before returning to DC."

But that might have been enough. The tire could have been tampered with when Carrie was visiting the lawyer. Easy enough for Gates to have an accomplice who handled the dirty work. Tyler needed to know more about the lawyer and how involved he was in the sergeant major's business.

Carrie felt as if she were having a bad dream that kept getting darker and darker. She wanted to pinch herself and wake up back in time, before George Gates's call, before she knew about her real father, before she had driven to Freemont and gotten involved with a murder investigation.

Thinking of all that had happened, she shivered.

"Cold?" Tyler reached for the heater control on the dashboard.

"Not physically, but I feel cold inside and empty, as I mentioned at the cemetery before someone tried to kill me. If not the chaplain's assistant, then who fired the shot?"

"The same person who took the lug nuts from your tire. He wants to scare you."

"He succeeded." She laughed ruefully. "But I'm grateful he isn't a better shot."

"He only fired once, Carrie, which means he probably had no intention of injuring you."

"That's doesn't reassure me. Besides, how can you be certain that he wasn't aiming at you?"

Tyler almost smiled. "All of us in law enforcement have plenty of people who would like to do us harm, but the lug nuts weren't taken from my car. You're the target."

"Which doesn't bode well for my staying in Freemont."

"Could anyone from DC have followed you here? Is the senator working on a new bill or resolution that has a lot of opposition? An angry constituent might turn his ire against you, especially if he had trouble accessing the senator."

"Doesn't it seem more than a stretch to have something the senator does in Washington impact me here in Georgia?"

"Yet it's worth considering. Have you had problems in DC?"

"A few prank phone calls. Some tweets and Facebook comments that are hateful, but nothing like this. Nothing that ended in violence."

"Do you remember the names of the people on social media?"

"It was months ago, Tyler. I really don't think they have any bearing on what's been happening here. Free speech, remember? Folks can say anything they want. This is different."

Different and deadly, she wanted to add.

Tyler lowered his speed as they neared the Freemont city limits.

"Let's stop by the lawyer's office and tell George

Gates about the missing lug nuts," Tyler suggested. "He'll deny knowledge, even if he was involved, but I'd like to see his reaction when you tell him."

Approaching the center of town, Tyler turned onto the side road and pulled into the parking lot behind the law office. They entered the building through the rear door. A woman sat at a desk in the outer office that had been vacant earlier today.

She looked up as they approached. The nameplate on her desk read Flo Beacon.

Carrie introduced herself. "I was here earlier today and need to talk to George Gates again. Is he in his office?"

Flo was middle-aged with overly made-up eyes and a heavy smear of blush that darkened her full cheeks. "You're Jeffrey Harris's daughter?"

Carrie nodded. "That's right. Did you know my father?"

"Of course. He stopped by the office a number of times, especially a few weeks before his death." Her eyes widened. "I'm sorry about your dad. My condolences."

"Thank you."

"George left the office a short while ago, Ms. York. Can you come back in the morning?"

"Probably not. I wanted to find out if anyone strange had been hanging around the office earlier today. My tires were tampered with when my car was parked in the lot out back."

"Oh my." Flo patted her chest. "I'm so sorry. We've never had any problem before. I'll let George know. Did you contact the police?"

"They know about the situation." Tyler stepped closer to the desk. "You said Sergeant Major Harris visited the law office frequently leading up to his death. Was he working on his will or estate planning?"

Flo batted her eyes. "I'm not sure, nor am I at liberty to discuss his legal dealings."

"We wouldn't want you to divulge anything you shouldn't," Carried reassured the receptionist.

"And I wouldn't," Flo said with a smile. "But it is fortunate for you that your father didn't sell the property a few weeks ago when a buyer came forward."

"For the entire property or just the house?" Carrie asked.

Flo shrugged. "I thought the entire estate was for sale."

"Do you know who made the offer?" Tyler asked.

"There were whispers around town of an outside development corporation that was interested in the land. You might want to talk to Nelson Quinn. He's a local real estate agent. Seems I heard he was involved in the offer."

Carrie glanced at Tyler, then back at Flo. "What time do you expect Mr. Gates tomorrow?"

"He's usually at his desk by nine in the morning. I'll tell him you stopped by."

Before they left through the rear door, Flo called out to them. "In case you're interested in local history, the Freemont Museum is open this afternoon. If you haven't been there yet, you might enjoy learning a bit more about our local area."

Tyler glanced back at her. "I didn't know there was a museum."

"It's newly opened. The Historical Society has been gathering objects for display. A lady named Yvonne runs the place. The sergeant major donated a few things from the Harris home."

"It's close by?" Carrie asked.

"Across the street in the old train station." Flo glanced at her watch. "It's open from two until five each afternoon. You've got about an hour until it closes for the day."

"Let's pay the museum a visit," Carrie said when they stepped outside.

Tyler's phone rang. He glanced at the screen. "It's Everett."

Lifting the cell to his ear, he said, "Did you talk to the men?" He nodded. "Right."

Carrie waited, eager to hear what the other CID agent had learned.

When Tyler disconnected, he turned to her. "The chaplain vouched for his assistant. The men had been working on a new program for married military families, along with two of the sergeants from the engineer battalion. No one had left the office since we were there last. Everett's running background checks, but he's confident they couldn't have driven to the cemetery and fired the shot."

Carrie sighed. "Which takes us back to square one."

Tyler pointed down the street. "Let's wait to tour the museum. There's a real estate office on the next block. I'd like to see if Nelson Quinn works there and find out what he knows about the development corporation."

A receptionist welcomed them to Freemont Real Estate and quickly explained that Mr. Quinn was out of town and not expected back for the next five to seven days.

Carrie couldn't help feeling frustrated at another delay. If they continued to find doors closed, the investigation would take forever.

"Do you know anything about an out-of-town corporation that was interested in buying the old antebellum home on Amish Road?" Tyler asked the receptionist.

"A beautiful house," she noted. "I'm not aware of any offer on the home, but I'll tell Mr. Quinn to call you when he returns to work."

Tyler provided his contact information before he and Carrie walked outside.

"I'm beginning to think we'll never learn who's responsible for the attacks."

"Police investigations take time, Carrie. The local cops and the CID are working on the case. Something will break."

She didn't share his enthusiasm, but she tried to appear encouraged as they crossed the street to the small depot that had been turned into a visitors center.

A sign pointed them to the Historic Freemont Museum in the rear where a number of freestanding glass cases displayed an assortment of artifacts and historic memorabilia. Yvonne, the visitors center greeter, who doubled as the museum's docent, welcomed them. When Carrie mentioned her father's donation, the woman directed them to a glass showcase near one of the side windows.

A number of antique farm implements and a few kitchen items were tagged as having been gifts from Jeffrey Harris, along with two sheets of stationery, yellowed with age. The swirled handwriting on the heavy paper was beautifully scripted but hard to read. Carrie leaned over the display case to get a clearer view.

Tyler glanced over her shoulder. His nearness stirred a sensation deep within her that Carrie couldn't explain. Not anxiety or fear but unsettling just the same. She scooted sideways to give herself space as she studied the fluid script.

"My Dearest Son," the missive began. The letter recounted local farm activities as well as the health and well-being of family members.

"Word has come to us about the Northern forces' advancement," the writer of the letter continued. "We will stand firm and be vigilant, yet all the while taking precautions and preparing lest they come this far south. As we discussed before you left, dear son, your mother and I have secured our family treasures from enemy hands and have placed them where they cannot be pillaged or found. I have left a map to the whereabouts of our precious items and worldly wealth in my desk, which I pray to God you will find and not the Northerners. Even should they surround the house and take me captive, you have my solemn word, my dear son, that I will fight to the death to protect our land and our treasure.

"Your affectionate father,

"Jefferson Harris."

"Jefferson must be a distant relative." She glanced at Tyler. "Interesting that he mentions treasure and wealth."

"Which could be anything of worth to a family in those days. Actually your father's gift of the letter and farm and kitchen implements to the museum was very generous."

Tyler's comment gave her pause. She glanced at the number of objects in the Harris collection. "You're right. My father's gift was generous."

Together she and Tyler viewed the other items on display that chronicled the change in the area from a land of cotton fields to small farms that now dotted the countryside. Old photos showed Fort Rickman's beginning days as a training camp for soldiers heading to Europe in the 1940s. A series of photos and graphs chronicled the recent growth to the area owing to the fort's expansion, along with short write-ups about the friendly partnership between the military and civilian communities. A newer section of the small but informative museum mentioned the arrival of the Amish families and the positive role they played in the development of the outlying areas.

When Yvonne politely reminded them that the museum would soon close for the night, Carrie and Tyler said their farewells and hurried outside. Eyeing the end-of-the-day traffic flow, Carrie saw something that made her heart lurch. A military guy in uniform pulled out of the law firm parking lot just as she and Tyler were ready to cross the street.

She tapped Tyler's arms. "Isn't that the chaplain's assistant?"

Tyler followed her gaze and nodded. "You're right. I wonder what Jason Jones is doing in town."

"Making an appointment with George Gates?"

"Maybe, but why would a soldier need a civilian lawyer when the military provides JAG services on post? The timing has me concerned. He must have left Soldiers Chapel soon after Everett's visit."

They crossed the street, and Tyler pointed to the law office. "Let's pay Flo Beacon another visit and see what she can tell us about Jason."

Carrie reached for the door and found it locked. The hours of operations on the wall read Mon–Fri, 9 AM–5 PM.

"We're not making progress," she said with a sigh.

"Not yet, but something will break soon. I'm sure of it."

Once they settled into his car, Tyler called post. Everett's phone went to voice mail, and Tyler left a message about seeing the chaplain's assistant.

"Jason Jones needs more scrutiny," Tyler warned. "Let me know if anything surfaces from your background checks."

Disconnecting, he glanced at Carrie. "If the soldier is involved, Everett should be able to pick up the trail."

"At least we know he didn't fire the shot at the cemetery."

Tyler nodded. "But I'm still concerned about his connection with George Gates."

Carrie was concerned, as well. What was happening in Freemont, and why did it involve her?

Traffic was heavy as Tyler drove through Freemont, but it eased once they turned onto the country road that led to the Amish community. As they passed the spot of Carrie's accident, she turned to stare at the ditch.

"Have you heard from the mechanic?" Tyler asked.

"Not yet. Maybe he's having trouble finding a tire that matches the other three."

"You might want to call him."

"I'll do that in the morning."

The rolling hills and fertile fields were such a stark contrast from the hustle and bustle of small-town Freemont they had just left. Transferring back to the States after three years overseas, Tyler had yearned for the peace and calm he had grown to enjoy in rural Germany. He'd been drawn to the Amish community when he learned of a house for rent. Now the serenity of the area had been disrupted with the murder. Maybe he had picked the wrong location.

Turning onto Amish Road, he studied the farmhouses that dotted the area. Wash hung on clotheslines and blew in the breeze. A buggy passed them on the opposite side of the road. The *clip-clop* of the horse's hooves on the pavement served as a not-so-subtle reminder of the differences between the *plain* and *English* ways of life. The bearded man holding the reins raised his hand in greeting as the buggy passed.

Had Carrie's father found respite in the Amish community with the rolling hills and bucolic farms? Or had he taken up residence in the old homestead for another reason?

Approaching the Harris home, Tyler turned into the driveway and pulled the car to a stop at the side of the house. A man appeared, seemingly from thin air. He was tall with broad shoulders, a thick beard and a black hat.

Alarmed by his presence and worried about Carrie's safety, Tyler hopped from the car. "May I help you?"

"I am Simon Plank. My son said you questioned his care of the chickens."

Instantly relieved, Tyler stretched out his hand. "You're Eli's father?"

"Yah." The man accepted the handshake.

Carrie stepped out of the car and moved closer. "I am grateful for your son's help, Mr. Plank. Special Agent Zimmerman was concerned about finding a stranger on the property this morning. You've probably heard about the soldier who died here last night."

Simon nodded. "I learned of this today. My son had nothing to do with the dead soldier or any of them."

"By any of them, do you mean soldiers from Fort Rickman?" Tyler asked.

"Not from the fort, but from someplace nearby. They try to talk our young boys into doing things that God forbids."

Tyler looked at Carrie. "What type of things, sir?"

"Playing cards and movies that are not suitable for anyone to watch, especially for the young."

"Sir, can you give me the names of the people who have approached the boys?"

"I do not have names. I have only heard about what has happened. I do not want this to happen to my boy."

"I'm in complete agreement. If Eli hears of anyone upsetting the youth in this community, please tell me. I'll personally find the soldiers involved and talk to them and have their superiors counsel them, if necessary."

"What about the care of the chickens?" Simon asked. "Eli helped Isaac Lapp as a favor while they were gone."

Glancing at Carrie, he added, "My son said you wanted to pay him to do the job."

"That's right. As you probably know, my father died a little less than two weeks ago. I could use Eli's help, and I will pay him for his work."

"The job is still available?"

"Yes, I'd enjoy having his help," Carrie said.

"*Gut*. Eli will save the money. He is young and dreams with his eyes open."

Tyler smiled. "Most kids do, but I don't think you have to worry about Eli."

"A father always wants his child to follow God's way. That is my desire." He nodded to Carrie. "I will tell him he can accept the job."

After a nod of farewell, the Amish farmer crossed the road and walked toward his house. Simon's words played through Tyler's mind. *"A father wants his son to follow God's way."*

Tyler's own father would have said the same thing. He had been strict, almost to an extreme, but also committed to the Lord. His dad had expected Tyler to embrace the beliefs he held dear, yet his tragic death had sent Tyler's world into chaos. How could a boy continue to believe in a God Who had allowed such darkness into his young life? To Tyler's way of thinking, God had abandoned him when his father died.

Or had Tyler been the one to close his heart to the Lord?

"Are the Amish naive about their faith, or do they have it right?" Tyler stared into the distance and watched as Simon entered his farmhouse.

Carrie sighed. "I'm not sure."

Hearing the fatigue in her voice, he touched her arms. "I know you're tired. Go inside. Lock the doors and windows. I'll stay outside and keep watch for a while."

She shook her head. "I appreciate your thoughtfulness, but that's not necessary. As you mentioned at the cemetery, the shooter tried to scare me instead of doing me harm. Go home, Tyler. Get some rest. I'll call you if I hear anything or become fearful."

"I can drive you to the garage tomorrow if your car is ready. Or if you want to talk to Gates."

"Aren't you going to post?"

"At some point, but I can also work from home." He didn't mention that he'd been tasked to ensure her safety and to find out if she had additional information about the case.

When she unlocked the door, Bailey bounded outside and barked with enthusiasm.

"You've been cooped up for too long," Carrie laughed. "Sorry, boy."

His tail wagged as he paused for her to rub his neck, then scurried to greet Tyler.

"Hey there, Bailey. What have you been up to?"

The dog barked playfully. He scampered around the yard before bounding across the road.

Carrie called to him, but Bailey ignored her. Instead he raced to where Eli walked along the road, coming back to the Harris home.

"Looks like your new hired hand is ready to get started on his job," Tyler said with a smile.

"With Bailey's help."

The dog and teenager crossed the road and approached where Tyler and Carrie stood. Eli nodded in greeting. "My *Datt* said you still want me to care for the chickens."

"Yes, thank you, Eli. If Bailey gets underfoot I can call him inside."

The boy scratched Bailey's ears. "He likes to help, and the chickens do not worry about him when he is outside the fence."

The boy and dog walked toward the barn to get the feed. Carrie turned as if ready to go inside.

Much as Tyler didn't want to leave her, he said goodbye and climbed into his SUV for the short drive home. He pulled into the driveway of his house and killed the engine. As he exited the car, he glanced at Eli and Bailey sauntering toward the chicken coop, relieved the day would end better than it had begun.

Once at his door, Tyler wiped his feet on the mat. Before he turned the key, he heard Eli running back to the Harris house.

Even at this distance, Tyler could tell something was wrong. Bailey followed close behind the boy with his head down and tail between his legs.

Tyler ran across the green space between the two

homes. Carrie stepped onto the porch, her face drawn as she watched the boy run toward her.

"Chickens," Eli called. "Ten of them. Blood. Feathers. Their necks have been broken. They are dead."

Chapter Seven

Tyler and Officer Inman inspected the chicken coop while Eli sat on the front porch with Bailey. Carrie fixed the teenager a glass of lemonade and brought cookies for him to eat, insisting that he stay close until Tyler and the police officer finished checking the damage.

Glancing at the police car in her driveway, she was glad Inman hadn't sounded his siren or flashed his lights. She didn't want the memory of last night to return. Had it only been twenty-four hours since she arrived in Freemont?

So much had happened and none of it good.

"Have another cookie," she encouraged Eli.

"I dropped the feed bucket. It spilled. I should not be so wasteful."

"That's not a concern, Eli. I can get more feed. I'm more worried about you. I know seeing the chickens upset you."

"Why would someone do that to innocent animals?"

"I don't know," she answered truthfully.

"My *Datt* said someone was killed here last night."

She nodded. "A soldier who lived in a trailer in the woods. Did you know him?"

Eli's eyes widened. "A friend of mine saw two soldiers arguing on the hill. He stayed back so they would not see him. He said the soldiers were angry, and he feared for his own safety."

"When was that?"

The boy shrugged. "Maybe two weeks ago."

"Who's your friend?" she pressed.

"I should not say things that he told me."

"The police need to know. The arguing soldiers could have been involved with the soldier's death last night. You wouldn't be wrong to share your friend's name."

The boy thought for a long moment, then shook his head again. "I cannot."

"Does your friend live near here?"

"Not far."

"Had he seen the soldiers before?"

"Not my friend, but I have heard other boys talk about the soldiers."

Tyler and Officer Inman approached the porch.

Carrie stood. "Did you find anything that might point to who did it?"

"I'm afraid not," Inman said with a discouraged shake of his head. "The wire on the side of the coop was cut. More than likely, the person knew you weren't home since he acted in daylight."

The officer glanced at the neighbor's house. "They must have known the Lapps were gone too."

Carrie shared what Eli had told her.

Tyler glanced down at the teenager. "If you won't tell us your friend's name, Eli, then encourage him to come forward. The information could help us find some bad people who have hurt others. Do you understand?"

The boy bit his lip and nodded.

"Go home, Eli, before your father gets worried about you," Officer Inman said. "But if you think of anything else, tell Ms. York or Special Agent Zimmerman. They'll pass the information on to me."

Eli downed the lemonade and looked at the plate of cookies.

"I'll get a plastic bag, and you can take the rest of the cookies home," Carrie suggested.

"That is too much. May I have one more?"

"Of course. And come back anytime, Eli."

"I will clean the coop before I go."

Tyler held up his hand to stop the boy. "I'll take care of the cleanup. You can come back tomorrow and feed and water the chickens that weren't hurt."

"I will." He took a cookie.

"Take another one," Carrie encouraged.

He nodded his thanks, took the second cookie and hurried home.

Tyler turned to the police officer. "We need to find this guy."

"He seems to be everywhere."

"As if he knows my schedule." Carrie shivered and wrapped her arms around her waist. "Could my phone be telling him where to find me?"

"Might be smart to turn off your cell when you're not using it," Inman suggested. "You can't be sure about this person..." He hesitated. "Or persons. They could be making good guesses. You said the soldier in the chaplain's office heard that you planned to stop at the cemetery. Then you saw him at George Gate's office?"

"After we visited the museum. The lawyer's receptionist mentioned that my father had donated items I wanted to see."

"Hate to tell you, but I haven't had a chance to stop by the museum. It's only been open a short time. One of the ladies in town did most of the work on getting the project off the ground. What did you find?"

"Some old farm and kitchen tools and a letter that talked about family treasure."

Inman nodded knowingly. "Folks have been spreading rumors about treasure since I was a kid. A Southerner's worst nightmare was having the Union soldiers pillage his farm and home. Hiding valuables was universally done south of the Mason-Dixon Line." He scratched his chin. "Thing is, we don't know what was hidden. Everyone dreams big. Talk is there were gold coins, but that's probably not the case."

"Have you uncovered anything new on Corporal Fellows's death?" Tyler stated the question everyone wanted answered.

Inman sighed. "I'm afraid not. His trailer was clean. The only thing we found were some shrubs that needed to be planted around his trailer."

Carrie gazed at the farmland that paralleled the road and stretched all around her father's property. Her property. She failed to think of it as such.

"I'm heading back to headquarters," Officer Inman said. "Keep your eyes open. No telling what this guy or group of men might try next, so be cautious." He pointed to Tyler. "You've got this guy next door. Don't hesitate to call him."

Once the officer had left, Tyler touched her arm. "I'll hang around outside for a while."

"I was thinking about fixing something for dinner. Maybe burgers and a salad. I've got more than enough for you to join me, if you don't already have plans."

He smiled. "Burgers sound great. I saw a grill behind the house, if you want some help."

"Perfect. Thanks." She opened the door and motioned him to follow her inside. Opening her purse, she drew out her phone and placed it on the counter.

"Is your GPS turned off?" Tyler asked.

"I can't remember if I ever turned it on."

Tyler stepped closer. He picked up the cell and handed it back to her. "The GPS would pinpoint your location whenever you post on social media. Check your settings. You should be able to find it."

She sifted through a number of screens. "Here it is. No, it's off."

"That's good. You might want to turn the cell off when you're not using it, as Officer Inman mentioned, just as another precaution."

"I'll do that after dinner. I'm waiting for a phone call from my office."

"Have you had any time to work on the senator's speech?" he asked, following her into the kitchen.

"Not yet. I'd hoped to get some guidance from him first."

"Who's he speaking to?"

"A veteran's group."

"Then he probably wants his antimilitary rhetoric toned down a bit."

"He's not antimilitary, Tyler. It's more about spending and the defense budget."

"You can't have a well-trained military without supplies and technology and battle-fighting capabilities,

Carrie. The senator likes to pretend he stands with the military, when he undermines them by cutting their funding."

"The budget has grown far too large."

"I agree, but look at social spending within the US. The national defense budget pales in comparison."

"Maybe we should change the subject," she finally said, pulling a package of ground chuck from the refrigerator. "Or agree to disagree."

"Stay away from politics and religion, right?"

"That might be wise."

"While you make the burgers, I'll bring the grill around to the kitchen door."

Tyler stepped outside and then glanced back to her. "First, I'd better bury the chickens and get the coop cleaned out."

"I feel indebted."

"Don't. One of the foster homes I lived in was in the country. I know my way around a barnyard."

"Thank you, Tyler." She watched him walk away, heading for the chicken coop and a job she didn't know if she could have handled. Tyler helped her in so many ways, but then, she was an assignment to him. He needed to stay close and ensure that she didn't get hurt. At least, that was what he had probably been told. For a moment, she wished their relationship could be something more.

Grabbing another hunk of ground beef, she forced herself to think of other things rather than the handsome special agent who was off-limits. Too soon, she'd be driving back to DC and her job. She didn't have time to get involved with someone in Georgia, especially a special agent who was all business. Bottom line, she needed to be strong and keep up her guard, especially when Tyler was around.

* * *

Tyler walked away from Carrie before he could say something that he'd later regret, something about how she looked at home in the kitchen and how having dinner with her this evening sounded special.

Carrie was a city girl. She had undoubtedly worked hard to land the position with Senator Kingsley, even if Tyler didn't espouse the politician's beliefs. Once she decided what to do with her father's estate, she'd head back to the hustle and bustle of Washington and leave her antebellum roots behind.

Finding a shovel in the barn and a small cardboard box, he placed the remains in the box and buried it in the wooded area. He fed the remaining chickens, ran fresh water into their trough and repaired the fence to keep them safe from animal predators. If only he could keep Carrie safe from the two-legged kind who kept attacking her.

Once finished, he tapped on her kitchen door. His chest hitched when she peered outside, looking flushed.

"I'll shower and return shortly," he said, taking a step back to distance himself from her alluring charm. "Is there anything you still need?"

"Just some charcoal, if you have extra."

"I've got a full bag from the last time I stopped in the commissary."

After a quick shower, Tyler returned wearing khaki trousers and a button-down-collar shirt and a pullover fleece. He carried a ten-pound bag of Match Light charcoal and arranged the charcoal in the grill. As the fire caught, he knocked on her door.

"Thanks again for the invitation," he said when she invited him inside. She'd done something to her hair that made it curl over her shoulders and had slipped into slacks and a colorful long-sleeve blouse.

"The burgers are ready for the grill whenever the fire's hot."

He laughed when he saw the plate piled high. "Looks like enough to feed an army."

She smiled. "Did I overdo?"

"I'll eat two."

"We'll have leftovers."

Was that another invitation?

Once the charcoal was hot, Tyler grabbed the plate and headed out the door. Bailey followed on his heels but quickly bounded toward the Amish house next door.

Eight-year-old Joseph Lapp stood in his front yard and fell to his knees as the dog slid into his warm embrace.

"I missed you." The boy dropped his head to Bailey's neck and scratched his back.

"Joseph, you must help your mother," Isaac said as he walked toward Tyler.

The boy waved goodbye and hurried back to the house.

"Welcome home." Tyler stretched out his hand. "How was your trip?"

The farmer looked tan and relaxed. "*Gut*. But I have twice the work to do now."

Tyler chuckled. "I know the feeling." He pointed to the coop in the backyard. "Eli Plank has been feeding the chickens. Thanks for arranging for his help."

Isaac smiled. "Eli is a fine boy and a hard worker." Carrie stepped from the house and approached, smiling. "You must be Isaac Lapp." She introduced herself and shook hands with the tall Amish man. "You were visiting family?"

"We went to Florida. Some of my wife's family met us there."

"What part of Florida?"

"Pinecraft. It is an area that adjoins the city of Sarasota."

"On the Gulf Coast," Carrie said. "I usually go to Daytona or Cocoa Beach on the Atlantic side."

Ruth came from the house. Isaac motioned her forward and introduced her to Carrie. "Our son, Joseph." He pointed to the young boy standing near his mother. Bailey took a tennis ball to the boy, who threw it into the backyard.

Carrie laughed. "It seems that Bailey's missed you."

"Joseph has missed the dog even more," Ruth said with a knowing nod. "After your father was gone, the house was dark and lonely. We are sorry for what happened, but we are glad to see the house is open again."

"You've been traveling all day?"

"On a charter bus." Ruth gazed at the countryside and inhaled deeply. "The fresh air of home is good."

"It's dinnertime. I'm sure you're hungry. I made too many burgers, but it looks like the number is perfect if you join us?"

Ruth looked at her husband. "We were going to have some cheese and bread, Isaac. The meat would be nice after the trip."

He nodded to Carrie. "You are generous. *Denki*, but we have work to do. The bread and cheese will satisfy us till morning."

"The meat will take about thirty minutes to grill," Carrie insisted. "We can bring the burgers to you when they're done. If you don't have time to eat with us, at least you could share the food so it doesn't go to waste."

Ruth watched for her husband's reaction. He hesitated

for a long moment and then nodded. "*Yah, Gott* would not want us to be wasteful."

"Thank you for your generosity," Ruth said as she turned to follow her husband back to their house. "Joseph, you may play with Bailey until dinner is ready."

After they had taken the extra burgers to the Lapps and had dinner themselves, Carrie and Tyler stepped onto the front porch. "The stillness is comforting," she said as her gaze took in the surrounding farmland.

Turning, Tyler glanced at the old freestanding kitchen hugging the main house as well as the barn and the chicken coop. Even the field behind the house where he'd viewed Corporal Fellows's body seemed peaceful tonight. Was he being lulled into believing everything would be all right?

"It's late, Carrie. You need to get some sleep. Thanks again for inviting me to join you for dinner."

She smiled. "We'll do it again."

"Good." He hesitated a long moment and looked down into her pretty blue eyes, the color of the sky on a summer's day. A breeze stirred her hair, and the light scent of gardenias wafted past him. As much as he wanted to touch her cheek and feel the smoothness of her skin, he kept his hands at his sides and willed himself to step away.

"I'll see you tomorrow." A heaviness settled in his heart. What was wrong with him? He was thinking foolish thoughts that could ruin their somewhat strained relationship. There was no room for romance when a killer was on the loose.

He walked back to his house, thinking of the openness of her expression and how much he had wanted to draw her into his arms.

Chapter Eight

Carrie sat on the edge of the bed, exhausted. Before turning out the light, she checked Tyler's number on her phone, relieved that she could call him if she needed help.

Bailey whined and pranced around the room. She beckoned him closer and patted his head. "Is something wrong?"

Glancing out the window, she saw the chicken coop, the barn and the old kitchen house. The moon peered through the cloud cover and cast its glow over the field where the soldier's body had been found.

The memory of what she had seen played through her mind. Needing to push away the too-graphic thoughts, she headed for the bathroom and drew water into a glass, then drank it down. Padding into the second guest room, she eased back the curtain and peered out the other side of the house, seeing Tyler's ranch next door. A light glowed in one of the windows. Was he working late? Or staying awake to protect her?

She dropped the curtain back in place and returned to her bed. Bailey settled on the floor nearby. Eventually, Carrie drifted into a fitful sleep.

Again the memory of finding the body returned, only this time she raced after Bailey toward the mound of a digital-patterned uniform. Circling the victim, she looked down and screamed. The soldier wasn't the man she'd found but Tyler.

Her eyes jerked open. She gasped for air. Looking around the room, she tried to get her bearings.

Sitting up, she wiped her hand over her eyes and shook her head to detach herself from the horrific dream. Dropping to her feet, she inhaled.

A chill tangled along her spine.

Smoke.

Bailey?

Standing, she glanced out the window.

Terror gripped her heart.

Fire!

The kitchen house was engulfed in flames.

Grabbing her phone, she screamed for Bailey, slipped on her robe and ran to the stairs. Taking them two at a time, she stumbled down the stairs, almost falling. Bailey stood at the door, barking.

She hit the speed dial for Tyler. The call went to voice mail. Where was he?

She disconnected, her fingers stiff, unyielding. The smoke drifted into the house. She coughed. Hit his number again.

"Please," she moaned. "I need help.

The phone rang in her ear. She threw open the front door and raced into the night.

Flames shot from the freestanding kitchen and licked the top rafter of the second story of the main house. The bedroom where she had slept just minutes before would quickly be engulfed in flames.

The house.

Her father's house.

"Carrie!" Tyler's voice came from the phone. "What's wrong?"

"Fire. Help me, Tyler."

"Fire, fire, fire."

Carrie screamed in the night as Tyler raced across the yard. She was too close, holding the garden hose and trying to put out the blaze with a mere trickle of water.

"Get back," he warned, pulling her away from the dancing flames.

A door slammed. Isaac ran to the bell behind his house. He tugged on the rope. The toll of the bell sounded in the night over the crackling fire.

"The men will come." Isaac grabbed buckets from his barn and pulled water from the well.

Just as he had promised, men ran from the neighboring houses and raced to the Harris home.

Tyler called 911. "Fire on Amish Road." He gave the address. "Tell the fire chief to hurry."

Eli Plank and his father, Simon, ran from across the street. They grabbed buckets and tossed water on the blaze. Other Amish men joined them and formed a bucket brigade, dousing the kitchen house.

Tyler looked at the hose. "It's been cut," he told Carrie as he turned off the spigot. "Find duct tape. In the barn."

She disappeared into the building and returned carrying a silver roll. Tyler wrapped it around the split hose. Not the best repair but good enough to feed water through.

He turned on the faucet. Water poured from the nozzle. Tyler wet down the side of the main house. A portion of the wood had blackened from the lick of flames, but the house hadn't caught.

He glanced at the bedroom above, knowing too well how close the fire had come.

More men filled the gaps, even some of the women, all helping.

Sirens screeched in the night; two fire trucks pulled into the driveway. Firemen dressed in turnout gear quickly attached their hoses and poured water onto the flames.

Once the fire was under control, Tyler glanced around for Carrie and found her standing with eyes wide. "He wanted to burn down the house," she said, her voice no more than a whisper. "He wanted to trap me inside."

She was right.

The attacks had turned violent. Someone didn't just want her to leave the area. He wanted her dead.

Carrie sat on the front steps and watched the firemen roll up their hoses and carry them back to their truck. Although her heart was heavy about the damage to the kitchen house, she was grateful for all those who had worked to save at least a portion of the structure. The huge fireplace, hearth and one of the two adjoining walls were still intact. When rebuilt, the structure would still maintain its historical significance, which was a relief, but she was most thankful that the main house had been saved.

Bailey lay at her feet and watched the firemen.

His tail wagged as Ruth Lapp approached carrying a sleepy Joseph in her arms.

Carrie smiled at the sweet boy. "Did the noise wake you?"

He nodded and wiggled free from his mother's hold. She placed the boy on the porch step and watched as he wrapped his arms around Bailey's neck.

"Joseph was awake and worried," Ruth said. "He feared Bailey had been hurt in the fire."

"They're fast friends."

"*Yah*. He would like a dog, but Isaac is not interested in having an animal in the house."

The little boy looked up with big eyes. "I told *Datt* I would take care of the dog."

"I know, Joseph, but your father knows what's best."

"I talked to *Gott*. He said a dog would be good for the family."

Ruth smiled. "You hear your own mind, Joseph."

"No, *Mamm*. I hear His voice."

Ruth turned as her husband approached.

"The fire is out, but I will watch tonight," Isaac said. "We do not want sparks to start anew."

Carrie stood. "Thank you, Isaac, and please thank our other neighbors. If it hadn't been for your help and theirs, the main house would have caught fire." She let out a ragged breath as she gazed up at the Harris home. "I can't imagine what would have happened."

"The house would have been quickly engulfed," one of the firemen chimed in as he approached. He nodded to Isaac. "Appreciate the help, Mr. Lapp. The water cooled everything down and kept the flames from spreading."

Tyler and the fire chief neared.

"Looks like it was a set fire, ma'am," the chief told Carrie. "A trail of accelerant led partially toward the house. The arsonist may have been interrupted."

"Bailey started barking, which must have scared him away. I looked outside as soon as I woke but didn't see anything at first. Then the flames caught." She glanced at Tyler. "That's when I called you."

"I'm sorry, Carrie." Tyler's face reflected the regret she heard in his voice. "I was talking to Everett and didn't realize you had phoned."

"Ruth heard Carrie's screams and woke me," Isaac interjected. "I saw no one. Only the fire."

"I'll bring the fire marshal out this way tomorrow," the chief said. "If you give me your cell number, Ms. York, I'll call you ahead of time to make sure you're home."

"That might be a problem," Carrie said. "I'm going to town in the morning to meet with my lawyer."

"Not to worry. We don't need to go inside the main house. I just wanted you to know I'd be on the property in case you came home to find two strange men prowling around your backyard."

The fire chief didn't realize the significance of his comment.

"Sir." One of the firemen hurried toward the chief. "We checked the chimney and fireplace in the old kitchen house and found a loose brick."

He glanced at Carrie. "When we tried to replace the brick, we found a small journal that looks old."

Carrie took the leather-bound book from the fireman's outstretched hand. He raised a flashlight and pointed to the page where a fragment of ribbon marked the spot.

"The book fell open as we pulled it free. A few of the guys and I couldn't help but notice the script," he told her. "You don't see writing like that these days. From the looks of the brittle pages, the journal has to be old."

Another fireman stood nearby. "Guess we were caught up in the moment, ma'am, and read a bit of the script.

The page we saw mentions buried treasure and actually tells where it's located."

Tyler looked over Carrie's shoulder and read from the journal, "…turn at the twisted oak and walk toward the row of blackberry bushes…"

Isaac rubbed his beard. "I'm not aware of a twisted oak."

Tyler nodded in agreement. "The tree's probably long gone."

Carrie turned the page. "There's more."

"You might want to check your property," one of the firemen suggested. "Most folks believe gold is buried around here."

Joseph pulled on his mother's skirt. "What if someone found the treasure, *Mamm*?"

"They would give it to Carrie, Joseph. This land is hers now."

She smiled at Ruth. "I still consider it my father's property."

Tyler's face darkened. No doubt he realized she was distancing herself from the land and the confusion that continued to haunt her. If she got rid of the property and the house, would she be able to leave the memory of her father here in Georgia when she returned to Washington?

Ruth stood and nudged her son. "I must get you home, Joseph."

The boy hugged Bailey and then placed his small hand in his mother's. *"Guten nacht,"* he said with a wave of his hand.

"Guten nacht," Carrie repeated back to him.

As she watched Joseph and his mother walk toward their house, Carrie sighed. Contrary to what she had wished the boy, the night wasn't good, because an evil person had struck again. Carrie had been saved from harm, but would there be a next time, and if so, would she escape alive?

Tyler helped the firemen load equipment onto their trucks and raised his hand in farewell as they pulled out of the driveway. Then he joined Carrie, who'd been watching from the porch.

Isaac stepped closer once the fire engines had turned onto Amish Road, heading back to their station. "I will check the kitchen house to make sure it is as the firemen said."

"Thank you, Isaac." Carrie smiled. "And again, thank you for coming to my aid."

"Neighbors help neighbors. The fire could have destroyed your house and mine. Fire is always a concern. *Gott* woke you in time."

Tyler felt the warm grasp of the farmer's friendship as they shook hands. "Thank you, neighbor."

"*Yah*, we are that."

Isaac nodded his farewell and walked toward what was left of the kitchen house.

Tyler turned to Carrie. "I'm sorry that I didn't answer your initial call for help."

"You couldn't have known."

"But I told you I'd be there for you."

"And you were, Tyler, although I'm concerned because the attacks are escalating. He wants to scare me away, yet I'm determined to stand my ground, at least until I decide what to do with the house."

"Maybe you should move to a hotel in town," Tyler suggested.

"No." She shook her head. "I'm staying here, in my

father's house. He won't strike again. At least not tonight. Plus, knowing you're next door is reassuring."

She turned toward the door. "I should go inside, although I don't think I'll be able to sleep."

He pointed to the aged journal she still held in her hand. "You could read yourself to sleep."

She smiled and raised the small leather-bound book. "Catching up on family history sounds like a good idea."

"How soon do you plan to return to DC?"

"I'm not sure. I'll know more after I talk to George Gates. What time did you want to go to town tomorrow?"

"How does nine o'clock sound?"

"Fine. I'll call the garage in the morning. The new tire should be in. If nothing else needs to be worked on, I'll be able to get my car back. Then I can travel to town on my own."

"That may not be the best idea. You need to be careful."

She nodded. "I'm all too aware of the danger."

In the distance, Isaac climbed the steps to his porch and entered his house. A soft glow of an oil lamp lit the downstairs window, only to be extinguished a few minutes later.

"I'll walk around the house a few times during the night to check on things, Carrie, so don't worry if you hear someone outside. I want to ensure that the fire remains out and that no one tries to pull something like that again."

"How will I know it's you and not someone out to do me harm?"

"Call my cell, if you're worried. I'll answer."

"On the first ring?"

He raised his right hand to his chest. "Cross my heart."

From the look that washed over her face, he knew his words had touched a place deep inside her.

"My mother used to say that," Carrie shared, her voice low and melancholy. "The funny thing is that she was talking about how much she loved me and how much she believed that my father would have loved me if he had been alive."

She glanced down. "Only she wasn't telling me the truth, Tyler. She was telling me lies."

"From what I've seen, your father did love you. He kept the house and property so he could pass it on to his only child. That's love. Your mother may have had problems of her own, and your childhood wasn't what you would have wished it to be, but she loved you. Your father—in his own way—did, as well."

"I'm not sure." Carrie clutched the leather journal to her chest. "Maybe I'll find something in the pages of this old journal that rings true. At least now I belong to a family. That's something I never had before."

"You have ancestors and a history."

"I hope it's a good history, of good people of whom I can be proud."

"Your dad was a good man, Carrie. You can be proud of him."

"I hope you're right, Tyler." She hesitated for a long moment and stared into his eyes.

He saw vulnerability and a woman who wanted to find her place in the history of this family. First she had to open her heart to her father. From everything that Tyler had heard, the sergeant major was a dedicated soldier and an honorable man, but he'd made a mistake in not contacting his daughter. If only Carrie could find the reason the sergeant major had stayed out of her life. If she knew why, she might be able to see beyond her pain and forgive her father.

Then he thought of her boss, the senator, and realized some mistakes were too big to be forgiven.

After Carrie went inside, Tyler circled the house and checked the old kitchen outbuilding, all too aware of the nearness of the main house and the danger that could have trapped Carrie inside. Looking up, he saw light glowing in the bedroom window directly above the outbuilding. The black charred marks on the main structure were a chilling reminder of what had happened tonight.

Flicking his gaze to the surrounding woods, he listened and watched for anything more that could bring her harm. The investigation was important, but Carrie's safety was his top priority. Tyler had to ensure that no harm came to her. He couldn't let down his guard, not when her life depended on him.

Chapter Nine

Although tired, Carrie crawled into bed determined to read the journal the firemen had found. Her eyes quickly grew heavy as she held the book and tried to decipher the writing. The script, although beautiful, was difficult to read, with its fluid swirls and flowering prose that people used in days long past.

The diary belonged to a young woman who longed for her husband's return from war. She had children at home, Anna and Benjamin, and an older son fighting alongside his father.

Carrie woke the next morning with the book still in her hands. She placed it on the nightstand, planning to read more after she returned from town. Quickly she dressed and headed to the kitchen for coffee.

Her cell chirped. Checking the caller ID, she saw her office number and answered the call. The senator's senior adviser's deep voice clipped a curt greeting. "We haven't heard from you, Carrie. I thought you were returning within forty-eight hours."

"It's taking me a bit longer to decide what to do with the property, Art."

"Sell. You don't want to be tied to some backroads area of Georgia."

"It's beautiful here."

"Maybe, but don't get sidelined by pretty countryside. You're a city girl with a career you need to grow. The senator is waiting for that speech."

"I told you I'd have it ready in the next day or two. Senator Kingsley usually doesn't look at his speeches until a few days before each event."

"This one is important. He wants more emphasis on cutting the military budget."

"I doubt that's a good idea at this time with the threats to national security coming out of the Middle East."

"Are you doubting the senator?"

She bristled. "Of course not. I'm just wondering if you have the right take on what he said."

"I heard him, Carrie, and I know what he wants, but if you insist on talking to him—"

"That might be a good idea."

Art sighed. "You know his busy schedule. He doesn't have time for you today."

"Then why did you mention it?" Frustrated, she paused for a moment before asking, "Are you sure he can't squeeze in a phone call?"

"I'm sure."

"I'll write the speech. Then maybe he'll have time to talk to me."

Hot tears burned her eyes as she disconnected. Art Adams wasn't speaking for Senator Kingsley, she felt sure. The senator was usually concerned about her well-being. She had expected him to call and find out personally how she was doing, especially if the staff had told him about the murder on her father's property.

They must not have informed him.

Unwilling to accept what Art said, she dialed the senator's private number and left a voice mail. "Senator Kingsley, I wanted you to know that things are going a little badly here in Georgia. I told you I didn't know my father, and now I'm trying to sort through what is true and what is not. You can understand the difficulty. I'm working on the speech, but I'd like to clarify a few points. Art said you wanted to emphasize the need for additional budget cuts for the military, but I'm not sure if that's what you really want or if that's Art's interpretation. Let me know, sir. I'd like to hear it from you."

She hung up feeling better and hurried into the kitchen. Hopefully she hadn't seemed needy, which was something she never wanted to be. She'd grown up with a mother who needed so much more than Carrie had been able to provide—support and love and affirmation. Whatever she did to help her mother, it had never been enough.

The sense of unworthiness she had felt as a child still resonated in her spirit, especially at times like this when she was enmeshed in the memories.

Determined to be strong, Carrie pulled bread from the wrapper and stuck it in the toaster, appreciating the high-end appliances in the newly remodeled kitchen. Had her father prepared the house for her? Or had he been getting it ready to sell as Gates had mentioned?

She put her head in her hands. If only she knew what to do and what would be the best for her own future and for this house.

In a strange way, she was beginning to see the man who had lived here. His books, his Bible, the devotionals and plaques with inspirational sayings that decorated his house. She had hoped to find a picture of herself. If only.

They'd never met, or at least she didn't think they had ever met. How could he have turned his back so completely on his own child when he had no one else? Especially since he seemed to have a relationship with the Lord. Could a godly man disavow his daughter?

He left you his estate.

The inner voice chastised her, yet she didn't want her father's house or his land. She wanted to know him, to have a relationship with a real person and not the memory, which wasn't even that. How could she have a memory when she didn't know him?

The toaster buzzed, but when the slice of bread popped up, the outside was too dark.

Was that her father's preference? She opened the cabinet seeing the rich roast coffee. No sugar. No fancy creamers. No tea or hot cocoa.

His refrigerator held hot sauce and pickles and horseradish mustard and a half-empty jar of yellow peppers.

Spicy food. Black coffee. No frills. No fuss. Was that her father?

She threw the toast in the trash and poured coffee into a mug, adding a heavy dollop of half-and-half she'd bought at the grocery and a rounded teaspoon of sugar. Evidently she hadn't followed her father's taste in coffee. Lifting the mug to her lips, she inhaled the rich aromas and sipped the hearty brew.

Mmm. Good. Not the mild roast she was used to. Maybe her father could teach her a thing or two after all.

She almost smiled.

Glancing out the window, she raked her fingers through her hair and straightened her blouse when Tyler stepped outside and glanced her way. Surely he couldn't see her through the window. She took a step back and peered ever so carefully over her mug, watching as he stretched.

Dressed in athletic shorts and an army T-shirt, he looked muscular and tall, and a curl of interest twisted through her insides that was mildly disconcerting. She didn't need to notice anything of interest in the special agent. He was investigating the soldier's death and was a neighbor. Nothing more, she told herself as she tried to glance away.

Her eyes returned to watch Tyler jog out of his driveway and along Amish Road. In the distance, she spied the Plank Farm. A man wearing a dark hat waved as Tyler passed.

Weren't the Amish usually standoffish? Perhaps the recent danger had brought them all together. Either that or they'd had—as Tyler had mentioned yesterday—a good relationship with her father that carried over.

She pulled a second slice of bread from the wrapper, stuck it in the toaster and turned down the timer. The result was light brown toast, the way she liked it.

Opening the fridge, she pulled out a stick of butter and strawberry jelly that appeared to be homemade. The seal on the top of the jar was from the Amish Craft Shoppe. She'd have to ask Ruth about the store, imagining the fresh vegetables and baked goods she might find there.

Tyler returned soon after she had eaten the toast and finished her coffee. She stuck the mug and plate in the dishwasher and again paused to watch him stretch to cool down.

Even from this distance she could see the ruddy hue to his flushed skin and his tussled hair. In spite of his workout gear, he looked exceedingly attractive.

Maybe there was a less formal, less by-the-book side

of him. If only he would let down some of his guard at times so she could feel more at ease around him.

After wiping the counter clean, she ran upstairs to put on makeup and comb her hair. Returning to the main floor, she let Bailey out to run and waited on the front porch until he bounded back to her.

Joseph tumbled out of his house as if he'd been waiting for the dog. The two met in the grassy area between the homes.

"I'm going into town for a bit, Joseph. If you want to play ball with Bailey, I know he'd enjoy the exercise before he has to go back inside."

She tossed the boy the ball, and the two frolicked in the yard. Bailey's barks mixed with Joseph's laugher and brought a sense of well-being to her heart.

If only coming to Freemont could have been different.

The sound of footsteps caused her to turn. Tyler walked toward her, dressed in a crisp cotton shirt and navy slacks. The blue windbreaker had CID on the left breast, reminding her that there was an ongoing investigation.

"Looks like Bailey's getting lots of good exercise," he said with a smile as he watched Joseph and the dog.

"Joseph said he wants a dog, and God told him he'd get one, but evidently Isaac isn't interested."

Tyler laughed. "I have a feeling Joseph might be able to change his father's mind."

"I…I don't know what I'll do with Bailey when I sell the property."

Tyler glanced at her. "So you're putting the house on the market?"

She shook her head. "I don't know."

"You've got a career to go back to, Carrie. I'm sure you worked hard to get where you are, and while I don't have anything good to say about the man you work for, landing a speechwriting position in DC is to be admired."

"I don't understand your feelings about the senator. You've just heard things through the news. You don't know him. If you'd met him, you'd have a different opinion."

"No, Carrie." Tyler shook his head. "Nothing can change my mind about Drake Kingsley."

She bristled, unable to understand such a one-sided viewpoint. That was Tyler's problem—he formed opinions that didn't necessarily bear out. If only he could soften a bit and see the way things really were.

"I'll get my coat." Turning back to the house, she realized she didn't see clearly either. No matter what people said about her father, she couldn't believe he was a good man.

Maybe she and Tyler had that in common. Two controlling people who held on to their beliefs too tightly.

"Bailey, it's time to come inside."

The dog wagged his tail and waited as Joseph patted his ears; then, holding the tennis ball in his mouth, Bailey raced into the house.

"I won't be gone long," she told the dog as she grabbed her purse and coat. Stepping outside, she closed and locked the door behind her.

Another day to learn more about her father. Another day with Tyler Zimmerman, a man who focused on facts and evidence instead of people.

She didn't belong here. She belonged back in Washington, DC.

Or did she?

* * *

Tyler remained quiet as he drove Carrie into town. He didn't want to talk about the senator and the man who had changed his past and not for the better.

She wouldn't understand. Carrie was focused on the senator as a boss and maybe an older man who stood in a father's place. She was mistaken. Royally wrong, but she needed to learn the truth about him by herself.

Hopefully she wouldn't be hurt from her mistaken allegiance to someone who wasn't worth her praise or adulation. If only she could have seen the man Kingsley had been years earlier.

The memory of what had happened that fateful night still burned within Tyler.

"Did you want to go to the lawyer's office first?" he asked, needing to focus on the present instead of the past.

She nodded. "If you don't mind. I want to talk to George about my father's land. He said there was a buyer and that my father was interested in selling."

"Didn't his receptionist say that your father had changed his mind?"

"She could have been confused, Tyler."

"Maybe, but I wonder if Gates was seeing things through his own financial gain."

"Meaning what?" Carrie asked.

"Meaning he wanted to negotiate the sale and earn a nice paycheck. He may be thinking of his own pocketbook instead of what would be the best for you and the property."

"Then I'll ask for the buyer's name and contact the person myself," she insisted.

"Flo mentioned a corporation that was interested in the land, Carrie. When a big buyer is on the horizon, everyone wants to get into the action. That could be a problem."

She drew her hand protectively to her neck. "Surely you don't think someone in the corporation is attacking me."

"More likely it's a local person who sees himself as a middleman and wants you out of the picture."

"Are you accusing George Gates?"

"I'm not accusing anyone, but I'm being truthful, Carrie. Someone's out to do you harm."

"Which I'm well aware of," she said. "It's just that I'm not sure who's on my side."

"I'm on your side, and I'm here because I'm concerned about your safety."

"That's not totally true, Tyler. You're here because you were assigned to watch me as part of the investigation."

"I'm assigned to ensure that you aren't harmed." He saw a flash of confusion in her pretty eyes. "I won't let anything happen to you, Carrie."

She pulled in a ragged breath and shook her head. "I'm sorry if I sound antagonistic, but I'm worried and confused, and I don't know who I can trust."

"You can trust me, Carrie."

She stared at him for a long moment. "I...I hope I can."

He gripped the steering wheel tightly, frustrated that she questioned his desire to keep her safe. If only she would open up and share more with him, but she remained closed and reserved.

He pulled into the Gates Law Firm parking lot and killed the engine. Carrie was out of the car before he could open her door.

"Did you want company when you talk to Gates?"

She shook her head. "I'll go in alone."

"You're sure?"

She nodded and headed for the back door. Tyler glanced around the lot, realizing too quickly that he didn't want to wait outside. He followed Carrie into the building and nodded to the receptionist.

Flo was equally as made-up as she had been the day prior and smiled widely as they entered.

She pointed to George Gates's office. "You can go in, Ms. York. Mr. Gates is expecting you."

Carrie glanced at Tyler over her shoulder. "This won't take long." She opened the door to the lawyer's personal office and closed it behind her.

Tyler smiled at Flo and then glanced at the people sitting in the adjoining waiting room. "Busy place."

She batted her eyes. "Mr. Gates has a lot of clients."

"There was a soldier here yesterday. Jason Jones. He works for the chaplain on post."

Flo nodded. "Jason's my nephew."

"Really?" Tyler hadn't expected the connection.

"He stops by to see me when he comes to town." She closed a manila folder on her desk before asking, "Did you visit the museum?"

Tyler nodded. "Thanks for telling us about the displays."

"You saw the items the sergeant major had donated?"

"And the other memorabilia, as well."

"What about the letter written by Jefferson Harris? The hint of buried treasure always gets folks' attention."

"I'm sure it does," Tyler agreed. "I was struck by Jefferson's love of family and home. I'd hate to see the Harris property go to someone who didn't appreciate the family history."

Tyler paused before adding, "You mentioned that a

corporation from out of town was interested in buying the land. Do you have any additional information?"

"Not about the corporation, but there's been talk that the mayor's wife wanted to turn the house into a B and B. In fact, Mrs. Gates said she wouldn't mind doing the same. The property has a lot of potential."

"I'm sure. There's enough acreage to build some houses too."

Flo lowered her voice. "A mall is what I heard."

The receptionist's comment took him by surprise. "A shopping mall?"

"But with an Amish theme. Craft shops, small restaurants, a grocery mart that sells Amish items."

"Do you know the name of the corporation?"

"No." Flo shook her head. "I don't have a name, and I've probably said too much."

Tyler held up his hand. "Nonsense. You've just been neighborly. I've enjoyed learning some of the local news."

The receptionist smiled as if pleased by his comments. "That's prime real estate if you ask me. Anyone would love to buy the land. Folks are interested in Amish areas now. A resort, a hotel or boutique shops catering to tourists would do well there."

"I doubt the Amish would be happy."

The phone rang.

"Perhaps not." She lifted the receiver.

The door to the lawyer's office opened. George Gates stood in the doorway.

Tyler moved closer. "If you've got a minute, sir, I'd like to talk to you along with Ms. York."

Gates glanced at his watch as if to make an excuse.

Ignoring the lawyer's attempt to shove him aside, Tyler looked at Carrie. "We need to discuss the buyers who are interested in your father's property."

"George mentioned a large construction company had talked to my father," Carrie explained. "He was initially interested but then declined the offer."

"Were there other offers?" Tyler looked at the lawyer.

Gates splayed his fingers. "As I told Carrie, I'm sure a number of local people would be interested in acquiring the property. The home is lovely and has been well maintained. The acreage provides a lovely setting in the midst of the Amish area. Perfect for folks who want a quiet environment to raise their families."

"Or change the home into a bed-and-breakfast," Tyler countered.

"I'm not following you," the lawyer said.

"Isn't that why the mayor's wife wants to buy the land?"

"She's expressed some interest," Gates admitted, "but I'm not sure that's what Carrie wants."

She shook her head. "I don't want a business venture to disturb the Amish way of life."

"What about a shopping center?" Tyler threw out.

Gates wrinkled his brow. "You're imagining things."

"Am I? Isn't that what some folks are interested in doing?"

"I would never agree to that," Carrie said. "Anything that would bring more traffic to the area would hurt the Amish neighbors, who have been so helpful to me."

She looked at Tyler. "I told George about the fire last night."

"Any idea," Tyler asked, "who might want to burn down the historic home? The fire chief claimed it was arson."

Gates tugged on his chin. "Have you found anything more about the soldier who was murdered? Perhaps military personnel are involved."

A stab at Tyler for sure. "The investigation is ongoing. Let me know if you hear anything from the townspeople or anyone else who is interested or disgruntled because Ms. York doesn't want to sell the property."

"But she is interested." George smiled at Carrie. "You need to inform the special agent about your plans."

Tyler was confused. He looked at Carrie. "You're planning to sell?"

She tilted her head. "At this point, I'm just gathering information."

"Someone's trying to get you to leave town, Carrie. You said yourself that if you do so, they've won. That's not what your father would want."

"Right now I'm not sure of anything involving my father. What he wants is not my concern, Tyler. I have to determine what's best for me."

"And the Amish neighbors?"

"Of course, I'll take their needs into consideration, as well."

Tyler glanced at the lawyer. "Thanks for your time." He opened the rear door and held it for Carrie, who said goodbye and then hurried to the parking lot.

"I don't know why you sound angry," she said once they had settled into Tyler's car.

"I don't like that guy. He seems to know more than he's letting on. From the way it looks, he's probably going to make a nice profit from the sale of your father's property. We'll know more once he tells you the names of all those interested."

"There's got to be more involved than just the land."

"Add buried treasure to the mix, Carrie, and you have a good motive for murder."

"Corporal Fellows or my father?"

"Maybe both."

Chapter Ten

Carrie couldn't understand Tyler's bad mood. Maybe he was upset because he hadn't been able to solve Corporal Fellows's murder.

"Have you heard anything more from the local police?" she asked.

"Not this morning. Let's stop at the garage first and check on your car. Then we can visit the police department. I'd like to talk to Phillips."

The garage wasn't far. Tyler pulled in front of the shop and killed the engine.

From the sign on the door, Earl Vogler, the mechanic on duty, was the owner, as well. The beefy man nodded as they stepped from the car. "Be with you folks in a minute."

He turned back to the attractive woman in stiletto heels, a low-cut top and a skimpy skirt with whom he had been previously talking. From the sour look on her face, she was evidently upset.

Earl shrugged his broad shoulders. "I can work on your car first thing tomorrow morning, ma'am, but not before."

She pursed her lips. "That's ridiculous."

"Actually it's because the part is still in Atlanta and won't arrive until close of business today."

"Then work late."

"Ma'am, my grandsons are playing ball tonight. I want to watch their games."

"If that's the case, I'll be forced to spread word around town that you're not a good mechanic."

He sighed with frustration. "Mrs. Gates, my garage is the best in town, but you can go to my competition, if you so choose. They won't be able to get the part any faster than I can."

She huffed. "Then I'll bring my car back in the morning. You can work on it then."

"I open at seven-thirty."

"I'll be here at nine-thirty, after my aerobics class at the gym."

"It's first come, first serve. I can't guarantee my workload by that point, ma'am. It might be afternoon before your car will be ready."

She let out a lungful of frustration. "Tomorrow morning then at seven-thirty. I may have my husband drop the car off. You know George Gates, don't you?"

"Can't say that I've met Mr. Gates."

"Of Gates Law Firm."

"I'll look forward to meeting him tomorrow."

She hurried to her car and peeled out of the parking lot, no doubt still frustrated.

The mechanic shook his head as he approached Tyler and Carrie. "Takes all kinds."

"That was George Gates's wife?" Carrie asked the man.

"You know him?"

"He was my father's lawyer."

"Gates does a good job from what I've heard, but his wife thinks she's entitled to special privileges." He sighed. "Might save me a lot of headaches if she takes her business elsewhere. I have a feeling she'll never be satisfied with the work I do."

He shook his head regretfully. "'Course you're here about your own car. I looked it over yesterday. It's good to go except for needing a new tire. My distributor is trying to find a match with your other three. Soon as the new one comes in, I'll put it on and have the car ready for you. Might be tomorrow or the day following."

Carrie looked at Tyler. "Which means I'll have to beg more rides from you."

"Not a problem." Glancing back at the mechanic, he said, "I heard Mrs. Gates runs a home design business."

The mechanic nodded. "She calls it a boutique. Real pricey stuff from what folks have told me. She takes old homes and restores them, then decorates them with the high-end furnishing from her business."

"I'm surprised she has many customers in a small town like this," Tyler said.

The mechanic smiled. "Don't let Freemont's size fool you. We're got some industry here. The fort brings in a lot of folks, as well. Military retire in the local area. Some of them start their own businesses. The moneyed folks live in the country club community. Big homes with even bigger price tags. Too pricey for my budget."

"What about the mayor and his wife? Do they live there?"

"They have a house in town, but she works in Mrs. Gates's boutique. There's talk they might start flipping homes on the side."

"Who would do their demo and reconstruction work?"

"Sorry, I don't have a clue. The wife and I moved in with her mother after we married. We've never had to buy a house." He nodded to Carrie. "I'll call you when that tire comes in."

"An interesting mix of folks," Tyler said as they returned to his car. "And they all have something to gain by acquiring your father's property."

"Now I understand why Gates encouraged me to sell. His wife wants to buy the property."

"Which means he's not providing sound advice about your father's estate. Let's stop by police headquarters and talk to Phillips. He'll be interested in what we've learned."

Tyler drove to the Freemont Police Department, hoping they had uncovered more information that could end the case and bring the guilty to justice. If only the information they'd learned at the garage would fit somehow into the mix, or at least provide clues as to who was attacking Carrie.

The CID had researched Corporal Fellows's background and found a low-key guy without much history. He had gotten in trouble with a superior once during basic training, but since then he'd kept his nose clean.

Why he had rented a trailer at the sergeant major's property was the question Tyler kept asking. Did he have anything to do with the sergeant major's so-called accidental death?

Officer Inman had taken the day off, but Phillips ushered them into his cubicle and invited them to sit down and have a cup of coffee. The brew was hearty, and both

Tyler and Carrie were eager to share what they had found about Mrs. Gates's home design business.

Phillips listened to the information and nodded when Tyler finished talking. "Mrs. Gates's business is out of my range, for sure, and anyone here in the PD, but she's attracted folks from as far away as Macon and Columbus."

"Do you find it strange that she's interested in the Harris property when her husband is handling the estate?"

Phillips took a swig of his coffee, then set the cup on his desk. "Nothing wrong with Mrs. Gates running the business or wanting to buy the property. I don't like her husband being secretive about the interested buyer, but that would eventually come to light when the property went to sale. Unless, of course, he used a corporation name, and Mrs. Gates didn't come to the signing."

Carrie sighed. "Meaning he'd keep me in the dark or tell me it was an out-of-town venture, which is evidently what my father thought."

"I'm not saying there wasn't an interested buyer from outside the area," the cop added. "But Gates certainly has a vested interest in his wife buying the property."

"Do you know about any construction team that might work for her?"

"Nelson Quinn is a local real estate agent. He's flipped a few houses on the side. I heard he sometimes works with Mrs. Gates."

"So we've got a real estate agent, a designer who stages the homes for sale and a lawyer who handles the paperwork and ensures that every *i* is dotted and *t* is crossed." Tyler ticked off the various people involved on his fingers. "Looks like Gates and his wife have a nice business going."

"Which is perfectly legal," the officer pointed out.

Carrie tilted her head. "But what if my father initially planned to sell and then changed his mind?"

"Which sounds like what happened," Tyler added.

Phillips rubbed his chin. "Again there's nothing illegal about him changing his mind."

"But," Carrie said, "what if his accidental death wasn't an accident?"

Phillips glanced at Tyler. "That puts a different slant on things."

Tyler leaned forward. "You mentioned that a teen found the sergeant major's body."

"That's right. An Amish kid." Phillips swiveled his chair to face his computer. He tapped the keyboard and pulled up a file on the monitor. "Here it is. The dispatcher got a 911 call from Matthew Schrock, age fifteen, who discovered the body in a wooded area. The boy had smelled something. Saw turkey vultures overhead and took a closer look."

"Where did he find a phone?"

"Probably the Amish Craft Shoppe. It's located at the northern corner of Amish Road. They've got a pay phone there. As you probably know, the Amish don't allow phones in their homes, but they sometimes have them in their barns to use them for business purposes. A couple of the dairy farmers sell their milk to larger dairies and communicate by cell phone. Also, they use them for emergencies."

"Anything else in the report?"

Phillips studied his computer screen. "The deceased appeared to have slipped down the hillside to his death. He had a lump on the right side of his head."

"Any sign that he'd been in a fight?"

"'Abrasions to his face and hands consistent with having fallen through the bramble' is what the report says."

"What about his clothing?"

"He was wearing a hunting vest, cargo trousers and a plaid fleece shirt. Hiking boots."

"A hunting vest? What did it contain?"

"Hmm?" Phillips pursed his lips as he read the online report. "Seven rounds of ammo in the pockets, .30-30 caliber."

"Anyone find a rifle?"

"The officer on-scene searched the surrounding area, but found nothing else. Emergency rescue retrieved the body and transported it to the morgue."

"Was an autopsy done?"

"It was. Cause of death was trauma to the head and a broken neck."

Carrie gasped. "A broken neck? Was the officer who retrieved the body convinced it was an accidental fall?"

"A good question that we need to answer." Phillips reached for his phone and tapped in a number. "See if Officer Wittier is available. Tell him I want to talk to him."

Disconnecting, he pushed back from his computer. "He's in the building. Ray's a good kid with an excellent record in law enforcement. I'm sure he was thorough in his search of the area."

Ray Wittier quickly arrived. He was tall and lean but with a softness to his features that made him look young and immature. Tyler guessed him to be midtwenties, although he could have passed for a teenager.

Phillips quickly filled him in on what they had already discussed.

"Did you give any thought to a possible homicide?" Carrie asked.

"No, ma'am. The injury to the body seemed consistent with a fall. That hill's steep. Lots of leaves. We'd been having rain, so they were slippery. Easy enough for a person, even someone used to wandering the trails in that area, to lose his footing and tumble down that hill. The autopsy revealed a broken neck."

"What about his hunting vest?" Tyler pointed to Phillips's computer. "The report said ammo was found in his pockets. Did you look for a weapon?"

"I did. I even walked to the top of the ridgeline from where he must have fallen. An area of leaves was disturbed. Looked like he slipped and tried to right himself, then lost his footing and toppled to his death."

"Did you see signs of a scuffle?"

The young cop thought for a moment. "In hindsight, that could have been the case, although I never thought of a struggle at the time."

"The Amish boy you talked to—"

"Matthew Schrock," Ray volunteered.

"What did he say?" Tyler asked.

"Only that he had been walking through the woods and smelled something that had died. He decided to investigate and saw the body."

"Did you ask him about a rifle?"

"No. But at the time, I didn't think there was any reason to ask the question."

"Did Matthew's father come with you when you retrieved the body?"

"Yes, sir, along with the teenager."

"Did the father give any indication that his boy might have held back information?"

Ray shook his head. "The Amish are hesitant to call in

the police, but we've never had a problem with prevarication." He looked at Phillips. "Wouldn't you agree, sir?"

"That's right. They may not provide as much information as we'd sometimes like, but a lack of honesty is never something we worry about." Phillips stood. "Thanks for talking to us, Ray."

Tyler pointed to Carrie. "Ms. York wants to learn as much as she can about her father's death. I'm sure you can understand her concern, seeing how Sergeant Major Harris's death was so tragic."

"I am sorry for your loss, ma'am." Ray turned to Officer Phillips. "Let me know if you need anything else, sir."

"Will do, Ray. Thanks for your help."

Tyler stood once the younger officer left the room. "We'll talk to the Amish boy. Do you have an address for him?"

Phillips checked the computer. "It just says Amish Road. Want me to call Ray back?"

Tyler held up his hand. "We'll find the kid. You've done enough already."

Carrie stood, and they both shook hands with Officer Phillips before they left the headquarters and drove back to the Amish community.

"We're going to talk to Matthew?" she asked.

"Exactly. I want to hear what he saw and compare notes. Isaac and Ruth will surely know how to locate him, but the Amish Craft Shoppe isn't far from where we intersect Amish Road. If we turn north and ride a couple miles, we'll find it. Let's stop there."

Carrie smiled. "Might be a good time to get to know the shop owner. He may have known my father. Seems everyone did. I only wish someone could provide more information about his death. I can't see how a man who had deployed numerous times to the Middle East could trip and fall down a hill to his death."

Tyler had to agree. "A lot of people have a little piece of the puzzle of his death. We need to keep searching for the various parts and then try to put them together."

"And Corporal Fellows's death?" Carrie asked. "Will that fit into the puzzle, as well?"

"We'll have to wait and see."

"I'm running out of time, Tyler."

"Because you're ready to go back to Washington?"

"Because I need to decide what to do about the land."

"Gates can't force you to make a decision if you're not ready," Tyler insisted.

"But Senator Kingsley needs me back in DC."

"You don't have to go, Carrie."

"I do, if I want to keep my job."

This was only an investigation, Tyler realized. As much as he wanted Carrie to stay on the property, she needed to return to her job, working for a man who had caused so much pain in Tyler's life. He had hoped Carrie would see the senator for who he truly was, but she saw what she wanted to see.

Unfortunately the senator was a sham. Her mother had created a fictional tale about her father, and Carrie had created her own fictional impression of the senator.

Both were wrong.

But he wouldn't tell Carrie about her mistake. She would have to find that out for herself, probably long after she left Freemont.

Tyler would have moved on to a new assignment by then, but he'd always remember the pretty speechwriter who had tugged at his heart.

Chapter Eleven

The Amish Craft Shoppe looked as if it had stepped out of the pages of time. Carrie smiled when she spied the wraparound porch, welcoming hand-painted sign over the door and the winter pansies that circled the front of the building. Tyler braked to a stop on the gravel lot in front of the small establishment, and they quickly entered.

Long, hand-hewn tables were covered with freshly baked breads, pies, cakes and cookies as well as jars of jam and vegetables. On the shelves behind the counter were bolts of fabric in subdued colors, no doubt in keeping with Amish rules of dress found in the *Ordnung*, the Amish guide as to how they were to live their lives. Felt hats for winter, straw for summer hung from a free-standing wire shelf, along with suspenders and sewing supplies.

Thick quilts stitched in intricate patterns were draped over racks. Others were neatly folded and piled on a side table. Farther along the wall were bins of potatoes, both golden and sweet, onions, bunches of carrots and turnips and other tubers.

A young Amish man stood near the counter with broom in hand. "*Gut* morning. May I help you?"

"I'm sure I'll find a number of things to buy." Carrie glanced at Tyler.

He stepped closer and held up his identification. "I'm with the Criminal Investigation Division at Fort Rickman. I'm looking for Matthew Schrock."

"Matthew sometimes works here but not today. Is there a problem?"

Tyler shook his head. "Nothing that reflects poorly on him. He found a body in the woods about two weeks ago, and I wanted to talk to him about what he saw."

"Mr. Harris." The clerk nodded, his face somber. "Everyone was so sorry to learn of his death."

"Did Matthew mention anything about calling the police?"

"I was here when he and his *Datt* came to the store to use the telephone. Matthew was emotional, naturally. Uncovering a dead body would be very upsetting."

"Do you know where we can find the boy?"

"You should find him at home."

Tyler nodded. "Could you direct us?"

The clerk raised his hand. "Along Amish Road. Turn south when you leave the parking lot."

"Is it far?"

"Three or four miles at most."

As Tyler talked, Carrie gathered potatoes, onions, a loaf of bread and an apple pie. She placed them on the counter.

"Did you find everything you wanted?" Tyler asked.

"I did. Plus some. From the amount I'm buying, it looks like I'm staying in Freemont longer than a day or two."

Tyler smiled. "If you buy too much, you can always invite a neighbor over for dinner."

She laughed. "That sounds like a good solution. Do you like apple pie?"

"Doesn't everyone?"

"My *Datt* prefers peach pie," the young man said, joining in the discussion.

"Shall I get a peach pie, as well?" Carrie asked. "I could take a pie to Ruth. They've been so nice, and I'm sure she's busy unpacking and washing clothes after their trip."

"I doubt Isaac or Joseph would object."

Carrie added a second pie to the counter and paid the clerk once he had totaled the bill. Tyler helped carry the food to the car and opened the door for her.

"Did you notice the beautiful quilts?" she asked as she slipped onto the passenger seat. "I'd love to take one back to DC with me."

A muscle in Tyler's jaw twitched, which she'd noticed every time she mentioned returning to DC. She wasn't sure what it meant, but his enthusiasm had waned and his expression had grown somber.

"Are you okay?" she asked.

"Of course. Let's drop the food off at your house before we talk to the Amish boy. It sounds as if his house isn't far from your dad's place."

"That's fine with me." She hesitated a moment before adding, "There's one thing that bothers me about leaving the area."

Tyler turned expectantly and stared at her. "What's that?"

"Leaving my Amish neighbors. Ruth is a lovely lady,

and although I don't know Isaac well, he's a good man, and Joseph has stolen my heart. Such a sweet little boy."

"The Lapps are good folks, and Joseph is a cute little boy." Tyler's muscle twitched again. "But what about the neighbor on the other side?"

Surprised by the question, Carrie didn't know what to say and laughed to cover up her mixed emotions.

"I'm blessed with good neighbors on each side," she finally added, hoping to deflect any more comments.

Tyler seemed focused on the investigation and nothing else, but perhaps she was wrong about him. Maybe there was something more to the special agent than solving crimes.

Tyler pulled into Carrie's drive and carried the produce and baked goods into the house.

"Shall I fix sandwiches?" she asked. "It's almost lunchtime, and I'm getting hungry."

"We should have stopped in town. I could have bought you lunch."

"That wasn't necessary." She opened the refrigerator. "Ham and cheese on wheat sound good?"

"Better than I'd have at home."

She pulled the meat and cheese from the refrigerator and placed them on the counter. "You're not a gourmet cook?" she teased.

"I can grill. Does that count?"

"Sure. Those burgers were delicious last night. A couple of them are left over, if you'd prefer that for lunch."

"Surprise me."

"Let's do the ham and cheese. If you want, we can have leftover burgers tonight."

"I'll need a rain check. I've got a meeting at CID headquarters. They often run longer than expected. I wouldn't want to hold you up."

"And I didn't mean to insert myself into your schedule."

"No, it's nothing like that."

But it probably was. Carrie had failed to consider that Tyler might have a special someone on post. Someone he saw on a regular basis. Next time, she would keep her ideas for a shared meal to herself.

She fixed the two sandwiches, added chips and a pickle and placed them on the small table near the window, along with two glasses of iced tea.

"Good view of my house." Tyler laughed as he sat down and glanced out the kitchen window.

"I hadn't noticed." Her cheeks burned.

He stared at her for a long moment before he reached for his sandwich.

"I don't usually say grace," she blurted out. "But being around the Amish and seeing my father's Bible, it seems right."

Tyler returned the sandwich to the plate. "My dad never let me eat without giving thanks to the Lord for the food, as well as for those who had prepared the meal. He often prayed that the food would do good and not harm us in any way."

"Sounds like your dad was a good man."

"He loved the Lord. As I got older, I realized he loved me, as well." He shrugged. "Raising a child alone is tough on guys."

She thought of her mother. "On women too."

"Sorry, of course, your mom raised you alone."

"But she wasn't God-fearing, and she didn't teach me to pray. I got it from an osmosis of sorts visiting friends who had more stable home lives. Sometimes I'd go to church with them, but never with my mother."

"I'm sorry."

"At the time, I didn't think I was so far out of the norm. Later, in college, I realized other moms weren't quite as neurotic as mine, nor did other moms have a need to constantly be the center of attention."

"You could never measure up to what she wanted?"

"Exactly." She bowed her head. "Father God, thank You for bringing me to Freemont and for all those who have lived in this house. Bless the farmers who grew the food we are about to eat and the people who prepared it for sale." She glanced at Tyler. "Let it be good for our bodies and do no harm."

"Amen." He bit into the sandwich and smiled. "Delicious."

"You're just hungry."

"I never lie."

She laughed. "That's a quality I admire."

"You haven't mentioned the journal."

"I was so tired last night that I didn't get much read. The journal belonged to a woman named Charlotte Harris, who lived during the Civil War. She loved her family, and she loved to write."

"Like you."

"Perhaps I inherited my appreciation for the written word from her. Charlotte had an older son fighting in the war along with her husband. A younger son and daughter lived at home with her."

"Any mention of treasure?"

"I started at the beginning so I haven't gotten to the page the fireman noticed. She wrote about hiding some of the family keepsakes, which is different from buried treasure. Plus, there was no mention of gold coins."

"But there could have been coins."

"Of course. I'm wondering if the letter we saw in the Freemont Museum was penned by her husband, perhaps before he went off to fight."

"Or he could have come home injured before the end of the war or before the Union forces headed into Georgia. The letter mentioned his concern about Northern aggression taking what rightfully belonged to his children."

Tyler reached for the second half of his sandwich. "Have you looked at any of your father's things? He may have a family tree tucked away with his papers."

"There's an office in the back of the house with French doors that lead outside. I thought it might have been a screened-in porch that someone turned into a sunroom. He has bookshelves and a beautiful antique rolltop desk."

"Have you found anything of interest there?"

She placed the rest of her sandwich on the plate and wiped her hands on the napkin in her lap. "I know it sounds foolish, but I haven't wanted to infringe on the private areas in the house."

"You haven't opened the desk?"

"Nor have I gone in his bedroom or through his papers. I'm living as if I were a guest in a home that rightfully belongs to me, or will when all the paperwork is completed."

"You're not ready to accept him as your father?"

"Maybe that's the problem, but it seems a bit foolish of me, since he is my father, whether I claim him or not."

"Are you hesitant to embrace your father because of some skewed allegiance you have to your mother?"

Carrie titled her head. "I never thought of that as being the problem, but perhaps you're right."

"The people were nice at the first foster home I went to after my father's death, but I wouldn't open myself to them for fear I was dishonoring my dad. No one could or would take his place. At least that's the way my childish logic worked. I was struggling with a lot of things—anger, guilt, grief. Eventually the family sent me back, saying I wasn't willing to accept them into my life. Which was true at the time. Only—"

She waited. "Only what, Tyler?"

"Only that was the best home foster care could offer me. The next people were a whole lot worse, which only made me even angrier. I was kicked from home to home because of who I was. Each place was a step down, and my hate escalated."

"Sounds as if you were on a slippery slope to self-destruction. How'd you turn that around?"

"A high school coach saw something in me. Plus, he needed a lineman for the football team. For whatever reason, I let him into my pain. He loved God and tried to get me to join his church. I never went that far, but I listened and some of it rubbed off on me. He encouraged me to join high school ROTC, and I found my spot. We worked with the local police, and for a number of reasons, law enforcement and the military drew my interest."

"Did you enlist after high school to join the CID?"

"First the military police. Then I got a degree in criminal justice, thanks to Uncle Sam, and applied to be in the CID. I wanted to investigate crime and injustice done against military personnel and their families."

"You're a success story."

"Maybe, but I still harbor a grudge against the past."

"At your father?"

"At the man who killed him."

Carrie looked puzzled. "I thought your dad lost his life in an auto accident."

"He did, but the man driving the car that killed him was drunk."

She reached out and touched Tyler's hand. "I'm so sorry."

"It happened long ago, but I still remember how the guy staggered from his car. He reeked of alcohol and slurred his speech when he asked me if I was okay."

"You were in the car?"

"Luckily in the backseat. My forehead was cut." He touched a small scar that was probably a constant reminder of what had happened.

"He went to jail?"

Tyler laughed ruefully. "If only the world were a perfect place."

"You mean he wasn't found guilty?"

"He wasn't even accused of wrongdoing, Carrie, because he was a man of influence who knew the right people."

"Is there anything you can do now?"

Tyler shook his head. "What's the Bible say about vengeance?"

"As I recall, something about *vengeance being mine, sayeth the Lord.*"

"I'm waiting for God to bring the guilty to justice in my father's case and working hard to help the Lord in the cases I can handle."

He reached again for his sandwich. Carrie took a sip of iced tea and tried to imagine what Tyler had gone through. She had thought her own childhood was hard, but it was nothing compared to his.

As soon as they finished eating, she cleared the table and both of them rinsed the dishes and placed them in the dishwasher.

Her phone rang, a local number she didn't recognize. "I should take this."

Tyler nodded. "I can go in the other room if you need privacy."

"No, stay."

Once she answered, Sergeant Oliver identified himself as the soldier she had talked to outside the headquarters of her father's former unit. "Ma'am, I wondered if you found any photos of your dad that we can use in the upcoming ceremony."

"Oh, Sergeant Oliver, I haven't had time. I'm so sorry. Give me another day or two if you don't mind."

"Certainly. Why don't I stop by tomorrow night? As I told you yesterday, we have a few military pictures, but I think some personal photos would be nice, as well."

"You're so kind to think of my father and to want to make the ceremony special. I promise I'll search through his papers and let you know if I find anything that might be appropriate."

"Appreciate your help, ma'am. It must be difficult going through his things."

"I'm not moving as quickly as I had hoped."

"No problem. Call me and I can pick the photos up anytime."

"Thank you, Sergeant Oliver." She hung up and informed Tyler of the sergeant's request. "I guess that means I have to go through his desk."

"If you want to look now, I could drop the pictures at his unit when I return to post this afternoon."

"But you wanted to talk to the Amish boy. Let's do that first. I'll check for photos later."

"Whatever you want."

She picked up the peach pie. "I want to take this to the Lapp family before Ruth bakes a pie of her own."

"I'll go with you," Tyler said. "I need to ask Isaac if he knows anything about Matthew Schrock."

The doorbell rang. Carrie looked quizzically at Tyler. "I don't have a clue who that could be."

Tyler led the way into the dining room and peered out the window. "It's Isaac and Joseph."

She called Bailey. "Joseph will want to say hello to you." When she opened the door, she realized the little boy wasn't here to play. His face was blotched from crying and his lower lip quivered.

"Isaac, is there a problem?" she asked, looking from the tearful Joseph to his stern-faced father.

"*Yah*, there is." He tapped his son's shoulder. "Tell her, Joseph."

"I am sorry for taking something that did not belong to me."

"Whatever are you talking about?"

Tyler came and stood behind her.

The little boy stretched out his hand and opened his fist. Lying on his palm was an old coin, covered with Georgia clay.

"I found this on your land. *Datt* said I should have given it to Mr. Harris."

"When did you find it?" she asked.

"Before Mr. Harris died. He is with the Lord now, so

I kept the coin. *Datt* said I was wrong to keep anything that was not mine."

She held out her hand. The boy dropped the coin into her palm.

"You have been a very brave boy and done the right thing," Carrie said. "Thank you, Joseph, for returning what you found. Now I don't think you need to cry anymore."

"I am sorry."

"I know you are, and I have something that might help you dry your tears."

She stepped away from the door and grabbed the pie from the table. "Do you think your mother would like to serve peach pie tonight after you've eaten your dinner?"

He bobbed his head, the tears forgotten. *"Yah, ist gut."*

"Can you carry it home?"

His eyes widened. "I will be careful."

"You do not need to do this," Isaac said.

"It's a small token of my appreciation, Isaac. I'm grateful to have such fine neighbors. Thank you for helping my father and for helping me."

"That is what *Gott* would want us to do."

Tyler stepped onto the porch and pulled Isaac to the side.

"Joseph, take the pie to *Mamm*. Tell her I will be home soon," Isaac said.

When the boy was on his way, Isaac turned a worried gaze on Tyler. "Is something else wrong?"

"Matthew Schrock found the sergeant major's body. Do you know the boy?"

"Of course, I know him."

"Is the teenager truthful?"

Isaac nodded. "You can believe what he says. He is almost a man. What do you need to know?"

"Did you ever see the sergeant hunting on his property?"

"Often."

"What gun did he usually take with him?"

"Jeffrey had many guns. You have seen his gun cabinet?"

Tyler turned to Carrie.

"It's in his office," she shared.

"He told me he had recorded all his weapons," Isaac continued. "Many were old. Some antiques. He took pictures of them and wanted to be accurate in his details. There should be a binder with all the information about his guns."

"I'll look for the binder."

"I must go now and talk to Joseph. I do not want him to think that he is forgiven because he takes home a pie."

"But I have forgiven him, Isaac," Carrie assured the boy's father.

"The wrongdoing is forgiven, maybe, but he needs to make reparation for his actions. Sin carries a residual wrong that needs to be made right. He must help his mother and me until he has restored himself in our eyes. Then he will know he is forgiven. If forgiveness is given too easily, he will feel the sting later and the guilt will hang heavy on his shoulders. The next time he thinks of doing something wrong, he will remember if we do not make it too easy on him today."

"Don't be too hard on him, Isaac." Tyler took the coin from Carrie and rubbed away some of the red clay. "It's an old coin, but not that old. Joseph may have thought he'd found gold, but he didn't."

"If Joseph thought it was gold," Isaac said, "I fear he might have told his friends about the treasure he found. More rumors are not needed."

"He's a good boy," Tyler tried to assure him.

"*Yah*, but he will be a better boy when he learns to obey his father." With a nod of farewell, Isaac turned and walked back to his house.

"Forgiveness is tricky," Tyler said, watching the man enter his home.

"I'm not sure I've forgiven my mother."

Tyler understood. "That's the way I feel about my father's death. Maybe we both need to make reparation."

"Meaning?"

"Maybe finding out how and why your father and Corporal Fellows died will bring peace. War was fought on this land. Many of your ancestors were wounded or killed in battle. Those traumatic deaths could pull the family apart for generations, until some type of healing takes place."

He looked at Carrie. "Maybe you're here to heal your family's past."

"And you, Tyler? Will you heal yours, as well?"

"I'm not sure."

Chapter Twelve

"Let's check your father's office," Tyler said as he followed Carrie inside. They headed through the main living area to a rear hallway that led to a room with large windows, bookcases, a filing cabinet and, as Carrie had mentioned, a mammoth rolltop desk.

Tyler ran his hand over the rich hardwood, appreciating the workmanship and quality of the furniture. "It's old and has probably been in the family for generations."

"It could have been the desk Jefferson Harris mentioned in his letter, where he planned to hide a map to the treasure."

Tyler walked toward the side wall where a tall gun cabinet stood. "Your father had quite a collection of firearms. Just as Isaac said, some of them are antiques."

"I don't know guns, but I'll take your word for it."

"We need to find that binder."

Carrie turned around in a circle and threw up her hands. "Where should we start?"

"The desk." He glanced at her, knowing she was hesitant to delve into her father's personal items.

She stepped forward and slowly rolled back the top.

The surface was clear of papers. She pulled open one of the small drawers and gasped.

Tyler moved closer. "What is it?"

"A picture of a woman holding an infant child." She stared down at the photo.

Tyler peered over her shoulder.

Her face clouded. She dropped the photo on the desk and turned away.

He rubbed his hand over her shoulder. "Have you seen that picture before?"

She nodded, her voice husky when she spoke. "My mother had a copy on the dresser in her bedroom. It was taken when I was three months old. She must have sent him a copy of the picture."

Tyler's heart broke for her. Her mother had manipulated a story that was untrue. "He kept it close, Carrie. That should bring you comfort."

She sniffed and shook her head as she turned to face him. "It brings more questions to bear. If he loved God so much, why didn't he try to find me, to have a relationship with me? All the years, he could have been in my life, but he remained distant and didn't try to see me. That's what I don't understand. It hurts not to be wanted."

"He kept the picture. He didn't exclude you from his heart."

"His actions don't prove that to be true, Tyler."

"He left you this house."

"Maybe he felt guilty as he aged. Or maybe as Isaac mentioned, it was reparation for abandoning me. Money or possessions weren't what I wanted growing up. I wanted a father."

Seeing the confusion and the pain on her face and the

tears that filled her eyes, Tyler couldn't stop himself and pulled her into his arms.

She was soft and pliable and molded to him. The tears fell. He felt her tremble and rubbed his hand over her shoulders as she cried.

Her grief tugged at Tyler's heart. He remembered the loss he had felt as a child at his own father's death. Carrie was grieving for a father she had always yearned to know.

For the first time, Tyler saw himself as the fortunate one. He knew he was loved. Somehow over the years he had forgotten the importance of that love.

At the moment, a stirring welled up within him of another type of feeling, a desire to protect and care for this woman who had been thrust into such despair. More than anything he wanted to right the wrongs and fix the hurts. If only he could.

He rested his head against hers and let her cry for the past, for the loneliness she had felt growing up, for her struggle with a mother who had been untruthful and for a future that probably confused her at this point.

Tyler knew deep within himself that he wanted her to turn to him in her need.

Was he asking too much?

Carrie wanted to remain wrapped in Tyler's arms. The pain she felt about finding the picture and knowing her father hadn't tried to contact her eased as Tyler pulled her even closer. Surrounded by the strength of him, she felt her grief start to ease. Perhaps she would be able to sort through her current confusion and find her way, with Tyler's help.

Selling the house didn't matter as much as finding who she was in relation to her father. Had he loved her from afar? As Tyler mentioned, at least her father had kept the picture of her close.

"Shhh," Tyler soothed. His voice caressed her heart and healed some of the brokenness she had felt for too long.

If only—

Realizing she was enjoying his nearness far too much, she drew back, unwilling to let her heart be swayed by a military guy. She didn't want to follow in her mother's footsteps. Carrie had to be careful, especially with a family history of betrayal.

Was that what had happened? Had her father betrayed her mother's love?

Knowing her mother's manipulative ways, she wondered if her mother had been the one to blame.

"I…I'm sorry," she stammered as she stepped out of Tyler's embrace. She felt an instant sense of loss, and the swirl of confusion returned to cloud her mind again.

She glanced at the photo. "I didn't expect to react so strongly. It's probably a combination of everything that's happened."

"You're allowed to be emotional, Carrie, seeing the picture of you as a baby and knowing your father had treasured it all these years."

She shook her head. "He probably stuck it in the desk long ago and forgot he even had the picture."

Tyler took the photo from her hand and turned it over. "What do you see on the back of the picture?"

"Smudges, darker patches."

"Caused by—"

"I'm not sure."

"Caused by the oil on his fingers. He had touched the

photo countless time, Carrie, probably pulling it close to stare at his precious child."

She shook her head. "Yet he never contacted me."

Tyler let out a breath. "Maybe he didn't know where to find you. Did your mother move? Perhaps she had given him the wrong address. The world was a different place back then, before computers and social media. Telephones and letters were the only ways to connect long distance. If your mother moved or changed her phone number, your dad could have lost track of both of you."

She sniffed and wiped her hand over her cheeks, feeling heat from her tears. "You might be right."

"I know I am." He carefully returned the photo to the desk drawer. "Why don't you make a cup of tea and sit for a while? I'll look for the catalogue of your father's weapons."

"But I need to help you, Tyler. There might be other things of interest that we'll be able to find together."

"Only if you feel up to it."

As much as she appreciated his thoughtfulness, she had to look through her father's things. The search would be easier having Tyler working at her side.

"Where shall we start?" she asked.

"The larger side drawers on the desk."

Together they opened the drawers and sorted through the files and papers, looking for anything that might mention the sergeant major's weapons or provide other clues as to her father's past.

Carrie found a number of sales receipts for work he had contracted on the house, for the kitchen renovations and the half bath downstairs. "I wonder if he did the remodeling because he planned to sell the house."

"Then changed his mind," Tyler added.

"Maybe we'll find something that gives us a clue of where he would have gone if the house had sold. From what most of the people I've met have said, my father seemed to be happy in Freemont."

"George Gates could have thought your father was more interested in selling than he really was. Now he's encouraging you to sell."

"Probably because his wife wants to change this into a bed-and-breakfast." Carrie looked through the windows to the hill at the rear of the property, the chicken coop and barn and what was left of the kitchen house. "I don't want strangers walking through this house or on this property, until I'm ready to say goodbye."

"You don't have to sell."

She nodded. "I know. But the estate tax will be significant. I'm not sure I can pay it."

"That's often the plight of farm families too and those who inherit a mom-and-pop business. The high taxes force families to sell land or a business just to have the money to pay the government. That's something you should convince Senator Kingsley to work on changing."

"You're right."

"Did you father have any other assets?"

"A few things that Gates said need to go through probate court. At least my father had the foresight to put my name on the deeds for the house and land so they go to me outright without having to be held up in court."

"Gates is providing information piecemeal, Carrie. You need to sit down with him and go over everything."

"He never has time and always says we'll cover the rest of the inheritance in a day or two."

"We can drive back to his office this afternoon."

"I'd rather talk to the Amish boy. I need to know how my father died."

Tyler glanced at his watch. "Let's search the office for half an hour. If we come up empty-handed, we'll visit Matthew and return later to continue looking."

"Didn't you say something about a meeting on post?"

"Later this afternoon. Do you want to come with me? You could wait in my office."

She smiled, appreciating his attempt to keep her safe. "I'll be fine. Bailey will be my watchdog. It's warmed up this afternoon. Maybe we'll go outside and see if Joseph wants to toss the ball. The thought of sitting in the rocker on the front porch would be a nice change of pace."

"As long as Isaac and Ruth are next door. If I'm tied up after dusk, be sure to come inside and lock the doors. Call me if you're worried."

"I'll be fine."

"Mind if I check the closet?" Tyler opened the door and glanced at the top shelf. "I may have found what we're looking for." He pulled down a large three-ring binder and placed it on the desk.

"Let's hope it provides the gun records," Tyler said as he opened the front cover.

The pages had plastic protective covers. "'A Collection of Weapons from the Harris Family,'" he read. "Exactly what we needed to find."

Flipping through the pages, he stopped a number of times to read the information about the various guns. "Your dad had lots of antique firearms. A few of them were passed down in the family. He purchased others at gun shows in the local area."

"Does anything stand out?"

Tyler came upon a photograph that made him pause.

"Here's a picture of a Winchester Model 1894. Your father noted that it was his favorite gun to carry when he walked in the woods. The .30-30 caliber ammunition the police found in his vest would fit the rifle."

Turning the page, he found a photo of the sergeant major's gun cabinet. He lifted the binder off the desk, carried it to the wall and compared the photo to the actual guns on display.

"The Winchester is in the photo but missing in the gun rack."

"Is that proof enough that he had a gun with him the day of his fall?" she asked.

"No, but it provides a clue."

"If so, then what happened to the weapon?"

"That's what we need to find out. The rifle was old. Probably manufactured some time between 1894 and 1918, by the Winchester Repeating Arms Company in New Haven, Connecticut. In good shape, it could sell for over six thousand dollars."

Carrie's eyes widened. "Reason enough for someone to take the gun."

"Exactly. If the weather's good tomorrow, I'll hike up the hill and see what I can find."

"I'll join you. Bailey can tag along too. I'm sure he'd like to romp in the woods."

"And chase squirrels." Tyler smiled.

Carrie glanced at her watch. "Why don't we postpone looking for the photos of my father until later so we can visit the Amish boy?"

Tyler nodded. "Let's go now. Hopefully we'll find him at home."

Returning to the foyer, Carrie lifted her coat off the

hall tree and turned to Bailey. "We won't be gone long." She nuzzled his neck.

As Tyler helped her with her coat, his hands lingered ever so lightly on her shoulders, causing an unexpected warmth to curl along her spine.

She stepped away from him, somewhat flustered. Her cheeks heated, and she glanced quickly at the hallway mirror to make sure she wasn't blushing.

"Is something wrong?" he asked, evidently oblivious to her unease.

"Just thinking of what we might learn today." True though her statement was, she was even more agitated by Tyler's touch. The memory of being wrapped in his arms was still so fresh.

When she had cried, he had comforted her, as any caring individual would do. She shouldn't read anything else into his embrace. It had merely been a compassionate response to her unexpected reaction after finding the photograph. Hadn't Tyler said as much?

Fumbling with the buttons on her coat, she stalled for time until her cheeks cooled and she could readjust her mindset.

Steeling her resolve, she reached for her purse. "Ready whenever you are."

He followed her onto the porch. She locked the door and walked with him to the car. Again he touched her arm as she slipped into the seat. Biting the inside of her cheek, she focused on the discomfort in her mouth instead of the ripple of response from his touch.

In DC, she had distanced herself from most men, other than those with whom she worked. They were older and married, except for the senator's senior adviser, who was recently divorced. Senator Kingsley was, as well.

In his early fifties, the senator had seemed more like the father she never knew rather than a boss. Although perhaps she had read too much into their relationship, especially since he still hadn't called to check on her.

Finding her cell in her purse, she glanced at the phone log to ensure that she hadn't missed his call.

"Has the garage phoned concerning your car?" Tyler asked as he started the engine and navigated out of the drive and onto Amish Road.

"I was checking. Not yet." Disappointment fluttered over her. Perhaps the senator hadn't received her message. She'd try to call him again later today.

"Did Isaac give you more specific directions to the boy's house?" she asked.

"He just said it wasn't far."

Finding the turn, Tyler pulled onto an intersecting dirt road that wound through a thick patch of forest. A clearing on the right revealed a small one-story house with a porch and side chimney. Chickens pecked at the grass, and a goat stood tethered near the house. The animal glanced up as Tyler turned onto the property and braked to a stop.

"The place needs paint," Carrie said, eyeing the slope of the front porch, the torn screen door and the window patched with cardboard. "And maybe a renovation crew."

Tyler nodded in agreement. "Looks like the Schrock family is struggling to hold on."

"There, Tyler." She pointed to a teenager who peered from the nearby barn. "That might be Matthew."

The boy approached as they stepped from the car. He wiped his hands on a rag and then tossed it over a nearby fence post. He wore the traditional Amish garb of a solid color shirt and black slacks, held up with suspenders.

A warning tingled Carrie's neck. She had seen the boy before, in town when she pulled out of the lawyer's parking lot the same day the lug nuts had been removed from her tire.

She glanced at Tyler and tried to silently warn him that something was very wrong about the house and surrounding land and especially the teenage boy with a pronounced limp who came to meet them.

Chapter Thirteen

One look at Carrie's face and Tyler knew something was wrong. He held her gaze for a long moment, then turned back to the Amish teenager limping toward them.

"Afternoon," Tyler said in greeting. He gave his name and introduced Carrie. "Are you Matthew Schrock?"

The boy glanced warily from one to the other. "What is it you want?"

"The police said you found Sergeant Major Jeffrey Harris's body in the woods. We want to ask you a few questions about that day."

"I told everything to the police."

"Ms. York is the sergeant major's daughter. She would like information about how her father died."

The boy kicked his foot into the dirt. His eyes held little compassion as he turned to her. "I do not know how your father died, but I'm sure his death was *Gott's* will."

Carrie didn't seem to buy in to his statement, but she nodded her thanks and then added, "You found him at the bottom of a hill?"

"That is right. I was in the woods and smelled death." He turned to Tyler. "You have smelled a dead animal? I thought it was a deer. I held my nose and stepped closer. At first, I did not understand what I saw. So I walked around the body. On the other side, I could see the face."

"Was it bloodied?"

"Scratched and scraped from the fall. *Yah*, there was blood."

"Did you see anything that might indicate a fight had taken place?"

Again, the teenager glanced down and kicked a rock with his shoe.

"Matthew, did you hear me?" Tyler pressed. "Were there signs of a struggle?"

"The body fell down the hill."

"Yes, but could you tell if the deceased—the dead man—had been in a fight?"

"How could I tell that?" His glance was furtive as he looked from Carrie to Tyler.

"What was he wearing?"

The boy shook his head. "I do not remember."

"A hunting vest. Do you remember if it had a camouflage pattern?"

"Perhaps it was a vest."

"Did you see a rifle or any type of weapon lying nearby?" Tyler asked.

Again he shook his head. This time too hard and too quickly. "I did not see a rifle."

"How long did you stay with the body?"

"I did not stay. I ran to get help."

"You called the police?"

The teen nodded. "The Amish Craft Shoppe has a telephone. I called from there."

"Did you return with the police?"

"I had to show them where I found the body."

"Why were you walking in that area?" Tyler asked.

Again the furtive look. "I like the woods."

"But it wasn't your property, Matthew."

The boy's eyes widened. "I did not see signs about trespassing."

"You've taken that route before?"

The boy nodded. "Sometimes."

"Is there a friend you visit nearby?"

"Not friends. Just the woods. I like to be alone."

"Have you seen anything else in the woods when you walk?" Tyler asked. "Has anyone bothered you?"

Matthew frowned. "I do not understand."

"Have you seen soldiers or men fighting?"

The boy shrugged. "Maybe not."

"What does that mean, Matthew? Have you seen soldiers?"

"Sometimes."

"Have they talked to you?"

"Not to me, but to other Amish boys."

"What do the soldiers talk about?"

"About making money by doing jobs for them. Sanding, roofing, cutting lumber. They work on homes."

"Flipping houses?" Tyler asked.

"I'm not sure what they do."

"But they never asked you to help them?"

Matthew dropped his gaze. "Perhaps they do not think I can work hard."

"You know Eli Plank?"

"Yah."

"He said one of his friends saw two men fighting in the woods. Was that you, Matthew?"

"I saw something once. Through the trees. Two men

appeared to be fighting. I turned away. It was getting dark. I needed to be home."

Tyler leaned closer. "Were the men in military uniform?"

"I could not tell."

"Was one of the men Jeffrey Harris, the man whose body you found?"

The boy glanced at Carrie. "I did not see their faces."

"When was the fight?" Tyler asked.

Matthew shrugged. "A day or two before I found the body."

"Was that why you returned to the area? Did you know someone had died?"

Matthew shook his head. "That is not why I was in the woods."

"Did you see a rifle when the men were fighting? Did you go back to find the gun?"

"I told you before. I did not see a rifle."

"Are you telling the truth, Matthew?"

A sharp dip of his head. "Why would I not tell the truth?"

"I don't know, but you won't get in trouble by telling us," Tyler said, hoping to reassure the boy. "I'll keep any information confidential. Do you understand?"

Matthew remained silent.

Tyler stared at the boy for a long moment before asking another question. "Did the soldiers invite you or any of the other boys to the cabin?"

Matthew's face paled. "What cabin?"

"Where soldiers watch movies and play pool. Have any of your friends gone there?"

"I do not see many people. There is much work to do at home."

"What about on Sundays, after services?" Carrie asked.

"My *Datt* does not always want to go. We must work."

"Matthew." The boy turned at the sound of his name. An Amish man stood on the top of a small rise and stared down at the three of them.

"It is my *Datt*. He needs me."

"I live across the road from Eli Plank," Tyler said. "If you think of anything else, he'll know how to find me."

"I have nothing else to tell you."

"And I live in the old house next to Isaac and Ruth Lapp," Carrie added.

"And Joseph?"

"That's right. If you think of anything else, please let me know."

"Matthew," the father called again, his voice sharp and insistent.

"I must go." The boy turned and limped up the hill to where his father stood.

The man's hands were on his hips. He ignored his son and stared down at them.

"Might be time to leave," Tyler said, touching her arm. "Mr. Schrock doesn't seem friendly."

"Maybe he didn't like us talking to his son."

Getting in the car, Tyler turned to glance again at the hill. The boy had disappeared, but his father continued to watch them from the rise.

"I need to learn more about Mr. Schrock and his son," Tyler said once they were back on Amish Road.

"The boy may be keeping secrets," Carrie said.

Tyler nodded in agreement. "The father may have secrets, as well."

* * *

"Are we on for exploring the wooded area and hill tomorrow?" Carrie asked as they rode back to her house.

"What time?"

"Whenever you're free. Call me in the morning and we can decide." She looked at the dark clouds overhead. "If the weather works in our favor."

Tyler turned into her driveway and braked. He hurried around the car, opened the door for her and walked her to the porch.

"Did you want to come in?" she asked as she unlocked the door.

He glanced at his watch. "I need to get to post. My boss likes everyone in their seats and waiting for him ahead of time."

"You'll be back before dark?"

"I never know. Sometimes he gets long-winded. Shall I call you when I get home?"

"Sure, unless it's really late."

"I'll call if your light is on."

When he hesitated, she stepped closer. "Thank you, Tyler."

He touched her hand. "See you tonight."

Her heart fluttered when he smiled. Did she notice a dimple? For the first time. What was wrong with her? Had she been so distracted that she hadn't noticed? She needed to make sure she didn't miss anything as noteworthy in the days ahead.

She stepped inside and waved from the window as he drove out of the drive and onto Amish Road.

Bailey stood with her, whining.

She leaned over and rubbed his back. "You need a little attention, don't you, boy?"

The dog barked, making her laugh.

"Is it dinnertime?"

He barked again.

"I know, you're hungry. So am I. Let's get dinner started."

Bailey trotted beside her and filled the stillness with his warmth. She patted his head again and then filled his bowl with dog food. Bailey ate while Carrie pulled chicken breasts from the refrigerator.

"I'll cook extra in case Tyler is hungry when he comes home." The dog was much too interested in his food to respond to her comment.

Quickly she fixed a casserole, shoved it in the oven to bake and set the timer. She patted her leg for Bailey, who had finished his food and was sniffing around the oven, no doubt hoping for some chicken treats too.

"Let's look for those pictures Sergeant Oliver requested," she said to Bailey as she headed into her father's office. In the file cabinet, she found a manila folder marked "Photographs." She pulled it out and opened it on the desk. The photos were of her father, some in uniform on post and others in civilian attire in town. One was taken at the old train station and appeared to have been a ribbon cutting ceremony when he had donated the items to the new Freemont Museum. The docent they'd met stood next to her father.

Digging deeper, she found older pictures of her father as a younger man, tall and strong and handsome. No wonder her mother had fallen in love with him. Toward the bottom, she found a photo that tugged at her heart. Her father was standing with his arm around her mother, staring into her eyes. Both of them looked so very much in love.

Selecting a few of the more recent photos, she placed them in an envelope and wrote Sergeant Oliver's name and "Photos" on the front. She gathered the older pictures, including the one with her mother, and tucked them in her pocket so she could look at them later.

After returning the file, she and Bailey headed to the front door. "Get your ball, and we'll sit on the porch and play."

The evening was peaceful with the smell of fresh earth and the first hint of spring. Bradford Pear trees were sprouting buds, and circles of daffodils were unrolling their leaves. Georgia was farther south than Washington, and Mother Nature, in spite of the cool temperatures, would soon burst forth.

Sitting on the porch, she tossed the ball into the yard and watched Bailey race to grab the toy and then bring it back to her and lay it at her feet like a trophy. She had to smile, and her outlook lightened at the dog's playful antics.

For an instant, she glanced at the other rocker and imagined her father—the man in the pictures—sitting next to her. If only she could hear his voice and see his facial expressions, more than what had been captured in the photos. She pulled the pictures from her pocket and looked at them again, trying to memorize the angle of his square jaw, the arch of his brow, the curve of his full lips.

A crow cawed, causing her to turn her gaze left to Tyler's neatly trimmed yard and pruned shrubs. A few daffodils had already opened, and the burst of yellow warmed her heart like sunshine peeking through the clouds.

Tyler was a good man and hardworking. He seemed to care about her and the plight she faced about whether to stay or sell the property. She sighed, thinking of sitting with him on the porch, seeing the firm set of his jaw as he surveyed the land she knew he loved as much as her father must have. She could see him turn to her and smile, showing the dimple in his cheek and the tenderness in his eyes that she noticed when he'd held her in his arms.

Again, a warmth swept over her, and she felt a serene peace and rightness envelope her, like his strong arms. His heart had beat loudly enough for her to hear the rhythmic pulse. Funny that she should think such thoughts of him when she'd started out questioning whether he could have been involved in the corporal's murder.

Within just a few days, she'd come to a new realization about many things, her father and Tyler and her mother. Carrie knew the importance of forgiveness. If she failed to forgive her mother, anger would fester and grow.

Bailey brought the ball and dropped it at her feet. Instead of playing, he returned to the yard and started chewing on something he found in the grass. Probably a stick or piece of bark.

"Bailey." He failed to acknowledge her call.

"Don't eat that," she chastised, brushing what looked like the last tiny remains of a piece of meat out of his mouth. "No, Bailey. Sit on the porch." He sat, nuzzled his ball and eyed a flock of birds that were swooping over a distant field.

Carrie breathed in the cool air and watched the twilight descend upon the farmland.

"Time to go inside," she finally said as the night turned chilly.

The dog eyed the Lapps' house as if waiting for Joseph.

"He's probably helping his mother with the dishes," Carrie said, thinking of Isaac's words about reparation.

Strict as Isaac seemed, his love for his son was evident. Ruth doted on the boy like most mothers. Would there be other children? Most Amish families were large. Surely Ruth and Isaac wanted more children, not that Carrie would broach the subject. She had been an only child and had longed not only for the father she had never known but also for brothers and sisters.

If she ever married and had a family of her own, she hoped for a number of children. Although reclusive women who closed men out of their lives couldn't expect to find someone special.

Again, she glanced at Tyler's house, then quickly turned her gaze back to Bailey. Rising from the rocker, she patted her leg. "Come on, boy."

The dampness of the night followed them inside where long shadows darkened the house. Carrie reached for a light switch and turned on the lamp. Even in the soft glow, she felt uneasy and returned to the door to check the lock.

The rich aroma of baked chicken and rice in a mushroom sauce drew her into the kitchen. Opening the oven, she peered at the bubbling casserole.

"It's almost ready." She smiled at Bailey, who sniffed the air.

Once the table was set, she pulled the casserole from the oven and covered it with foil to keep it warm.

"Everything's ready, Bailey. Let's wait in the living room?"

He stood at her side and wiggled with appreciation when she rubbed his back. "Tyler's meeting must be taking longer than he expected."

Glancing again around the kitchen and satisfied the dinner could wait, she turned off the light and headed for the comfy couch in the main room. Her father's leather-bound Bible sat on a side table. She pulled it onto her lap and opened the book. A paper fell out. She reached to retrieve it from the floor and startled at the handwriting she recognized. The return address confirmed what she had realized. The letter was from her mother.

Scooting closer to the light, she pulled the yellowed paper from the envelope addressed to her father, all too aware of her mother's script.

Dear Jeffrey,
You inquired about Carolyn and requested visiting me so you could see her. As I told you when you called, I do not want you to contact me again, and I do not want or need your help. Even more important, Carolyn doesn't need you in her life. You have been gone too long. I know you were overseas, but your inability to see her after her birth confirmed what I had always thought, that you weren't interested in our child. I insist that you stay away from us. We are moving. You won't be able to find us, so don't try. If you do try to contact us, I'll call the police and tell them that you have been causing problems. I know you had hoped my feelings would have changed, but they haven't. I thought you would get out of the military. When you accepted your overseas assignment, I saw you for who you really were, and that wasn't someone I wanted associating with my child.

Carrie's heart broke. Her father had wanted to see her, but her mother had stood in his way. After returning the letter to the envelope, she tucked it back in the Bible along with the photo of her mother and father.

Her eyes burned. Through the veil of tears, she retraced her steps to the kitchen and put the casserole in the refrigerator before she climbed the stairs to the bedroom. Bailey trotted at her side.

How could her mother have been so thoughtless to separate her from her father's love? The pain swept over her and clamped down on her heart. She pushed open the bedroom door and fell onto the bed. Bailey dropped to the floor beside her.

Hot tears fell from her eyes. She pulled tissues from the box on the nightstand and held them to her eyes. She cried until her head throbbed and she had no more tears, only shallow sobs that caught in her throat.

Her swollen eyes hurt. Her heart hurt even more. She didn't want to stay in Freemont, yet she didn't want to leave. All she wanted to do was forget today had ever happened and cry herself to sleep.

Chapter Fourteen

The howling wind woke Carrie from a fitful sleep. She groped her hand across the nightstand, searching for the electric alarm clock that usually lit the night.

Touching the lightless clock, she fidgeted with the dials, but to no avail. Raising her hand, she searched for the lamp switch and turned the knob. The room remained dark.

A quiver of concern wrapped around her throat. She sat up and listened. Bailey lay at the side of the bed, his breathing deep and labored.

"Bailey?" She touched the dog, who failed to respond. "Bailey, wake up."

Her worry turned to fear when he didn't move.

Again she groped her hand across the nightstand. Relief washed over her when her fingers touched her cell phone.

The screen lit. She found the flashlight app and shone the light on Bailey, yet he failed to rally. She touched his nose. Cool and moist. Was that a true indication of a dog's health and well-being?

Searching her phone log, she hit Tyler's number. Surely he was home by now. The call went to voice mail.

"It's Carrie. Something's wrong. I can't wake Bailey. And the electricity is off. I was asleep. There must have been a storm. Call me."

Stepping around the dog, she padded across the bedroom and opened the door to the upstairs hallway. Peering over the railing, she glanced at the first floor entryway, but saw nothing except the faint outline of furniture below.

The house was in the country where power outages were probably a norm. Perhaps a faulty generator or a malfunction of some sort. She'd find the number to the electric company in the kitchen phone book and notify them of the problem.

Again she turned on the flashlight. The light dimmed. As she checked the battery, her heart sank. Her battery needed to be charged. Without electricity, she wouldn't be able to use her phone.

She glanced at her phone again. Why hadn't Tyler returned her call?

Grabbing the banister, she started down the stairs. A sound made her pause halfway to the first floor.

Nerve endings on high alert, she turned her head toward the rear of the house. What had she heard?

The settling sounds of an old house?

Or something else?

The sound came again. Like a drawer opening.

Her neck tingled and her stomach roiled.

Another creak. A footfall?

Someone was in the house.

Heart pounding, she hurried down the stairs and

turned toward the kitchen, determined to leave through the back door and run to Tyler's house.

If he was home.

Footfalls sounded in the hallway, coming closer.

Her chest tightened. Fear strangled her throat and escalated her beating heart.

No time to flee. She needed to hide. But where? In spite of the darkness, she felt exposed.

Another creaking floorboard. Close. Too close.

She ducked behind the sofa and hunched down. Her body trembled, and her heart pounded too loudly.

A series of footfalls moved into the main room. She held her breath. He grunted, as if more animal than human. Fear clung to her. She wanted to whimper, but any noise would draw his attention.

Another step, then another.

He was so close she could smell him.

Stale beer and sweat.

Afraid to breathe, she crouched even lower.

He walked in front of the couch, two feet from where she was hiding. If he went into the kitchen, she'd make a dash for the front door. Could she make it in time? The lower lock would need to be turned and the dead bolt released.

Grip the knob, twist and pull the door open. Run.

The Lapps' house would be the closest. Were they home? Awake? Would they hear her pounding on the front door, and if so, would they come to her aid?

What about Tyler?

Tied up with a meeting on post.

Now or never. She started to rise. Her cell phone trilled. Glancing down, she saw Tyler's name on caller ID.

The intruder turned, lunged. His hand caught her shoulder.

She screamed and fumbled with her phone, trying to answer the call.

"Carrie?" Tyler's voice.

The intruder knocked the cell from her hand.

"No!" she screamed.

He grabbed her hair and jerked her head back. She thrashed her hands to strike him.

He raised his hand and slapped her across the face. She reeled and crashed against the wall. Air whooshed from her lungs.

Groaning, she crumbled onto the floor and crawled away from him, sobbing with fear.

He kicked her in the ribs.

She moaned, rolled into a ball. He kicked again.

Knowing she had to fight back, she grabbed his shoe and twisted his foot. He fell against the couch.

Scrambling to her feet, she ran. He followed, his footfalls heavy on the hardwoods.

Unsure of herself, Carrie took the corner to the kitchen too fast. Her feet slipped, slowing her down.

His hand clamped down on her arm. He threw her against the doorjamb. The hinge dug into her back.

"Oh!" she gasped, then ran forward. On the counter was a knife that she had used earlier to slice the chicken.

Grabbing the handle, she turned and raised the blade.

He caught her hand in a death grip and tightened his hold, bringing tears to her eyes and making her legs weaken. She sank to one knee, fighting to keep hold of the knife that was raised precariously over her head.

She...didn't...have...the...strength...

He twisted her arm.

She screamed in pain.

The knife dropped. She shoved it across the floor before he could stoop to retrieve it, then struck him in the face.

He growled and went for her neck. She backed against the counter. His grip tightened. She couldn't breathe and gasped for air.

Tyler!

She had to open the door and scream for help.

Tyler would save her.

But hands tightened on her throat, and her lungs burned like fire.

She couldn't scream, she couldn't move, she couldn't see and as she slipped into another place, she realized she wouldn't live to breathe again.

Irritated that the CID meeting had taken so long, Tyler increased his speed after leaving Fort Rickman. Glancing at his phone resting on the console, he debated calling Carrie, then checked the clock on the dashboard. Ten o'clock. Too late.

Carrie was tired and probably in bed sound asleep. The last thing he wanted was to wake her. They'd talk tomorrow.

But he couldn't stop himself from reaching for his phone. Using his one hand, he punched in his security code and swiped to access his screen.

A new voice mail.

Concern swept over him. He'd turned his phone to vibrate during the meeting and placed it in front of him on the conference table, yet he had missed the incoming call.

Tyler touched the prompt and raised the phone to his ear.

"Something's wrong with Bailey... The lights are out."

His pulse raced. He pressed down on the accelerator and pushed Call.

She answered, but what he heard sent chills through his heart.

Carrie's scream, along with the sounds of a scuffle or worse.

He tossed the cell aside, gripped the steering wheel and raced through town. He had to get to Carrie.

Never had the drive seemed so long or the road so winding.

He breathed with relief when he reached Amish Road, but his heart stopped when he saw the Harris home in the distance, standing dark against the night. He screeched into the driveway and jumped from the car, his weapon raised and at the ready.

Pounding on the front door, he screamed her name. Circling the house, he saw the French doors open and a man, running into the woods. Much as he wanted to pursue the intruder, he had to find Carrie.

"Carrie!" He tried the light switch that didn't work and raced into the main part of the house.

The sound of the dog's footfalls came from overhead. "Bailey, come. Where's Carrie?"

The dog failed to appear, which added to his concern. Tyler ran from room to room, fearing the intruder had harmed Carrie and her faithful pet.

Entering the kitchen, he stopped short seeing her on the floor. He knelt beside her and touched her neck. Relief swept over him when he felt a pulse.

Hurriedly he called 911. "Emergency. Medical help needed now."

After providing the necessary information, he disconnected and rubbed his hand lightly over Carrie's cheek, seeing the welt and marks from the assailant's hand. A cut on her lip was oozing blood, along with a scrape to her forehead and another to her hand.

She moaned. A good sign.

"Carrie, it's Tyler. I'm here. The intruder's gone. You're safe with me. Open your eyes. Talk to me."

She moved her hand.

"I know you're in pain. The ambulance will arrive soon. You'll get medical care, but you need to let me know you can hear me. Open your eyes, Carrie. I need to see your eyes."

Her eyelids fluttered.

"That's right, hon. Open your eyes."

He gripped her hand, relieved when she squeezed his fingers. "I know you can hear me."

"Ty—"

"Good job. I'm right here. Open your eyes."

Again, her eyelids fluttered, then opened for a second before closing again. He lit a candle and placed it on the counter.

"Try again," he encouraged.

Her eyes opened ever so slightly. He smiled. "I see you."

Her lips twitched as if she wanted to smile.

He patted her hand. "I'm going to check your pupils."

Gently he pulled back the eyelid on her right eye and then the left one. The pupil and iris looked normal. No severe dilation. Hopefully that meant no concussion.

At least that was in her favor.

Sirens sounded in the distance.

Footsteps on the front porch. Someone pounded on the door.

Carrie's face twisted with fear.

"I'll check it out. It's not the assailant. I saw him running into the woods. I'll be right back."

More pounding.

Tyler raced into the foyer, peered through the window and was relieved to see Isaac.

"Carrie has been hurt," he said as he opened the door. "An ambulance is on the way."

"I saw your car. The door was open, and the lights were on. I knew something had happened."

"Someone broke in and attacked Carrie."

Isaac's face clouded. "They hurt her?"

"I'm afraid so. She was unconscious when I arrived, but she opened her eyes and tried to let me know she could hear me."

The two men hurried to the kitchen.

Tyler bent down next to Carrie. "Isaac is here. The ambulance is close. Hang on."

She nodded, almost imperceptibly.

"Did you see your attacker?"

She shook her head. "Mask."

"He wore a mask over his face?"

She nodded.

Flashing lights invaded the kitchen.

The sound of car doors and men climbing the front steps. Isaac hurried into the foyer and pointed them to the kitchen.

Tyler stepped aside as the EMTs entered, hauling medical bags and a stretcher. He quickly filled them in on what he knew.

"An intruder. Looks like Ms. York was beaten. He ran from the house as I pulled into the driveway."

Knowing Carrie was in good hands, he stepped into the foyer and met Officer Phillips there.

"Did you see the perpetrator?" the cop asked.

"Only as he was running into the woods," Tyler said with regret. "I could have chased him, but I was worried about Carrie and rightfully so. He wore a mask and messed her up pretty badly."

"What happened to the power?"

"He must have cut the line." Tyler thought suddenly of Bailey. "And tranquilized the dog."

Borrowing a flashlight from one of the officers, Tyler headed upstairs and found Bailey lying in the hallway. He appeared sleepy but otherwise all right, which was a relief. If the perpetrator had given the dog a sedative, it had been short-lived.

Tyler checked the bedrooms and saw the aged journal on the nightstand near the bed where Carrie had been sleeping. Had she heard a noise and gone downstairs to check it out?

Returning to the hallway, he patted his leg. "Come on, Bailey. Let's have the medics look you over after they finish with Carrie."

The dog slowly rose and padded after Tyler, who kept his hand on his collar in case Bailey's legs buckled under him. Thankfully the dog went down the stairs without any problems. He trotted into the kitchen, whined at the cluster of people around Carrie and wiggled his way to her side.

Her hand rubbed against his fur. "Are you okay?" she managed to ask.

He wagged his tail.

"Looks like the dog may have been given something

that knocked him out," Tyler told one of the medics who took Bailey aside and examined him.

"He seems okay, sir. His eyes are clear. His reflexes are good."

"What about Ms. York?"

"We're taking her to the hospital in Freemont. The doc may order a CT scan. Her vitals are good, but she's got a knot on her head, a bruised cheek and what may be a couple broken ribs."

"I'll follow in my car."

He found Isaac. "I'm going to the hospital with Carrie. Would you stay here with the police?"

"Of course. Tell Carrie we are praying for her recovery."

"Thanks, Isaac. She needs prayers."

Phillips motioned for Tyler to follow him to the rear of the house. "Check out the sunporch. Looks like your intruder was looking for something."

Tyler hadn't noticed the chaos earlier when his thoughts were on finding Carrie. Now he saw the scattered papers and books and other memorabilia tossed about the room.

"Wonder if he found what he came searching for," Tyler mused.

"No telling." Phillips picked up an old plat of the property that had fallen out of a manila envelope. "Did you see this?"

After stepping closer, Tyler studied the plat. "It's of the Harris property."

Opening the drawer on the desk, he was relieved to find the photograph of Carrie still in place.

"Something important?" the officer asked.

"One of Carrie's baby pictures."

"What about the journal the firemen found the other night?"

"It's upstairs in one of the bedrooms," Tyler said. "I wonder if that's what the guy was looking for. She probably came downstairs never expecting someone was in the house."

The cop flashed his light over the porch door. "Looks like he got in through the French doors."

"And Bailey wouldn't have heard because he was drugged, which meant the guy had to have been in the area earlier. Carrie had planned to sit outside and let Bailey play. He may have found something edible laced with sleeping medication."

Returning to the living area, Tyler approached Isaac. "Did you see anyone hanging around the house today?"

"The boy who fed the chickens. Matthew Schrock came with him."

"Anyone else?"

"Not that I saw."

Phillips signaled to Tyler. "The EMTs are ready to transport her."

"I'll follow the ambulance. Isaac Lapp will stay in the house until your folks are ready to leave."

Tyler hurried to his car in time to pull behind the ambulance as it raced back to town.

In the rearview mirror, he could see the flashing lights of the police sedans for miles. The strobe effect added a chilling reality to the dark night.

Someone was after Carrie. He—or she—had almost killed Carrie tonight. Tyler hadn't been there, which frustrated him.

As a boy he'd wanted to help his father, but he'd been unable to save him. The reason he went into law enforcement had been to help people in need. Carrie was in need, and Tyler had been worried about her security, yet he hadn't been able to protect her.

What did that say about his ability?

As the Amish said, he was *dummkopf*. Stupid. Not worthy of wearing the uniform and not able to keep Carrie safe.

Chapter Fifteen

Carrie didn't like hospitals, especially when she was the patient. The emergency room doctor was thorough in his evaluation and had ordered a CT scan to ensure that her injuries weren't life threatening.

Much as Carrie's body ached, she was all right. A few scrapes and bruises, a sore rib and a pounding headache that made her grit her teeth and clench her fists, but she would survive.

Thanks to Tyler.

She peered out the door of the examination room when the doctor left and smiled when she saw Tyler standing in the hallway.

He stepped closer. "Do you want company?"

"That sounds good, although I'm not much for conversation at this point. My head's throbbing, and I keep telling myself that I should have been smarter. How's Bailey?"

"Doing fine, the last I saw him. Isaac stayed at the house to watch over everything. The doc will let you go home as soon as the blood test results are back."

"What happened to the electricity?"

"The guy cut the line coming into the house."

"He wanted me in the dark."

"Your dad's office papers were scattered about. He may have been looking for the diary."

She nodded. "It was upstairs in the guest bedroom."

"When I pulled into your driveway, he must have exited through your dad's office."

"Good riddance."

"Exactly, but we need to find out who it was and why he was there."

"Land or treasure would be my two guesses," Carrie said through half-closed eyes.

"He may have been after you."

Carrie kept thinking of Tyler's comment as he drove her home. Had the intruder entered the house to do her harm? If she hadn't gone downstairs, would he have climbed to the second floor and attacked her there?

She shivered thinking of what could have been on his mind. Biting her lip, she blinked back tears as the memory of his vicious blows swept over her again.

Tyler touched her arm and worked his hand to hers. His fingers tightened as if he read her mind and wanted to comfort her. "You've been through a lot, Carrie."

"All my life, I longed to know about my father. I never expected information about him to come with such a high price."

"Your father didn't want this to happen."

"But was he involved, Tyler? I keep thinking it can't be coincidental."

"Have you found anything in the journal?"

"Only that things were hidden somewhere on the property. Charlotte called them her treasures, but she never mentioned gold."

"Yet her husband's letter at the museum mentions coins that needed to be secreted away."

"Could all of this—the two murders and the attacks, my tires, the chickens—" She glanced at Tyler, hoping he could make sense of what she was trying to say. "Could they all have been caused by one man's greed?"

"I'm not sure at this point. Your father's death could have been accidental, yet Eli said his friend had seen men fighting. The sergeant major usually carried his rifle when he walked in the woods. It wasn't recovered when his body was found. Did someone kill him and take the rifle?"

"Maybe Fellows."

Tyler nodded. "That could be, but if so, then who killed Fellows and why?"

"What if the corporal was searching for buried treasure? Someone else could have been working with him," Carrie mused.

"The guy who eventually killed him."

She nodded. "If everyone's after the same thing, and they thought my father knew how to find it, they could have been fighting among themselves."

They rode in silence as Carrie thought back over the events that had led to this point in time. Tyler seemed equally lost in thought.

He let out a deep breath when the outline of the old antebellum home appeared in the darkness. After parking at the side of the house, Tyler opened the driver's door.

Isaac walked toward the car, Ruth hurrying along behind him.

"She is all right?" the Amish man asked.

"Thankfully nothing was broken. She'll be sore for the next few days, but it could have been so much worse."

"Thanks be to *Gott*," Ruth said.

Carrie could hear them talk even though the windows were raised. Opening the door, she waited. Tyler hurried to help her from the car.

Ruth stepped closer and wrapped Carrie in her arms. "We were so worried." The Amish woman's embrace had a motherly quality that brought comfort and a sense of homecoming.

"You cannot stay alone in your father's house," Ruth said. "Isaac and I both insist that you sleep at our house. We have an extra room. You will be safe there."

Isaac nodded in agreement. "No one will think to look for you in our house."

Carrie glanced at Tyler. "I don't want to give in or let the attacker think he's won."

"Your safety is our first consideration," Tyler said. "I don't want you staying alone in your father's house after someone was able to get inside. Tomorrow I'll fix the back door, install more security and get the power turned on, but for now you need to stay with the Lapps."

"What about Bailey?" Carried asked, glancing at the house.

"I brought him earlier into our home," Isaac assured her. "I wanted to watch him through the night because of the drugs he had in his body. He didn't seem as playful as usual, and I was worried about him. He is in Joseph's room, curled up on the floor by his bed. The boy loves him, and the dog is happy there. I will check on both of them later."

Relieved that Bailey was in good hands, Carrie realized she needed to accept the Lapps' offer and stay with them.

She turned to Tyler. "You'll be all right?"

"Of course. I need to contact the local police and CID on post and try to put together any new information they've received. Plus, I'll keep an eye on your house, Carrie, while you rest."

She shivered as wind blew through the trees, and a sliver of moon broke through the clouds. Tyler was right, but she didn't want to leave him.

Stepping closer, she said, "Thank you, Tyler, for coming to my rescue today."

He wrapped his arms around her and drew her close for a moment. His embrace warmed her.

"I'll see you in the morning," he whispered, dropping a kiss on her forehead before he pulled away.

Ruth took her hand. "Come, Carrie. We'll go to my house now."

Carrie glanced over her shoulder as she walked with Ruth. Tyler waved and gave her an encouraging smile visible in the moonlight.

For one frightening moment, she wondered if she'd see him again. Then shaking off the thought, she followed Ruth into the house. The smell of fresh-baked bread and the oil from the lamps greeted her.

"You would like something to eat before you go to bed?" Ruth asked, her eyes filled with concern.

"I'm fine, but tired. Are you sure you have room for me?"

Ruth nodded. "Upstairs. I have a nightdress you can wear and soap and water if you would like to wash your face and hands."

She lifted a small lamp from the nearby table and motioned Carrie to follow her up the wooden stairs.

The door to the first room was open. Ruth paused

and pointed to the bed where Joseph slept. "Look where Bailey is."

Carrie peered inside. The dog rested on a small rug at the side of the boy's bed.

Ruth smiled. "Joseph will be surprised when he wakes in the morning."

Bailey opened his eyes. Spying Carrie, he walked to the door, tail wagging as he nuzzled her leg. She bent to pat him, finding comfort from his welcome.

"Good to see you, boy," she whispered so as not to wake Joseph. "I was worried about you."

"Your room is this way." Ruth pointed to the end of the hallway.

Bailey followed the two women into the small but pretty guest room. A single bed was covered with a quilt. Two fluffy pillows were encased with white pillowcases embroidered with tiny spring flowers. A newly laundered nightdress lay folded on the nearby washstand that also held a basin and pitcher of water. A package of wrapped toiletries added a thoughtful touch that Carrie appreciated.

Curtains covered the windows in a delicate subdued print that matched some of the quilted patches on the spread. Wall pegs provided a place where Carrie could hang her clothes.

"If you need anything, just call for me. I will be sleeping across the hall. Isaac will be watchful throughout the night. You do not need to worry. Our doors are locked, and Isaac will not let anyone intrude. You are safe here."

"Thank you, Ruth. You and your husband have done so much for me."

"We are grateful for your friendship. Your father helped us when we first moved here. He sold some of his land so Isaac could have a nice farm. That meant so much to us."

She placed the lamp on the stand.

"Sleep well," Ruth said as she left the room and closed the door behind her.

Bailey whined.

"You want to go back with Joseph?" Opening the door, Carrie watched the dog walk to the end of the hallway. He glanced back as if to ensure that she was all right before he entered the boy's room.

Overcome with exhaustion, Carrie went to the window and pulled back the curtain. She could see her father's house and a corner of Tyler's one-story ranch beyond. A light came on in one of the rooms, and even from this distance, she could see someone standing at the window and staring out into the night.

She doubted Tyler could see her, and she wondered what he was thinking. She didn't know her own mind at this point, but her heart reached out to Tyler. Grateful as she was for the Lapps, she was even more grateful for him. Tyler had tried to protect her and keep her safe. But someone was still out there.

Her gaze moved to the dark stand of trees at the rear of her father's house and the spot where she'd stumbled upon Corporal Fellows's body. After all that had happened, the police were no closer to finding his killer. Nor did they fully understand the reason for her father's death or who was attacking her.

Should she stay longer and risk her own life? Or should she return to Washington? In DC, she wouldn't have to worry about a killer in the night, but that meant leaving Tyler.

Would he care if she left?

Carrie thought again of the comment he'd made when she mentioned not wanting to leave the Lapps. "What about the neighbor on the other side?" Tyler had asked.

Perhaps he wanted her to stay after all.

Tyler looked out the window and stared at the Amish house. While most of the dwelling was blocked from view, he could see one of the upstairs rear windows where a faint light glowed. In his mind's eye, he envisioned Carrie at the window staring back at him. Foolish to imagine such a thing. Tired as she was, Ruth had probably already tucked her into a bed piled high with handmade quilts and fresh, dried-on-the-line linens.

As much as Tyler wanted to believe otherwise, Carrie wasn't thinking of him. If she was thinking of anything, it would be her job in DC and the speech she needed to write for Senator Kingsley.

Had the senator changed over the years? Surely since his drinking had been such a significant problem back then, he would have sought treatment and stopped the addictive behavior by now.

The memory of his father's death returned with the screech of tires, the crash of metal and the horrific sound of his father's scream as he called Tyler's name. Along with the wail of sirens and the flashing lights came the memory of a closed-casket funeral and of a young boy who wanted to see his father again.

Tyler turned from the window as his cell rang.

Seeing Everett's name, he connected and raised the phone to his ear. "Anything new on the case?" he asked in greeting.

"I got a call from the first sergeant at the engineer battalion. One of the guys in the unit started talking. Evidently a few of the men had visited a cabin not far from Amish Road. They'd check out of post on a three-day pass to work for a guy in town who flips houses. He's got a cabin where the soldiers stay so they don't have to drive back and forth to Fort Rickman. The construction boss stocks the fridge with beer and wine, and provides X-rated movies to entertain the men at night. From the way the soldier talked, it sounds like it's in the vicinity of the Harris home."

"Was Fellows involved?"

"He helped sometimes. Guess the money was good. They were paid in cash so everything went into their wallets with nothing taken out for Uncle Sam."

"Is the soldier willing to share names?"

"Not yet, but we plan to haul him in for questioning."

"I'll head to post sometime tomorrow." Tyler filled Everett in on what had happened at Carrie's house. "She's staying with one of the Amish families tonight. I need to find out more about that cabin. I'll call the local police and see what they can uncover."

After disconnecting, Tyler called Phillips. "You're working late," he said when the cop answered.

"Sounds as if you are too. How's Ms. York?"

"I'm guessing that she's fast asleep at the Amish neighbors' house. Staying in her father's place again was too risky."

Tyler explained about the soldiers and the cabin where they crashed and then asked, "Do you have any knowledge of a cabin and who might own the property?"

"I'll search the county records and get back to you," Phillips said. "We don't show anything on our maps of the area. The guy must keep information about the cabin off the radar. As you know, there are a number of dirt roads that twist through that area. They have to lead somewhere."

"Check out Nelson Quinn."

"The real estate agent?" Phillips asked.

Tyler nodded. "Quinn sometimes flips houses. Also check on Mrs. Gates and the mayor's wife."

"Will do. By the way, I contacted a friend who will reconnect the power first thing tomorrow."

"Thanks. That saves me time and means I can hike Harris's property in the morning."

"Let me know what you find, and, Tyler—"

"Yeah?"

"Watch your back," Phillips warned. "The attacks are escalating against Ms. York. I have a hunch the killer's becoming desperate, and we both know that when a killer's cornered, he often strikes again. I don't want you in his crosshairs."

"I'll be careful. My main concern is Carrie. She didn't plan on being a target and keeps wondering if it involves her father."

"That's been my question as well," the cop said. "But everything I've learned about Jeffrey Harris is positive. The guy kept to himself, was unassuming and was the first to lend a hand when someone was in need."

"Let's hope you've got it right."

Tyler disconnected and began searching the archives of the local paper for any history of the area that might have a bearing on the investigation. Sometime after midnight, he found a picture of the Harris home as it was when the sergeant major's elderly aunt had lived there, until her death.

By then, the house had fallen into disrepair. The restoration must have been extensive and costly. How had Harris, on a sergeant major's paycheck, afforded the work? Maybe Carrie's hunch would prove true. Maybe her father was involved in something corrupt. Could he have taken part in the weekend construction projects that involved the soldiers in his former unit?

As much as Tyler didn't want anything negative to surface, he needed to learn the truth.

Reading through a feature story about the renovation, he found mention of a builder, named Ulmer, who had helped with the project.

Where had he seen that name?

Tyler poured a cup of coffee and stared again at the house next door. Once he'd downed the strong brew, he grabbed his jacket and walked around the Harris home, checking that the doors were locked and the property secure.

The sounds of the night surrounded him. In the distance, an owl hooted, its deep call adding to the sense of unrest he felt. He glanced at the wooded area behind the house and the hill beyond. Was there a cabin out there someplace, and if so, was the killer holed up inside, waiting and perhaps watching?

Lord, help me solve this case. The words slipped through Tyler's mind and surprised him. He had closed the Lord out of his heart since his father's death, but being with Carrie had renewed his faith, at least a little.

He stared at the Lapp house. His gaze homed in on the upstairs rear bedroom where he'd sensed Carrie's presence.

He had changed since her arrival. For the better.

Maybe after all these years, it was time to leave the past behind and make his way into the future unencumbered by the anger and distrust that had hovered over his heart for too long.

"Forgive me, Lord, for not being able to forgive another." Perhaps forgiveness would come in time. Right now he was grateful for being open to the Lord.

If he remained around Carrie, he might find his heart soften even more. She had an effect on him. A good effect. She forced him to look beyond his own broken past and see the potential of a future free of resentment, a future based on love.

He shook his head. Carrie brought feelings of protectiveness and an almost constant desire to be near her. Was that love?

Only time would tell. Would she stay in Freemont long enough for Tyler to make sense of his emotions or would she return to DC and to the senator who wasn't worthy of her attention?

Chapter Sixteen

Carrie woke with an aching body. The bumps and bruises she had received from the intruder seemed even more painful this morning. Groaning, she dropped her feet to the floor and stood, feeling the blood leave her head. The room swirled around her. She grabbed the headboard and waited until the dizziness passed. As if sensing her presence, Bailey pushed open the door and stepped into the room.

"How are you?" Carrie patted his nose and scratched his back. "Did you sleep well in Joseph's room?"

Hearing his name, the boy knocked lightly on the door and peered into the room. "Is Bailey with you?"

"Come in, Joseph." The boy was all smiles as he entered and knelt on the floor. Wrapping his arms around the dog's neck, he whispered, loud enough for Carrie to hear, "I couldn't find you, Bailey."

The boy's words touched Carrie's heart. That was how she felt about her father. She couldn't find him, couldn't find who he really was. Then she thought of everything people had told her. Why couldn't she accept what they had said? Instead she continued to question whether her father was involved in something corrupt and illegal.

How foolish of her. As if blinders were removed from her eyes, she saw more clearly. Her father was a good man. He had wanted a relationship with his only child, but he had honored her mother's wishes. Perhaps he felt at fault for not being the father he should have been, for not marrying her mother and for forcing her to raise a child outside of marriage. For a man who embraced the Lord and scripture, that could have been a heavy burden to carry that would have brought a sense of unworthiness.

She felt unworthy as well and was overwhelmed with a desire to connect with her heavenly Father. *Lord, forgive me for accusing You of not loving me, when I was the one who rejected You. Open my heart to love You more.*

Thoughts of her mother came to mind, a lonely woman who was never satisfied with her life or her daughter. Carrie didn't feel anger or resentment, but a sadness that her mother had never experienced the peace Carrie felt at this moment.

Joseph leaned back against the bed and brushed against her leg. Bailey snuggled close, enjoying the boy's hugs.

Carrie's heart opened even more completely to the goodness she felt in this house, to the warm embrace of love from the Lord and her new appreciation for both her earthly father as well as the God of heaven and earth.

Love filled her for her father, for the Lord and—

The face that came to mind made her startle.

Tyler?

He had worked so hard to protect her and keep her safe. He made her smile, and she felt protected and totally at home in his embrace.

Was it… Could it be love?

"Joseph," Ruth called to her son.

The boy jumped to his feet. "You're staying for break-fast?" His eyes were wide and hopeful.

"I would like to, Joseph."

"Can Bailey stay too?"

"If your parents agree."

"I'll ask *Mamm*." The boy scurried out the door.

Bailey looked up at her with his big brown eyes as if needing her consent. She laughed and hugged him. "Go with Joseph. I'll be fine."

The dog hurried from the room.

Carrie slipped into the clothes she had worn yester-day and folded the nightgown Ruth had provided. After making the bed and smoothing the quilt covering, she moved to the window and pulled back the curtain. In the distance, she saw Tyler heading into the thick woods be-hind her father's house. No doubt, he was in search of the cabin the Amish boys had mentioned, knowing she wouldn't feel up to hiking across her father's property this morning.

Keep him safe, Lord. Let him find the cabin and in-formation about my father's death so the case could be solved and the investigation ended.

A sadness swept over her as she thought of what that would mean. Tyler would move on to the next case, and she would return to Washington and the life she knew. She'd sell the house and forget about Freemont and the Amish community and the family legacy she had found in South Georgia.

Would she… Could she forget about Tyler?

Grateful for the old plat Phillips had found in Carrie's father's office, Tyler followed the markings on the brittle yellow paper. He discovered a path, probably where deer ran, and followed it to the steep rise from which Carrie's father had fallen. Glancing over the drop-off, he was all too aware that a fall could have broken the sergeant major's neck. A soldier, trained in hand-to-hand combat, would have known how to inflict the same injury, as well.

He glanced again at the plat and noted the end of the sergeant major's property, but continued walking for half a mile farther. Peering through the woods, he saw a structure in the distance and had a surge of exuberance, knowing he might have found the cabin the Amish boys had talked about and the soldiers had mentioned.

A path, wide enough for a single vehicle, led toward the main road. He and the Freemont police had searched, but the woods were vast and dense and the trail had eluded them.

Nearing the cabin, he glanced through the windows. A number of cots filled the main room, along with a large-screen television and pool table. Chances were the refrigerator was stocked with beer.

Spying something else, he pulled out his cell and called Phillips. "I've found a cabin that needs to be checked. Through the window, I can see a rifle. Looks like a Winchester 1894, the model the sergeant major carried when he was in the woods. Ammo was found in his pocket, which means Harris was probably carrying the rifle. The person who took the Winchester could have been the man who fought the sergeant major. If we find the owner of the cabin, he might lead us to the killer."

By noon, Phillips and his men had gotten a search warrant and had scoured the cabin for evidence. The rifle appeared to have belonged to the sergeant major, although ballistics testing would confirm ownership. The gun, like the rest of the cabin, had been wiped clean of prints. When the police wrapped up their investigation, Phillips gave Tyler a drive back to his house.

"Thanks for your help," he said as Tyler stepped from the car.

"Carrie will be glad we found the cabin and the gun. I'll tell her now."

He hurried to her house and tapped on the door. She answered looking tired. Bruises darkened her cheek and forehead.

"How are you feeling?" he asked, stepping inside.

"Better than last night."

"Were you able to get a good night's sleep?"

She nodded. "Which was what I needed. Ruth insisted I stay for breakfast, and I ate more than I have in years. Her ham and eggs and fresh-baked biscuits and gravy were wonderful. If I lived with them long, I'd weigh a ton."

She tried to laugh but grimaced. Raising her hand, she brushed her fingers along her jaw. A dark mark outlined one of the strikes against her face and brought Tyler back to the subject at hand.

"I found the cabin," he said. "The police retrieved what we think is your father's missing rifle."

"Who owns the cabin?"

"We don't know yet. Phillips is trying to find the records for the property. He's concerned that the deed for the land may go back further than the recorded county documents. They may need to access some of the old records in the county courthouse."

"So we don't know who the attacker is yet?"

"Soon, Carrie. It will all be over soon."

"Do you want some coffee?" she asked.

"Sounds good. Evidently your power's back on."

"For which I'm thankful."

On the way to the kitchen, he saw her laptop on the dining room table and a few papers scattered close by. "You've been working?"

She nodded. "On the speech for Senator Kingsley."

He let out an exasperated breath.

"I know you don't like him," she said.

"He's not a good man, Carrie."

After grabbing two mugs from the cabinet, she poured coffee and handed a mug to Tyler. "The senator is not against the military."

"I'm not referring to his present political stand. I'm referring to something that happened years ago."

She looked confused. "What are you talking about?"

"I told you about the car crash that killed my father."

Carrie nodded.

"I never told you who was driving the other car."

Her gaze narrowed. Her voice weak when she spoke. "Drake Kingsley?"

Tyler nodded. "He was drunk, Carrie, and staggered from his car. My father was dying, I was cut and bleeding and Kingsley called someone who picked him up. The next I knew he was exonerated from any wrongdoing. He killed my father and walked away without being prosecuted."

"That's why you went into law enforcement," she said.

He nodded. "And why I don't want you involved with the senator."

"But that was years ago, Tyler. He's a changed man."

"Is he?"

"I've never seen him drunk."

"Maybe he's reformed. I hope so, but I still question his judgment and integrity. Tell me you'll quit your job."

She took a step back, seemingly perplexed by his comment. "I...I can't do that."

"If you stay here, you could find another job. Maybe on post."

"It's not the same."

"You mean it's not Washington. That's it, isn't it? You're not interested in small-town Georgia."

"You said it yourself, Tyler. I've worked hard to get where I am. I can't throw it all away."

He smiled ruefully. "I wouldn't want you to throw your career away, Carrie. I just want you to think of what you've found in Freemont that you won't have in Washington."

She looked around the house. "I've found an antebellum home that I don't want to live in alone, Tyler. Yes, I know more about my past, but that's not enough moving forward. I need something else in my life."

"You need Washington."

His cell rang. It was Phillips. "We've got a name," the cop said. "Karl Ulmer. His wife, Yvonne, comes from an old Freemont family. The cabin belongs to them. We're going to haul them both in for questioning."

Tyler disconnected. "They found the connection." He told Carrie the names and that the woman was old Freemont.

"Yvonne is the docent at the museum," Carrie said.

Tyler nodded. "I knew I recognized the name. Her husband did some refurbishing for your father after he acquired the property when his elderly aunt died. Ulmer must have seen the potential then. When your father retired, folks thought he'd leave Freemont. Ulmer wanted to buy the house and land. He's probably the person who Flo mentioned that wanted to turn this area into a recreational site."

"Which the Amish would never want."

"Are you still planning to sell?" Tyler asked.

"Not to them, but I'll find a buyer, someone who will care for the house."

"Really, Carrie? Who's to say the next buyer won't sell to someone else for the right price? Your legacy will be gone, cut up into a housing development or even shops and restaurants like these people planned to do. Think about Isaac and Ruth Lapp. That's not what they want for this area."

"I can't take care of everyone, Tyler. I have to take care of myself."

Tyler bristled at the sharpness of her tone. "That isn't what I wanted to hear."

He turned his back on her and strode to the door. "I need to go back to post and inform the CID what's happening. The Ulmers had a motive and appear to be involved in your father's death. You should be safe, since the couple is in custody. Still, keep your doors locked." He glanced around. "Where's Bailey?"

"He stayed with Joseph. I plan to give the dog to him when I leave."

Tyler's gut tightened hearing her say the words that cut into his heart. This had all been of so little value to her, when it had meant so much to him.

He glanced at the table by the door and saw the envelope for Sergeant Oliver. "You found photos of your dad?"

She nodded. "Last night."

"I'll stop by the unit and get these pictures to Oliver."

Opening the door, he turned to stare back at her. "Looks like everything's over, Carrie. You can make arrangements to leave. I'll watch over your property until it sells."

He stepped outside and heard the door slam behind him. Hurrying across the yard to his car, he struggled with a mix of regret and heartache, which he hadn't expected. Carrie had finally made up her mind. She was leaving Freemont and leaving him.

Slipping behind the wheel, he pulled onto Amish Road and never looked back at the Harris home or the woman who would leave him and return to DC, taking his heart with her.

Chapter Seventeen

Tyler found First Sergeant Baker at the unit and handed him the photos. "These go to Sergeant Oliver. They're pictures of Sergeant Major Harris."

The first sergeant scratched his head. "That's strange."

"Why?" Tyler asked.

"Oliver and the sergeant major were at odds," the first sergeant explained.

"Since when?"

"Since the sergeant major discovered Oliver arranging payday loans with some of the guys in the battalion."

"Where'd Oliver get the money?"

The first sergeant stepped closer. "From what I heard, his brother-in-law was the source of the loan money. Oliver was the middleman. Of course the interest rate was sky-high."

"Using soldiers who worked under him for his own personal gain is against regulations," Tyler said, stating the obvious.

"Yes, sir. That's why the sergeant major brought the situation to the commander, who gave Oliver an Article 15, which meant he didn't pass his promotion board.

Without a promotion, Oliver couldn't reenlist. He's leaving the military at the end of the month."

"But he's working on the ceremony honoring Harris at the end of the month?"

The first sergeant shook his head. "That's something I haven't heard. Oliver is an ornery guy who can pick a fight at the drop of a hat. I can't see him working on a project that would honor the sergeant major."

A sick feeling settled in Tyler's midsection. "Where's Oliver?"

"He signed out on a three-day pass. He mentioned visiting a friend in Florida."

"Do you know his brother-in-law's name?"

The sergeant thought for a moment. "I should. Seems he earned his money in real estate."

"Quinn?" Tyler offered. "He's got a real estate business in Freemont."

"Maybe." The first sergeant pursed his lips. "But I can't be sure. I'll think of it in a minute. Are you going to be around?"

"I'm heading to CID headquarters." Tyler gave the first sergeant his cell number. "Call me if you remember the name."

Carrie's heart had broken when Tyler walked out the door. The story about his father's death troubled her deeply. Could it be true?

She stared at her computer monitor for long enough to know that she couldn't move forward until she talked to Senator Kingsley. Finally she reached for her cell and called Washington, hoping to learn the truth.

The senator's senior adviser answered.

"I want to talk to Senator Kingsley," Carrie demanded.

"No can do, Carrie. What's the problem?"

"Why isn't he returning my phone calls?"

"The senator's tied up."

"Something's going on, Art, and I don't like it."

"What about the speech?" he asked.

She glanced at her laptop and the blank screen on her monitor. "I'll have it done in time."

"I want it ahead of time, Carrie."

"I've never missed a deadline," she said, feeling frustrated and somewhat helpless. "I need to talk to the senator. Now."

"I told you—"

"Look, Art, there's something important from his past that I need to discuss with him."

"What's it involve?"

"A two-car accident some years ago."

The adviser sighed. "Who told you?"

She didn't understand his change of direction. "Who told me what?"

"You're talking about the accident that killed a single dad who had a ten-year-old son, right?"

"Is it common knowledge?" Carrie asked.

"It may be soon enough. Some news reporter called the senator for a statement. He plans to feature the story in *The Washington Post* this weekend. That's why the senator finally decided to take matters into his own hands."

"I don't understand."

"Do I have to spell it out for you, Carrie?"

"I guess you do."

"Rehab." Art's tone was sharp. "The senator checked into a treatment center for alcohol addiction."

His words felt like a stab to her heart. "I…I never thought he had a problem."

"You never socialized with him, Carrie. He was on his best behavior at political functions. Socially and away from the office was a different story."

"What about the speech I'm supposed to write?" She glanced again at her laptop.

"He'll be out of rehab by then. So write it, Carrie, and send it to me as soon as it's finished so I can be sure it reflects the senator's wishes."

"All this time, Art, have you been the one pushing the antimilitary sentiments?"

"I've counseled the senator."

Anger welled up within her. "You've controlled him."

"The senator needed someone."

"He didn't need your hateful feelings about the military. Why can't the senator voice his own mind?"

"Because he's weak, Carrie. I'm the power behind Drake Kingsley."

"Shame on you."

"You may not realize, Ms. York, that the world is filled with lots of people who can write speeches. Jobs are hard to come by in this downward economy. I wouldn't be quite so quick to express an opinion contrary to your boss."

She steeled her spine. "My boss is Senator Kingsley."

"I'll tell him how you feel."

"Fine, but I'll write the speech and email it prior to the deadline. Tell him I'm praying for his return to good health."

She hung up tasting the bitter bile that rose in her throat. Art was hateful. She'd had blinders on her eyes all this time, like some of the horses that pulled the Amish buggies. How could she have been fooled by the senator? Thinking back, she realized Art was right. She had never socialized with the senator or any of his staff. The few functions she attended had been job related when, evidently, he was on his best behavior.

Thankfully the senator was getting the help he needed. *Oh, Lord, help him.* She sighed.

The doorbell rang.

Expecting to see Joseph and Bailey, she hurried to open the door.

"Sergeant Oliver." She took a step back, surprised. "I didn't expect you this early."

"I told you I'd stop by for the pictures."

"Tyler Zimmerman took them to the unit. I'm sorry you had to make a trip for nothing."

He stepped inside, although she hadn't invited him in. A sense of déjà vu filled her.

"It's not a problem," he said. "Besides, I wanted to talk to you about something else."

"Oh?"

"The treasure."

She tried to smile through stiff lips. "Which probably doesn't exist."

"You know where it's located," the sergeant insisted.

"Rumors in town have gotten out of hand," she assured him. "That was long ago, and I doubt there would be anything of value to find, even if there had been treasure."

"Corporal Fellows told me he had found a coin."

A tingle curved along her spine. "You mean the soldier who was killed?"

Oliver nodded and stepped closer. "He'd found the stash, but he wouldn't tell me where it was located."

She took a step back and glanced at the table where

her cell phone lay. The memory of the attack last night swept over her.

"Tyler might know about the treasure." She reached for the phone. "I'll call him."

Oliver slapped the cell out of her hand. "Don't try that again."

Her eyes widened. "You were here last night."

"Looking for the maps that I couldn't find. The letter at the museum in town said Jefferson Harris would leave a map for his son, only there weren't any in the desk. Where are they?"

She turned and fled into the kitchen, hoping to reach the side door. Surely someone would hear her if she got outside.

He grabbed her hair.

She screamed and fought back.

His hand rose, just as last night, and she tensed, anticipating the blow that rocked her world.

The pain made her gasp for air. She doubled over. He kicked her in the stomach. Air *whooshed* from her lungs.

She collapsed onto the hardwood floor, thinking of the women of old who had washed the floors by hand.

She'd never finished reading the journal or learned what happened to her ancestors. Before she could think anything more about the past, darkness swept over her, wiping out the pain and the memories.

Before he got to CID headquarters, Tyler's phone rang. "Zimmerman."

"Sir, this is First Sergeant Baker with the engineer battalion. I remember the name of Oliver's brother-in-law. It's Ulmer."

Tyler's gut tightened. "You're sure?"

"Yes, sir."

Tyler thanked the first sergeant and tried Carrie's phone, but it went to voice mail. As he headed off post, he called Everett and quickly filled him in. "Put out a BOLO for Sergeant Frank Oliver. Supposedly he's heading to Florida on a three-day pass, but that could just be a cover. I'm driving back to Amish Road to warn Carrie."

Next he contacted Phillips. "See what Ulmer has to say about his brother-in-law. I need to warn Carrie. She's at the house alone."

"I'll send one of our men to check on her," Phillips assured him.

Tyler arrived at the house before the police. He pounded on the door and then circled to the rear and broke through the French doors, just as the intruder had done.

"Carrie," he screamed.

The house was empty, but he found her cell phone on the rug and spattered blood on the kitchen floor. Heart in his throat, he retraced his steps.

Joseph was in the backyard.

"Go inside, Joseph. Tell your dad that a soldier from post may have taken Carrie into the woods. Stay with your mother. Tell her to lock the doors."

Fear clouded the boy's face. Tyler hated to scare him, but the boy needed to be kept safe.

Tyler raced toward the woods. He had to get to Carrie. He had to get to her in time.

"Tell me where the treasure is buried," Oliver insisted. His voice was low and menacing.

He had brought her to a dark, dank cave on the side

of the hill where her father must have fallen to his death. Fallen or been pushed.

She squared her shoulders, looking defiantly at the sergeant. "I don't know anything about treasure."

"I heard one of the new volunteer firefighters in town was reprimanded for talking about a journal that mentioned buried treasure."

She shook her head. "The clues provided in the little book have long since disappeared. One was a twisted oak, the other a hedge of blackberry bushes. Both are gone."

He raised his brow. "A twisted oak. There's one not far from here. Two trees have grown together. The trunks wrapped one around the other."

"Then maybe that's where you should look," she suggested, hoping to turn his thoughts to anything except her.

He grabbed her arm. "You're going with me."

"No." She shook her head. "I can't help you."

"Of course you can. You can dig, and then when the treasure is unearthed, you can crawl into the hole and I'll bury you."

Fingers of fear clutched at her throat. "No," she whimpered.

He grabbed a shovel and pushed her toward the mouth of the cave.

She screamed. The sound was chilling, but who would hear her?

Not Tyler. He was at Fort Rickman tying up the loose ends of the investigation.

Oliver slapped her face. She grimaced with pain but remained upright, determined to appear strong and in control.

"I know about the cabin," she said, hoping to focus

the sergeant on anything except killing her. "It belongs to Karl Ulmer."

Oliver sneered. "Karl's my brother-in-law. He had big plans for developing your father's land."

"With a shopping mall."

"That's right. Until the sergeant major found out he was related to me. Then your father decided to keep his land. Karl blamed me when the deal went south. I had to prove that I could take care of myself, and I wanted my sister to be proud of me."

"By stealing what belongs to someone else? Fellows found a buried coin, and you thought it was part of the treasure. Is that why you killed him?"

"Fellows found a coin when he was planting shrubbery. He'd seen the light on in the big house and was headed there to tell you about his find."

"So you did kill him."

"I had to," Oliver insisted. "Fellows planned to tell you about my search for the treasure. He knew I'd argued with your father. He thought I'd killed the sergeant major even though I told him it was an accident."

"But you did kill him," Carrie insisted.

Oliver smirked. "I wanted him to die after what he did to me. I shoved him, knowing he wouldn't be able to stop his fall."

"You're a murderer."

With a shake of his head, the sergeant added boastfully, "I'm a man trying to provide for my future."

"By killing two innocent people."

He slapped her again. She fell to the ground.

"Drop the gun, Oliver."

The sergeant turned at the sound of his name.

Tyler stood in the clearing, his weapon raised.

The sergeant grabbed Carrie and shoved the gun to her head. "I'll kill her if you take one step closer."

Tyler's gaze narrowed. "You won't succeed."

"Try me," the sergeant taunted.

Carrie struggled to free herself.

"Bailey." Joseph's voice.

Ice chilled her veins. Out of the corner of her eye, Carrie spied the boy standing wide-eyed, openmouthed.

"Joseph, run home. Fast." Tyler's warning.

Bailey growled and raced forward. He nipped at Oliver's leg.

Carrie jabbed her elbow into the soldier's gut and shoved him hard.

He fired.

The bullet hit the ground just inches from her foot.

She kneed his leg, throwing him off balance. He pulled her down under him. She grabbed his wrist, unable to gain control of the weapon.

Tyler clamped his hand down on the sergeant's shoulder, lifted him off Carrie and kicked the weapon out of Oliver's hand.

"Augh!" the guy screamed, his hand limp.

Picking him up by the collar, Tyler jammed his fist in his gut.

Air rushed from the soldier's lungs. Oliver collapsed on the ground, holding his stomach and moaning in pain.

Raising his weapon, Tyler took aim. "You move, Oliver, and you die. Understand?"

The sergeant nodded.

Tyler reached out a hand of support for Carrie. "Are you all right?"

She steadied herself against his sturdy frame. She hurt all over, but she was alive and so was Tyler.

"Where's Joseph?" She searched the bushes, worried about the boy.

"I am here," he said, waving at both of them.

"Joseph?" Isaac's sharp call came from the path.

The Amish man stepped into the clearing and opened his arms for his son. "You were to stay home."

"Bailey got out. I had to follow him. He knew Carrie was in danger."

The police were right behind Isaac and quickly took Oliver into custody.

Tyler holstered his weapon and wrapped both arms around Carrie. "Are you sure you're not hurt?"

"I'm fine now," she said, resting her head on his shoulder.

The fear that had surrounded her eased. In Tyler's arms, she was safe.

Officer Phillips approached. "When my patrolman found the Harris home deserted and the French doors standing wide-open, he called for backup. Sorry it took so long to find you." He glanced at Joseph with his arms around Bailey. "If not for those two, we might have gone in the wrong direction."

"Oliver pushed my father to his death," Carrie told them. "He also killed Corporal Fellows."

"The sergeant had a reputation of being a hothead," Tyler shared. "Even without your father getting involved, I doubt he would have been promoted."

Officer Phillips nodded in agreement. "Your father had declined the offer Ulmer made, Ms. York, but not because of Oliver. Your dad wanted to hand the property on to you, his only child. When Oliver learned the deal wouldn't go through, he became irate. Ulmer feared that he'd sought out the sergeant major and pushed him down the steep incline to his death."

"Matthew had witnessed the fight and went back later to check on your father," Tyler mentioned. "Oliver hadn't seen him."

"Unfortunately Ulmer didn't go to the authorities with the information about his brother-in-law," Phillips added. "That won't bode well for him when he comes up on tax evasion charges. Plus, he took part in Oliver's payday loan schemes."

"What about his wife?" Carrie asked.

"The two of them were probably working together," Tyler said. "I'm not sure what the judge will decide, but I am sure of one thing. He'll throw the book at Oliver. The sergeant won't have to worry about what he'll do after retirement from the military, because he'll be doing time."

Phillips lifted his phone. "If you'll excuse me, I need to notify the chief."

He stepped away, leaving Tyler and Carrie to themselves.

"Seems we were interrupted a bit earlier." He smiled.

"Interrupted?" she asked.

"That's right. Officer Phillips interrupted us. You were in my arms, and I was planning to kiss you."

"I wouldn't want to spoil your plans," she whispered, moving closer and lifting her lips to his.

His kiss was warm and lingering and took her breath away. When he pulled back, her knees went weak, and she grabbed his arms to keep from falling.

"You're not okay."

"I'm fine, just light-headed, but it doesn't have anything to do with my injuries."

"Then what caused the problem?" His lips curved into

a knowing smile that showed his dimple and warmed her even more.

"It must have been your kiss."

"I know of only one solution for that problem, ma'am."

"Oh?" she asked, feigning innocence. "What's that?"

"Another kiss." He lowered his mouth to hers and they melted together in a long and luxurious embrace that made the world stand still and everything else fade into the background.

Why had she thought of leaving Freemont? She'd found her home. She was at home in Tyler's arms.

Chapter Eighteen

Tyler paced in front of the War Memorial. He was part of the contingent of military police and CID special agents waiting for the ceremony honoring Freemont veterans to begin.

He checked his watch and searched for Carrie. "Have you seen her?" he asked Everett.

"Be patient, my friend. She won't miss this occasion."

Tyler couldn't help being nervous. He'd been tied up on post yesterday and returned home too late to call Carrie last night. The large, stately home had been dark, and at the time, he thought she was already in bed asleep.

This morning, he'd driven to post early to coordinate the military police presence at the ceremony that would honor the local veterans. General Cameron and CID Chief Wilson wanted to ensure that nothing, no matter how seemingly insignificant, detracted from the solemnity of the day.

When Tyler had called Carrie earlier, her phone had gone to voice mail. Now he was frustrated that he hadn't knocked on her door last night to ensure that she was all right.

She still wasn't sure about whether to return to Washington, especially because of the senator's important speech. Carrie had spent the last few days fine-tuning the talk. Hopefully she hadn't been forced back to DC at the behest of her boss.

The army band stood at parade rest near the grandstand. The bandleader tapped his baton and called them to attention. On the count of three, they began to play a jaunty military march that had the people gathered in the seating area tapping their feet in time to the music.

Again he glanced at his watch.

Everett beckoned him forward to help with the video screen. "Let's adjust this a bit higher so everyone can see the slide program. Didn't you say they were planning to honor Carrie's dad?"

"That was the plan, but with Oliver in jail, no telling what the photos will highlight."

"The first sergeant said he's got it covered," Everett assured him.

"I hope so."

The *clip-clop* of horse hooves sounded. Tyler turned toward the main street. What he saw made him smile.

Joseph waved from the buggy and sat next to his father in the front. Bailey was tucked in at the boy's feet.

Behind them sat Ruth and next to her was Carrie.

Tyler hurried to help Isaac harness the horse to a post, and then he helped Carrie down. His hands lingered on her waist as he lifted her effortlessly to the ground. "I didn't know if you were still in town."

"I wouldn't miss this," she said with a smile. "Ruth and Isaac asked if I wanted to accompany them. After all they've done for me, I thought it would be fitting."

"There are seats reserved for you and enough for the Lapps, as well."

Tyler escorted them to the front of the VIP area.

Bailey sat between Carrie and Joseph. "You'll join us, Tyler?" she asked.

Everett overhead her question and smiled at Tyler. "You're on the guest list, my friend. Your place is next to Carrie. You don't want to disappoint the lady."

Carrie handed him a sealed envelope when he sat down.

"What's this?" he asked.

"A letter from Senator Kingsley. I got one too. Open it. You have time to read it before the ceremony begins."

Unsure of what the letter would contain, Tyler tore open the envelope. The handwritten letter expressed the senator's sorrow at the accident so long ago that had taken Tyler's father's life. The senator claimed full responsibility for the accident. He had gone to rehab and was trying to restore the brokenness he had caused. Knowing that nothing could replace Tyler's father, the senator had decided to step down from public office and donate a sizable contribution to the creation of a program to help kids at risk. He had been a kid without a father to guide him, and he had taken Tyler's father from him. He wanted to help other young men overcome the anger that could lead to a life of addiction, anger and dependency.

He planned to name the organization the Zimmerman Alternative in honor of Tyler's father. In the closing paragraph, the senator asked Tyler's forgiveness.

The anger Tyler had felt for so long disappeared.

He turned to Carrie. "I never expected this."

"Neither did I. This morning he gave the speech I

wrote—a patriotic and pro-military speech. At the end, he included a special statement and texted me the video."

She pushed a few prompts on her phone. Senator Kingsley stood on a podium with an American flag at his back and concluded the speech Carrie had written for him. The applause was instant and heartfelt.

"I have something to add," the senator said to the audience. "I need to ask forgiveness for my actions years ago." He went on to talk about his condition that night, and the accident that had taken an innocent man's life. "What I did was wrong. That I didn't turn myself in was wrong, as well. That's why I'm turning myself in today and asking the state to try my case so that justice can be served. I am stepping down from my senatorial seat. I am not worthy to follow in the footsteps of honorable men who have served before me, and I ask your forgiveness. Whatever the verdict, I pray that no one will suffer like the Zimmerman family, and especially Special Agent Tyler Zimmerman, who lost his father years ago."

Carrie's smile was wide as she reached for Tyler's hand and held it tight throughout the ceremony honoring the local veterans and especially commemorating her father, Sergeant Major Harris.

When the slide show concluded, Carrie turned to Tyler. "I know my father was a good and honorable man who loved the Lord and worked to help others whether through the military or civilian life. He did his family proud, and I'm proud of him."

She squeezed Tyler's hand. "I'm proud of you, as well."

George Gates approached them. "Mind if I interrupt?"

"Not at all," Carrie said as she and Tyler stood.

"Did you check out the safe-deposit box?" the lawyer asked.

Carrie nodded. "And the savings account at the bank. My father had done well with his investments as you mentioned."

"All the paperwork has been filed, and the rest of the estate should go through probate soon. You won't have long to wait until everything belongs to you. I presume you're keeping the house and property."

"That's right." She glanced at Tyler and smiled. "I'm staying in Freemont for a long time."

Back at the house following the event, Carrie prepared a lovely lunch and invited the Lapps to join them. The neighbors recounted heartwarming stories about the sergeant major that brought more than a tear to Carrie's eyes. By midafternoon, the neighbors had said their goodbyes. Tyler helped Carrie with the dishes and then told her to change into walking shoes so they could go for a hike in the woods.

"But why?"

"Trust me."

Which she did.

Hand in hand, they crossed the field where Corporal Fellows's body had been found and entered the wooded area.

"We're going back to the twisted tree?" she said.

Tyler smiled. "That's where Oliver thought the treasure was buried. But I read the journal found in the kitchen house, and with the help of the old plat realized the twisted oak wasn't the end of the treasure hunt but the beginning."

"If we're going to dig for treasure, we should have brought a shovel," Carrie said, wondering what Tyler had planned.

"I don't think we'll need one."

Finding the twisted oak, Tyler pointed west. "What do you see?"

"The steep hill that we're going to climb?"

"Exactly." Tyler ushered her to a side path that led almost to the top.

"What do you see now?" he asked once they stopped to rest.

"The entrance to the cave."

"Which was hidden for years. I noticed it on the old plat. When Oliver tore through the vines and undergrowth, he did us a favor."

Carrie peered inside the dark opening.

"Follow me." Tyler motioned her forward.

"This doesn't bring back good memories."

He squeezed her hand. "You may change your mind."

Turning on the flashlight, Tyler angled the light into the far recesses of the cave where a small opening appeared. "Hope you're not frightened by small spaces."

"Would it make a difference?"

"You could stay here and wait for me."

She shook her head. "No, Tyler, we're in this together."

His smiled widened. "I like that."

He hesitated for a moment and lowered his lips to hers. "Excuse me, ma'am, but I thought a kiss was in order."

Not that she objected.

She would have rather stayed and continued kissing him instead of bending low and entering the smaller confined area.

The flashlight played over the interior chamber.

Tyler sighed with discouragement.

"What's wrong?" she asked.

"I thought—"

The light caught on a dirt-covered object. "There." He pointed and motioned her to follow him to where a small rectangular box sat.

Kneeling, Tyler brushed his hands over the surface. A cloud of dirt and dust filled the air.

"It's a trunk," she gasped, realizing what they'd found.

Tyler undid the latch and slowly lifted the lid. He shone the light into the interior.

Carrie pulled out a faded quilt and unwrapped a teapot that had been carefully nestled within the fabric. The weight of the pot and the tarnished facade made her realize it was probably sterling. Quickly she unwrapped a coffee urn and cream and sugar accompanying pieces.

"Charlotte Harris wrote about her tea service." Carrie glanced up at Tyler. "We've found her keepsakes."

He angled the light into the truck. "There's more." He handed her two objects.

"Silver candlesticks," Carrie said. "They're beautiful."

A small box lay nestled in table linens. Carrie gasped when she opened it, seeing the cameo brooch surrounded by seed pearls. "It's exquisite."

"No gold coins, but treasures nonetheless." He drew out a leather-bound Bible.

Carrie read the names listed inside. Charlotte Jones and Jefferson Harris and their children.

"It's a family tree," she said to Tyler.

He put his arm around her shoulder and drew her close. "It's your family, Carrie."

"But I want a real one, Tyler. Not just the memories."

He hesitated and then his face softened. "We haven't known each other long, but I want a family, a family with you, Carrie. You can say no if you want to go back to Washington, but I hope you want to stay here. I want you to be my wife."

"Oh, Tyler," she sighed.

"We can take our time, but I love you, and want to spend the rest of my life holding you in my arms."

"That's what I want too."

She glanced at the Bible. "We'll write our names in the family tree. Tyler Zimmerman and Carrie York Harris wedded into married life."

"There's space for the names of our children," Tyler added with a smile, before he kissed her.

Slowly they walked back to the Harris home. Carrie wore the cameo, and Tyler carried the trunk filled with the family treasures.

In the field behind the house, they spied Joseph running toward them with Bailey at his heels. "Guess what?"

"You're so excited, Joseph." Carrie laughed. "Do you have a surprise?"

"*Yah. Gott* is giving me a baby brother or sister."

Carrie's heart burst with joy at the good news. "Oh, Joseph, that's wonderful."

"I told *Mamm* I'd been praying for a baby harder than I was praying for a dog."

"It sounds as if God answered the best prayer of all," Tyler said, smiling at the boy.

"He answered both prayers." Joseph motioned them forward. "Look what's in the box on the front porch."

Tyler placed the trunk inside the house and then joined Carrie on the Lapps' porch.

Peering into the box, she smiled.

"It's a puppy," Joseph squealed. "An Irish setter like Bailey. *Mamm* said they will be best friends if you stay here."

"Don't worry, Joseph." She took Tyler's hand. "I'm staying here. I wouldn't leave this area for anything." She looked at the house and the small boy and the dog and then into Tyler's eyes. "Everything I love is here."

Then as Joseph and Bailey played and the puppy frolicked nearby, Tyler and Carrie sat in the rockers on the porch of her father's house and enjoyed the evening breeze and the smell of the flowers blooming as spring arrived in Freemont—the first of many springs they would have together. They'd be together for a lifetime of seasons that would take them from today across the years when children of their own would play in the yard. They'd add their names and the names of their grand-children to the family Bible so the rich heritage of the Harris-Zimmerman family would continue on…forever.

* * * * *

Love Inspired

Save $1.00

on the purchase of any
Love Inspired®,
Love Inspired® Suspense or
Love Inspired® Historical book.

Available wherever books are sold, including
most bookstores, supermarkets, drugstores
and discount stores.

Save $1.00

on the purchase of any Love Inspired®, Love Inspired® Suspense or Love Inspired® Historical book.

Coupon valid until August 31, 2017. Redeemable at participating retail outlets in the
U.S. and Canada only. Limit one coupon per customer.

52614851

Canadian Retailers: Harlequin Enterprises Limited will pay the face value of this coupon plus 10.25¢ if submitted by customer for this product only. Any other use constitutes fraud. Coupon is nonassignable. Void if taxed, prohibited or restricted by law. Consumer must pay any government taxes. Void if copied. Inmar Promotional Services ("IPS") customers submit coupons and proof of sales to Harlequin Enterprises Limited, P.O. Box 3000, Saint John, NB E2L 4L3, Canada. Non-IPS retailer—for reimbursement submit coupons and proof of sales directly to Harlequin Enterprises Limited, Retail Marketing Department, 225 Duncan Mill Rd., Don Mills, ON M3B 3K9, Canada.

U.S. Retailers: Harlequin Enterprises Limited will pay the face value of this coupon plus 8¢ if submitted by customer for this product only. Any other use constitutes fraud. Coupon is nonassignable. Void if taxed, prohibited or restricted by law. Consumer must pay any government taxes. Void if copied. For reimbursement submit coupons and proof of sales directly to Harlequin Enterprises, Ltd 482, NCH Marketing Services, P.O. Box 880001, El Paso, TX 88588-0001, U.S.A. Cash value 1/100 cents.

5 65373 00076 2 (8100)0 12282

® and ™ are trademarks owned and used by the trademark owner and/or its licensee.

© 2017 Harlequin Enterprises Limited

LIINCICOUP0517

"Noah, where are you? I need to speak to you."

Working near the back of his father's barn, Noah Bowman dropped the hoof of his buggy horse Willy, took the last nail out of his mouth and stood upright to stare over his horse's back. Fannie Erb, his neighbor's youngest daughter, came hurrying down the wide center aisle, checking each stall as she passed. Her white *kapp* hung off the back of her head dangling by a single bobby pin. Her curly red hair was still in a bun, but it was windblown and lopsided. No doubt, it would be completely undone before she got home. Fannie was always in a rush.

"What's up, *karotte oben*?" He picked up his horse's hoof again, positioned it between his knees and drove in the last nail of the new shoe.

Fannie stopped outside the stall gate and fisted her hands on her hips. "You know I hate being called a carrot top."

"Sorry." Noah grinned.

LIEXP0517